THE MENAGERIE OF JENKINS BAILEY

MATTHEW S. COX

The Menagerie of Jenkins Bailey
A novel

ISBN: 978-1-949174-00-7 (ebook)
ISBN: 978-1-949174-01-4 (paperback)

View the map online: http://www.matthewcoxbooks.com/wordpress/books/the-menagerie-of-jenkins-bailey/the-menagerie-map/

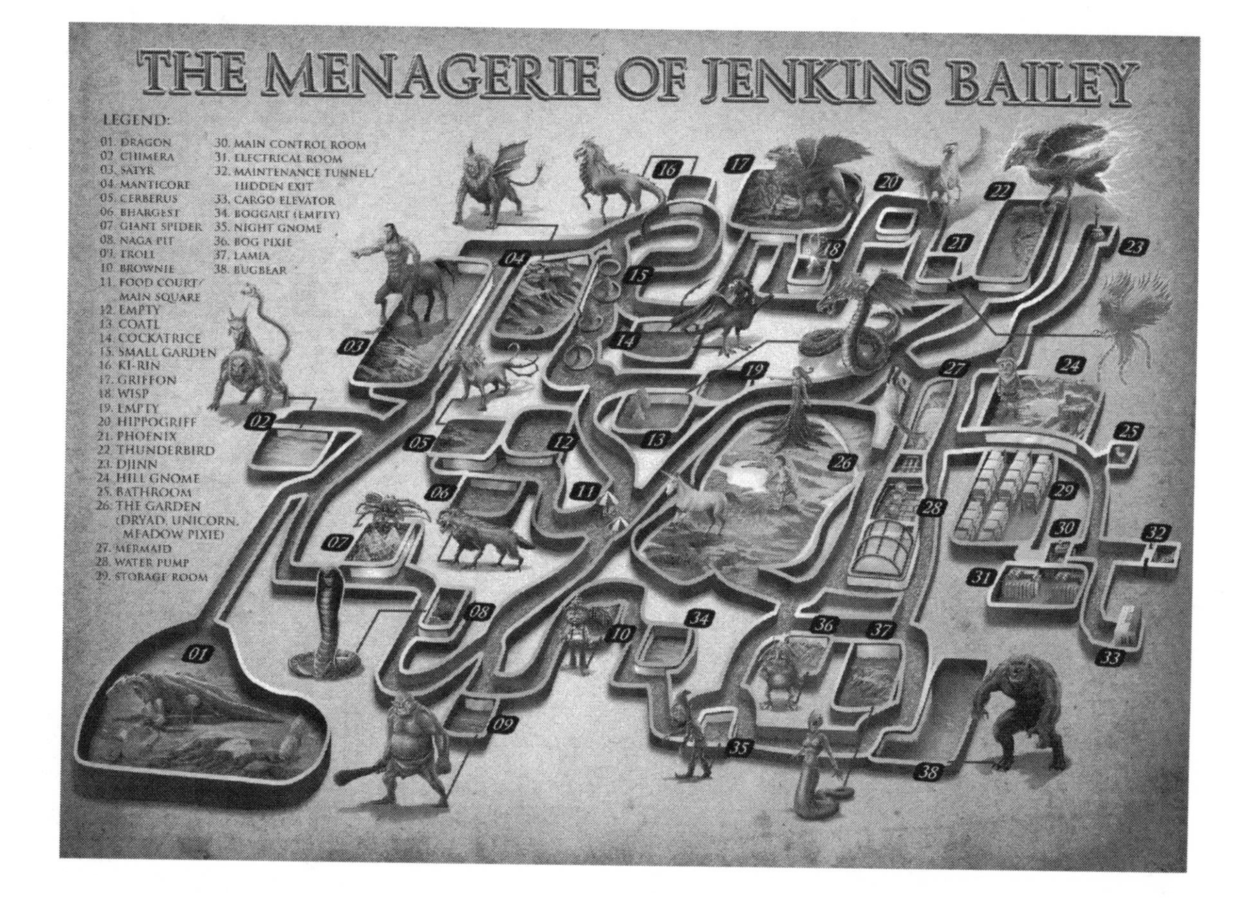
THE MENAGERIE OF JENKINS BAILEY
LEGEND:
01. DRAGON
02. CHIMERA
03. SATYR
04. MANTICORE
05. CERBERUS
06. BHARGEST
07. GIANT SPIDER
08. NAGA PIT
09. TROLL
10. BROWNIE
11. FOOD COURT/ MAIN SQUARE
12. EMPTY
13. COATL
14. COCKATRICE
15. SMALL GARDEN
16. KI-RIN
17. GRIFFON
18. WISP
19. EMPTY
20. HIPPOGRIFF
21. PHOENIX
22. THUNDERBIRD
23. DJINN
24. HILL GNOME
25. BATHROOM
26. THE GARDEN (DRYAD, UNICORN, MEADOW PIXIE)
27. MERMAID
28. WATER PUMP
29. STORAGE ROOM
30. MAIN CONTROL ROOM
31. ELECTRICAL ROOM
32. MAINTENANCE TUNNEL/ HIDDEN EXIT
33. CARGO ELEVATOR
34. BOGGART (EMPTY)
35. NIGHT GNOME
36. BOG PIXIE
37. LAMIA
38. BUGBEAR

CONTENTS

1

THE LAST WILL OF JENKINS BAILEY

Moping in sullen silence, Piper kept her head down, counting the frayed holes in her threadbare jeans. They didn't bother her, nor did the occasional mockery her drab wardrobe caused at school. She'd never cared about fancy clothes or possessions, and wished as hard as she could that the strange old man had never made that phone call.

For all twelve years of her life, she had been quite content to wear thrift store offerings or hand-me-downs from Mom. Her clothes' patches had patches, but she had become fond of the comfort. The well-worn feel of her world had been saturated in the kind of love one couldn't simply buy with a designer label hung on it.

Each moment she remained stuck in the back seat of Dad's pickup truck, crammed between a stack of cardboard boxes on her left and a mound of trash bags containing clothing on the right, drained her hope a little more. Every mile they travelled away from Syracuse made her heart heavier and her tongue sharper.

Precisely why she kept her tongue locked up behind her teeth. Mom was already giving her the silent treatment after the last protest. Truth be told, Piper *had* gone too far. Telling her mother she'd 'gotten so old she forgot what having friends was like' had slipped out faster than she could think to stop herself.

But she had to do *something!*

Some old man had called midway through May, claiming her father had inherited the entire estate of his late father, Jenkins Bailey. However much money that meant, it wasn't worth never seeing her friends again. It certainly wasn't worth Dad uprooting them all and rushing way off into the woods to some creepy old house.

Piper would give anything to be able to go back home. She missed her tiny little house and the battered kitchen table that had held everything from cereal breakfasts to Christmas feasts. But most of all, she missed her friends.

Her friends, now almost two hours away, would be hanging out and enjoying the summer—like she had been looking forward to doing all year. At least until that stupid phone call threw Dad over the moon.

Piper sighed, frowning at her scratched iPhone 4. Someone had actually sold one to Goodwill, and Mom snagged it for her—mostly so she could stay in contact with her parents. Her closest friends, Jamie and Gwen, were all the way back in Syracuse—and she'd probably never see them in person ever again. Did her parents really expect her to be thrilled about that? So what if her family became rich overnight? She wanted her friends back, her home back, and her bedroom back.

Eyes closed, she tried to remember how her room smelled: the faint wet-dog fragrance of her carpet, the overly fabric-softened bouquet of her bedding, even the stale wood aroma that lurked in her closet.

She'd been happy with their meager suburban life. Her flimsy canvas sneakers wouldn't win any style awards, but they were comfortable. It didn't bother her that she often dressed like she'd stepped out of a time machine from the 1980s. True, some kids picked on her, but she never paid attention to them. At her age, Dad had *made* holes in his jeans on purpose because he thought it made them look cool. He even still listened to the same music he did back then, which currently blared from the radio.

Somehow, having nothing but trees surrounding the road outside made the stereo feel louder.

Although… an enormous house deep in the woods of upstate New York *might* be interesting. Houses like that often had ghosts, secret passages, or other fun things to explore. Of course, she tried her hardest not to let curiosity rise up. Whenever she caught herself thinking there *might* be something fun or interesting about the new house, she concentrated on her friends and how she *couldn't* hang out with them, throwing herself deliberately back into a cloud of glum.

The truck swerved with Dad's futile effort to dodge a pothole. Yet again, the poorly arranged stack of cardboard boxes buckled to one side, nearly burying her. Yet again, she rammed her elbow into it, fighting to protect her little bit of space. A compact disc fell out of the topmost box, bounced off her head, and hit the floor. With a growl, she shoved the stack a little too hard, toppling it the other way and spilling flat plastic cases against the window. Piper fumed, feeling like yet another object crammed into the back seat that her parents brought on a trip she had no interest in. Scowling at the back of his head, she tried to make her father turn around through sheer willpower.

"Sorry!" yelled Dad. "The road's a bit rough. Hey, hon, grab that CD, would you?"

"A *bit* rough? Maybe they don't fix it because only one car drives on it per year," muttered Piper past a frown. After a sigh, she stretched to retrieve the CD from the floor. "*Caress of Steel*? Wow Dad, people haven't listened to music off these things since dinosaurs roamed the earth. And you've already got them all digital. Why do you even keep these?"

"It's a compact disc."

She looked it over. "I know that. But it's like old and stuff."

"It's music!" yelled Dad over someone wailing about Bastille Day.

"That's debatable," mumbled Piper, too low to hear. "What are they doing to that cat? Is that a guy singing or a woman?"

"Ha. Ha. The singer's voice is high." Dad peered at her in the rearview mirror for a second. "You're one to talk about strangling cats… that stuff you listen to." He grinned.

She looked away before he could catch her starting to smile. Smiling didn't go along with being whisked away from her entire life. She'd have to wait at least a week or two before she could show any sign of not being miserable. With luck, Mom's opinion would prove correct. Her mother didn't trust the whole inheritance thing. 'Too good to be true' had been her first reaction. Maybe her mother would be right, and they could run home to Syracuse before anyone bought their old house.

Piper glanced down at a nickel-sized spot of skin showing from a hole on her jean thigh. She picked at the denim frays, sighed, and checked the iPhone on the seat beside her again, not expecting anything to have changed. Sure enough, it still displayed a 'no signal' tag, as it had for the better part of the last hour, reinforcing the whole 'middle of nowhere' aspect of the new house.

Mom hadn't spoken a word in over forty-five minutes. She hammered at the keys of her laptop, clicking loud enough to hear over the blaring music. Her thick, auburn hair hid her face, and any clue of her mood. Piper hadn't exactly yelled at her, but she figured her mother kept quiet because she also didn't like the idea of moving—but had to do that whole 'unified parent' thing. She couldn't disagree with Dad in front of her, so she said nothing.

Piper fidgeted at the hole in her jeans, stirring a little guilt into the cauldron with her homesickness. Hopefully, Mom's silence came from moving in general and not at their minor argument.

At least it beat Mom constantly telling her to cheer up.

Trees… endless trees rushed by on both sides of the narrow road taking them deep into the Black River forest. She vaguely recalled her father calling it Route 214. The cardboard mountain at her left shifted on a brief bend in the road. Piper raised her elbow, but the boxes didn't attack her again.

The song changed, her father batting his hands on the steering wheel to the beat of something stupid about going bald. *Really? Who writes a song about losing their hair?* Piper sighed and kept her head down.

A little past ten in the morning, they rolled into a town so small it looked like a production set for a movie. She craned her neck to peek over the pile of backpacks and blankets on her right. A gas station, grocery store, a couple houses, post office, more houses, and a street going off to the right shot by in less than a minute.

No one lives out here. She sighed into her lap. *This is going to suck so much.*

"You okay, hon?" asked Dad.

"Oh, fine," she muttered. He probably couldn't even hear her over the music.

Ever since her father had bought himself a five-year-old iPod, he'd had his entire Rush collection on loop/repeat wherever he went. Piper didn't dislike it as much as she hated having it *constantly* on. The man never listened to anything else.

He turned down the volume. "Sorry, what?"

Piper looked up at the thick mass of dark brown hair covering the back of his head. "I said, 'oh, I'm fine.' It's not like I've just abandoned my best friends and I'll never see them again or anything."

"Oh, Piper…" Dad kept drumming his fingers on the steering wheel. "You'll see them again. We're not *that* far away. Besides, this is an unbelievable opportunity."

Mom glanced at her with an expression of concern and annoyance before shooting a quick stare at Dad, then resumed punishing the laptop keyboard.

"Unbelievable is right," said Piper. "What was wrong with our home? People don't just get phone calls and craploads of money out of the blue like that. I'm with Mom. I don't trust it."

He smiled at her in the mirror on a straight patch of road. "People don't get opportunities like this often. Once we get settled in, you can invite your friends over for a week or two. We're more than capable of feeding them now."

Piper folded her arms, staring into her lap. Money seemed to be the only thing Dad cared about lately.

"We're almost there." He leaned to his right and poked the GPS device. The power wire running to the cigarette lighter port (accessorized with duct tape) sometimes lost contact and made it go dark. The screen came to life after a few taps, showing a little car symbol moving down a road. "Fifteen minutes."

"Hey, when school starts again, can I stay at Jamie's during the week?" asked Piper. "And like only go back to nowheretown on weekends?" She bit her lip as soon as she finished asking. That might've sounded like she didn't want to be around her parents anymore… "I mean, I don't… Umm… Not like mad at you guys or anything, but… I don't wanna change schools, and my friends and… Sorry."

Dad laughed. "Piper, you don't even have to go to school anymore. We can hire a tutor to come to you."

"Alan…" Mom stopped typing with a sigh. "You can't just throw money away like that. All those people who win the lottery and wind up broke again in a year? That's going to be us if you're not careful. Besides. She needs social interaction."

"Yeah, that. Social interaction." Piper gestured at Mom while concealing a smile behind a wall of hair. She'd inherited Dad's color and some of Mom's curliness, resulting in a dense, wavy chestnut brown mane. She called it the comb-killer, as she broke one or two a month.

Mom had refused to quit her teaching job and intended to commute back to Syracuse… or transfer to Utica to be a little closer. She clearly didn't expect this whole mansion-in-the-woods scenario to last long.

Dad pulled left off Route 214 onto a bouncy dirt road. One of the trash bags full of clothes fell on Piper's head. As soon as she stuffed it back into place, the truck hit a rut that toppled the cardboard onto her from behind.

"Aaah!" shouted Piper, her face mushed into plastic.

She grunted, pulling herself out of the bags, and rammed her back into the boxes, fighting not to be buried. When the truck hit level paving again some minutes later, she had her right foot braced against the bags, her left shoulder against boxes, left foot pressing into Dad's seatback, and both hands holding up a waterfall of compact discs. *Caress of Steel? More like Waterfall of Plastic.*

"We're here," said Dad.

"You stink at packing." Piper grumbled, rammed her elbow into the boxes, kicked the trash bag, and shifted to sit normally.

"Oh, my God," muttered Mom.

Another CD case bounced off her head and clattered to the floor.

"Argh!" She almost stomped on it, but stopped herself. "Why did you pack all this crap back here with me? You got that giant truck, and—" Piper's jaw hung open at the view out the windshield. An ornate black gate spanned the road in front of them. Beyond it, a winding driveway led up to a paved circle around a huge fountain, surrounded by grassy field. A pair of carved stone griffons adorned the fountain, both spitting water into a basin below. A massive manor house stood at the far end of the courtyard, like something straight out of some stuffy Victorian period drama. "Whoa…"

"There it is!" said Dad past a grin. "Home sweet home."

Piper scooted forward into the gap between the two front seats, gawking at the 'house' her father had inherited. The walls, once white, showed stains from age and rain, but they lent it an almost castle-like quality. Three stories tall, it looked wider than ten of the house she'd grown up in (so far). The reddish tinted roof had a row of dormer windows at evenly spaced intervals, no doubt connected to the attic or perhaps a smaller fourth story. Every twenty feet along the front wall, manicured bushes jutted upward like soldiers at attention, tapered ovals reminiscent in shape to a football stretched ten feet tall. All but the attic windows had fancy curtains, but wherever they parted, they revealed only darkness inside.

Her entire class could all move in and there'd probably be rooms left over.

"I don't need to go to school, because this place *is* a school. It's huge!" whispered Piper. "Are you sure this is the right address?"

Mom whistled. "Alan, this is so much… Are you sure about this? The property taxes… maintenance… we'll be out of money in a year."

"We'll work it out. My father kept this place for years, so it can't be impossible. How much can the taxes be this far out in the middle of nothing?" Dad patted Mom on the shoulder. "You've been teaching math for fifteen years, you ought to know your way around a budget."

Mom rolled her eyes. "Accounting and trig aren't similar."

"No?" Dad opened his door. "Both involve numbers. So… math. Hence, you are good at it."

She sighed.

Piper couldn't stop staring at the place. It went way beyond anything she expected. "It's huge."

Mom reached up and took her hand. "We'll be okay."

"If we have so much money, can we maybe *not* sell our house?" Piper looked downcast. "I miss home."

"Well… I suppose we could talk about that," said Mom.

Dad approached the gate. After looking around for a mechanism, he grabbed the middle bar and tugged, but couldn't budge it. He pulled and pushed for a little while before snapping upright with a raised finger like he'd just remembered something.

Piper grinned at her mother. Sensing opportunity, she pounced. "It could be like a vacation house or something. Only, we can live there when school's on, and come out here for the summer. That way you don't need to leave the teaching job and I don't need to go to a different school and miss all my friends, and you don't have to wake up at like 4:30 in the morning for a two-hour ride."

"How long did it take you to come up with that sales pitch?" asked Mom, a bit of a smile forming on her lips.

A loud *clank* outside drew Piper's gaze back to Dad, who stood beside the truck at a small metal box mounted atop a post. He'd driven a little too far for it to line up with his window, and evidently hadn't seen it before he hopped out. The gate opened inward, two motorized halves gliding out of their way on small wheels. Sunlight sparkled from delicate silvery engraving on the black bars.

"Umm. Not long. I just thought of it." She tilted her head, mesmerized by the glittering light.

Dad climbing back into the truck snapped her out of it. "Forgot the key card was in my pocket. Duh."

While the truck rolled past the gate and onto the grounds, Piper climbed over the bags of clothing to peer out the side window. Every bar in the gate bore a line of ornate silver scrollwork. Even sitting in the shade, the engraving sparkled like diamonds in the sun. She had the oddest feeling it *shouldn't* have been glowing like that since the gate sat in the shade.

This place is creepy.

She sank back into the middle of the bench seat.

Dad parked between the house and the fountain and shut off the engine. Her parents got out, but rather than unbury her, walked around behind the truck to take Mom's Camry off the tow rig. Piper looked left and right at the junk packing her in and decided to crawl into the front seat. She escaped via the driver's side door into a cooler-than-expected breeze, heavy with the fragrance of forest. A steady whispery hiss came from the trees, rustling in the wind. She thought it chilly for mid-June, but not so cold she wanted a jacket.

Long fields of meadow grass flanked the house on either side, beyond which the endless expanse of trees resumed. A sense of being watched came over her. Gripped by unease, Piper searched the dark, empty windows for any sign of a person, but found none. The house felt like a giant creature with many eyes staring right back at her.

She drew in a sharp breath when a curtain twitched, but no one appeared. Her throat tightened and her heart beat faster. "Dad?"

"Yeah?" yelled her father from halfway under Mom's car.

"Is anyone supposed to be in the house?" She took a step backward, unable to look away from the window where she thought something had been spying on them.

"Nope," yelled Dad. "Why?"

Piper stood motionless for a while, watching that window. Even the rush of wind in the trees had stopped, leaving her in complete silence. When a loud *clank* came from Mom's car, she jumped and clamped a hand over her mouth to keep from screaming. "Uhh… no reason."

"Movers ought to be here soon," said Mom.

The eerie feeling from the house faded. Piper took a deep breath and shook her head, then wandered over to the fountain. A coppery taste hung in the air on a fine mist, kicked up by the water pouring from the beaks of two griffon statues, each as big as a horse and carved from white granite dappled with dark green moss. The creatures circled each other as if in flight above a bronze basin lined with green tarnish.

"This sucks," she muttered. "I wish I could go home."

Piper dipped her fingers in the water, swishing them back and forth for a little while until they went numb from the cold. She turned around and sat on the rim, arms folded, watching her parents fight with the U-Haul trailer that had a death grip on the Camry's front wheels. It didn't matter that her father had been a mechanic for years, Mom defended her car like a second child, telling him to be careful, don't pull on that, don't push that, loosen *that* strap first, and so on. Since neither one of them looked at her, she grinned, laughing under her breath at the two of them acting like a married couple from a TV sitcom.

Heavy rumbling announced the arrival of the movers, in a truck only slightly smaller than a big rig. Her family's whole life, everything from *home,* sat inside the truck. The house back in Syracuse had been reduced to an empty shell. Piper's stomach tightened, remembering how it all went into boxes, and her last walk around the bare rooms that had choked her up as though they'd buried the family pet. She desperately missed her little bedroom—even the way she always whacked her knee on the desk whenever she got out of bed. If Mom actually went for the idea of keeping that house and living there during school, Piper would insist that they bring her furniture back. This giant mansion would never feel like home, so she'd sleep on any old bed.

Mom started backing the Camry off the trailer, but slammed on the brakes as the truck rumbled within inches of her rear bumper. The huge van came to a stop by the front door in a cloud of dust and diesel fumes. Mom glared death at them, but none of the movers saw her. Piper crossed her arms tighter and bowed her head.

"Hey," said Dad in a soft tone. "You okay?"

She looked up, sighed, and leaned against him. "Yeah, I guess. I miss home already."

"You'll get used to it. Lot of changes for all of us to adjust to." Dad put an arm around her, squeezing her in a hug. "It's not like you'll never see your friends again."

"We're out in the middle of nowhere." She scrunched up her nose at the front door. "Who was this guy anyway that left you the house? Do you think this is a scam like Mom said?"

"No, hon." Dad chuckled. "This estate used to belong to my father. He left my mother before I was a year old. Your grandmother always spoke poorly of that side of the family… called them snobs, eccentric—or crazy, when she wasn't feeling overly polite. I never really knew him."

"So… this father you don't even know leaves you his whole fortune and house?" She raised both eyebrows and tilted her head. "Really?"

"Guess there's no one else to give it to." Dad shrugged. "That or he felt guilty. I didn't get much of an explanation. The lawyer checked everything out and it looked legit."

She shied away from the windows again, clinging to him. "This place is creepy. I don't like the way it feels."

"It's just big… and strange."

"Yeah. Strange is right." She kicked the toe of her sneaker at the ground.

Five men emerged from the big van and approached.

"One sec, hon." Dad patted her on the back before walking over to meet the movers.

Mom drove the Camry around the fountain and parked in front of a four-car garage at the end of a short spur of road. She hopped out and went from one garage door to the next, but couldn't manage to get any of them open. Defeated, she leaned into the car, cut the engine, and joined Dad in talking to the movers.

Her father shook hands with one of the men and walked with him to the front door. Dad tried the knob, but it didn't open. After patting himself down, he sighed.

"Great, we can't get in. Oops, guess this isn't going to work after all, can we go home now?" muttered Piper to no one. She sat on the rim of the fountain again, staring down at her sneakers.

"The estate lawyer should be here soon," said Dad to the movers. "Sorry… I guess we got here a little earlier than he was expecting."

"No problem, man. We get paid by the hour." The man smiled and returned with the others to hang out by the truck cab.

As if on cue, a silver BMW appeared out of the forest in the distance, rolling up the road toward the front gate. It glided past the gate in a gentle turn around the fountain, coming to a silent stop by the steps leading to the porch.

An older, white-haired gentleman in a fancy black suit emerged without shutting the engine off. He eyed the house with a noticeable shiver before turning a forced smile toward Dad. "Mr. Bailey?" asked the new arrival, offering a hand.

"Yes," said Dad.

"Excellent. I'm Pritchard De Havilland, your father's attorney."

"Oh!" Dad grinned and accepted the handshake. "A pleasure to meet you in person finally."

"Indeed." Pritchard hurriedly removed an ancient, yellowed envelope from inside his suit jacket and held it out. "This is directly from Mr. Jenkins Bailey. Now, despite your instincts, I'd advise taking the contents seriously."

"Ooo-kay…" Dad took the envelope, looked it over, and let his arm fall slack at his side. "I hope you brought the keys."

"Of course." Pritchard rummaged a keyring from another pocket, which he almost threw to Dad. "There you are. Three copies of all the major house keys. There are some additional papers that need to be finalized whenever you can head into town."

Dad nodded. "Day or two all right?"

"Perfectly fine." Pritchard smiled, looking (and sounding) a bit like a posh English butler. "Well, now, if you'll excuse me, I must be off."

Piper smirked. *That guy thinks this place is creepy too. He can't wait to get out of here.*

The lawyer ducked back into his BMW. He drove the rest of the way around the fountain and back out the gate, which motored itself closed. Piper twisted to watch the fancy car disappear into the trees once again. Soon after the blur of silver vanished among the woods, the gate closed with a *clank*.

"Great. We're trapped here." She grumbled.

Dad fumbled with the keyring until he located a key that unlocked the grand double doors. He wandered inside, Mom close behind. The clatter of the moving van's doors swinging open against the sides echoed back from the woods, startling a few birds to wing. Piper didn't move, having less than zero interest being here, much less going inside. Every minute she could delay felt like a tiny victory.

Her T-shirt tightened like someone grasping a fistful of fabric behind her back, trying to pull her into the frigid water. She screamed and leapt to her feet, whirling to stare at the spot she'd been sitting. No one stood behind her, merely the two griffon statues. She clutched her chest, backing away and shivering.

"Piper?" called Dad, trotting back out the door.

She ran across the circle and up the stairs, jumping into a hug. "Dad! A ghost just grabbed me!"

His expression of worry shifted to amusement. "Ghosts?"

Mom rolled her eyes. "Piper… You're twelve years old now. Stop being melodramatic."

"But…" She opened her mouth to protest, but no words came. *I wouldn't believe myself.*

"What happened?" asked Dad.

"Umm." She fussed at her T-shirt. "It felt like someone tried to pull me into the fountain."

"Okay, I give you that this house is a little creepy, but you have an overactive imagination." Dad poked her in the forehead.

"Says the wannabe writer." Mom winked.

Dad faced her, holding his hands up in a 'hey, check me out' gesture. "She's gotta get it from somewhere. If her math grades are any indication, she got my creativity instead of your fondness for numbers."

"I got *one* C." Piper frowned. "And Mr. Rodwell hates girls. He even said it's pointless to teach us math. Gives us bad grades on purpose even when we get the answers right. Ask Mom. She took the test to the principal."

Mom scowled at the distant trees. "The man should've retired last century. I can't fault her that C."

"Why's an idiot like that still teaching?" asked Dad.

Mom threw her hands up in frustration and stormed inside. "Don't even get me started on that. If that was my school, he'd have been gone years ago."

Piper spared a moment to beg the powers that be that she never had to suffer the embarrassment of having her own mother as a teacher. She had plenty of time until sophomore or junior year of high school, but she'd been dreading winding up in Mom's class ever since fifth grade.

"Go on and pick a bedroom on the third floor," said Dad, nudging her into the house.

The doors led to a large foyer where archways on the left and right opened into sitting rooms. Straight ahead, a wide stairwell went up to the second floor. Despite the size of the place, the décor remained on the conservative side. A handful of paintings, a vase or three, and some small statues. Nothing looked overly expensive.

"That looks like the staircase from a horror movie where the woman from 1800-whatever died," muttered Piper. "Geez, Dad. Our entire house would fit in this room."

She didn't like the way her voice echoed. This mansion didn't appear to be a vacant house; all the furnishings remained, making it feel like they'd invaded someone's home. None of the people in the portraits looked familiar. They could've been dead relatives, historic figures, or paintings of random models for all she knew. At another prodding finger in the back, Piper trudged across the foyer and up the huge stairwell, tracing her hand along the white-painted banister.

On second floor, two long corridors went in both directions from the stairs with pale beige walls. Small tables here and there held little vases or decorative silver bowls. More paintings filled in some of the space between evenly spaced white doors. She shivered, thinking the hall eerily similar to the hotel from *The Shining*. About ten doors away on either side, two openings branched off toward the back of the house. Piper swung around the post at the end of the banister to her left and kept going up another set of stairs to the third floor.

Deep brown doors lined a hallway with matching wainscoting below navy blue wallpaper. Black-stained wood chandeliers with candle-shaped light bulbs hung from the ceiling every twenty or so feet, lending an air of creepy coziness. If not for the obvious hint of technology, she could've imagined herself in a medieval manor house.

A distinct feeling of being watched kept her pinned in place at the top of the stairs, gazing down into the burgundy carpet. "Hello?" whispered Piper. "Is someone here?"

Only the distant voices of movers and her parents downstairs filled the silence.

"Okay. This is just a big old house and I'm seeing stuff that isn't real."

She huffed a deep breath and walked to the right, peeking in door after door. The lack of dust surprised her. After pulling open a dozen knobs, she found two bathrooms, as well as a modest-sized room with a few wardrobe cabinets but no bed. Two windows on the wall opposite the entrance peeked out at the backyard, an expanse of grass big enough to hold several football fields. Forest didn't start up again for about a quarter mile or so, and near the edge of the woods, a suspicious-looking hill seemed at odds with the land around it. Too flat on top, the sides too sharp. It resembled one of those old bunkers from World War II covered in fake vegetation.

"Whoa. What's that?" She leaned on the sill and put her face up to the glass. "That's *so* fake. I wonder what's in there."

"Hon?" asked Dad, from the hallway.

"In here," yelled Piper.

A few seconds later, he poked his head in the door.

"Can I have this room?" She gestured around. "It's got enough room for my bed… and there's no bed here."

"It's so small." He smiled and walked up to her. "You've had such a tiny room… Come on, hon. You don't need to *settle* anymore."

"I'm not settling. I don't need a lot of space."

Dad took her hand. "It's fine. It's not going to cost more if you pick a real bedroom." He led her out into the hall, and down past a handful of doors to the last one on the left side. The doorway at the facing end opened into the master bedroom, which had to be three times the size of their old living room. "Your mother and I are in here. You're used to being right by us… and this one's right next door."

She couldn't argue that she liked being close to her Mom and Dad. Having a noticeable *walk* between her bedroom and theirs would kinda suck. "'Kay."

"This is… unbelievable," said Mom, from the master bedroom.

"Isn't it?" Dad grinned and went in.

Piper pushed the door aside and trudged into the room she'd been assigned. *Why did he even ask me to pick one?* A long bay window took up most of the inner wall, complete with a cushioned bench nestled in the part that extended out past the wall. The view of the backyard *was* much better here, but the spaciousness of the room left her open-mouthed. It had to be eight times the size of her old one, though in all fairness, her *real* bedroom had probably been intended as a large closet.

Her parents' conversation fell to indistinct vocal tones behind her. This room already had a bed in it, a giant four-poster queen size with white trimmings and little pink ribbons on the pillows. It looked like the sort of fluffery a Disney princess would sleep in. She bit her lip as excitement clashed with guilt. Clearly, her parents had gotten this for her already. Despite it feeling like too much, she couldn't throw a gift back in their faces. It would crush her father if she rejected it.

Well, I guess I can send my real bed back home then. She trudged over to sit on the cushioned spot in the bay window. Chin in her hands, elbows on her knees, Piper frowned at the giant place that had become her bedroom.

"I'm never going to get used to this."

2

THE LONELY BOY

Piper's new room had two white dressers, a wardrobe cabinet, bookshelf, a small fireplace, and a door that led to a private bathroom. Dad's handwriting adorned a Post-It note on the fireplace glass door. Curious, she got up and wandered over to read, "There will be no fires in here until you are sixteen or older."

"As if we're still going to be here then." She rolled her eyes at the note. "Ugh. What am I going to do with all this space?" The window bench caught her eye again. "That's a cool place for reading. I guess I'll be doing a lot of that… since I'll never see any of my friends again."

She plodded over to the window, sat on the peach-colored cushion, and stared out at the distant forest by the strange artificial hill. Jamie and Gwen would likely be having fun at that very moment, while she sat here lonely and bored. Well, perhaps not *completely* bored. The temptation to go exploring the huge house did exist, but lay trapped beneath her gloom. Stuff like this sucked to do alone. Especially when her two best friends couldn't hang out with her.

"Hon?" asked Dad, again leaning in her door. "Wanna grab your clothes out of the truck?"

"I guess. Do we really have to stay here?" Piper picked at the cushion by her leg.

He crossed the room. "Your mother is convinced we'll be out of here in less than a year."

"Why does this house have to be so far away?" She let her hands flop in her lap. "It's not fair."

Dad squeezed her shoulders. "I'd say something about life not being fair, but it's hard to use that after we just got all that money plus this house. There are lots of people who would be over the moon if the same thing happened to them."

"Well, they can have it then." She smirked.

"Piper…" Dad kissed the top of her head. "How do you think Gwen or Jaime would've reacted to their parents inheriting this place?"

She leaned her head side to side, thinking for a moment. "Jamie would've been like… *See ya!* And probably invited me and Gwen over for epic sleepovers. Gwen would've wanted us and Jamie's family to move in too."

He patted her shoulder. "I dunno about moving in, but we could certainly have your friends over for a week or two if their parents are willing. Come on, kiddo. Cheer up, 'kay? This is the life most people dream about."

"I'm not most people." She slid her legs off the cushions and stood into a hug. "Thank you for the bed. It's beautiful."

He squeezed her. "You're welcome, sweetie. We're putting your old one in one of the other rooms for now. Your mother tells me you want to keep the house in Syracuse."

"Please!" Her head snapped up with a pleading stare. "I don't want to go to a different school. Can we keep it like a reverse vacation home or something?"

"We'll think about it." He winked. "Go on, get your stuff."

Forgetting that her father could see her, she smiled before the required 'glumness period' ended. He grinned and returned to the master bedroom while she ran out into the hall and down the stairs to the front door. Weaving among movers carrying boxes in, she made her way outside and jogged up to Dad's pickup. Most of the trash bags in the back seat contained her clothing, except for two that held her parents' dirty laundry. Her 'forgetting' to pack resulted in a lot of last-minute bag stuffing.

Piper pulled the door open and gathered her stuff bag by bag, setting it out on the paving around her feet. She shoved the door closed, revealing a boy who hadn't been there before.

He smiled at her. "Hi."

"Gah!" Piper jumped back. "You scared the crap out of me!"

He tried to hide a grin. "Sorry."

She glared at him. He stood a little shorter than her, not quite as skinny, with longish black hair and striking dark blue eyes. The boy also rocked the T-shirt and jeans thing, but his looked new—no holes. He also had 'real' sneakers, not Walmart canvas specials.

"Umm, so you guys are moving in?" asked the boy. "I'm Tristan."

"No, you're just imagining us." Piper waved her hands about in a bad pantomime of being a spooky ghost. "We're not really here."

"Hah. Yeah, I guess that was dumb. Here's your sign," said Tristan.

"What?" asked Piper.

"Oh, it's a comedian my dad likes. I guess I asked a stupid question. This guy has a whole routine about that. Like people should carry signs saying 'pardon me, I'm stupid.' They get them when they ask a question with an obvious answer. You're here now, you weren't here yesterday, and there's a big moving truck. So, I guess it was dumb of me to ask if you're moving in."

"Oh." She looked around at the grounds, and the utter lack of any visible neighbors. "Where did you come from?"

Tristan pointed to the woods on the left side of the house. "Walked through the forest. We live about a mile away. Our house isn't this big though. Saw the moving truck from my bedroom and wanted to say hi."

"Umm. Hi." She looked him up and down. He seemed okay, at least close to her in age, and didn't give off any 'weird' vibes. "I'm Piper."

"Cool name." He smiled. "You need help carrying anything?"

Mom walked over to them. "Who's that?"

"Umm. This is Tristan. He's our neighbor." Piper pointed at the woods.

Mom blinked at the trees. "We have neighbors?"

"I know, right?" asked Piper, to no one in particular.

Tristan offered a hand. "Hello, Mrs...."

"Bailey," said Mom, accepting his handshake.

"I'm Tristan Wiley. We live over that way. My folks'll probably want to invite you over to welcome you or something."

Mom smiled. "Oh, that would be lovely. Everything all right here?"

"Yeah." Piper hauled a few bags up off the ground. "It's cool."

"Okay. It'll take the movers a bit to get your stuff up to your room." Mom set her hands on her hips and twisted around to watch the men for a few seconds. "Once you've got your clothes situated, try to stay out of their way… and don't touch anything that looks dangerous."

Piper fake-cowered from the house. "This whole place looks dangerous. Can we go back to Syracuse?"

"Nice try." Mom patted her on the head and walked away, back to direct the movers.

"Syracuse?" asked Tristan.

"Yeah." She kicked at the paving. "That's where we're from."

He picked up the remaining four trash bags. "Cool. Guess you're not happy about it, huh?"

"Thanks for helping." She started for the door. "And no, not really."

He followed her inside and up the stairs. "I guess it would stink to move away from all your friends and stuff."

"You guess?" asked Piper, rounding the banister and heading up to the third floor. "Have you lived here all the time then? Never been taken away from your friends?"

"I've never had any," said Tristan, in a matter-of-fact tone that didn't sound like a cry for pity.

She stopped halfway between the second and third floor. "What? You've never had any friends? How is that even possible?"

"No other kids live around here. At least, not close enough for me to walk." He shrugged. "You're the first. The old guy who lived here before didn't have any kids. Just a lot of weird noises."

She raised one eyebrow. "What kind of weird noises? And, don't you go to school somewhere?"

He shook his head. "No. My grandma homeschools me. She gets stuff from a school in Utica and I'm basically doing all the same classes."

"Oh, that's… lonely." Piper turned away and continued climbing stairs. "Do you *want* to go to school?"

"I wouldn't mind. But my parents can't drive me and the bus won't come all the way out here."

Piper headed to the right at the top of the stairs. Some of the little vases and statuettes on the tables looked different, like someone had rearranged them. She stopped short, staring at a Greek warrior next to the 'too small' bedroom she chose first, certain there had been vase there earlier.

"Whoa!" Tristan almost walked into her. "What'd you stop for?"

She gestured with two overloaded garbage bags at the table. "That wasn't there before."

"Oh."

"You said something about weird noises before. What did you mean?" She glanced back at him, then over his shoulder when a shadow darted across the hallway far off in the other end of the house. She gasped. "Did you see that!"

Tristan spun to stare down the hall. "See what?"

"Umm. I thought I saw someone run across." She lingered for a moment watching, but nothing else appeared. Nervous, she hurried all the way down the long hallway to her bedroom.

"Wow, this place is huge… and all sorts of noises. Screeching like a giant bird, screams like a woman, even a couple roars that sounded like bears or something. My parents think the old man who lived here worked for like a movie studio." He looked around at the walls inside her bedroom. "Wow. My whole house could almost fit in here."

"Mine too." She dropped the bags and folded her arms. "This is too much space. My old… I mean real house is small too. Mom doesn't think this is gonna last and we're going to have to go back."

Tristan tossed his bags on the floor by the others. "That sucks."

She opened her mouth to say 'no, it doesn't,' but stopped herself. To him, it *would* suck, since he'd go back to being the only kid in walking distance. "Well, I dunno. Dad thinks we'll be okay. I guess if he doesn't waste money on dumb stuff, it might last."

"So no more helicopter rides?" asked Tristan.

"I've never been on a helicopter." She blinked at him. "Where'd that come from?"

"Oh, sometimes helicopters would land in the yard." He walked over to the big window and pointed out. "There. But there hasn't been one in a while."

She sat on the cushion with her back to the glass. "Do you know what that big green building is?"

"Nope. This is the first time I've been here, but it's close to where it looked like the helicopters landed." His eyes went wide. "Think it's some kinda military thing?"

She shrugged. "I dunno. We could go look?"

"Sure."

"Or we could explore inside. I've only seen a few rooms upstairs."

Tristan scratched his head. "It's your house. You pick."

"Umm, guess house. Since we're closer."

He laughed. "So, you've never been in a mansion before?"

"Nope."

Tristan nodded. "Me neither. Guess that's why you don't dress like a rich girl."

"These jeans used to be my Mom's when she was a kid. I'm not a rich—" She closed her mouth. "Okay, I guess I am."

His eyebrows went up. "You sound mad about that."

"I'd rather have my friends back," said Piper.

"Seriously? Wow… that's pretty cool."

Almost to the door, she spun to look at him. "You're not teasing me?"

"No." He shook his head, an earnest gleam in his eyes. "My dad says people are too materialistic. That's why he moved out here to the woods. I think he'd like you."

She wandered into the hall. "That's cool. Yeah, I really would give up the money for my friends."

"Would you agree never to see them again if it would save their life?"

Piper again whirled around to stare at him. "What kind of question is that?"

He smiled. "Just a thought question. What-ifs. It's a way to get to know someone."

"Oh. Umm. Yeah. Of course. I'd rather be lonely than have them die. But that's kind of a dumb question since if they died, I'd be alone anyway. Both answers have the same result."

"Kinda."

"Well, I mean *I* would be alone in either case, but, yeah, I'd rather they were alive."

"Would you shoot someone to save the life of someone you liked?" he asked.

Piper glanced at him. "I can't answer that. I don't know if I could kill someone. You don't really think about doing it until you're stuck in that situation."

"Yeah, I guess that's true."

She peered into a sitting room with a bunch of divans, sofas, chairs, and landscape paintings. "Ugh. This place is boring. It's like for old people."

"An old guy did used to live here." He laughed.

"Alone?"

"I think so." Tristan crossed the room and fiddled with the mesh screen over the fireplace.

Piper turned around in place, taking in the décor. "How could someone live alone in a place this big? Didn't he have like maids and butlers or something?"

"Thought you didn't know rich people stuff?" He backed away from the fireplace and wiped his hand on his jeans.

"I don't. But I *have* seen movies." She walked out of the sitting room, but froze the instant her sneaker hit the carpet in the hallway.

Scampering came from the left, like a group of two-year-olds running away.

"What?" whispered Tristan. "You stopped again."

"Did you hear that?" asked Piper, without moving.

"Sounded like a little kid running."

She faced him. "You *did* hear it?"

Tristan nodded.

"I'm not crazy then." She leaned into the hallway. "Hello? Is someone there?"

After a minute without a reply or hearing any more sounds, she crept into the hall.

"This is so weird." Piper told him about the pull on her shirt at the fountain while they explored another sitting room and wandered into a guest bedroom.

"Could be haunted," said Tristan.

"You believe in ghosts?"

He shrugged. "I don't *not* believe in them. I'm open-minded."

"Would you rather ghosts existed or didn't?" asked Piper.

"Umm. I think it would be cool if they did, but not if ghosts are stuck being sad all the time."

"So what would a ghost do then, if their job isn't to be sad?" She ignored another three bedrooms and walked into a modest library. "Oh… score!"

"I dunno. Maybe they like being ghosts and scaring people." He traced his fingers across the wainscoting while following her around the library. "So what kinda stuff do you like? Music?"

"Umm. Whatever's on the radio I guess." Her excitement at finding books waned. She frowned at the titles on the shelves as she passed. None of them looked remotely entertaining. Atlases, encyclopedias, and the like. The few fiction novels among them appeared to be from the 1950s. "Taylor Swift, Ed Sheeran, Katy Perry. Sometimes I listen to my dad's stuff, but I don't like all of it."

"Cool. What's he listen to?"

"Eighties."

"Never heard of them."

Piper laughed. "I mean the 1980s. Music from then."

"Oh. Duh." Tristan slapped himself in the forehead. "How 'bout video games?"

"Nope."

He tilted his head. "Nope?"

"Don't play them." She shrugged. "I mean I *have* played 'em at my friends' place, but I don't have a system. Doesn't bother me."

"Wow, really?"

She nodded, sighing at the shelves. "Geez. This library sucks."

They continued roaming from room to room, exploring guest bedrooms, sitting rooms, and a huge atrium with ten floor-to-ceiling windows along the outer wall. At the middle of the row of windows, a pair of glass double-doors led out onto a veranda that overhung the second story.

"Whoa…" Piper opened one of the doors and poked her head out.

The elevated porch had a few small, round tables and some patio furniture. Oddly enough, none of it appeared expensive.

"Piper? Check this out," said Tristan.

She looked back. He squatted a few feet away by the window nearest the door, studying something. Upon taking a knee beside him, she noticed what had drawn his attention: a faint handprint on the glass, about the size of a toddler's. "Whoa."

"We heard a kid running before," said Tristan. "Think it's a ghost?"

"Do ghosts leave handprints?" Piper stood. "That's really messed up."

"I dunno. But there's movers and your parents. If a real kid is running around here, someone would've seen them."

Mom's voice floated in, directing movers toward Piper's bedroom.

She leapt up and ran to the door, leaning out into the hallway. Her mother stood at the top of the stairs, a good distance away. "Mom! Come here a sec. You gotta see this!"

"What, Piper? I'm a little busy."

"Just, come here. You need to see this." She waved rapidly, beckoning her mother over.

With a sigh, Mom marched over and stopped in front of her with folded arms. "What is it?"

"On the glass. There's a little handprint." Piper pointed at it, and hurried across the room with her finger still aimed. But the print had disappeared.

"I don't see anything," said Mom.

"It was *right* there." Piper shot a look to Tristan.

"I saw it too, Mrs. Bailey." He gestured at the now-pristine glass. "It disappeared. I guess it *was* a ghost. Unless you have ninja housekeepers."

Mom smirked. "Are you trying to be funny or spooky?"

"I'm not *trying* to be anything. I really saw it." Piper stared down. "This place is getting creepier."

"Look, Piper, I have to help these movers get everything where it needs to be. Please at least let us get settled in before you play pranks, okay?"

"Not a prank, but okay," muttered Piper at the floor.

"Honest, Mrs. Bailey. We weren't trying to play a trick on you," said Tristan.

Mom regarded the two of them with an expression that could've been annoyance or simple tiredness. She walked off, muttering apologies to the movers for making them wait.

"That sucked," muttered Tristan. "Sorry."

She shrugged. "Thanks for trying."

"I really did see it. What do you think happened?"

"Good question." Piper crouched by the window and exhaled, making a spot of fog. No sign of a handprint appeared. "So weird."

"Yeah." He scratched the back of his head. "Kinda freaky."

Piper, feeling unsettled at the large, empty room with giant windows, hurried out into the hallway.

Tristan followed. "So, like, what did you used to do for fun?"

"Hung out with my friends, read books, sometimes watched TV." Piper nosed around a corner into a hallway that ran toward the back face of the house. It had a handful of doors on both sides as well as a bronze one at the end with a seam down the middle. "Whoa. Is that an elevator?"

"Kinda looks like one." Tristan grinned. "That's pretty cool. Your house has an elevator!"

Piper jogged down the hall, ignoring the side rooms. A bronze plaque on the wall beside the door had a gem-like button set in it next to a downward-pointing triangle. "I think it *is* an elevator."

"Push the button."

She shrugged, and poked it. The clear button lit up purple, and a faint mechanical noise echoed from behind the doors.

"Whoa. It works!" Tristan gawked at her. "That's awesome!"

"The house has an elevator," deadpanned Piper. "Who puts an elevator in their house?"

"Old people," said Tristan. "Maybe your grandfather couldn't walk up stairs?"

The doors slid apart, revealing a closet-sized chamber with brass walls polished almost to the point of mirrors. A band of ornate engraved scrollwork circled the top. To the right of the door inside where an elevator's control panel would normally be, four thin copper tubes connected from the ceiling to a box with four gem buttons as big around as quarters. Engraved lettering marked the buttons as: 3, 2, 1, B.

"Huh, wow." Tristan leaned up to the inner wall, looking at his reflection. "This is cool."

Piper hit the gem marked '2.' The doors slid closed and the elevator sank in silence.

Ten seconds later, the doors opened to reveal the strange bright décor of the second floor, peach and coral, with white trim. It wouldn't have bothered her except for the third story being so dark and cozy and the first floor, relatively plain.

"This is messed up. Like grandpa couldn't decide how to decorate the place. Upstairs looks like a creepy old mansion. This floor looks like a horror movie—it's trying too hard to look welcoming and nice. And the downstairs is like… I dunno, middle-class or something, only huge."

He laughed and pushed the gem for the first floor. Again, the doors closed and the elevator moved without a sound to the ground level. "There's one more button."

She eyed the basement gem, but didn't really want to go down there. So far, the house had been eerie enough *above* ground.

Tristan glanced at her. "Scared?"

"A little."

"Me too." He offered a hand. "Curious?"

She couldn't deny being curious, and risking a peek at a spooky basement didn't mean she had to leave the elevator. Besides, she wasn't alone. Piper grasped his hand. "Yeah."

They stared at the last gem for a minute.

She looked at him.

"Your house. You do it," said Tristan.

"Aren't boys supposed to be brave?"

"Usually, but you're older. I'm only eleven." He put his finger on the gem without pushing it. "Together?"

"'Kay." Still holding his hand, she put her left index finger on the button next to his.

"Three… two… one."

The gem depressed with a faint *click*, but it didn't light up, nor did the elevator go anywhere.

"Broken?" asked Tristan.

Piper examined the control panel and noticed a small keyhole next to the 'B' gem, like for one of those old-timey skeleton keys. "It could be locked."

"Wicked," whispered Tristan. "I wonder what's down there that your grandfather made it require a key."

She let go of his hand and walked out onto the ground floor. "I dunno. Maybe there's stairs?"

"Maybe."

The idea that she lived in a house that had its own elevator would've been weird enough without a locked button. Her mind raced. She envisioned everything from a mad scientist's lab, to a James Bond style secret lair, to something Mary Shelley might've created. Piper grimaced while roaming down the first-floor hallway. Maybe she didn't want to see the basement after all. People tended to lock things for good reasons. But if Grandpa Bailey had a bunch of cool stuff down there, he might've locked it.

Did the lock protect the stuff from people, or people from the stuff?

"Is it wrong to sneak into a place a dead guy locked? I mean, he can't go there anymore, right? And my Dad owns everything now, so it's technically my Dad's stuff."

"Then it's not bad." Tristan nodded. "Unless your Dad tells you not to go in."

Piper opened the first door on the left and sighed at two sofas arranged catty-corner near a fireplace and a big television. Other than being large, the room didn't feel like it belonged in a mansion. Common furniture and ordinary decoration made it look like her friends' nice living rooms, only double the size. True, *her* living room had been small and packed with falling-apart furniture, but she still missed it.

Room after room on the ground floor followed that trend, including the kitchen, which could've come from any average suburban home. A few doors away from a dining room, the kids entered a den with dark burgundy wood-grain walls, a charcoal-grey marble fireplace in front of a pair of wingback chairs, and a giant desk, where Dad sat looking over paperwork.

"Hey." He smiled up at them. "Oh, who's your friend?"

"Hello, Mr. Bailey." Tristan walked up to him and offered a hand. "I'm Tristan. We live up the road a little."

"Nice to meet you." Dad shook his hand.

Piper looked at the mass of yellowing papers all over the desk. Most had sketches of animals, but no creature she'd ever seen before. One depicted a bird with an extremely long pair of tailfeathers, more like streamers. Another had a sketch of a winged snake. A third looked like a relatively normal dog, save for its aggressive posture and bared teeth.

"What's all this?" She tugged the dog drawing out from the pile and held it up.

"I think my father was working on a book of mythology," said Dad. "Or maybe he liked *Lord of the Rings* or something."

Piper grinned. "What's wrong with that?"

"Fantasy is overdone." Dad shook his head. "People want vampires."

"Ugh, Dad, really? *Everyone* and their mother writes about vampires. It's *so* boring, especially the way they keep falling in love with normal teenage girls."

Dad scratched at his shoulder. "I don't have to write about teen vampires. I could do something darker. More like Bram Stoker."

"Okay." Piper smiled. "That, I'd read."

"Maybe a retelling with a werewolf Van Helsing." He tapped a finger to his chin.

"I will do something horrible to you if you write that." Piper narrowed her eyes.

Dad laughed.

Tristan walked over to a display case in the corner full of small figurines.

"Why don't you try to give fantasy a shot?" asked Piper.

Dad shuffled the papers, trying to get them into a neat stack. The envelope the estate attorney had dropped off sat near the top of the desk by the base of a lamp. "I dunno, maybe. There's enough information here for me to build out an entire setting, but that would take so much time."

Piper folded her arms. "You quit working at the dealership. You've got nothing but time now."

"You sound like your mother. Like you're yelling at me." Dad laughed.

She held her arms out to the sides. "There's lots of people who want jobs and can't get them. You had a good one and you quit."

"Piper…" He poked one finger into her stomach and wiggled it until she grinned.

She scooted back, scratching the spot.

"I don't need to work. I can spend time with you and maybe finally chase that dream of being a writer."

"Why's Mom still teaching then?" Piper tilted her head to examine another sketch that resembled a mermaid, only the woman's face had been drawn with hideous giant teeth and a gaping mouth wide enough to take someone's head off. "Eww."

"Wow," muttered Tristan, beside her. "That mermaid really needs a dentist."

Dad shrugged. "Because she's convinced herself that this is all far too good to be true."

She shrank away from the horrible image and gave him a flat look. "Isn't it?"

He patted her back and kissed her on top of the head. "The funny thing about humans, hon, is that we have a tendency to make things happen because we expect them to. If you keep believing that this is too good to be true, you'll wind up making that reality."

Piper fidgeted. "That sounds like magic."

"Not at all, hon." Dad resumed trying to organize the piles of sketches and notes. "Think about an athlete about to run a marathon. If they convince themselves they don't have the endurance to reach the finish line, they're going to sabotage themselves subconsciously, and they probably won't make it to the finish line."

She leaned on the desk. "Okay, so how does me thinking that no one really winds up inheriting gobs of money and a giant house out of nowhere like this mean something's going to go wrong?"

Tristan looked back and forth between them.

"Well," said Dad. "You are a bit young yet… but maybe seeing you so sad and miserable will make me do dumb things out of guilt and waste all the money so we wind up back in Syracuse in that little shack."

"But I liked our house." Piper twisted her sneaker toe into the rug.

"You could barely turn around in your room. It had what? Three feet of space between your desk and bed?"

"Two. But I liked those two feet." She half-smiled for a moment, then looked up with worry all over her face. "I felt safe there. This place feels… scary. Like something's always staring at me."

Tristan snickered. "Maybe your grandfather's not really dead and he's hiding in the basement watching us on cameras."

Piper's stomach did a flip. "Don't even say that. That's *so* twisted."

Dad cringed.

"What happened to him?" She looked up at her father.

"I have no idea. That attorney never mentioned anything beyond that he'd died somewhere out of the country." Dad hooked his thumbs in his pockets. "I already told you, I didn't know the man. The last time I saw him I'd been not even a year old yet."

"They didn't find a body, did they?" asked Tristan.

"Stop!" Piper shoved playfully at him. "That's not funny." Out of the corner of her eye, she noticed the door on the glass cabinet in the corner hung open. "Oh, you left the door open."

Tristan glanced back at it. "I didn't open it."

The confusion and fear in his eyes struck Piper as real enough to freak her out. "Umm. Dad?"

"Oh, that's enough, you two." He ruffled her hair and shook his head at Tristan. "Go try and stay out of trouble. I have a lot of work to do." Dad walked to the corner and shut the cabinet.

A reflection flashed on the moving glass door, she glimpsed a tall man with shaggy black hair, misshapen yellow eyes, and rotting teeth standing right behind her and Tristan. Piper shrieked and spun around, leaping backward and bumping the desk with her butt.

No hideous creature stood there.

"Piper!" said Dad in an almost-shout, one hand on his chest. "What's gotten into you?"

Tristan had gone pale, though he stared at her, likely startled by the sudden scream, too.

"I thought I saw something in the door. A monster. When you closed it, like a reflection." She pointed a shaking hand at the cabinet.

Dad opened his mouth, likely to chide her for being silly, but hesitated. He opened the cabinet door and nudged it back and forth. She stared into the glass, but nothing strange appeared in the reflection.

"It's gone," said Piper.

"Hon, I think you've let the idea of 'creepy old house' get into your head and play games with you. There's no such things as monsters."

She looked down. "Sorry."

Tristan leaned close and whispered, "I believe you. This place feels weird."

"Thanks," muttered Piper, smiling weakly at him.

They left the den and spent the rest of the day exploring the house. The ground floor had three living rooms, two dining rooms, a big kitchen, pantry, a couple of sitting rooms, and a garden/greenhouse at the back left corner. A fountain there had a statue of a bronze fish spitting water straight up, and bizarre plants in the basin that resembled lily pads, only they spanned three or four feet across with upturned edges that made them look like pie plates.

From there, they went up to the second floor and stumbled across a room full of display cases. All sorts of gadgets sat on the shelves, from antique clocks to old toys, to unidentifiable steel contraptions affixed to leather harnesses that resembled backpacks of some kind. Tristan suggested jetpacks, but the metal part had nothing close to a rocket engine, only an assortment of fake-looking gems and something like a grapple hook that might spring out from the top.

By the time Mom showed up to announce dinner, Piper had grown fond of having Tristan around. Not that he replaced Gwen or Jaime, but since they couldn't be here, she figured they wouldn't mind her making a new friend. Not to mention, the boy seemed lonely, friendly, and they more or less had similar senses of humor and tastes in music. He liked country music in addition to the stuff they both listened to. Piper had never heard any, so she didn't recognize the bands he mentioned. As she and Mom walked him to the door, he offered to bring some over sometime… if Piper wanted to hang out again.

"Yeah, cool." She smiled at him. "Thanks for coming over."

"Awesome. See you tomorrow?"

Piper nodded, and stood there, half out the door, watching him race off across the grass toward the forest. A forest where this boy supposedly lived a mile away. She folded her arms, struck with a sudden, bizarre thought. This house seemed so alive, so strange… could it have sensed her want for a friend and made one? Tristan had an almost elven look to his features, and she hadn't seen much of his ears under his thick, black hair. Given how long he wore it (a bit past his shoulders) and that he ran off into the woods, might he *actually* be an elf? Perhaps a ghost or an illusion of some kind?

"Piper?" asked Mom. "Something wrong?"

She stepped back inside and eased the door shut. "Do you really want me to answer that?"

Mom sighed. "Come on, it's time to eat."

3

SECONDHAND LIFE

Piper sat at the table, which occupied a nook at the end of the giant kitchen, surrounded by blue-grey painted shelves full of plates, bowls, and cups. For a house this huge, she'd expected something more industrial, made for an army of kitchen staff like a cafeteria. It had an island counter with a second sink, cabinets wrapped around the opposite two walls over the main counter, and a big steel fridge. It didn't look at all like the kitchen of a great manor house, and by appearance, could've been in any ordinary suburban home—albeit a big one.

Her parents had always taken turns cooking, with Dad winding up behind the stove somewhat more often than Mom when she got stuck grading papers or working on lesson plans. He had initially suggested splurging tonight and ordering a pizza—something that hadn't happened since Piper had been nine years old. As it turned out, the little town they'd passed on the way in didn't have a pizzeria, nor anything at all that delivered prepared food. No place in Utica (the closest major city) would run a pie out here; one man had even laughed at Dad for asking.

Fortunately, the pantry had enough supplies for Mom to whip up a vegetable soup. The fridge had surprisingly fresh-looking produce, which none of them trusted. The phone call mentioning the death of Grandpa Bailey had come near the end of May, which meant the old man had to have died at least a month ago. Mom thought it strange for the fridge to still have intact perishables one to two months after the only person who lived here died. Dad suggested the lawyer stocked it up for them, but didn't sound like he really believed that.

Neither did Mom.

Dad found some bread in the pantry, also surprising in its lack of staleness. It smelled, tasted, and looked fine, so he'd set it out with Mom's soup.

Piper kept her head down, leaning her cheek against her left hand, elbow on the table, and lifted soup by the spoonful to her mouth in no great hurry. With Tristan gone, her mind had returned to dwelling on her absent friends, but she also couldn't help but question if the boy had been real. She obviously hadn't imagined him, since her parents both saw and talked to him. But who lives off in the woods in the middle of nowhere?

She frowned. *We do.*

"Something wrong with the soup?" asked Mom.

"No," said Piper, not quite at full volume. "It's good."

"She didn't complain when your parents made liver and onions either." Dad shuddered. "Maybe we *should* take her to see someone. Normal kids don't just eat whatever you put in front of them without protest."

"Oh, you're forgetting when she was small." Mom smiled. "She didn't get over being a picky eater until she was around seven."

"Old enough to understand we didn't have much money and be happy we had food at all." Piper sat up straight and let her left arm fall into her lap. "I'm not complaining."

"She's got your altruism," said Dad.

"Me?" Mom laughed. "You're calling me an altruist?"

"Well, you are working as a teacher. Who else but an altruist would deal with *that* much stress for so little money?"

Mom gave him a peeved stare, but didn't argue the point.

Footsteps thumped by overhead. Piper looked at the ceiling and dropped her spoon into the bowl with a *clank*. "Did you hear that?"

"Hear what?" asked Dad.

"I just heard footsteps upstairs." She peeled her gaze off the ceiling and stared at Dad.

Evidently, she looked frightened enough for him to get up.

"I'll go check it out," said Dad. He dabbed a napkin at his lip, stood, and walked out.

Piper pulled her legs up and wrapped her arms around them, sitting in a ball on her chair. "You didn't hear it?"

"No, I didn't notice." Mom looked at the ceiling.

They sat in silence, listening. A minute or three later, more footsteps passed overhead, likely from Dad. Something creaked in the distance, making Piper turn her head toward one of the archways leading out of the kitchen. The sound appeared to come from the ground floor, meaning it couldn't have been her father.

"Something's down here." She leapt out of her chair and ran around behind Mom. "A door creaked."

Mom soaked up some of her contagious worry. She stood and wrapped a protective arm around her. They waited, barely breathing, twitching at every groan or creak of the building. The tension in her mother's body lessened at the rumble of Dad coming down the stairs. He walked into the kitchen, raising his arms in a shrug.

"There's no one there."

"I think they're downstairs now. A door squeaked." Piper pointed.

Again, Dad walked off, heading through the second archway. Piper clung to her mother for a few minutes until he reappeared, looking equally confused.

"Nothing." He returned to his chair and sat. "We're alone. There's no one in the house but us."

Mom prodded her back to the table. Piper sat, head down, and hid behind a curtain of wavy brown hair while stirring at her soup, having lost her appetite.

A short while later, Mom sighed. "Piper, we know you're unhappy about moving. I understand, but making up stories to try and scare us out of here isn't the right way to confront your feelings."

"Give her time," said Dad. "Relocating isn't easy on kids. Only *our* daughter would be unhappy about us becoming financially independent."

"I'm like a two-hour ride away from all my friends who are so far away I'll probably never see them again. Why would I possibly be unhappy?" asked Piper, not looking up.

"Your father spent years putting in overtime just so we had a roof over our heads and food in the fridge. I know we weren't able to give you the same things your friends had, but we did the best we could." Mom reached across the table toward her.

Piper set her spoon down and stretched her right arm out to grasp Mom's hand. "I know."

"I'm sorry I missed so much of your life, hon." Dad reached for her other hand, which he squeezed when she took it. "That's not a problem for us anymore. At least you're still young enough for me to try and make up for it. Give me a couple years before you're 'too cool' to hang out with your parents? Huh?" He smiled.

Piper laughed. "Dad… You're such a dork. Besides, you guys dragged me out here. It's not like I can blow you off to go to the mall with my friends. We might as well be on Alcatraz island."

"I'm honestly surprised you haven't asked for anything," said Mom. "You were so thrilled when we got you that cell phone."

"Never saw someone cry over an old iPhone before." Dad grinned.

"Mom… I'm happy with my secondhand clothes. They're still good enough to wear. I don't care about computers or video games or designer shoes or electronic gadgets."

Dad glanced at Mom. "Maybe we ought to take her to a shrink. This kid is broken."

"Money doesn't make people happy. It makes them miserable." She squeezed her parents' hands tight. "I'm afraid it's going to change us. I like the family we have. I bet this grandpa I never met died alone and sad in this huge house. What did all that money do for him?"

After a short silence, the three-way handholding parted, and they resumed eating. Piper found a little bit of her appetite again and gnawed on a slice of bread.

"Well, I bet my father never had to worry about making rent on time, or affording food." Dad winked.

"The taxes on this place?" Mom shivered. "Probably four times our rent."

"Most likely that's why it's out here in the middle of nowhere." Dad ripped off a hunk of bread and swabbed the sides of his bowl with it. "You know, if you still want to be a vet when you're done with high school, *now* we can afford to send you to college. And a good one."

Mom shook her head. "Alan, let her finish seventh grade first."

"Sorry for being glum... and don't rush me back to school. Summer just started." Piper shot a somber look out the windows at the meadow behind the house. "If it's okay with Gwen's parents, can I maybe spend a week there before summer's over? Or can they come here?"

"We'll work something out." Dad smiled. "Contrary to what you think, this entire move wasn't engineered to make you miserable."

Piper looked around the room. "What about selling this place and getting a normal-people house back in Syracuse? You don't really expect Mom to clean this whole place, do you?"

Mom shot him a 'she's got a point' look. "It would take a staff to keep up with it. As much as our daughter's suggestion is coming from the hip, she raises a point worth considering."

Dad held his hands up. "Can we at least give it a month before we decide it unmanageable?"

"You're such a little boy." Mom laughed. "Big shiny new toy and you want to play with it."

"Oh, Dad, what's in the weird building out back?"

He looked over at her. "Weird building?"

"Yeah. It's way out by the trees. Big and square and covered with fake bushes and stuff, like someone's trying to hide that it's a building. I saw it out my window."

"Oh, that's curious." Dad glanced over his shoulder at the kitchen curtains. "That lawyer guy never mentioned anything about that."

"He didn't seem to like it here," said Piper. "Got the feeling he wanted to leave as fast as possible."

"Yeah, me too." Dad rubbed his chin.

Mom shifted her gaze back and forth between them. "Wonder why?"

"He probably knows what's haunting the place," said Piper.

Mom sighed. "Really, Piper? Will you please give that a rest?"

"Yes, Mom."

Piper gathered the dishes after dinner, as had been her job for the past few years. This sink had so much room she could fit them all in at once to wash, as well as a weird rubber plug in the drain, separated into triangular sections. "Mom, what's this?"

Her mother peered in. "Oh, umm. I think that's a disposer sink. Don't put your hands down the drain."

"Disposer sink?" asked Piper.

Mom pointed at a switch on the wall. "It's got a grinder that chops things up so they can go down the drain. Sharp and dangerous."

"Eep." Piper leaned away from the sink. "Why?"

"Supposed to be convenient, I guess." Mom rubbed her back. "It won't hurt you as long as you don't stick your hand down the drain."

"Right. I'll try to remember not to do something I've never done before." She rolled her eyes playfully and turned on the water, adding some liquid soap.

Mom walked off.

A few minutes after she started washing dishes, her mother re-entered the kitchen looking angry. Piper twisted around to give her a 'what's wrong?' face.

"Where's my laptop?"

Piper shrugged. "I dunno. I haven't seen it since we drove up here."

"This isn't amusing, Piper." Mom raked her hands at her hair and paced side to side. "I have work I need to do. I'm not like your father. I can't just walk away from my job that I've been doing for the past sixteen years. I need something normal to cling to. I don't appreciate your ghost nonsense."

"Uhh, Mom?" Piper's eyes widened, trying to project innocence. "I swear I didn't touch your laptop."

Mom stared at her for a moment, then the anger faded from her expression. "All right. I'm sorry. I believe you."

She relaxed. "I'll help you look when I'm finished with the dishes."

"I'm going to check the truck. Maybe I never brought it inside." Mom hugged her on the way out.

Piper turned back to face the sink and resumed scrubbing a bowl. "Okay, house. You're trying to get me in trouble. You don't want me here? Well, fine. I don't want to be here. Making my parents think I'm nuts isn't going to help. If you want us out of here, you'll have to do something obvious that they can't blame me for."

That strange feeling of being watched returned, stronger and darker. Piper pulled her hands out of the water, inexplicably terrified the disposer would turn itself on and somehow still hurt her even if she didn't reach down the drain. She clutched the edge of the counter, sending suds dripping down the cabinets. The sense of not being alone intensified. She twisted to look behind her at the large, empty kitchen.

Her attention fixated on the corner between the two archways: one opened to a hallway toward the front foyer, the other to a dining room. A shadow, as if a man stood in the corner, darkened the wall. Piper leaned away, shivering as a faint whimpery whine leaked out of her nose. Her knees threatened to give out. She clung to the counter, too frightened to scream, and too scared to stop looking at the mysterious shape.

After a few seconds, the shadow vanished.

It took her a minute to calm down enough to cry. Worse, she couldn't tell her parents what she just saw, or they'd cart her off to a psychiatrist—or think she'd made it up. She desperately wanted to run out of the kitchen and jump into her old bed, but forced herself to finish washing the dishes.

Piper plucked each piece out of the water and ran the sponge over it in midair, careful to keep her hands as far away from the hungry teeth of the disposer sink as she could. Every few seconds, she peered back over her shoulder, dreading she'd see the shadow—or something worse—behind her.

When Dad walked in, she couldn't help herself, and leapt into a hug. She grabbed a fistful of his shirt and stared over her knuckles at the corner.

"Piper? What's wrong? You're trembling." He held her tight, sounding concerned.

"You'll think I'm crazy or lying."

He swayed her side to side in a gentle rocking motion. "I promise I won't think you're lying. You've always been honest with us."

She looked up at him, her chin against his chest. "You didn't say you won't think I'm nuts."

Dad smiled.

"I thought I saw a shadow in the corner, like someone standing there. But it disappeared."

"This house *is* creepy. If I was your age, I'd probably be randomly scared of shadows too. It's all in your head, like a nightmare. You've convinced yourself that there's something wrong with this place, so your mind is playing tricks on you."

She frowned at the corner. "It felt too real. And something hid Mom's laptop."

"Hid?" He chuckled. "You're that sure she didn't misplace it?"

"If Mom was a superhero, her power would be organization. She's freaking out that it wasn't where she put it."

Dad raised an eyebrow. "Hey. Let's do something we haven't done in a while."

Piper scrunched up her nose. "I'm not sure I like the sound of that."

"Movie?" He nodded toward the hallway leading to one of the living rooms. "There's a giant TV in there."

She forgot the shadow, and grinned. "Okay. Lemme go put on PJs."

4

HOMESICK

It had taken Dad a few minutes to work out the satellite TV, but they eventually all snuggled on the sofa and watched *Zootopia.* After the movie, she went upstairs to her bedroom, but as soon as she reached the foyer, it felt like something followed her. She gasped and sprinted up the stairs, running most the rest of the way to her room. Once safe behind a closed door, she leaned against it gasping for breath, dreading that at any second something would pound on it.

After a few seconds of peace, she sighed at the cardboard-henge stacked up in one corner. All her stuff, which wouldn't have fit inside her old bedroom while boxed up, looked so small in here. She rummaged around until she found her stash of cosmetics and took a moment to debate between pink glitter or plain purple polish. Eventually deciding on pink, she sat on the rug with her back against her bed, and checked her phone. Much to her surprise, it had a signal.

"Holy crap!"

She dialed Gwen. Her friend picked up in a few rings.

"Pipes! Where have you been?"

"Middle of nowhere." She sighed. "I'm not even sure how I have signal now. Maybe this house has some kinda connection or something."

"Hang on…" Gwen clicked off. She came back on the line a moment later, with Jamie conferenced in.

Piper set the phone on speaker and painted her toenails while telling her friends about the house, the crappy drive, the strange lawyer, and how much she hated it here. Of course, her friends thought her crazy for not being thrilled to have so much money. At least they sensed her getting glum when they talked about spending the day at Gwen's in the pool, and changed the subject to Kyle Remmer (Gwen's crush) being in a car accident. Fortunately, he wasn't hurt beyond a sore neck, but his older brother who had been driving broke a leg.

While swishing her feet back and forth to dry the polish, Piper got started on her fingernails, as well as ghost stories. She told her friends about the scampering toddler-like footsteps, the handprint, the heavier footsteps, and the creepy hairy thing in the cabinet glass, saving the shadow in the kitchen for last. Both of her friends kept pin-drop silent the whole time (a true rarity). Gwen's mother had once joked that only an Armageddon-level event would've kept her from going more than six seconds without talking.

"So you think it's real?" asked Jamie.

"Has to be. At least, I guess I believe it. Gwen kept quiet for like a whole two minutes listening."

A raspberry came back over the phone.

"Hey, I'm trying to get my 'rents to let you guys come up for a week… if you want to," said Piper.

"Cool," said Jamie. "Or maybe you can stay at Gwen's instead since she's got a pool. Does your *new mansion* have a pool?"

"Umm. I dunno. If it does, I haven't found it yet," said Piper.

"That's cool. You can sleep in the closet under the stairs. Harry Piper style," said Gwen.

Piper bit her lip, unsure if her friend meant that as a joke. Gwen's house *did* have a storage area like that. "Okay, as long as you don't lock me in."

The girls laughed. Piper made the mistake of mentioning Tristan, and the interrogation began. Jamie insisted Piper 'now had a boyfriend.' Her face flushed red as she insisted that she'd only known him for a few hours and had no interest in a boyfriend yet.

"Is he cute?" asked Gwen.

Piper smirked. "He's okay looking. Big eyes and a small nose."

"She *does* like him," cooed Jamie.

"Shut up!" Piper laughed.

Mom knocked and poked her head in. "It's almost ten, hon."

"Okay, okay." Piper smiled at her mother while muttering, "Gotta go. Mom's raging."

"I am not 'raging,' Piper. It's bedtime." Mom chuckled and drifted off.

The friends exchanged good nights, and Piper reluctantly hung up.

She tossed the phone on her nightstand and went into the attached bathroom. Having a bathroom all to herself went beyond strange, never mind one with a bathtub so big it counted as a small pool.

"Geez. A band could hold a concert in here."

The toilet seat was so cold it made her yelp.

"You okay?" called Mom from out in the hall.

"Yeah," shouted Piper. "I'm fine. Cold seat."

She looked around at the towel rack, sink cabinet, bathtub/shower with a sliding glass partition instead of a plastic curtain, and a shelf to her right with little bowls holding decorative seashell soaps in pastel colors.

"That's weird. Why would an old man living alone have cute soaps?" She couldn't reach the shelf from the toilet, so merely stared at it. "That's like something Mom would buy… if we had spare money."

Trying to go in a bathroom so large took a while. She felt like she sat out in public. The one bathroom her old house had was so small, doing anything (except standing in the shower) involved being smushed against at least one wall or a cabinet. She didn't think overweight people could've even used the toilet in there, and Gwen (who was unusually tall for her age) constantly complained about no legroom.

Eventually, Piper relaxed enough to relieve herself. After brushing her teeth, she headed out to the bedroom. With the lights off, the creep factor magnified ten times, and she found herself running like a terrified five-year-old for the safety of her covers.

The new bed had more than twice the space of her old one, and felt like she'd crawled inside a cloud. She pulled the puffy white blanket up to her nose, only her eyes peering out at the dark room, as if the blanket and comforter would stop monsters.

Strange shadows drifted around in the patches of moonlight on the ceiling, despite the lack of trees near the windows. She shivered from fear, but couldn't explain exactly what had scared her. Since no one could see her at the moment, she didn't mind looking childish, and took comfort from hiding in her bedding.

Unable to escape the feeling that something had invaded her bedroom, Piper lay awake, staring at the ceiling. Despite the bed being the most comfortable thing she'd ever touched, hours dragged on with her getting no closer to sleep. At every shift in light above her, she snugged the blankets tighter at her chin. Whenever she thought she saw motion in darkness at the edges of the room, she trembled.

She would've sprinted to her parents' room and crawled in bed with them if it didn't require leaving the safety of her covers. Fear rose and fell; one moment, she felt like screaming for her father, the next, she wound up only a little nervous. The cycle continued for some time, until she realized she had to pee.

Oh, no way. She cringed. *I'm not getting out of bed.*

As if trying to fall asleep while terrified hadn't been difficult enough, the added discomfort of her body demanding a bathroom break made it impossible. She squirmed, then rolled on her side and curled up. The urge didn't qualify as an emergency, merely enough to keep her thinking about the need to go.

"Grr. Okay, time to grow up. There's no monster in my closet. Dad's right. I have an overactive imagination." She rolled flat on her back again, tilting her head to stare at her bathroom door. "I don't even have to go far."

Piper sat up and looked around. Blue moonlight made her formerly nice bedroom into something from a haunted house movie. It took her a few minutes, but she managed to convince herself that her fear came from being in an unfamiliar place so much different from the home she'd been used to. When she thought that the distance from her bed to the bathroom door looked longer than the entire upstairs hallway of her old house, she giggled.

"I'm being stupid."

She pushed the bedding aside and slid to the side of the mattress.

The instant her toes touched carpet, a frigid hand from under her bed grabbed her around the ankle.

Somehow managing not to wet her nightdress, Piper clutched the blankets and screamed as loud as she could. Her left knee pressed into the bed as she tried to pull her other leg up, but the icy fingers didn't budge. Still screaming, she tried to get a solid hold of the headboard, but her arms couldn't reach. Twisting and tugging at her leg, she scrambled for a grip on the comforter, pushing with her free leg to keep the monster from pulling her under the bed as it seemed to be trying to do.

"Piper?" called Dad in the hallway.

"Help!" screamed Piper. "It's got me!"

"Leave her alone!" rasped a small, gritty voice under the bed.

A faint, inexplicable sizzling *pop* accompanied a flash under the bed at the same instant her door opened. The hand released her ankle, sending her flying face-first into the middle of her mattress. Lights came on. Dad rushed in and sat on the edge of the bed. She curled into a ball and burst into tears.

"Shh," said Dad, rubbing her arm. "Just a bad dream."

Piper grasped her ankle, the skin cold to the touch. "There's a monster under my bed. It grabbed my leg."

He gathered her upright, cradling her against his chest. "You just had a dream, hon. There's nothing under your bed."

She pointed. "Feel my leg. It's ice cold."

Dad's hand settled on her right ankle, his touch as hot as a freshly-drawn bath. "A little cold, but you're out of bed in the middle of the night."

"Had to go." She eyed the bathroom, again afraid to leave the safety of her blankets. "Please look and make sure there's nothing under the bed."

He yawned, chuckled, and shook his head. "Wow. We're having a good month. Big inheritance, new house, our daughter found a potion of youth."

"Huh?" She blinked.

"I thought we had a twelve-year-old, not a *little* daughter." He winked. "Check under the bed for monsters?"

Her wounded, pouty expression convinced him to look. He took a knee, stooping to put his head down near the floor. After making a show of gazing around, he sat back up. "Nothing there. Must've been a doozy of a nightmare; you're actually shaking."

"It really happened." She tried to rub warmth into her leg.

"Moving... this is a big change for you. For all of us." Dad stroked her hair. "It's okay to be scared. I guess at your age, nightmares can happen. But dreams can't hurt you."

"I didn't make it up," said Piper in a small voice. She leaned over to look at her leg, but despite the iron grip that had held her, her skin showed no finger-like marks. "It can't be a nightmare because I didn't fall asleep. I've been lying awake all night."

"Understandable. Me too." He managed a weary smile. "I have trouble falling asleep in a new place. You probably got that from me. It's just a matter of adjusting and getting used to it."

Piper shifted to sit with her legs over the edge, feet dangling over the carpet. "What if I don't want to stay here long enough to get used to it? I think the house hates me. It wants us to leave."

"You haven't given it a chance. Our family received a wonderful, unexpected gift." Dad smiled.

"From a guy you never met who Grandma said was an elitist butthead. Maybe he gave us this house because it's cursed."

"Go to sleep, Piper. We can talk about this tomorrow."

"I can't. I gotta go to the bathroom."

She swirled between frightened, annoyed, and exhausted for a few seconds before finding the courage to slide out of bed, kneel, and peek underneath. Sure enough, nothing but carpet under the bed—and a whiff of singed hair. Her eyes shot open wide.

"Do you smell that?" asked Piper.

"I smell tired." Dad yawned.

"Smells like burnt hair." She stood. "Will you wait here with the lights on while I go?"

He nodded. "All right, fine. Hurry up."

Piper darted to the bathroom, dealt with the iceberg toilet seat, and ran back to bed. "Thanks."

He held up the blankets for her to climb under, and tucked her in. "Wow. You're still shivering."

She stared at him. "Tell me you wouldn't be freaked out if a freezing hand grabbed your leg when you got out of bed in a dark, creepy room."

"Nightmares can seem real, hon. You probably *did* fall asleep and had a bad dream that you were lying here awake." He leaned down and kissed her forehead. "C'mon. Try to get some sleep."

Piper nodded and closed her eyes. She flinched when the lights went off, but didn't dare open her eyes. A long period of silence passed with her no closer to sleep. Footsteps, heavy like a grown man, passed overhead in a slow, methodical trudge.

"Maybe Grandpa Bailey didn't want to leave his house." She risked opening one eye, and tracked the entity walking across her ceiling. "And he's pacing in the attic."

She rolled on her side and crawled to the edge by the nightstand, grabbing her iPhone long enough to check the time: 2:58 a.m. "Ugh." Again feeling like a little kid, she ducked completely under the covers and curled up. "What was that other voice? Something told the monster to leave me alone. Maybe there's a bunch of ghosts here and one is nice… or one isn't nice and the others aren't so bad."

A while of tossing and turning later, she rearranged herself to lie flat, but kept the blankets up to her chin. Minutes passed into a blur. Piper kept thinking *just a nightmare,* over and over. Eventually, her eyelids grew heavy, and she drifted off.

UNUSUAL WEIGHT ON HER CHEST WOKE PIPER TO A ROOM FILLED WITH early morning sun. She yawned and tried to reach up to wipe her eyes, but the blankets kept her arms pinned in place. Sitting up didn't work either. She twisted and tugged at her limbs, but couldn't move, as if her comforter had turned into a giant slab of stone too heavy to lift.

"Help!" wheezed Piper, barely able to breathe against the heaviness crushing her into the mattress. Pressure like a grown man kneeling with all his weight on her chest forced all the air out of her. "Ngh!"

Piper struggled, only able to wiggle her feet side to side, grab around with her hands, and lift her head up enough to stare at her outline in the puffy, white comforter. She felt (and looked) like a doll vacuum-sealed in a plastic package.

"I'll be downstairs," said Mom, likely to Dad, while breezing by outside in the hall.

"Mom!" wheezed Piper. "Help!"

Her mother evidently didn't hear her, as she didn't come back.

Rapid breaths made her dizzy in seconds. Piper strained to fight the force pressing her into the bed. Not being able to move would've been scary on its own, but the added dread of having such difficulty breathing made her fear for her life. No matter how hard she twisted or wriggled, she couldn't budge.

Panic kept her feebly thrashing for a minute or two until she passed out and woke back up.

Crap! It's trying to kill me!

Tears streamed down the sides of her head. She tried again to scream for help, but only emitted an asthmatic rasp. When Dad walked by outside like nothing at all was wrong in the world, her fear spiked so high she became calm. *Think! Don't be stupid!* She looked around at her normal-seeming bedroom. No creepy shadows, no looming figures.

"Please let me go," she whispered.

It didn't.

"Why are you doing this?" she whispered.

Nothing replied.

I have to do something. Piper tried to move her arms in close to push the ponderous blankets up from her chest so she could breathe, but she may as well have been trapped in a full-body cast. How could she possibly get her parents' attention without any air inside of her?

An idea hit after a few seconds. Sip by sip, she sucked in small breaths, using the pressure inside her lungs to fight the crushing force. After a moment, she felt like she had a decent chance of making noise, and let out a scream of, "Help!"

When no one responded, a flash of dread brought icy shivers. This house was so big her parents could be in the kitchen and they'd never hear her all the way up here.

Again, she filled her lungs with tiny sips and let out a scream for help.

Two minutes passed in dreadful silence, but when the thump of

Dad's footsteps approached in the hall outside, her heart swelled with hope.

"Piper?" Her doorknob rattled. "What's going on?"

"Dad! I can't breathe!"

Her door rattled again. "Hon, why did you lock your door?"

"I didn't," wheezed Piper. "Help! I can't"—she forced in more air—"get outta bed."

"Open the door, Piper. This isn't funny."

She took a few sips of air before shouting, "It isn't. I'm stuck!"

"What are you doing, hon?"

"Argh!" She thrashed around like a faerie stuck to flypaper. "Daddy!"

Dad stormed off.

She lay still, unsure if he planned to leave her trapped all day long or if he'd gone off in search of a key. It didn't matter if she got in trouble for locking the door, even if she didn't. If it would get her out of the bed, she'd accept any punishment.

Her father returned in a little while. Metal scraping came from the keyhole. Seconds later, the lock *clicked.* The instant the knob turned, the oppressive force released her blankets. Piper scrambled out of bed as her father walked in. She ran across the room and leapt into a hug, exploding into a fit of sobbing and shivering.

It took him a few minutes to calm her down enough to talk. He kept a straight face while she explained being trapped in bed, unable to move the sheets, blankets, and comforter, and swore over and over that she didn't lock the door.

"Are you sure that's what happened?" He raised an eyebrow. "You don't want to change that story at all? Maybe you had another bad dream or you're pretending there's a ghost so we move out and go back to Syracuse?"

Piper stared down at her bright pink toenails, glitter sparkling in a patch of sunlight. "I *do* want to go home, but I didn't make that up. I couldn't breathe. I think it was trying to kill me." She held up her hands, both still shaking. "Look at me. Do you think I'm faking it?"

He grasped her hands, holding them still. When he let go, she resumed trembling. "I think you had a really bad nightmare." Dad put an arm around her back and held her. "I don't think you're fibbing, but

I am worried that you seem not to be able to separate nightmare from reality."

"I..." She bit her lip. Did crazy people know they were crazy? Maybe she really did have a nightmare and couldn't tell the difference. "Maybe I did have a bad dream."

"That's my tough girl." He gave her a quick hug and wagged a screwdriver at her. "I don't want you locking that door again, clear?"

"I didn't lock it."

He gave her the 'really' expression.

"Well, if I did, I was sleepwalking and don't remember it. I swear I didn't lock it on purpose."

Dad's accusing stare turned worried. He sat in silence for a moment before hugging her again and standing. "G'won and get dressed. I'm going to go get started on breakfast."

"Yes, Dad."

She sat on the side of the bed watching him walk out. As embarrassing as it would've been to have one of her parents walk in on her while changing, she didn't trust that her door would open again if she shut it. After gathering a clean pair of jeans, T-shirt, underpants, and socks, she padded into the bathroom.

5

FANTASY NONSENSE

Her parents' voices in the kitchen stalled her right outside the arch. Piper leaned out of sight up against the wall, listening.

"I just don't know, Ames. She's never acted like this before, and it's got me worried."

Piper folded her arms. Dad only called Mom 'Ames' when he was either really happy, or frightened. Of course, that beat him calling her 'Amy.' That, she'd only heard once when they'd been fighting so bad she expected they'd get a divorce. She'd said something about his not doing enough around the house and his protest of working sixty-hour weeks hadn't been an adequate explanation for her.

"Well, you didn't really ask her how she felt about this move before committing to it," said Mom.

"She's twelve." Dad sighed, probably pacing around. "What kid wouldn't be thrilled to spend her summer exploring a giant house in the countryside? This place is right out of a storybook."

"Apparently, *our* twelve-year-old." Mom's nails clicked on the countertop. "Maybe moving out here wasn't the best idea. She doesn't have a lot of friends, and she is close to the few she has."

"Those kids tease her," said Dad.

"Her friends don't. She doesn't let the others get to her. You'd know that if you weren't always working." Mom's voice softened. "And I'm not being critical… just saying you haven't been around enough to notice. Yes, some of the kids at school have teased her over her out-of-style clothes, but she ignores them. Piper's quite resilient and doesn't need validation from anyone."

"That makes this more worrying," said Dad.

Mom clinked her nail against a cup. The sound made the scent of coffee register in Piper's mind. "You're right. Maybe that idea of hers is worth considering."

"Which one?" asked Dad.

"Selling this place and getting a more reasonable home back in Syracuse, where she can still spend time with her friends. We don't *need* a mansion to enjoy the inheritance. How are we going to even maintain such a big house? Even if I gave up teaching and cleaned full time—which is not happening—I'd never finish."

"We can afford to hire help."

"Is that who we are?" asked Mom. "A wealthy family with servants?"

Dad sighed. "We don't have to treat them like servants. They'd be employees, not lessers. But… did you notice something?"

"What?" asked Mom.

"This house has been vacant for what, two months? It doesn't look like it's been neglected at all. There's no dust anywhere."

Piper's eyes widened. Dad had a point and that did *not* make sense.

"All right. That's strange, but maybe the place is just so big the dust disperses, and it takes longer to show," said Mom. "I still don't trust that this isn't all going to fall to pieces. Some technicality in the will or we find out the whole thing is a prank."

"A prank?" Dad laughed. "What, Piper said she felt watched so you think there's cameras around? Like we're on some reality show?"

"Reality prank TV is certainly more believable than ghosts." Mom yawned. "Look, Alan… I'm not planning on giving up my position with the school. It's more than just money. I *enjoy* it. I'd go nuts rattling around a house like this all day with nothing to do."

"I never said you shouldn't keep teaching, only that you didn't *have* to."

Mom grumbled. "Yet you gave me a two-hour commute."

"Piper wants to keep the old house. Easily doable given our current financial situation." Dad's voice had a big grin on it.

"I still don't trust this. There's going to be some other heir coming out of the woodwork, challenging the money… or a legal technicality will rear up. What was in that letter the attorney gave you?" asked Mom.

"Oh, you should read it if you want a good laugh. I skimmed over it. Sounded like a bunch of nonsense. Something about horseshoes and salt… fantasy rubbish. The old man was clearly off his rocker."

"Do you think we should take Piper to see someone?"

Piper's stomach clenched up. The idea of being taken to see a psychologist made her uneasy. As if she didn't have enough trouble at school, being the girl in twenty-year-old clothes who didn't own a computer or even a PlayStation. Her ability to ignore stupid kids who thought that not having money made someone worthy of contempt managed to get most of them to leave her alone. However, if they found out she'd been to a psych doctor, the bullies would tease the hell out of her. What if even Jaime and Gwen got freaked out and avoided her, thinking her crazy? She pulled her right leg up and rubbed her ankle.

That really happened, didn't it? I'm not going nuts.

"Nah," said Dad. "She's a kid going through a big upheaval. I think we should give her some time. It's just an adjustment period. Hell, neither one of us slept well last night either."

"I could've slept if you didn't keep tugging on my hair."

"Umm. I don't remember doing that."

"Don't you start," said Mom, sounding annoyed.

Piper slipped around the arch into the kitchen. Both parents jumped at her sudden appearance. When they regained their composure, she muttered, "Sorry."

"Why are you sneaking around?" asked Mom. "Did you sleep? You look exhausted."

"Not much." She sank into a chair at the table. "I'm just freaked out about the move. The house is scary as hell and I miss my friends. Guess I'm having nightmares, too."

Her parents exchanged a concerned look. Dad headed to the stove, while Mom refreshed her coffee from the pot.

"Did you find your laptop?" asked Piper.

"No. Why? Do you have any idea where it might've gone off to?" Mom's tone didn't carry too much accusation, but a hint of it remained in her eyes.

Piper looked straight at her, shook her head, and said, "No. I didn't hide it on you. Just curious if you found it."

"You've never been a liar," said Mom. "Even as a little kid, you always admitted stuff. I don't know what to say."

"I'm not crazy, but I think there's a ghost in the house."

Mom opened her mouth, but closed it when her father laughed.

"Maybe it's Grandpa Bailey." Dad kept laughing while preparing omelets.

"Where'd those eggs come from?" asked Mom.

"Fridge." Dad pointed the spatula at the carton on the counter. "They look fine. Why?"

Mom got up and went over to the fridge, opening it. "Everything in here would've had to have been in here for at least two months."

"But nothing looks spoiled," said Piper.

"Right, and that doesn't make any sense." Mom shut the fridge door.

Piper smirked. *Neither does being trapped in bed by a ten-ton comforter.* "I'm not crazy. I don't need a psych doctor."

Her mother again opened her mouth, but before she could say a word, footsteps went by overhead. She looked up.

"Just the house settling," said Dad. "Boards creaking."

For a second, Mom seemed about ready to believe in ghosts, but gave Dad an 'oh, yeah, right' look.

Piper crossed her arms on the table and put her head down. *I hate this house.*

6

HAUNTED

Piper lifted her head as her mother approached the table. When Mom went to sit, the chair shot out from under her. Screaming, her mother fell on her rear end, tossing her coffee mug over her shoulder as she wiped out on the floor. The mug bounced off the island counter and shattered on the floor behind Dad, making him yell in surprise. Piper gasped, shaking in her seat, staring at the chair that had moved all by itself.

"Ow!" Shouted Mom, followed by a handful of nasty words.

Dad whirled around, spatula in one hand, pan in the other. "Ames?"

"Mom!" Piper darted over to kneel by her mother's side. "Are you okay?"

"What is *wrong* with you?" Mom glared at her.

Piper's lower lip quivered, but she didn't burst into tears. "I didn't do that."

Mom narrowed her eyes.

"I swear it moved by itself!" yelled Piper, starting to tear up a little. She pushed Mom's chair back in place, then returned to sit in the chair she'd been in. When she raised her leg as if to kick Mom's chair, her sneaker hovered at least two feet away. "I couldn't have even reached it, and why would you think I'd try to hurt you!"

Mom's anger evaporated to bewilderment. She shot Dad a nasty look for a second, but the stove was even farther away than Piper.

"What happened?" asked Dad.

"Something pulled the chair out from under Mom, and she fell." Piper got up to mop up coffee, but her mother caught her in a hug.

"I'm sorry for accusing you… I… this doesn't make any sense."

Piper exhaled with relief and squeezed her back. "I wouldn't do anything like that. It's not funny. Old people can get hurt from short falls."

"Old?" Mom yelled in a playful tone. "Who are you calling old?"

She giggled. "Everything after twenty is old."

"Ahh to be young again. When you're our age, 'old' will mean something altogether different." Dad yawned. "None of us slept well. Your mother's probably tired and just missed."

"I can see missing a chair on account of having too much wine, but tired?" Mom tried to fight the yawn caused by Dad's, but couldn't. "I'm not *that* tired."

Piper shared the yawn as well. "Mom being tired doesn't move a chair across the room. I saw it slide. There's a ghost here, and it's mad at us."

Dad glanced at the walls with an uneasy expression.

"Piper, please stop with the ghost stuff. You and your father both have too much imagination for your own good." Mom walked around the island counter and grabbed paper towels.

Piper took some as well. "Imagination doesn't drag chairs across kitchens. And the creaks of a settling house don't sound like old people walking around in the attic."

"If you're trying to scare us out of the house…" Dad eyed the omelet-in-progress. "You're starting to do a decent job of it."

Mom sat back on her heels, a collection of mug fragments in her left hand. "Don't encourage her. Coming here was your idea."

"I know." Dad smiled. "I think we're all just letting our imaginations run wild. You probably nudged the chair out of the way with your leg, not realizing it because you're exhausted."

Piper kept her head down. *I know what I saw. That chair flew away by itself.* If she pressed the ghost issue, her parents would send her to a psychiatrist, and everyone would call her crazy. If this house *did* have a ghost, that left her two options:

Either try as best she could to ignore it… or hunt it down and find out what it wanted.

7

GOING DOWN

After breakfast, Piper returned to her bedroom to unpack her stuff. She argued with herself on the way up the stairs about leaving everything in boxes, since putting her clothes and things away would feel too much like accepting she lived here now. On the other hand, if she unpacked all her stuff that would make moving back to her real home a lot more work, so doing it could jinx the universe in her favor. As much as she didn't want to 'accept' this house, unpacking could actually *increase* her chances of going home.

By the time she reached her room, she'd made the decision to unpack—not because she considered this place home, but because she dared circumstance to make her do all the work of re-boxing it.

She made it two steps past the door before the sight of her fully-made bed shocked her to a standstill. After being trapped in it, she'd run off as fast as possible. *She* hadn't made it, and she couldn't think of when either of her parents would've had the time to slip up here and do it. Once her brain started working again a moment later, she glanced to her right at the corner where the movers had piled all the cardboard boxes—and stared at bare rug.

"And… all my stuff is missing." She gnawed on her knuckles. Her life was going to suck when most of the school called her the crazy girl. Mom and Dad would think she did something to her stuff to 'act out.'

She couldn't tell them it just disappeared. Not a chance in hell existed they'd believe that. She'd go right to a padded cell and straightjacket. "Do they put all crazy people in straitjackets, or just the violent ones?"

Piper sighed.

"Only the violent ones," said a voice from under the bed, high-pitched like a recording of an old man played too fast.

"Hello?" asked Piper. "Is someone here?"

"Shh," whispered a different small voice. "Too soon."

"Are you a ghost?" Piper crept closer to the bed.

Whatever it, or they, were didn't answer. She waited a moment and took a knee, peering under the bed at open space. For no reason she could understand, she didn't feel threatened by those voices. They almost struck her as cute.

"Oh, this is too strange." She pushed herself upright, kneeling beside the bed. "What in the—?"

Cold air on her legs caught her off guard.

Piper looked down at her… bare legs. Her jeans had vanished. Everything else, including her socks and sneakers remained where it should be. Before she could question how her pants came off with her shoes in the way, she spotted the jeans draped over the back of the chair by the desk. Aside from being difficult to explain, it wouldn't have been *too* embarrassing for her parents to find her in underpants… but if the ghost decided to steal her jeans while Tristan was over, she'd want to drop dead. Heck. If the ghost stole his jeans, she'd be even *more* embarrassed.

"Ugh. This ghost plays *weird* pranks."

She stood, took her sneakers off, and hurried over to the chair to reclaim her pants. When she picked them up, she froze in astonishment. They no longer had numerous holes and patches. Not that they looked *new*, but all the damage had been repaired. Piper held them higher, turned them around to look at the rear, flipped them again, and blinked in disbelief.

"The ghost mended my jeans… but how? There's not even any thread marks or patches?"

"We're not ghosts," whispered a little voice behind her.

She whirled in place, but appeared to be alone.

The oddity of the situation made her laugh as she stepped back into her pants. Whatever this was, or these things were, couldn't be the same entity responsible for scaring the hell out of her that morning. Maybe these critters had been the ones who told the other thing to leave her alone.

"What are you?" asked Piper, while putting her sneakers back on. "And thank you for fixing my jeans."

No voice answered.

She waited a while before giving up and crossing her room to stand where the boxes weren't. "Ugh. I'm going to get in so much trouble."

Her closet door creaked open all on its own.

Piper drew a breath to scream, but when she saw her dresses hanging up inside, went from frightened to confused. She owned six dresses, all of which had belonged to her mother and leaned toward the somewhat formal side. They saw the light of day only for special occasions like holidays, one funeral, two weddings, and this one boring 'family reunion' thing on her mother's side where she didn't know anyone. One old woman there had too much wine and kept calling her Rachel.

Curiosity drew her across her room to one of the white dresser cabinets. She pulled a drawer open and gawked at piles of folded clothes. She went from drawer to drawer, then to the other cabinet. All her stuff had been put away already—not quite how she would have organized it, but still.

And even more unusual, she couldn't find a single hole, fray, tear, or patch on anything. Even a few of the T-shirts with 1980s prints (like the She-Ra one that got her laughed at in school) no longer appeared faded out.

She'd come to terms with the truth that her mom had been a nerd. Well, technically still was, but 'old people' didn't count as nerds. They counted as old people. Mom liked science fiction, comic books, superheroes, and *Lord of The Rings*. Piper hadn't quite gotten as much into sci fi, and not at all into comics, but she adored Tolkien and fantasy books. She *could* read sci fi, but only if the lead character wasn't one of those teens who was somehow great at everything, chosen to save the world, pretty, and ended up with two hot guys fighting over her, or some such nonsense.

Destined to save the world wasn't *so* bad if it made some sense, but a character being inexplicably awesome at everything without training drove Piper nuts.

A gong sound went off so loud it made her scream.

Her father shouted in the distance, too far away to understand.

Piper stepped out into the hallway.

"What on Earth was that?" asked Mom, emerging from the master bedroom.

"Loud." Piper shrugged. "I have no clue."

"Piper?" yelled Dad from the stairwell. "Your friend is here."

She jogged down the hall to the midway point of the house, where the stairs met the third floor landing. "Huh?"

"That boy?" yelled Dad.

"Oh." She hurried downstairs.

Dad stood by the open front door, with Tristan waiting outside in a plain black T-shirt, blue jeans, and white sneakers.

"Hey. Umm. Wanna hang out?" asked Tristan.

Piper looked up at her father.

"You need to get your room squared away some time soon, but other than that… sure."

"Okay." She smiled at Tristan, who walked inside.

"Morning, Mr. Bailey."

Dad nodded. "Morning. So polite out here. Must be a country thing."

"Umm." Tristan appeared bewildered. "Kids aren't polite to adults where you lived before?"

Dad patted Piper's shoulder. "Some are. Not all of them."

"That noise was the doorbell?" asked Piper, tilting her head toward Dad. "Check me. Are my ears bleeding?"

"Apparently." Dad cringed. "Gonna have to get that changed. That noise was so damn loud it blasted my pants off."

Tristan laughed.

Piper froze. "Literally?"

Dad smirked. "Of course not literally. Why are you looking at me like that?"

She peered at Tristan out of the corner of her eye and blushed. "No reason." Not waiting for the conversation to get any more awkward, she ran up the stairs. "Come on."

Once she got to her room, she waited for Tristan to walk in, then pushed the door almost closed. "The weirdest thing happened."

He grinned. "What?"

She told him about her stuff putting itself away plus the weird voices.

"Wow. That's… unbelievable."

Piper nodded. "Yeah, I know. But…" She pointed at the corner. "The boxes are all gone, and you saw them yesterday."

He twisted around to peer at the corner. When he faced her again, his expression had filled with awe. "Wow. What do you think did it?"

She sat cross-legged on the rug. "I don't know. But I think there's something else here. Something bad."

"Tell me." He sat nearby. "This is cool."

Piper explained the hand grabbing her leg and the heavy sheets that trapped her that morning. She did *not* mention her jeans disappearing right off her body.

"Whoa." Tristan appeared genuinely frightened. "That would've scared me so bad."

"My Dad thinks I had a nightmare." She picked at the carpet in front of her crossed legs. "I can't tell them about anything 'cause they're going to think I'm crazy and send me to a doctor."

"You're not nuts." Tristan shook his head, making his long hair swoosh back and forth.

She leaned closer to him. "Are you real?"

He blinked. "What's that supposed to mean? Of course I'm real."

"Well… All yesterday, before you got here, I was upset, missing my friends. Then you just walk out of the woods like some kinda Peter Pan or something. And you kinda look like an elf."

"Hah." He turned his head and pulled his hair away from his ear, revealing it to be non-pointy. "I'm not an elf. But thanks. You're cute too."

Her face warmed with blush. "Umm. I didn't mean it like that."

He tilted his head. "What did you mean?"

Before thinking, Piper blurted, "Well, if you put on a dress, you'd look like a girl."

"Heh. If you put on a dress, you'd look like a girl too."

She grabbed her mouth, mortified. "I… Sorry. I didn't mean…"

"It's okay. I know I look kinda skinny with big eyes, and the long hair doesn't help, but I like it anyway. Dad says it means I'm gonna either grow up into a movie star or an emo guitarist."

Piper laughed.

"Aha!" shouted Mom.

The kids exchanged a glance. Piper stood and wandered out into the hall. "Mom?"

Her mother stepped out of the master bedroom, laptop in hand. "It was on the desk in here. I don't know how on Earth I didn't see it until just now."

Piper forced a smile. *Probably because it wasn't* there *until now.* "Cool."

"Hello, Tristan," said Mom.

"Hi, Mrs. Bailey." Tristan waved.

"You can join us for lunch if you like today."

"Cool!" Tristan smiled. "That would be great. Thank you."

"Well, I need to finish unpacking." Mom sighed at the ceiling. "Sometimes I wish I was like Genie and could just wiggle my nose and make stuff happen."

Piper bit her lip, turning away before Mom saw the weird look on her face. "Yeah, that would be cool." After her mother went back into her room, she stared at Tristan. "Are you sure you're not messing with me?"

"Umm. I'm not messing with you?"

"You didn't even ask your parents if you could stay for lunch." Piper folded her arms. "You've got that elf cute thing going on, you came out of the woods on your own right when I was sad at not having any friends, and you don't ask permission to stay over? We like the same stuff, and we like the same kinds of humor. I think the house might me making me see you. Or you're a faun."

"What's that?" asked Tristan.

"Kinda like a satyr, but smaller."

"Don't they have goat legs?"

Piper nodded.

He looked down at his sneakers. "I don't have hooves."

"What do you want?" asked Piper.

"Umm. You're the only other kid in like fifty miles. I wanted a friend too." He looked down, thumbs hooked in his pockets. "I was hiding in the woods, watching the movers. I heard you yell when you were by the fountain, so I decided to walk over and say hi. I'm really a person. If you wanna see my house, we can go there."

She didn't feel any deception in his manners, so she nodded. "Okay. Sorry. There's so much weird stuff going on here."

"What do you think was talking to you?" Tristan went back into her room and peered under the bed.

"I don't know. House elves maybe?"

"What?" asked Tristan.

"You never read *Harry Potter*?"

"Oh!" He biffed himself on the head. "Right. Those aren't real, you know. It's just a story."

"Think about it." Piper's eyes went wide. "They sounded small. We heard scampering, and that handprint was kinda small too."

Tristan grinned. "I still think they're made up. It's gotta be something else."

"What else? Think about it... my grandfather lived here all alone and didn't have any housekeepers or anything. This place ought to be a complete mess. But it isn't. It's so clean, like a small army works here."

He cracked up laughing.

"What?" She folded her arms.

"*Small* army."

Piper rolled her eyes. "Puns are the lowest form of humor."

He held up his hands in surrender. "You're the one who said it."

"But I didn't mean it as a joke."

"That makes it even funnier." Tristan held his arms out wide. "You punned without knowing. That is the final step of enlightenment."

Piper rolled her eyes. "Still wanna check out the basement?"

He let his arms drop. "Umm. If you want."

"Scared?"

"Yeah." He took a deep breath and let it out. "Bet you are too."

Piper didn't think any of the boys she knew back in Syracuse would've ever admitted to being afraid. Not that she ever hung out with them. Thus far, all of her friends (which totaled about seven people) were girls. Jamie and Gwen, the most offbeat of the lot, had wound up her closest buddies. Though every one of them walked out of step with the popular crowd. She wasn't quite sure where to put Tristan. He definitely wasn't a jock, nor a geek. He edged close to a gothy outcast, but he smiled way too much for that. Then again, so far out here in the woods, maybe he didn't belong in any of them. No point in sorting kids into cliques when only one kid existed. She'd have to think of him as 'just Tristan,' and she liked his honesty.

"I am. I'm scared of this whole house," said Piper, eyeing her bed.

"Let's check out the basement then."

Piper took a deep breath. "Okay."

She led the way out into the hall and down to the first floor. They resumed their room-to-room exploration, but didn't spend too long at any one spot, trying to find a basement access door. The large pantry connected to the kitchen had a small door that led to a narrow passage. It cornered right, went a short distance, and turned left in a squared-off S bend. A knob jutted out of the wall at the end. Turning it opened a hidden door into the main dining room, which disappeared after closing behind them. Curious, Piper ran her hands back and forth over the patterned wallpaper until she found a small button concealed in the repeating blue dots. Pushing it made the door pop open.

"Probably so the servants could bring food here straight from the kitchen," said Tristan.

"Yeah. But I don't think my grandfather *had* servants. And I hate calling them that."

He shrugged. "Did he build this place or buy it?"

"I don't know." Piper pulled the secret door open and went back in, following the passageway back to the kitchen.

The door swung closed again with a *whump*.

"Ack! It's dark," said Tristan.

"Relax." Piper kept going. "It's not like we can get lost in a straight line."

Light leaking in around the door from the pantry helped her find the handle, and she emerged among shelves of canned goods, pasta, flour, and bags of beans. Tristan followed her out into the kitchen and then through another door into a smaller storage space that held mostly cleaning supplies. Unlike the rest of the house, everything in here looked decades old. The bottles and boxes of cleaners had brand logos she'd never seen before.

"Whoa, this stuff is old," said Tristan, while examining a box labeled 'Spic and Span.' "This is like older than my parents even."

She nudged his arm. "Put it down. It might be dangerous to touch."

He did, then wiped his hand on his jeans.

Piper crept past the shelves to the other side of the room, where it bent around a corner to the right. "Someone's been cleaning this place, but they haven't been using any of these supplies."

"What's that?" Tristan stepped past her and picked up a yellowed slip of paper with handwriting on it. "Maude's."

The top had the word 'Maude's' printed in red letters. Beneath it, much smaller black ink spelled out 'restaurant and coffee.' It appeared to be a receipt for a poached egg breakfast with toast and coffee, which cost someone eighty-five cents for the food, ten cents for the coffee. The date 3/18/62 had been handwritten in the top left corner.

"Wow." Piper whistled. "Dad would like this. He collects old stuff."

"Hey look." Tristan pointed at another small door on the wall. "Bet that goes to the basement."

Piper set the receipt on a shelf. At his quizzical glance, she said, "Don't wanna stuff it in my pocket and crinkle it all up."

He approached the door, but didn't go for the knob, keeping his hands at his sides.

Piper smirked. One look at his wide, innocent eyes made her feel protective toward him. Despite being only a year older (perhaps not even that, depending on where their birthdays wound up), she had a height advantage. Then again, a lot of the boys in her class looked small. Mom said something about growth spurts and girls getting taller faster. A year or two from now, Tristan would probably tower over her. She thought about Jamie calling him her 'boyfriend,' and whipped her head away, no longer looking at him.

She grasped the knob and twisted. The door stuck, but when she gave it a decent tug, it popped open in a cloud of dust that sent them both back a few steps, waving at the air.

"Guess no one's been down here for a long time," said Tristan.

Piper pointed a thumb back over her shoulder. "Why take the stairs when there's an elevator?"

The passageway down smelled like a wet sneaker. Walls of drab grey stone ran with drips and smears of mold in white, charcoal, and black. A wooden railing, only as big around as a fat broom handle, dangled on metal brackets to the left, as filthy and funky as the wall above it.

"Ugh." Piper pulled her shirt up to cover her mouth and nose. "We probably shouldn't go down there. It stinks. This mold might be dangerous."

"We found it. We should at least go to the bottom of the stairs." Tristan also pulled his shirt up to use for a breathing mask.

"Okay. Don't touch anything."

He nodded.

Piper eased herself onto the first step, got her balance, and looked around until she spotted an ancient light switch to her right: a rounded metal housing mounted on a narrow pipe that continued down along the wall. At first, the little lever didn't want to move, but the switch eventually gave way with a sharp *click*. The basement below lit up with weak light.

"Ow." She waved her hand. "It's got a really tough spring."

"Old," said Tristan.

The straight stairway led to a concrete-floored chamber with a few bare light bulbs dangling from wires. Straight ahead against the wall, a brown-and-gold console that looked like it had been stolen from the set of a 1960s-era science fiction TV show flashed and blinked with multiple colored lights. Two massive furnaces stood against the wall to the right. While the huge machines looked scary, this basement chamber didn't unsettle her as much as she'd expected it to.

Wide eyed, Tristan approached the flashing control station. More gem-buttons like those from the elevator covered the majority of its face, arranged in clusters. A few lever switches stuck out here and there next to two keyholes and a clear glass orb as big as a baseball set in a socket.

"What the heck is that?" Piper walked up behind him.

"No idea, but it's awesome." He traced his fingers over the buttons, but didn't push anything hard enough to activate. "It's on…"

"What does it do?"

Tristan twisted around to stare at her. "Why are you asking me? You live here."

"You lived in this area longer than me."

"Never been in this house before."

Piper pointed at the only gem on the panel lit up red. Letters had been etched into the metal below it, like handwriting. "Can you read that?"

"Umm." Tristan spit on his thumb and rubbed at the spot. "Looks like Boyyarl… The writing's bad."

"Boyyarl? That doesn't make sense." She glanced again at the furnaces, leaning back as though staring down a pair of hungry bears.

"Neither does finding this down here." He brushed at dust here and there. "That says 'outer ward.' And this lever's labeled 'inner ward master.'"

"That sounds creepy." Piper backed away. "Don't mess with it."

"I won't. My dad says only idiots push buttons they don't understand. That's how you wind up in the hospital."

She giggled, despite being nervous. "What's your dad do?"

"He works in a factory closer to Utica. Four days a week, but like all day."

"Oh." She tiptoed past the boilers. A doorway without a door in it led into another section of basement, lined with long shelves full of lumber and pipes. She hesitated by the edge, leaning in only enough to look around. The taste of old metal filled her mouth when she inhaled. At least thirty feet away past the end of the shelves, a workbench jutted out into the weak light from the room behind her. "It's dark in there… I don't see an elevator."

Tristan ducked under her arm and walked down past the long shelves.

"Wait." She shied away from the white and black patches of mold mottling the wall. After a few seconds, she darted ahead to stay with him rather than remain on her own with the menacing furnaces. "Don't go in there. It could be dangerous."

He stopped at the end of the shelves, gazing around. "It's not. Looks like a workshop, but I don't think anyone has been down here for a long time."

Piper edged up to stand beside him, not noticing she'd put an arm around him until a moment after she did it. Tristan didn't seem to mind. "This place is really scary."

"Yeah. Like a horror movie. Looks like the room where the killer takes the screaming girl."

She gulped. "Why did you say that?"

"I dunno. It just kinda looks like that." He stepped in further.

Unwilling to let go of him, she followed. "I want to go upstairs."

Tristan gestured at more, smaller shelves against the wall separating this room from the furnace chamber. Rusting cans of paint, tools, and wooden crates with random wood scraps all bore a thick coating of dust. The opposite corner, past the other end of the workbench, held a bunch of ancient gardening tools: grass-cutting scythes, hedge clippers hanging on pegs, and three lawn mowers with exposed, twisted blades that spun only if someone pushed the mower forward. Most of the metal parts of every tool had rusted. A short tunnel with a rounded roof next to the mowers led to a concrete stairwell with a thin stripe of sunlight shining down. Piper let go of Tristan and made her way over, ducking and swatting at cobwebs. Once she reached the much warmer air at the end of the tunnel, she peered up at a cellar-style set of double doors at an angle.

"This probably leads to the back yard."

"Yeah," said Tristan.

She went up a few steps until she could reach the metal door, and gave it a light push. It didn't move. A harder shove rattled it, triggering a wave of sand and dust falling on her head. She coughed and sputtered, but refused to stop. Afraid of going back into the basement, Piper rammed her shoulder into it and heaved.

With a great squealing screech, the cellar doors broke free and swung open, bathing the steep concrete stairs in sunlight. Piper leapt up and over the brick rim onto the grass. Tristan followed her, clapping his hands at his shirt and jeans to swat away pale grey silt.

"That's cool." He grinned back at the tunnel. "Guess that was like the gardener's office or something."

"This place doesn't have a garden." She pointed out at the meadow. "It's all grass."

"Hey, let's check out that funny building."

Piper nodded. Being out in a wide-open field was a *lot* better than a dark basement full of scary, ancient tools with blades on them. A ghost that could fling chairs could fling something much worse if it got angry. She set off on the long walk toward the big square building. "I wonder why he painted it green and covered it with fake bushes."

"He might've been crazy."

"Oh, I hope not."

Tristan looked over at her. "Why not?"

"Because. He's my grandfather. If he went crazy, crazy could be in the family and I might get it someday."

"Hope not."

She laughed. "Yeah. Me too."

The field spanned three-quarters of a mile, though the grass never got much higher than her knees. She stuck to a path where it remained trimmed to the height of a normal lawn. Who had been maintaining it? Whoever had to deal with mowing such an enormous field had certainly not been using the primitive push mowers.

When they neared the strange structure, grid lines on the walls revealed that it had been made of cinder blocks. It stood only one story tall, but had a raised section at the top angled inward in a poor attempt to recreate the slope of a hill, or a pyramid that had its point cut off. Plastic bushes and branches hung from small loops affixed to the cinder blocks with screws.

"This is really messed up." Tristan leaned back to gaze up at the roof.

Piper headed around to the right. On the east-facing side, she found a wide garage-style door, also painted forest green. It had no handle, but beside it on the wall sat a little control box with two plain plastic buttons and a keyhole. Nothing happened when she pushed the upper button, so she tried the other one, which also clicked without any effect.

"We need a key." Tristan indicated the keyhole. "Same as the elevator."

"Wonder what's in it." Piper walked along the door, banging a fist on the metal. The way it echoed suggested a single, large room. "Think it's a garage?"

He shrugged. "Either that or maybe a hangar for a small plane or helicopter."

"I don't think it's tall enough for that." Piper squinted into the sun while gazing up at the top of the roof. "A plane's tail is really high, and I think helicopters are big too."

"Oh, yeah." He followed. "Guess it's a garage then."

Piper walked to the corner and turned left along the north-facing side. A fat green-painted pipe, also covered with fake shrubs, came out of the wall and continued off into the forest. "Huh?"

"What?" Tristan bumped into her when she stopped short. "Oh, wow. That's a huge pipe. It must be for water." He pointed north. "There's a small lake that way not too far."

"I guess we get our water from the lake?" She scratched her head. "It didn't taste funny, so maybe there's machines or stuff in here that cleans it."

Again, Tristan shrugged.

She frowned at the lack of doors. "Stupid key. We should probably go back to the house."

"Okay."

They walked across the field, easily two hundred yards between the odd garage and the manor house. Upon entering the back door to the kitchen, Piper's parents corralled them over to the table for lunch. Her parents had made turkey-and-cheese sandwiches along with some frozen-in-the-bag French fries. Mom clarified that the food had *not* been sitting in the fridge, and her father had run off to the little town down the road to buy some groceries.

Between bites, Piper told them about the basement of old tools, as well as the weird green building and pipe.

"Odd. I'll have to check that out," said Dad. "The lawyer didn't say anything about a purification plant. That sort of thing doesn't just run on its own."

Mom fidgeted with her hair, something she always did when nervous. Piper figured she didn't like the idea of drinking lake water, or maybe she worried about needing to hire people to operate whatever equipment might be inside that building.

"Thanks for the food," said Tristan.

"You're welcome." Dad smiled at him before sending a hopeful look at Piper. "I'm glad you've made a friend so fast. That's a good sign."

She held back her glumness, muttered, "Yeah," and kept on a mostly false smile. Dad hadn't meant it in the way she took it: like Jamie and Gwen had been replaced, so she could forget them now. The other kids who used to tease her for her ratty clothes wouldn't know what to do with her since she'd become 'the rich girl.' If she managed to make it back to her school for seventh grade, it might be funny to watch them trip over themselves trying to be her friend. She wouldn't be mean, but Piper would definitely remember who her real friends were.

Footsteps again tromped over the ceiling while her parents discussed what to do about the 'green building.' Tristan glanced up, as did Piper, though Mom and Dad didn't react to the ghost walking around.

"Umm… we're gonna go upstairs, okay?" asked Piper.

"Sure, you've got a couple years yet before we ban you bringing boys to your room," said Dad.

"What?" asked Piper.

Mom turned red in the face.

Laughing, Dad waved her off. "Never mind. Go have fun."

She stood, put her plate in the sink, and walked into the hallway leading to the front foyer. Tristan jogged up behind her.

"Did I do something wrong?" he asked.

"No."

"Why wouldn't they let me go upstairs in two years?"

Piper paused at the start of the stairway long enough to shrug at him. "I dunno. I've never had a boy friend before, only girls."

He tilted his head. "I'm your boyfriend?"

"Uhh." She stopped again, four steps up from the bottom. "I mean a friend who's a boy. Not like… oh. That's what he meant."

"What?"

She blushed and hurried up the stairs. "Nothing. Just my Dad being a butthead."

"Right."

Piper returned to the elevator and wasted a minute poking the basement gem. "Grr. Now I really want to find out what's down there."

"Me too." Tristan grinned. "Hmm. Does the place have an attic? Sometimes ghosts hide up there too."

She tapped her foot. "It's got to… there's all these windows sticking out of the roof."

For an hour or so, they went room to room on the third floor checking everywhere except her bedroom and her parents' bedroom. She mostly ignored the guest bedrooms as it made no sense for an attic access to require walking through where someone would sleep. Once she felt certain they'd been everywhere without finding any way to go up, she stopped in the hallway and scowled.

"It's gotta be hidden. Like that passage to the dining room."

He gestured at one of the light fixtures on the wall. "Maybe it's a secret lever. Pull on the light and it opens."

A dull *thud* rattled the floor.

Piper jumped and wrapped her arms around Tristan. "What was that?"

"I think something fell… in the room at the end of the hall."

She twisted around to peer where he pointed. The last room on the right side, another sitting room, looked exactly like all the other rooms with sofas, chairs, and coffee tables. Except for the first floor where a few rooms had TVs, the rest of the house looked as though it had been built in an age before electronics, when the only things people could do for fun involved reading or sitting around talking.

"The bang came from that door," said Tristan.

"Umm." She shivered. "Do you think the ghost is in there?"

"Maybe." He tried to walk toward it, but didn't pull hard enough to drag her behind him or break free of her grip. "Come on. Maybe it's a helpful ghost."

She closed her eyes and took a few breaths before letting go, nodding, and walking behind him to the door. One of the wingback chairs near the fireplace had fallen over backward. "Holy crap!"

"Awesome." Tristan glanced around. "You really *do* have a ghost."

A loud *click* sounded behind the wall to the left of the fireplace. Piper twitched. With a slow, laborious *creeeeeak*, a door-sized panel of wall (and a section of the mantel top) opened outward to reveal a spiral stairwell going up.

"Uhh," said Piper, her voice shaking. "Is there a ghost in here making stuff move?"

"Yeah," said Tristan.

She frowned. "I wasn't talking to you."

He tilted his head. "How's a ghost going to answer you?"

"I dunno… knock on the wall?"

Tristan approached the doorway. "It's obviously a friendly ghost, since it helped us find the attic."

Before she could protest, he darted up out of sight. "Boys," muttered Piper.

Being alone in a room where two objects had moved on their own, one right in front of her, scared her more than the idea of an attic. She hurried up to the opening. A metal corkscrew of steps wobbled along with the soft squeaks of sneaker soles. White plaster oozed like cake icing between dark wooden slats on the walls around it.

"Do you see rats?" called Piper.

"No. It's a big attic. As long as the whole house."

He didn't sound scared at all, so she decided to go up. Her hand blackened from the sediment coating the thin metal railing. *This is small. Dad would have to duck to make it up here.* After three turns, the spiral ended at a dirty wooden floor. The attic stretched off into the distance, full of dust motes dancing in sunlight. The dormer windows lined both sides at even intervals, the brightness a pleasant opposite to the basement. Two rows of brick columns ran down the middle, around which stood dozens of wooden crates, boxes, and trunks. She stepped out and looked back at the stairwell she'd climbed, embedded in one of the columns. It appeared to be part of a huge chimney almost at the western end of the house. The house's outer wall sat a mere ten feet behind it.

"It doesn't feel creepy up here at all," said Tristan. He poked a dressmaker's mannequin. "What's this for?"

"Umm. I think they use them to make clothes." Piper went left to the nearest dormer window, ducking the angled roof to get her face up to the glass. From here, she could see the flat top of the strange building covered in fake bushes, but it didn't have any hatches, protruding pipes, or strange machinery.

"Check this out," said Tristan.

She turned.

He had found a sword in one of the piles of stuff, and pulled it a few inches out of the sheath. "Oh, wow. This is real!"

"Of course it's real, you're holding it."

"No." He looked at her, wide-eyed. "I mean it's like sharp. It's not a pretend sword." He drew it clear of the scabbard, struggling to wield it one-armed. Sunlight gleamed off the blade, which still had a mirror-like shine. "Ugh. It's really heavy."

"You shouldn't play with that." She walked over and helped him hold it up. Sure enough, the blade looked as deadly as any of their kitchen knives. "This is really dangerous."

"Yeah." He left her holding it in both hands, picked up the scabbard, and slid it over the blade.

Piper set it back where he found it and took two steps away. "Let's not play with any weapons, 'kay?"

"Right."

Taken by curiosity, Piper roamed down the right wall (where the windows faced the front courtyard and fountain) while Tristan searched the opposite side. Given the vast space of the attic, all the crates/boxes/trunks here didn't look like much stuff, but it probably wouldn't have fit in her entire home. The attic had plenty of open area and unused floor. A few boards shifted under her sneakers, but not so much she feared breaking any.

A giant steamer trunk, like something from the 1800s, contained coils of rope and bundles of long, metal spikes, cleats, and clips. It all looked old, probably from the seventies or so, but she recognized the equipment as what mountain climbers might use. None of it appeared valuable, or even all that interesting, so she closed the lid. Another trunk nearby had huge sections of folded canvas, likely massive tents.

"Whoa..." Tristan leaned around one of the brick columns. "I found guns."

"No weapons!" half-yelled Piper.

"I don't think they work. They're really old."

She trotted over.

Tristan led her up to the wall, next to one of the windows overlooking the backyard. A flat wooden case lay open atop a crate, with black velvet lining the interior. Two flintlock pistols flanked a well in the middle that contained several pale metal spheres with a dull sheen. Another well above that had darker ones that looked more like lead.

"Are those silver?" asked Piper.

Tristan picked up one of the lighter-colored balls. "Umm. Could be. I could ask my dad if you want. If they *are* silver, they're probably worth a lot of money."

"Why would someone make silver… umm. Do you call those bullets or something else?" asked Piper.

"Silver bullets are for werewolves," said Tristan, as smoothly as if stating a well-known fact.

"Except… that's made up."

He dropped the ball back in the well with the rest and closed the lid. "So are ghosts."

She stared at him.

"Hey, I don't know. Maybe your granddad was loopy and had them made *in case* werewolves are real."

"Yeah, maybe." She wandered back over to 'her side' and checked another trunk.

This one had been packed full of clothing that also appeared to be from the sixties or seventies. One dark tan suit jacket had four slashes down the sleeve, like huge claws. *Wow. Did grandpa get attacked by a bear?* A crate nearby held a bunch of books and maps about Eastern Europe, as well as English-to-Russian, English-to-Romanian, and English-to-Ukrainian dictionaries.

"I don't think my grandfather spent a lot of time actually living here. No wonder he didn't have a staff."

"Hey, I found a little elevator," said Tristan. "It's like kid-sized."

"What?" She shut the trunk of clothes and wandered out toward the middle of the attic.

Tristan had gotten a bit ahead of her, close to the center of the house. At a blank spot where a window should've been but wasn't, he'd found small sliding door to a chamber about half the size of a standard, non-rich-person refrigerator.

"Oh, that's a dumbwaiter."

"A what?" asked Tristan.

She shook her head. "It's like an elevator, but they used to use them to send food or drinks up and down multiple floors in big houses and castles. It probably goes all the way down to the kitchen."

"How do you know that?"

Piper quirked an eyebrow. "That it goes down or what it is?"

"What it is."

"I read a lot. They love to use them in Victorian novels."

He leaned in. "There's ropes going up and down, a pulley. I think I see the elevator part."

"Tristan, get away from there before you fall."

The boy started to lean back out, but lurched forward in a blur. His scream echoed out of the opening in the wall for a second or so before a splintering, wooden *crunch* echoed back up.

Piper shrieked, "Tristan!" and ran to the dumbwaiter. She braced her hands on the wall at either side, cringing, and gingerly stuck her head in to look.

"Ow," he muttered.

The boy lay upside down with his legs in the air, covered in pale grey dust. Old rope and a pulley sat on top of his chest, having broken off the top above her. She didn't see any obvious blood. She patted her chest, trying to get her heart to start up again.

"Are you hurt?" whispered Piper.

He looked around. "I don't think so. I'm afraid to move 'cause I think the elevator's gonna fall if I do. Maybe I should stop breathing. It's slipping."

An image of rope coils came to mind. "Hang on. I'm gonna get rope."

"I'll, umm, wait here," said Tristan.

Wow. He's so calm. I'd be losing my mind. Piper ran to the first giant trunk she'd opened, with the climbing gear. She leaned over the edge, gripped a coil of rope—and right as she started to stand back up, someone grabbed her legs and flipped her up and over, throwing her face first into a pile of canvas backpacks. She didn't even have a chance to scream before the lid slammed closed. She rolled over onto her back and kicked upward, but the lid didn't open.

Something metal *clicked* near her head.

I'm locked in!

"Help!" she yelled while pounding her heels at the lid. "Dad! Mom!"

Tristan shouted something, but between his being down a shaft and her stuck inside a closed trunk, she couldn't understand him.

No... he's gonna fall and get hurt. She looked around in complete darkness, and tried not to surrender to panic. *I could suffocate in here. We're both in a lot of trouble.* She shouted for her parents a few more times before deciding it a waste of air. Kicking and attacking the lid also burned oxygen, but she couldn't just lie there and wait. Her parents had no idea where they'd gone off to, and what if the stupid ghost closed the hidden door to the attic stairway again?

It's trying to kill me! It's not a helpful ghost... it led us up here so it could do this!

"Think... think..."

Piper scooted to the left, metal rattling from her motion. She stomped at the side, hoping it might be weaker than the lid. Anger, terror, and desperation lent strength to her leg, but she may as well have been kicking a brick wall. Amid the flurry of screaming and pounding sneaker, the continuous clatter of metal bars crept into her awareness.

She stopped to listen, and the rattling ceased as well. The rasp of her breath seemed like the loudest sound in the world, reminding her of the ticking clock leading to suffocation. At some point, she'd heard someone say that kids could die if they got stuck in trunks like this. Maybe her father said it back home when she'd been little. She pressed up on the lid, but it didn't budge.

"Dad! Mom!" shouted Piper.

Both were probably on the ground floor, if even still in the house. They'd never hear her. She kicked the side again, and metal *clinked* behind her.

The spikes!

Piper twisted around and patted her hands about, searching the pile of rope and backpacks. When she brought her hand down on cold metal, she practically squealed with delight. Ten or twelve pitons, tied together with twine, all had sharpened points at one end. She tugged at one until it slipped free of the bundle, and held it like a small spear.

Again and again, she jabbed it at the side of the trunk, trying to hit the same spot. Eventually, the old wood gave way and she made a hole about as big around as Dad's thumb. A few more jabs around the spot enlarged it.

"Tristan?" shouted Piper out the hole.

"Yeah," he yelled back. "What happened?"

"I fell in a trunk and the lid closed."

"Did something push you?"

"Yeah. Hang on. I'm almost out."

Piper stabbed the piton into the wood, no longer worried about air since she'd made a decent sized hole. Once she created a network of little punctures, she reared back and mule-kicked with both legs, breaking out most of the side panel. She tossed a rope bundle out, then crawled after it. Nearly out of breath from her battle for freedom, she trudged over to the dumbwaiter, but kept a healthy distance in case the stupid ghost tried something else.

"Hang on."

"Hanging," said Tristan. "Or sitting, technically."

Piper ran to the nearest column and tied the rope around it. That done, she tossed the coil into the dumbwaiter shaft. "Grab that."

"Ow!"

She leaned in to look at him. "What happened?"

He had one eye closed, his nose scrunched up. "The rope hit me in the face."

"Grab it before you fall!" shouted Piper. "I'm gonna go get Da—"

'Dad' stretched into a scream as a hand shoved into the middle of her back, knocking her headfirst into the shaft. Piper flipped over without intending to and caught herself by bracing her sneakers against the sides. Heart pounding, she couldn't bring herself to move for several seconds. Tristan lay about one story below her, clutching the rope, which ran up behind her back to the opening overhead.

Piper looked up, staring at the rectangle of sunlight above her.

"I don't like this ghost," said Tristan.

She coughed on the dusty air. "No. I'm starting to get angry."

"You don't sound angry. You sound kinda scared."

"I just got shoved into a dumbwaiter shaft. I'm allowed to sound scared." She winced. "It's strong. I thought I had a good grip on the wall. Grr. I *knew* it was gonna do this."

"Thanks for trying to save me."

Piper reached over her head and grabbed the rope with both hands. "I'm not finished saving you yet."

She tightened her grip until her hands hurt, then kicked off the wall, spinning around to face the rope. Her sneakers scuffed the sides, catching again to hold up her weight.

"Gah! Dust."

"Sorry," muttered Piper.

He coughed. "It's fine. I'll take a face full of dust any day over falling."

A sliding door in the wall a little ways below her looked tempting, but she didn't know if it would even open from this side, and the dark shaft didn't give much of a view. Opting for the already-open attic door, she pulled on the rope and scooted her feet up the sides, climbing inch by inch upward.

She grabbed the bricks at the bottom of the opening, and dragged herself up enough to get her head out.

A metal scrape from the right nearly froze the blood in her veins. Not wanting to look, but unable to resist, she turned her head.

The sword Tristan had found, out of its sheath and gleaming, floated straight at her.

Piper screamed, re-filled her lungs, and muttered, "Oh, crap. Oh, crap. Oh, crap!" Too frightened to move, she stared, transfixed while the blade rushed closer and pivoted upward, as if in the hand of a man about to slice her throat wide open.

At the last second, Piper recoiled with a shriek. The blade came down with a *clank* on the bricks, inches in front of her face, severing the rope. Her attempt to jump back made her sneakers slip on the walls, and with the rope no longer supporting her—she fell.

Screaming, she plummeted. Her left shoulder banged into something hard; Tristan let out an *oof* when she crashed down on top of him. His arms circled her from behind, clinging tight. Chaos surrounded her. Tristan yelled in her ear from behind. Loud scraping came from everywhere, wood grinding on stone. The square of sunlight above her raced away, shrinking smaller and smaller.

Their motion came to an abrupt halt with a wooden *crunch.* A dull pain throbbed in her left shoulder, and the back of her head hurt. A narrow shaft of artificial light shone in from behind her, illuminating Tristan's right sneaker and a stone wall.

He moaned.

"Are you okay?" whispered Piper.

Tristan wheezed.

She felt around, by touch learning that she'd landed sitting on top of his stomach, probably crushing the wind out of him. "Eep! Sorry!"

"Breathe," rasped Tristan. "Can't… breathe."

Piper squirmed around, pushing smashed pieces of dumbwaiter cab out of her way. Her new friend lay crumpled with his shoulders against another sliding door, which had cracked open from the force of their landing. The wood appeared quite thin, barely a quarter inch. She peered up at the spot of sunlight.

"Wow. That's way higher than four stories. We're deep underground."

He groaned.

"Close your eyes," said Piper. "Dust and splinters."

Tristan braced an arm across his face.

Piper reared back and kicked at the flimsy door, knocking it out with two stomps. Light flooded the shaft, and she squinted at the brightness. Wherever they'd landed had working fluorescent lights in the ceiling. After a few seconds, her eyes adjusted. Wood scraps clattered to the floor of a large, round chamber lined with empty storefronts. Dull red floor and plain stone-grey walls reminded her of something between a mall and a science museum. Three large corridors led away from the circular room, each wide enough to accommodate a car.

Tristan pushed at her.

She slid past him to the floor outside, turned, and helped pull him out to his feet. "Are you hurt?"

He looked himself over and swung his arms around, twisted side to side, and bent forward. "Sore, but I don't think I broke anything."

Long gouge marks in the dumbwaiter shaft hinted that the smashed cab had probably acted like a brake, slowing them down. "We got *so* lucky."

"This is lucky?" He finally looked at the room. "Whoa. Okay, this is kinda cool."

"I mean… the broken dumbwaiter box scraped the walls the whole way down. It made us fall slower so we didn't go splat."

His already pale face got even whiter. "Oh. Yeah. That is lucky."

Piper turned in place, gazing over empty storefronts, benches, and a few potted trees. The room had to be almost a hundred yards across, and had several freestanding displays like the maps at the mall, only these were blank. "I think this is some kind of… or was going to be some kind of museum or something. It's not finished yet."

"Tables and chairs." Tristan pointed to the left. "Looks like a food court."

"Yeah it does. Who builds a mall underground?" The stores didn't appear abandoned, more like they'd been built new but never occupied. She noted a fourth passage to the right of the dumbwaiter opening. Not far away, on the left, stood a familiar-looking bronze set of elevator doors.

"Crazy old grandpas do." Tristan chuckled. "So, umm. Where are we?"

Piper pointed at the elevator. "I think we just found where that locked button goes."

8

THE MENAGERIE

Piper wandered a few steps into the 'food court'. Faint tickles all over her body, like she'd walked into cobwebs with no clothes on, made her squirm and swat at nonexistent bugs. Looking down at herself confirmed whatever had happened in her room had not happened again—her jeans remained in place, as did her shirt. Even if she stood still, the odd tingles continued.

"Do you feel that?" asked Piper.

"Like bugs crawling all over you?" Tristan scratched at his side.

She nodded.

Tristan pulled his T-shirt off, revealing his scrawny chest and a small dreamcatcher amulet. He snapped the shirt a few times as if to shake bugs out of it, then examined the fabric close. Seeing nothing, he turned to put his back toward her. "Anything on me?"

"Uhh…" Piper cringed at a few fresh bruises, and brushed her fingertips over one over his left shoulder blade. "Just some bruises from the fall. No bugs."

"Still feels like stuff is walking on me." He fidgeted and put his shirt back on. "Maybe it's like static electricity in the air?"

Piper felt some degree of comfort in knowing that she hadn't been covered in fleas. She squinted up at the ceiling. "Maybe. These lights are *so* bright."

Tristan walked past a large island of dirt where two small trees and some white wildflowers grew inside a ring of benches. "This is like the mall." He headed across the room in a straight line, into the tunnel.

"Where are you going?" called Piper, not quite willing to walk away from the known exit.

He stopped where the passage met the chamber and spun to face her. "This way. We've been trying to see what's down here for two days. Let's at least take a look."

"We almost died falling down an elevator shaft! We need to tell my parents."

"What if they don't let us back down here?" He flailed his arms. "We should explore a little bit first."

The reality of finding a place like this under her house *did* have an undeniable element of awesome to it. If not for *how* they found it, she probably would've been as eager as he to run around checking it out. She closed her eyes and tried to set aside the memory of plummeting down the dumbwaiter shaft. *That ghost could've stabbed me in the face, but it cut the rope… maybe it wanted us to find this place? But… why did it lock me in the trunk?*

Anger at the ghost for trapping her in a box pushed aside her nervousness at exploration. Hands balled into fists, she hurried after Tristan. A little poking around couldn't hurt. *The elevator is right here, it's not like we'll get lost.*

Tristan waited for her, then walked at her side. The passageway leading out from the circular area (which she'd decided to call the food court) reminded her a bit of the corridors at her school, wide and grey. It curved around to the right at enough of an angle that they couldn't see far.

"Wow, this is long," said Tristan.

"Yeah." She studied the red tile floor, which looked old as well as clean. "I think this has been here for a long time, but that doesn't make any sense."

"Why not?" He hopped up onto a bench along the right side, walking on the cushions.

"Because all the booths in the food court are like brand new. If this place is old, why don't any of those places look used?"

He jumped off the other end of the bench, shrugged, and kept walking. "We're in a giant underground... something beneath your house. Rich people are weird. Who knows?"

Piper glanced over at him.

"You're not weird." He smiled. "You're not 'rich people.' You're 'normal people who found a lot of money.'"

She decided to smile. "There's a difference?"

"Yeah. Rich people have always been rich, and they don't really understand what it's like for anyone else." He slowed his stride, looking over at her. "I hope you don't change."

"I hope so too." She almost said she'd give it all up if she could go home to her friends, but that would also mean she'd be too far away to see Tristan. Frustration kept her quiet. Why did the world have to force her to choose between a new friend that seemed really cool and the friends she'd known for a couple years already?

After what had to be more than a hundred yards, the constant rightward curve bent left and straightened out. The next section looked at least as long as the part they'd already walked, only they could see all the way to the end. Two huge glass windows on the right, and one on the left, reminded her of the reptile house at the zoo.

"Tristan?" whispered Piper. "Do you think this is a zoo?"

He raked his hair off his face and tucked it behind one ear. "Kinda looks like it... but why would someone put a zoo underground?"

The nearest enclosure was on the right. Piper crept up to the glass, peering into a massive, featureless concrete room about fifty yards deep and sixty across. The ceiling extended about two stories up. She braced her hands on the window and leaned close, staring up at light fixtures and pipes on the ceiling. When she looked down, a sparkle of silver caught her eye. Intricate scrollwork ran along the bottom of the window where it met the stone, exactly the same pattern as what had been on the front gates.

"Hey look," said Piper, pointing at the fancy marks. "This same is engraving is on the gate too."

"Check this out." Tristan waved her over. He stood near the middle of the enormous window, pointing at a yellow sign with green writing on it.

Piper walked up to stand next to him.

The Menagerie of Jenkins Bailey

(Empty)

Reserved for an honest politician, if such a mythical creature can be located.

She grinned, then a worried thought caught hold in her head. "Wow. I hope this is a joke. Was my granddad really going to put a person in a cage?"

"I think it's a joke." Tristan laughed and traipsed off down the corridor to the next enclosure, on the left. "Wow…"

Piper turned.

The window looked into a gloomy forest with black trees, low-lying fog, and a dark, nighttime sky aglow with a bright moon. She leaned back, clutching her hands at her chest. The landscape looked perfect for the woods right outside Dracula's castle.

"Wicked," muttered Tristan.

"It's like a nightmare in a box…" She hesitantly approached behind him. "That's the scariest forest I've ever seen… I'm glad it's fake."

Tristan leaned up to the window, which had the same silvery scroll-work running along the bottom edge. "It doesn't look fake."

"Obviously, it isn't a real forest. And that's not the real moon. We're underground… and it's not dark out."

He walked along the glass, gazing in at the shifting fog and twisted trees. "There's something in there."

"You see it?" asked Piper.

"No, I feel like I'm being watched." He stopped at a sign.

Piper rolled her eyes. "I've felt watched since I got to this house." She crept up beside him and read:

Bhargest

Found: Northern England

The Bhargest is often regarded as a harbinger of death. When a soul is to move to the afterlife, the creature leads a procession of all the hounds in the village to the person's doorstep, announcing their imminent demise with howls and barks. It is said wounds caused by the Bhargest's claws never heal, bleeding and festering for eternity. Good thing, then, that it will only attack someone who attempts to keep it from its quarry. Bhargests are rumored to avoid crossing rivers and can become invisible whenever they desire.

"Oh, sure." Tristan folded his arms. "It's invisible. Ha. Ha. I think your grandfather was a con artist."

"What do you mean?" Piper leaned up to the glass, peering into the creepy forest.

"I bet he built this zoo, tells people there are creatures down here, but they're all 'invisible' so they don't really exist."

"Oh. Yeah, maybe."

A flash of orange light deep in the forest caught her attention.

Piper stared at the spot, her gaze tracking a pair of luminous spots gliding along. They floated out from behind a tree, hanging like eyes without a body. As if sensing her watching, they pivoted toward her. She swallowed, her throat tightening.

Shadows gathered around the spots, coalescing into the form of a large mastiff dog with infinitely black fur and massive paws with silver claws. Glowing fiery eyes flared brighter as the creature stalked out of the woods, approaching the window.

Vertigo washed over her, and she felt herself falling through the earth. An instant later, she sat on the floor of a square concrete-walled pit. Tristan lay a short distance away, his cheeks sunken in and pale. Intense hunger sliced across Piper's stomach, her aching body too weak to move. The clothes hung off her skeletal-thin frame. Shaking from fear, she lifted her shirt and gasped at her sunken stomach and prominent ribs.

The shock of it made her yell and jump, once more in the corridor outside the Bhargest's enclosure. Strong hunger remained for a few seconds, but faded away.

Tristan grasped her hand. "Did you just see something scary?"

"Yeah." She pulled her shirt up a little to examine her stomach, and breathed a sigh of relief when it looked normal.

"Is it going to kill us?"

"I don't think so." She pointed at the sign. "It's a harbinger of death."

"Does that mean it's gonna kill us?"

She swallowed. "No… a harbinger is like an omen. It's just telling us we're going to die… I think we're going to starve."

The Bhargest nodded at her. As if content with what had happened, the creature turned and padded off into the woods once more, its body vanishing into a whorl of shadows, leaving only its fiery eyes drifting among the trees. Seconds after it disappeared, a blood-chilling canine howl sounded over the woods.

"Did that really happen? Did we really see a big dog just vanish?" asked Piper.

"I saw it too, so if it's crazy, we're both crazy."

Piper stood there for a while, holding her gut with both hands, unsure how to cope with going from starvation-hunger to normal so fast. Queasiness rumbled in her stomach and all the hairs on her arms stood on end. She simultaneously wanted to eat but couldn't bear the thought of food. That, plus seeing a creature that shouldn't exist do something that shouldn't be able to happen freaked her out to the point she couldn't do anything but stare at the creepy forest for several minutes.

Again, she found herself examining the silver scrollwork. Her grandfather had somehow captured a mythological creature and stuffed it in a zoo. That it resembled a dog only made her angrier. "That's so cruel!"

"Yeah." Tristan rubbed his stomach. "Starving is a horrible way to die."

"No, I mean…" She pointed at the enclosure. "Locking animals up like that. Zoos are horrible! Animals belong in the wild."

"You're a tree hugger?" Tristan grinned.

She rolled her eyes. "Not really. I just… have a thing for animals. I want to be a veterinarian."

"Vets put animals in cages all the time."

"Sure, when they're sick and recovering from surgery. They don't keep them there for years and years." Piper leaned up to the glass. "I'm gonna let you out so you can go home."

"Umm, that dog just threatened to throw us in a pit and starve us to death," said Tristan.

"No he didn't. He showed us something that *might* happen."

He tilted his head. "I don't want to die, but are you sure it's *might* and not *will*?"

"Yeah." She pointed down the corridor. "The elevator is right there. That place where we fell looks just like these hallways, the same grey concrete. There's probably somewhere here that's dangerous, and we can fall in and no one will ever find us. But, if we get out of here now, we won't fall and die."

Tristan nodded. "I like not falling and dying… but there's another window."

She sighed, reluctantly following him to the last enclosure in this hallway on the right.

The window peered in on a hilly landscape, with short scrub brush and patches of open brown dirt. On one side, a few sparse trees formed a grove. The other had a rocky wall with a cave mouth, in which slept a three-headed dog as big as Dad's pickup truck.

"Holy crap!" said Tristan. "Look at that thing…"

Piper gulped. "It could eat us in two bites."

He poked her in the ribs. "Still wanna set it free?"

"Well, it *could* be friendly…" She crept over to the sign.

Cerberus

Found: Greece

The three-headed dog of legend, often said to guard the gates of Hell, is actually a surface-dwelling canid that lives in isolated pockets of forest, far from prying eyes. It is likely that a long-ago sighting of one of these magnificent beasts inspired its role in Greek Mythology. An interesting fact about the Cerberus is that each head retains a unique personality, like having three individual dogs. These animals are fiercely territorial, and will often attack anything they believe threatens their home.

Sensing their presence, the giant dog stretched up on its legs and trotted over to the glass. Its central head snarled at them. The right head conveyed a sense of guarded curiosity, while the leftmost head let its tongue loll out like a vapidly friendly canine.

"See?" whispered Tristan. "It's just like a normal dog... only huge."

She took a step away from the glass. "The middle one doesn't like us. I wonder which one controls the legs."

He shrugged. "Hi, doggie."

Friendly head licked the glass. Suspicious head sniffed at it, and the middle head continued emitting a low growl. The Cerberus raked its claws at the window. Each time its nails scraped down the glass with an ear-piercing squeal, the silvery scrollwork around the border of the window gave off light.

"Magic?" she asked, pointing at the decorative marks. "It has to be magic... A dog that big should be able to break this glass easy."

He scratched his head. "You believe in magic?"

Piper grabbed his head in both hands and forced him to look up at the enormous dog. "That's a three-headed dog the size of a Chevy. I think we can assume magic might be real."

He offered no protest to her grip, and shrugged. "Okay."

"We should get out of here before something bad happens." She let go of his head. "We have to tell my parents about this place."

Tristan laughed. "Yeah, right. They'll believe us."

"We have to try. I can't just leave these creatures down here to starve."

He scratched at his stomach. "I don't wanna starve either."

"Come on. We have to get out of here."

"Are you scared?" asked Tristan, in an honest tone.

"Yes. No one knows where we are. If something happens, they'll never find us." Since the passageway dead-ended, she walked back toward the food court. "We just go upstairs, find my parents, and show them this place. They'll know what to do."

"Right." Tristan stuffed his hands in his jean pockets and followed.

Piper jogged back to the large circular room, navigated the tables and islands full of plants, and approached the elevator. She jabbed her finger into the gem like a dagger, and waited.

"It didn't light up," said Tristan.

"I know." Her voice faltered with worry. "Maybe the light's just broken."

"Or the elevator won't come down here without the key."

Piper closed her eyes. "Maybe the light's just broken and we're not trapped down here with no way out."

Tristan took her hand. "There has to be more than one way out."

"Yeah." She defiantly mashed the button a few more times, scowling at the shiny brass doors. Her hope of simply leaving gone, worry that the Bhargest's vision might become reality made her shiver.

"Let's look around for another way out. If we can't find one, we can yell up the dumbwaiter shaft. There's doors on every floor of the house. Your parents will eventually hear us."

Piper took a breath, held it, and let it out her nose. That made sense. The sliding doors *were* thin. His backup plan fell short of perfect, but it did offer enough hope for her to swallow fear. "Okay."

She spun in place and randomly chose the next corridor out of the food court, to the right of the one leading to the bhargest. Piper realized she still held Tristan's hand a few minutes later as they walked, but decided to continue. Not being alone made being stuck underground *much* less scary.

"I wonder what kind of stuff your grandpa has down here. Do you think it's all monsters?"

"I dunno. I hope not."

They traversed more plain grey corridor and red tile floor, passing several benches and water fountains, where they stopped to have a drink. She tried to understand the vision the bhargest gave her: had something locked them in a cell as another exhibit, or did they fall into a hole? Already it had become indistinct in her mind, with only the feeling of hunger persisting. Grey concrete walls, Tristan looking *so* thin, but she couldn't remember how big the chamber had been. Worried that she'd stumble to her doom because she couldn't see it coming kept her creeping along, frightened that any individual piece of floor would collapse out from under her.

The corridor continued for quite a while before it swept around to the right in a sharp curve. At the bend, one offshoot went to the left, while the path they'd been following ran on ahead. Another dead end more than a hundred yards away held an empty enclosure. A long window on the right-side wall about halfway down glowed with sunlight.

Piper took the left turn, having little interest in gawking at trapped creatures until she found a way out of here. A dead-end corridor with two cages would not contain a way out. The hallway bent left, went straight for a while, then curved sharply to the right into a large, long chamber with irregular walls like a bunch of circles stuck together. Red tiles formed a walkpath that slalomed among circular garden areas full of bizarre flowers and plants. Brackets stood here and there, presumably to hold signs identifying the different species of flora, but none of the actual signs had been installed.

While it looked possible to cut across the gardens and proceed in a straight line, some of the plants (bright red or orange) had big thorns or looked dangerous. Erring on the side of caution, Piper stayed on the walkway, weaving around one circular garden and the next.

"Ow!" shouted Tristan, letting go of her hand.

She stopped short and looked over.

Tristan stood with his back toward her, right arm raised to protect his face, and a bright red taco-sized Venus-flytrap-style leaf clamped onto his forearm. Black spines as big as cats' claws dug into his skin, drawing blood. He leaned away, trying to pull his arm free, gasping and whining out his nose.

"Ack!" shouted Piper. She moved in to help, but three more giant flytrap mouths thrust themselves at her, making her leap away.

Another tried to bite Tristan on the forehead. He punched it aside while sidestepping one going for his leg.

Piper darted closer, grabbed the fanged leafy mouth on his arm, and pried it open. One snapped for her face; she turned in time to give it a mouthful of hair. Its claw-teeth raked like a comb, pulling away as she ran with Tristan down the path, out of its reach.

"Ow." He frowned at his arm, covered in little red dots.

She moved in front of him to study the injury, which didn't look all that bad. "Did it sting you?"

"No... just sharp like thorns." He rubbed it. "I've gotten worse from Nibs."

"Nibs?" asked Piper.

He grinned. "My cat. Nibbles, but we call him Nibs. He's a biter, but he only plays."

"You sure you're okay?"

"Yeah it surprised me more than hurt." He wiped a blood trail from his forearm. "Just a scratch."

She took his hand again and pulled him onward, rushing past the remaining gardens to plain corridor some minutes later. The hallway ended at a T, forcing her to decide between a left or right turn. After a quick side-to-side glance, she went to the right.

Another enclosure on the left contained a beautiful bamboo forest with a layer of ethereal fog. Somehow, it looked like a snow-capped mountain range spanned the distant horizon, miles away under bright blue sky and a shining sun. It had to be a huge picture, since her grandfather couldn't possibly have built an entire mountain range underground… much less sky.

"Wow…" Tristan pointed. "What is that!?"

Piper twisted to follow his finger.

A creature the approximate size and stature of a deer walked among the bamboo. Rather than fur, its body shimmered with metallic gold scales. A single backward-curving horn, also bright gold, protruded from the forehead, above a face that mixed features of dragon with canine. It walked upon gold hooves, and had a long, flowing white mane down the length of its back, which continued into a fluffy tail. Glowing ruby eyes regarded them with a sense of irritation and contempt.

Piper's heart sank. She rushed up to the glass and put her hands on it. "I'm sorry you're stuck in there! I promise I'm going to find a way to let you out."

The creature's standoffishness lessened. It approached, head tilted in curiosity.

"It's from Japan," said Tristan.

It took her a long moment to do so, but Piper peeled her gaze away from the creature and examined the sign.

Ki-Rin

Found: Japan (Okinawa)

Considered one of the most powerful beasts in Japanese folklore, the ki-rin shares ancestry with the Chinese Qilin. It is believed that in ancient times, the ki-rin have selected emperors and foretold great events.

Despite their frightening appearance, these magnificent animals are peaceful and considered benevolent, able to sense a person's goodness or evil. According to some Buddhist traditions, ki-rin fly or trod upon clouds so as not to injure even a single blade of grass.

Piper looked back up at the ki-rin, her eyebrows twisting up. Sadness at seeing such a creature confined made tears gather at the corners of her eyes. A voice emanated from the enclosure. Japanese words formed from delicate crystalline notes like wind chimes. Despite not understanding the language, she sensed that this creature understood her repulsion to its captivity.

Assuming it wouldn't know what she said if she spoke English, she leaned close to the glass, stared into its eyes, and concentrated on how much she wanted to set it free—but didn't know how. It bowed its head, then nodded to the left, ruby eyes brightening with trust and knowing.

"He doesn't belong here," said Piper.

Tristan muttered, "Yeah. I think he wants us to hurry up and let him out, too."

She looked back and forth along the glass, searching for any doors or panels, but the wall appeared solid. "There's got to be another passageway or something in the back, like at a normal zoo that only people who work there see."

He nodded.

Piper put her hand on the glass again and locked stares with the ki-rin. "I won't leave you trapped here."

It bowed its head, and again nodded to her right.

Piper fumed about her cruel grandfather as she stormed off. No wonder Grandma never said anything nice about him, or that part of the family. If all the money her family inherited came from these creatures' misery, she didn't want any part of it. Though, it would probably be easier to convince her parents to donate some to animal charities rather than give it *all* up. They loved her, but she doubted they'd walk away from such a fortune because she objected to how grandpa made the money.

This place never opened... The food court isn't finished. Maybe he didn't make money on it. He would've needed money to build it and run around the world catching this stuff. All the random things in the attic made sense now. Grandpa Bailey had spent decades roaming the globe in search of animals that most people thought to be myths.

"Tristan?"

"Huh?" He stopped walking and looked at her.

"Are these real? I mean… could they be really good holograms or something? Like a show? Maybe these aren't windows, but really giant TV screens."

He made a series of faces while thinking. "Maybe… but if it's fake, how'd we both get that scary dream from the big dog?"

"I dunno. Maybe it's like some kinda electronic thing that can transmit into our heads." She peered back toward the ki-rin's enclosure. "It felt real. But, it's behind glass. It could be all like computer movies. Like what if they're not windows, but giant screens?"

"Maybe." He shrugged.

"We still need to get out of here." She resumed walking.

The corridor swept around in another rightward curve, then left in a gradual S bend. Piper's legs ached from all the walking, exactly as they had when her parents took her to an actual zoo. She'd been about seven or eight at the time, and no less horrified at captive animals then as she felt today. What her parents intended as a nice day trip turned into a lot of crying and comforting. *Okay, maybe I* am *a bit oversensitive, but it's still mean to keep animals in cages.*

Another enclosure came up on the right side, this one's window stretching for about forty yards. The scenery inside appeared to be an ordinary pine forest that could've been from anywhere temperate. Motion caught her eye some distance in, where an ostrich-sized bird pranced about. Its feathers ranged from deep emerald green along its back and outer wing surfaces to seafoam green on the belly. Indigo legs held its pod-shaped body far up off the ground, both feet tipped with sharp black claws. It had a long, dark blue beak and huge eyes, somewhat offset from each other, giving it an expression like a cartoon chicken that had been hit over the head and gone cross-eyed.

Caught off guard by the manic, whimsical creature, Piper giggled.

"Don't look at it!" yelled Tristan. "The sign says it can kill you!"

"What?" She spun to face him.

He pointed at the sign, and kept reading. "Oh... never mind. It can't do it through the glass."

She trotted over to read.

Cockatrice

Found: Wales, County Gwynedd

The cockatrice is a fabled creature that has adorned the pages of literature for centuries. In the wild, these magical beasts hunt by means of their enchanted gaze, which turns living creatures to stone that the cockatrice eats. Natural rocks appear not to interest the creature. Fear not, gentle visitor, for the wards upon the enclosure glass protect you from its petrifying gaze. Should you find yourselves in the company of a cockatrice in the wild, do not make eye contact.

"That's kinda hard to believe," said Tristan. "Maybe you're right, and this is really just a giant computer screen playing a movie."

The enormous bird paced around among the trees, oblivious to their presence. It didn't appear to have any more smarts than an ordinary animal, and either didn't see them or didn't care. When Tristan tapped on the glass, the cockatrice stopped like a statue. He tapped again, and the bird swung itself around toward them, waving its head side to side.

"It can't see us," said Piper.

"It wouldn't if it's a video. Unless it's like a computer game and it can react to us."

Piper pointed. "It looks cross-eyed. Maybe it can't see well."

"It needs glasses!" Tristan laughed.

She giggled.

The cockatrice trotted up to them. When it pecked the glass, the silver scrollwork flared with light again. Piper put her hand on the window, as did Tristan. The second time it hammered the glass with its beak, she felt a definite impact, and leapt back with a yelp.

"Whoa," muttered Tristan.

"If that's fake, they really did a good job."

Tristan walked back and forth, the huge chicken's eyes mostly following him. "It can see me… Umm. Maybe it isn't fake."

"They could've programmed it to be interactive. You know, to amuse kids."

"Are you amused or scared?" asked Tristan.

Piper nibbled on her thumbnail for a moment. "Little of both."

"I'm starting to get hungry," said Tristan.

"Don't say that." She walked away down the hall. "Look for a way out."

"Right."

About sixty yards and a left curve later, they reached a small door marked 'Employees Only' on the right wall. The corridor kept going past it until it reached a ninety-degree rightward bend. Piper rushed over and grabbed the door handle, but it didn't budge. The keyhole looked ordinary, not like the old-timey one from the elevator.

"No!" yelled Piper, banging on the door.

"Calm down." Tristan added a kick to the door for good measure. "We don't even know if this is a way out. It could be like a closet or something. Maybe a way in to the back tunnels."

She backed up, sighing. "You're right. A way out would have an exit sign, right? For fire?"

"Do crazy rich people who make secret zoos bother putting exit signs up?" asked Tristan.

Worried that she'd never see the real sun again, Piper walked faster. Around the bend, she found another huge window, spanning the entire left wall before the corridor bent to the right again at least sixty yards away. This enclosure contained a mixture of rocky crags and windblown sand dunes. Dark mountains loomed in the distance, though they looked too real to be a painting. The sheer size of the chamber made Piper's jaw hang open. It extended well beyond the corridor to the left, and had to be a hundred or more feet tall with plenty of open 'sky.'

Seeing nothing but rocks and open space inside, Piper moved over to the sign near the center of the window.

Griffon

Found: North Africa

Griffons live in the arid climes of Egypt, Greece, and Persia, though some have been documented in Europe. According to legend, these creatures mate for life, and should their companion die, they will continue the rest of their existence in solitude. The mated pair in this enclosure was a fortuitous find. Upon capture of the male, the female presented herself without resistance.

"Aww!" Piper sniffled. "That's so sad!"

"Wow. I hope this is made up." Tristan glanced at her.

Wham!

Piper screamed and jumped back as a tremendous crash shook the window. Tristan also shrieked, and leapt into her, though she couldn't tell if he tried to protect her or clung like a scared boy.

A great creature had collided with the glass, evidently having attempted to dive at them. Stunned, it staggered from side to side. Its head resembled that of an eagle, only huge, with golden-brown feathers spreading down over the shoulders of a leonine body, becoming fur behind the front legs. Its forepaws, shaped like the legs of an eagle, bore massive talons longer than the sword in the attic. The rear two-thirds of its body had the appearance of a lion in every detail but size.

Once the initial shock of the slam wore off, Piper approached the glass, her hands still shaking. "Can you understand us?"

The griffon shook its massive head back and forth, dazed.

Tristan cracked up laughing.

"What?" Piper stared at him.

"It flew into a window like a bird. I don't think it's smart like a person."

She smirked, and turned back to face the creature. "It's a magical beast. It could be anything."

A second, slightly smaller, griffon swooped in to land next to it, nuzzling beak to beak.

"Aww, she knows he hurt himself." Piper patted the glass. "You don't belong here. I want to help you go home." Thinking that the female allowed herself to be captured so she could stay with her mate got her choked up and wiping tears.

"They don't understand you. Even if they did speak, they'd be like talking in North African or whatever... not English." Tristan put an arm around her back.

"It's so sad..." She watched the female tend to her mate, not even caring that she almost played the part of the field mouse in an eagle's dinner.

The female griffon swung her head around and peered at Piper. Bright yellow eyes fixed on her, but not with malice. For a moment of silence, they stared at each other, then a plump tear swelled and fell from the griffon's face.

Piper cried at the sight. "She's sad. They don't want to be in there."

"I don't either. They'd eat me," said Tristan.

"I'm serious. We have to help them."

"So they can eat us?"

She shook her head. "No. She's smarter than we think. I think she knows I feel sad for them. Look, she's crying too. The griffons will understand when I let them out. They'll go home."

When the griffon resumed nuzzling her mate, Piper dragged herself away from the glass and trudged on down the corridor. Tristan walked beside her, hands in his pockets.

"This place is so big," muttered Piper. "I hope we don't get lost."

"Yeah."

The hallway curved right, went past two merchandise booths full of figurines depicting griffons, ki-rin, cockatrices, another creature that looked to be half eagle and half horse, phoenixes, and another type of bird she didn't recognize that didn't have any non-bird parts, but did have fancy plumage.

"Wow, there's phoenixes?" Tristan's eyes went wide, like a little boy. "I wanna see it!"

"This place is bad!"

"I mean." Tristan grabbed her hand. "We gotta find it so we can help it."

She nodded and kept going.

A small enclosure on the left wall, merely thirty yards across, peered into a boggy landscape partway between swamp and forest. Numerous orbs of light, some blue, some yellow, some green, glided about among the trees, skimming the surface of the muck or hovering in the upper branches.

Piper headed straight to the sign.

Will-o-Wisp

Found: Ireland, Scotland, Wales

Wisps are creatures composed entirely of spirit energy that take the form of eldritch lanterns or dancing lights. They are rumored to lure travelers to a watery death by drowning in the swamps and peat marshes around where they dwell, though other rumors say the sight of a wisp is a good omen. These legends tell that wisps may lead those fortunate enough to find them to their heart's desire or destiny—if one believes in such things as fate.

The many drifting light orbs inside the enclosure showed no reaction whatsoever to Piper and Tristan watching them. They did have a mesmerizing quality that caused her to stand there gazing at them for a little while, before the urge to escape this place came back. She tugged Tristan along and rounded a leftward bend. It went for a long way down a plain stretch before bending back to the right.

Piper flopped on a bench opposite an enclosure that contained a temperate-looking forest. Like the griffon's, it had an impossibly tall ceiling at least five stories up. "This place is too big. My feet hurt."

"Yeah." Tristan sat beside her, one hand on his stomach.

She wanted lunch too, but thinking about being hungry reminded her too much of starving in a hole. Of course, the more she tried *not* to think about food, the hungrier she got.

A screech made her jump.

Moving among the treetops, another fantastical creature glided into view, cruising from right to left. Mottled blue-grey, it had a head like a hawk, and all four of its legs resembled those of a slender horse. Great, feathered wings beat in a steady rhythm, and a long tail glided along behind it like a pennant. The majestic creature flew back and forth in lazy figure eights, screeching every so often at nothing in particular.

Piper rubbed her aching thighs. Eventually, she made her way to the sign.

Hippogriff

Found: France

These beautiful creatures are said to be the offspring of a griffon and an ordinary mare, which under normal circumstances are quite fierce enemies. Thus, many regard these creatures as a symbol of love's ability to conquer all.

The hippogriff didn't seem at all concerned with a pair of children watching it, so Piper continued walking down the corridor. Each time her sneaker struck red tile, she resolved again to set everything in here free. Exactly how she'd get them back home, well… that she might need to ask her parents for some help on. Creatures like the griffon and the hippogriffs, they ought to be able to just fly.

She followed the corridor around another pair of opposing turns. "I guess my grandfather had a mortal fear of straight lines. Why do all these corridors keep bending back and forth?"

Tristan laughed.

A small enclosure (compared to the others) on the left contained a mountainous wall and a stretch of desert or hard-packed dirt. Upon a scraggly branch perched a flaming bird somewhat larger than the eagle it physically resembled. Beneath a coating of fire, bright red feathers adorned its back, with golden-yellow plumage down its belly. Even if it hadn't been *actually* on fire, the rich orangey-gold of the chest feathers glimmered like flames. Glowing sapphire eyes fixed on Piper.

"That's gotta be a phoenix," said Tristan, his voice a half-whisper of awe.

The phoenix leaned toward them and emitted a soft cry.

Fogginess swept over Piper's mind for an instant and faded away, leaving her somehow knowing the bird's intention. "Wow… He knows I want to help him get out of here."

"Huh?" Tristan glanced at her.

"It stared at me and I just know it's friendly." She pressed a hand on the glass. "I promise I'll help you go home."

It cooed again.

"Can you tell me where the exit is or how to get you out?"

The phoenix tilted its head. Again, without understanding why, Piper knew she should keep walking the same way she'd been going.

"Thank you. I'll be back as soon as I can!"

The phoenix made a noise like two pieces of slate scraping together.

Tristan cringed. "Is it talking to us?"

"Yes, but not with sound. Come on."

"Oh wow." Tristan blinked dazedly. "He likes that I think he's beautiful."

Piper hurried onward. The corridor curved slightly to the left before straightening out with wide enclosure window along the left. Flashes of lightning from inside filled the hallway. Opposite the sign at the middle of the window, another hallway led off to the right in a T. The glass continued, wrapping around the corner to the left, following two sides of a massive square cage.

The landscape within looked a bit like the desert from cowboy movies, with mesas and tumbleweeds. Dark clouds overhead flickered with jagged streaks of electricity. Piper felt like she ought to go down the T, but surrendered to curiosity and approached the sign.

Thunderbird

Found: American West

According to Native American tradition, the thunderbirds preside over the upper world. They throw lightning from their talons or eyes, and each flap of their wings can create thunder. Considered wise protectors, these beasts are regarded as divine beings by the indigenous peoples of the region in which they live. Mortal enemies of the Misikinubik (great horned snakes, which I have yet to find), they will attack them on sight.

Piper grumbled. "What was *wrong* with him? He had no right to lock these things up like this."

"Yeah. How'd he build this place anyway? It looks like real sky in there."

"I don't know. I'm still not… no, I am sure they aren't computer images. The phoenix like spoke to my brain. Movies can't do that. They're real."

A pair of birds as big as small airplanes glided down from the clouds, their feathers a mix of dark blue, white, red, and yellow. Threads of lightning crackled around their bodies, rushing off into the clouds with sharp *snaps*.

"Oh, this is too much…" Piper shook her head.

"I know. But *saying* it's wrong won't help. We have to find a way out." Tristan tugged on her hand.

"This way." Piper headed down the T.

After a long walk along plain corridor, they approached a branch to the left. Piper followed a strange urge and kept going straight. Over a hundred yards later, a huge archway opened, again on the left. A sign above proclaimed it, 'The Grand Garden.'

Whatever the phoenix had done to her pulled her toward it. She didn't resist, and walked in. The chamber on the other side of the arch was so massive, she felt as though she'd gone outside. Great, puffy white clouds drifted across a bright, clear sky. Sunlight real enough to warm her face bathed a storybook-perfect woodland and meadow. Soft grass tempted her to kick her sneakers off and run around. Beautiful twisty trees formed the lushest forest she'd ever seen, like nothing from this Earth.

"Whoa." Tristan blinked. "Are we outside?"

Piper grabbed his hand and squeezed. "No… I think we went into a cage… only a huge one. Whatever's in here… there's no glass protecting us."

"Wait. Don't you wanna free them? Why are you worried about being protected?"

"I am. I also think lions and tigers don't belong in zoos, but I don't want to run over and hug one."

"Okay. That makes sense."

She trusted the feeling inside her and walked deeper into the garden. "Whatever is in here must not be dangerous if it's out in the open like this where people can just walk by."

"Let's hope."

A whiff of grilled chicken went by on the breeze.

"I smell food," said Piper.

"Me too. Steak." Tristan nodded.

"Chicken." She narrowed her eyes.

"I smell steak." He looked at her.

"Weird."

Piper followed her nose to a bizarre giant bush, with purple leaves and rounded olive-drab fruits as big as softballs. She leaned close and sniffed one, mystified that it smelled exactly like a grilled chicken sandwich.

"They smell like steak." Tristan patted one.

She stared at the relatively ugly fruit, trying to make sense of it having such an appealing fragrance while looking like an Army canteen.

"We can eat them. Look. A sign." Tristan pointed at a plain yellow square on a metal post.

Chimera Fruit

These faerie-fruits are found in the deepest forests of Europe, where civilization has not yet spread. They are sensitive to shifts in energy caused by humans' non-belief in magic, and tend to die off when exposed to large numbers of humans who cannot accept faeries' existence. These fruits are a delight to eat. Magic within the pulp causes them to taste like whatever you desire at the time. Please check with management before picking.

"Well, I guess since my family owns this place now, I'm management, and I say, let's eat one."

"Cool."

Piper grabbed one of the fruits and tugged until it snapped off the vine. The rubbery rind surrendered to her fingernail, and she split it open around the middle, exposing a golf ball-sized pit and fruit flesh with the texture of peach. The smell of grilled chicken and cheese made zero sense, but as strong as it hit her, she couldn't resist taking a huge bite.

About halfway through the fruit, the flavor changed to salty French fries, and her last two mouthfuls became chocolate milk. Thoroughly confused, she tossed the rind on the ground by the stem for compost. Tristan, his cheeks smeared with orange liquid, stared at her.

"What?" asked Piper.

"That. Was. Weird."

"Yeah." She pointed. "You've got juice all over your face."

He wiped himself clean. "It started off tasting like steak, but changed to garlic and potatoes, then brownies."

"I'm not hungry anymore." She patted her stomach. "Come on."

Not far from the chimera fruit bush, they found a strange tree with a trunk that looked an awful lot like a woman holding a strange ballet pose. Upward pointing branches had a shape similar to arms, but instead of hands, they split into multiple thinner branches full of leaves. Ivy 'hair' hung from a wooden lump that vaguely resembled a head, but the shape of her bosom and hips had far too much similarity too to a person to be an accident.

"That tree has boobs," said Tristan.

Piper blushed a little, though she couldn't help but nod. "Yeah. That's really weird."

Curious, Tristan walked up to it and put his hand on the bark, by the silhouette's waist. "It's a tree."

"Duh," said Piper, approaching behind him.

The tree twisted itself around and straightened in posture. Branches shrank into the arms, taking on the shape of human hands.

Tristan jumped back with a shout of surprise. Piper grabbed on to him from behind to stop herself from fainting.

Though her skin continued to look like tree bark, a short, delicate-featured woman with pointed ears, moss for eyebrows, and hair of ivy and flowers offered a smile. Below the knees, her legs remained fused like a tree trunk. She reached toward Tristan and grasped the petrified boy's right arm, where the plant had bit him.

Seconds later, when the tree woman let go, the puncture wounds had vanished.

Awestruck, Tristan stared back and forth between his arm and the woman a few times before stammering, "Thank you."

"Are you a dryad?" asked Piper.

The woman faced her and nodded. Her expression fell sorrowful.

"I'm sorry you're trapped here. My grandfather was cruel. I'm going to help set everything free." She stomped. "Ooh! This is horrible! Why would he do this?"

With a crackling sound like twigs crunching, the Dryad's legs separated. She stepped up out of the ground and away from where she'd been rooted. Though she clearly had the shape of an adult woman, she didn't stand much taller than the kids. A rough hand caressed Piper's cheek. The Dryad's eyes, aglow with green magical light, radiated gratitude. As soon as she *felt* the sorrow in this creature's heart, Piper resolved to do whatever it took to undo her grandfather's crimes.

"I swear I'll help." She hugged the Dryad, the wood spirit's body as hard as if she'd embraced a literal tree, her skin coarse like tree bark. Despite that, the arms encircling her conveyed tenderness and love. "We need to find the way out."

The dryad pointed to the side.

"Go that way?" asked Piper.

She nodded, ivy-hair rustling.

"Okay. Thank you for helping Tristan."

He smiled at the dryad. "That was awesome of you."

The dryad bowed, took a step back, and raised her arms skyward. In seconds, branches extended where fingers had been, her facial features blurred away, and she again took on the appearance of a person-shaped tree.

Piper hurried in the direction she'd been pointed in, not caring to admire any of the beautiful trees, flowers, or bushes. Having sky overhead despite knowing she'd gone underground unsettled her, so she made it a point not to look up. It had to be some kind of complex illusion or lighting trick.

"Well, we know it's real now." Tristan held up his arm. "Movies can't fix claw marks or hug people."

"Yeah." Piper stopped walking, and shivered. "No one is going to believe us. We can't tell anyone. The government will come in, take them all, and put them in even worse cages. At least Grandpa Bailey tried to give them habitats."

He nodded. "We'll have to at least tell your parents."

She fidgeted, unsure how they'd react. They already thought she'd started 'acting out' and would probably think she made it all up. "Maybe. If we don't have another choice."

"Huh?"

While they walked through the woods, she explained about her parents, the ghost, and how they wanted to take her to a psychiatrist. A few minutes later, they reached the end of the giant garden and entered a short stretch of corridor that led to another T intersection.

Piper decided to go left. Not far from the garden exit, they found an enclosure window on the right that glimmered bright blue. Unlike the others, this one had a normal-sized door next to the start of the window. The chamber interior appeared to be full of water, more like an exhibit at Sea World than a zoo. A wall separated the tank from wherever the door went, which she figured a good thing since that door didn't look watertight. Near the bottom on the left, a sea cave opening contained a barred door, like a jail cell.

"What the hell?" Piper muttered. "That's really weird."

"Maybe it's like for sharks and divers? So the people who work here can go in the tank and be safe from whatever's swimming around." Tristan shrugged. "Must be something dangerous in there."

"It looks empty. Just water." Piper approached the glass.

Motion stirred in the darkness beyond the bars. Tristan edged up to stand next to her. They stared in engrossed silence for a few minutes. Eventually, a woman's face appeared in the murk, beneath a cloud of flowing blonde hair. She looked about eighteen, with wide, innocent blue eyes. From the waist down, she had a long, graceful tail like a fish that ended in a gossamer fluke glittering with teal, purple, and pink.

"A mermaid," whispered Tristan.

The young woman grasped the bars, staring pleadingly at them. Her lip quivered. Piper couldn't help herself and choked up at the sheer cruelty of it. She locked eyes with the mermaid, who appeared to be begging for help.

"I… can't even." Piper shook her head and pivoted toward the door. "I'm letting her out right now."

9

OF LIES AND MEN

The mermaid's sorrowful expression brightened in an instant to surprise. Still gripping the bars, she grinned.

"You can understand me?" asked Piper.

Blonde hair billowed about in a cloud as the mermaid nodded emphatically.

"Wait." Tristan elbowed her in the side and pointed at the sign. "Read that."

Mermaid

Found: Atlantic Ocean (near Iceland)

Long thought of as myth, the mermaid is a creature of legend. These beings have been a deadly threat to sailors since the beginning of ocean travel. With the appearance of innocence and incomparable beauty, they lure men to their deaths. They have the power to charm men and take away their free will, then drag them beneath the waves and feast upon them. Admire her beauty from afar, but dare not get close, for she will devour any man she touches. Do not trust her innocence or her lies, for these creatures want only one thing: the fresh meat of humans.

When Piper looked up from the sign, the mermaid banged her hands on the bars and shot her an imploring stare.

"I'm gonna go in."

"No." Tristan grabbed her. "She'll kill and eat you."

Piper looked at him. "I'm not a man. The sign says she eats men."

The mermaid shook her head.

"See? I'm right." Piper marched over to the door and grabbed the knob. "Please open."

"The sign said she lies." Tristan fidgeted. "Do you think she'd tell the truth if she was going to eat us?"

Piper walked back in front of the glass. "Will you hurt me?"

The mermaid shook her head.

"What about him?"

She shook her head harder.

Tristan folded his arms. He looked worried, but also sympathetic.

"You're technically not a man either… yet."

Tristan leaned up to the glass. "Do you eat people?"

A note of anger tinted the mermaid's features as she shook her head again.

He tapped his foot. "Adults lie all the time. Except my dad."

"She's not an 'adult.' She's a mermaid… and she's like still in high school."

The mermaid's expression went confused. She pointed at the sign and shook her head again, pointed at Tristan, and nodded.

"Is she saying the sign's a lie?" asked Tristan.

The mermaid nodded and held her hands together in a praying pose.

"I trust her." Piper grabbed the knob and yanked the door open.

A plain set of concrete steps filled a space the size of a closet. Piper scampered up to a platform that ran along the edge of the tank, her sneakers splashing in puddles from water that lapped up onto the deck. The chamber reeked of salt water and fish, with most of the fishy smell coming from a large plastic basin that had a few loose scales stuck to the side.

"She eats fish," said Piper, pointing at it. "But who's been bringing her food?"

The mermaid peered up at them from behind the bars, thirty or so feet beneath the surface on the far side of the room.

Piper crouched at the edge, staring at the cage door. "We probably need a key." Any trace of fear or worry she'd had at being stuck down here disappeared as pure anger took over. "I have to find a key to open that. Do you know where it is?"

The mermaid pointed up then pantomimed an old man walking with a cane.

"He's dead," said Piper. "And it won't bother me if you are happy about that."

The mermaid looked worried. She made a key turning gesture and clasped her hands again in a begging motion.

"Yes. I will let you out… but I have to find the key first. It's horrible that you're stuck in there."

Tristan, his eyes still narrowed in suspicion, squatted beside Piper. "Why are you locked up?"

The mermaid pointed at them and made a diving motion, then raked her arms like she dragged herself on land.

"You tried to run away?" asked Piper.

She nodded, making her hair bloom around.

"Ooh! I hate him so much." Piper stood upright. "My grandfather was a butthead!"

"Wait a minute." Tristan grasped her shoulder. "Can you charm people?"

The mermaid nodded.

"Why didn't you charm Old Man Bailey?"

She traced around her neck, indicating an amulet.

"He had a protection charm," said Piper.

The mermaid gave a thumbs up.

"How do you know that?" Tristan gawked at her. "Do you do magic too? Is it in your family?"

She shrugged. "No, but I've read *Lord of the Rings*, and other fantasy novels. There's magic items and stuff. Since mermaids and griffons and phoenixes and stuff are real, maybe they are too." She looked back down into the water at the mermaid. "I'm sorry that I can't open that right now, but I think I know where I can find the key. It's upstairs. I'm going to go get it and come right back, okay?"

The mermaid stared at her, long and pleading, then nodded.

"I promise," said Piper. "I won't leave you here."

"Okay." Tristan stood. "I trust you too."

Piper trudged down the stairs to the hallway. "Come on."

10

BEHIND THE CURTAIN

The corridor past the mermaid's enclosure split into a Y. Piper turned right without thinking about it. Fifty yards later, another right turn led off along the other wall of the mermaid tank, past a window, while the corridor continued straight ahead to a distant left elbow.

Piper turned, walking past the mermaid tank again. A minute or so later, she turned left, following her gut. After a long stretch of plain hallway, an opening on the left looked in on a verdant green hillside dotted with tiny doors and windows, like miniature houses had been dug into the hillsides. The enclosure had to be two-hundred yards long, and it bothered her for two reasons.

One: it had no glass.

Two: nothing appeared to be in there other than the mini houses.

"Wow. That looks kinda like hobbit houses, only way smaller." Tristan grasped the rim of the opening and leaned in. After a seconds' consideration, he jumped over the wall and ran up the hill to the nearest door, which only came up to his thighs. "They're super tiny!"

"Get out of there! It could be dangerous!" yelled Piper. "Remember, falling in a hole and starving?"

She hurried to the right, hunting for a sign, but the area didn't have one.

Tristan jogged along, staying in the grassy field inside the display. "It smells like pie in here."

"Weird. Do you think it's unfinished, or did stuff escape?" asked Piper.

"If stuff escaped, wouldn't there be broken glass?" Tristan jumped the low wall, back into the corridor, his sneakers squeaking on the red tiles. "You're not tempted to crawl into one of those houses and look?"

"Nope. I'm not doing anything until I get the key and let that mermaid out. She's in a cage!" yelled Piper.

"So is everything down here."

Piper smirked at him. "I mean a literal cage with bars. Because she tried to escape! That's really, really wrong! It's like kidnapping a *person* and locking them up. She's not a zoo animal."

"I agree, calm down. Don't get angry with me. Your face is all red now."

She looked down and took a few breaths.

"So, you know where this key is?"

"Yeah. I think so. The day we got here, this lawyer guy gave my Dad an envelope. If the key is anywhere, it's probably inside there, 'cause Dad said the letter was all fantasy nonsense. Remember that room where my dad was, with all the drawings?"

"That drawing of a mermaid had giant teeth," said Tristan.

"So? It's a myth. Maybe grandpa drew what he imagined it would be, not what he really saw. That girl looks… so lonely and sad."

"What do you think was going to go in there?" Tristan pointed at the hillside houses.

"No idea. Leprechauns?"

He laughed.

Uninterested in delay, Piper tromped onward. The corridor kept going straight along the pastoral hillside enclosure, but entered a gradual right curve once they passed the end of the window. A short offshoot on the left led to bathrooms that resembled the big, public ones from the mall.

Tristan tugged on her arm. "Can we stop real quick?"

"Sure. Fine."

They split up to make use of the respective facilities. The ladies' room smelled like a hospital, making her wonder if it had ever been used. Tristan was waiting for her in the hall when she emerged. From there, they continued to a T. To the right, another 'Employees Only' door occupied the dead end about ten feet away. The corridor to the left stretched on for a long way, and didn't have much light.

Since the much closer door scared her far less than a long, dark tunnel, Piper jogged over to it and pulled on the knob. Much to her surprise, it opened. Inside, the walls glowed with multicolored light cast from the controls and buttons of a console similar to the one they'd found in the house basement, only four times as big. Several chairs, where workers might sit, were all empty. On the far right end, a bunch of modern-looking electrical components connected by wires and glass tubes to a network of glass vessels, crystals, and bronze clockwork in a wooden cabinet.

"Wow! Look at this!" Tristan zipped over to the corner. The smallest of the electric boxes could've held him standing up inside it. "This is like… technology plugged into, uhh, magic." He pointed at the wooden cabinet with gems, bottles, and tubes, the various glowing crystals bathing his pale face in patches of pink, purple, and yellow light "I have no idea what that is."

"Don't touch it," said Piper. "I think we're behind the curtain."

"Huh?"

"*Wizard of Oz*," said Piper. "This is the great wizard's machine."

"Oh. Yeah, but he was all fake. This isn't fake."

She crept up to the console. Many of the controls, gems for buttons or little wells holding glowing gases, appeared far more magical than technical. The occasional tiny lightning bolt danced down the glass tubes of the giant contraption.

"Hey, over here." Tristan pointed at dozens of notebooks arranged on a table near the middle of the room.

Piper backed away from the controls, careful not to bump anything, and hurried to the table. The first notebook she picked up had sketches of crystals and bottles, with notes that generally seemed to explain a method to use electrical power to supercharge 'containment wards,' allowing for much cheaper creation of large protected areas. Most of the magical terms went right over her head. She skimmed it for a bit, but stopped when she found an ornate pattern sketched out that looked exactly like the silver scrollwork that lined all the windows of the enclosures, as well as the gates outside.

"What is it?" asked Tristan.

"Umm. It looks like there's magic keeping these creatures locked up… and it normally takes a lot of rare substances to make work, but grandpa found a way to replace all that rare stuff with electricity." She looked up, blinking. "That's why the fancy engraving is in silver. It's got electricity in it."

"This book's got notes on creatures." He pointed at a three-inch-thick book with handwritten pages. "So do those."

All the books appeared quite old and yellowed. They had notes on a wide assortment of 'mythological' creatures, which didn't seem so mythological to Piper anymore. She got the feeling he spent quite a while researching each creature before setting off to capture one, but couldn't tell what he'd been working on last.

"I think he died trying to capture something that didn't want to be captured," said Piper. "He wasn't *that* old, and if he knew he was going to die, he would've told us about the zoo or made contact with Dad sooner."

"Oh, boy." Tristan whistled. "Your father's not going to believe us unless we drag him down here to see for himself."

"Yeah…"

"Hey!" Tristan pointed. "Elevator."

In the corner opposite the electrical boxes, another brass-doored elevator taunted her with freedom.

"It's not going to work." She trudged over and poked the gem button, barely reacting when nothing happened. "See? We don't have the key yet."

"Maybe there's one in here?" Tristan pointed at the console, which had a few drawers.

They spent a while searching, but found little other than a box of graham crackers, a set of dentures floating in blue liquid, and a canister of orange fiber drink (for old people).

"Eww." Piper shied away from the teeth. "That's so nasty."

Alas, their search turned up no key.

"Dark hallway," said Piper.

"Huh?" He blinked at her.

"It feels right."

"Okay, whatever." He shrugged.

Piper went out the door and walked straight past the corridor they entered from, toward the poorly lit passageway. An offshoot to the right, also dark, had a bunch of flat pushcarts lined up against the wall, probably for moving heavy things.

"This is like an employee only area. Where workers would go. There's gotta be a way out."

He nodded. "Yeah."

"Up here." She kept going past the tunnel of carts, deeper and deeper into the dark.

After about five minutes of fast walking, the corridor ended at a plain grey metal door. It, too, had a keyhole, but hadn't closed all the way due to a slightly warped frame.

"Yes!" Piper yanked it open, revealing a stairwell made of short sections like the one at school. Ten steps up, ninety-degree turn, ten more steps, and so on. "This is a way out!"

Tristan cheered.

Piper scrambled up the switchback stairs, going around and around until *running* upstairs wore her out. The last half of it or so, she walked, gasping for breath. Eventually, the stairs stopped at a metal ladder that led up into a rounded shaft.

"So weird," said Tristan. "Want me to check it out?"

"'Cause I'm a girl?"

"Because I would rather get hurt than you get hurt. Not because you're a girl." He smiled.

She sighed. "Thanks, but I got it."

"'Kay."

Piper climbed the ladder into a small, round chamber, standing with her feet on either side of the hole in the floor on a ledge only inches wide. She turned around, examining the walls, and found a metal box with a button on it at chest level, about where a doorknob would be. When she pushed it, a flap of wall opened outward, revealing grass.

"It's safe!" Piper leapt out and held the door, which turned out to be the side of an artificial (but quite real looking) tree.

Tristan clambered up the ladder.

"I don't see any way to open it from this side… it must be an emergency exit." Piper grumbled. "If we don't find the key, we won't be able to go back down there."

"You want to go *back* down?" asked Tristan, blinking.

She stared at him like he'd said the dumbest thing ever. "Yeah… that mermaid is still trapped… and everything else."

He rolled his eyes. "Why do girls like mermaids so much?"

"I'm not super into mermaids, Tristan. I'd want to save you if you were stuck in a cage like that too."

Tristan widened his eyes and tried to make the same 'please help me face' the mermaid used on them. For an instant, he looked so cute she felt all weird.

"Wow. If you ever gave my mother eyes like that she'd do you whatever you asked."

"Are you blushing?" asked Tristan.

"No." Piper looked down, worried she probably *was* blushing. "Come on. Let's get that key."

"Wait." He ran off to grab a hefty stick, which he used to keep the fake tree door from closing all the way. "We can get back down this way."

"Cool." Piper spun around to get her bearings, and realized they'd emerged a short distance into the woods to the west of the mysterious green building. "Oh, wow. That water from the lake isn't what we're drinking in the house. I bet that's going to the mermaid's tank."

He shrugged. "Maybe."

Piper set off at a fast walk over the meadow toward the manor. It felt like late afternoon, so she hadn't been underground as long as she thought. She headed to the back door and the kitchen, intending to bee-line right to the den in search of the envelope.

"There you are," said Mom, hurrying in from the front hall. "We've been looking everywhere! I thought I heard a loud crash hours ago. I've been worried to bits."

She tolerated a short, smothery hug, grateful to be alive and no longer trapped in a dumbwaiter shaft. "We were outside."

Dad approached, wearing a relieved smile. "Come on, hon. We're heading down to Utica for a little while to meet the estate attorney. Hop in the car. Mom's driving."

"But, Dad..." Piper pointed at the door. "I know why this place feels so weird. There's a whole, like, zoo underground full of mermaids and monsters and stuff. I can't go to Utica now. I've gotta help them."

Mom frowned. "Piper... what is going on with you?"

"I told you they wouldn't believe it," muttered Tristan.

"Hon?" Dad raised his eyebrows.

"We have to help them. They're *so* sad. Grandpa Bailey was a really mean old man. This mermaid looks like a teenage girl and he locked her in a cage."

Mom whistled. "Maybe we should do this another time. It won't go over well if she makes a scene in front of the lawyers."

"I'm not 'making a scene.' I'm serious." Piper attempted her version of pleading mermaid face.

"Pritchard seemed rather insistent we meet him as soon as possible." Dad folded his arms. "Can you contain this... zoo nonsense for a few hours?"

"I can stay here with her." Mom looked at her with pity.

Dad nibbled on his lip. "We both need to be there."

"Umm. I'll be okay 'til you get back." Piper smiled, hopeful.

"Not at twelve, missy. We're not leaving you alone just yet." Mom shook her head.

"Uhh, she can come over my place. My parents are both home," said Tristan, giving Mom the cute eyes.

Piper snapped her head to the right to stare at him. "Yeah, that's a good idea."

Mom pulled out her cell phone. "What's your home number?"

Tristan recited it.

Mom wandered off around the island counter. A moment later, she stopped walking. "Hello. My name is Amy Bailey. We just moved in, I think next door to you? Your son Tristan is here."

A voice warbled from the earpiece.

"Yes, that's right. Piper's not coping with the move very well, and she's a bit emotional. My husband and I need to run down to Utica to deal with some paperwork and we don't want to leave her alone."

The voice warbled again.

"Thank you, all right." Mom hung up and looked at Piper. "Well, if you want, you can spend the rest of the afternoon over there, but we are going to talk about this little outburst when we're back."

Piper looked down. "Okay."

"Come on," said Dad. "Well drop you two off."

"We can walk." Tristan pointed. "It's not that far. It's way shorter than driving."

"I'd feel a lot safer not sending you two off into the woods alone." Dad nodded toward the front door. "C'mon."

Piper gave Tristan a trapped stare, but followed her parents out to the front.

Tristan hopped in the back seat of the Camry next to her, with Mom behind the wheel and Dad in the passenger seat.

"Go right when we hit the road," said Tristan.

Mom followed the estate's tremendous dirt-path driveway for a few minutes before it met Route 214, where she turned right.

"It's a few minutes off. Look for another dirt trail by a tree with an orange reflector." Tristan leaned into the front and pointed at the right side of the road, thick with trees.

Piper kept her head down, too worried about the mermaid to think about anything else, and petrified that they'd wind up trapped for hours with Tristan's parents unable to help her.

"There it is." Mom turned onto another dirt trail, following the windy path for a little while until they rolled into the front yard of a large, but normal house.

Tristan's home, other than being in the middle of the woods, looked like any other big house in the suburbs. Pale beige, two stories, with a two-car garage on the right. Her parents got out, following them to the front door.

A black-haired man in a T-shirt and red shorts opened the door. He introduced himself as John Wiley, while shaking hands with her parents. Tristan and Piper stood off to the side, not making a sound while the adults had a quick conversation about the area, welcome to the neighborhood, and so on.

"We should be a couple hours. I'll call when we're getting close," said Mom.

"All right." Mr. Wiley nodded.

Dad grasped Piper's shoulders and looked her in the eye. "Are you sure you're okay staying here? This is, well, a little out of character for you."

"I'll show you when you get back. I'm not making it all up."

He pulled her into a hug, as tight as if a doctor had told him his daughter had cancer or something.

Piper grunted. *Crap. He thinks I'm crazy.*

"All right." Dad let go and took a step back. "You're sure."

"Yes, I'm sure. Go do lawyer stuff. I'll be fine." She smiled.

It took her parents an annoyingly long time to stop staring at her and walk back to the car.

"Well, hello." Mr. Wiley smiled at Piper. "Nice to finally meet my boy's first friend."

Tristan fidgeted, his cheeks showing a tint of red. "Can we go out back? I wanna show her the creek."

"All right, but don't get too close. I don't want you falling in again."

"Sure thing, Dad. I don't wanna fall in again either." He took Piper's hand and tugged her along, heading into the woods around the end of the house.

Of course, they didn't go to the creek.

11

GRANDPA BAILEY'S LETTER

Tristan led the way into the forest, occasionally climbing a fallen log or jumping across narrow trenches full of roots. Piper hurried along behind him, her slightly longer legs making it easy to keep up. The woods looked the same in all directions, but he didn't hesitate or seem lost. Maybe ten minutes or so after leaving his house, they reached the edge of the woods where it bordered the field to the side of the Bailey mansion.

They approached from the west, along the narrow face of the house, able to see both the front and back at the same time. Piper took the lead and went around back, but found the kitchen door locked. She'd expected as much, so clenched her jaw tight and kept going.

"Locked?"

"Here's your sign," said Piper.

"Huh?"

"You asked a dumb question." She winked at him. "If it wasn't locked, I'd have gone in."

"Oh." He laughed. "You remembered that."

"Yeah."

She hurried to the cellar door, which opened easily. "Ugh."

"Ugh? It opened."

"Yeah, but we have to go into the scary basement."

He gulped. "True. But think of that sad mermaid."

Piper closed her eyes. "You're right. So what if there's a ghost trying to kill me."

"I don't think it's trying to kill you. Just be annoying."

She stepped over the bricks at the bottom of the cellar door and onto the first step. "How are you sure?"

"Because it didn't use the sword until you were hanging on the rope. It could've stabbed you before that, but didn't."

"Huh. Okay, good point."

Piper eased herself down the steep staircase and shimmied through the narrow passage to the workroom. Not bothering to look at any shadows, she rushed past the shelves into the boiler room, hooked a left, and went up the stairs to the kitchen.

"Does it count as breaking in if you live here?" asked Tristan, his voice echoing behind her.

"Umm. I don't think so, but I'd still get in trouble with my parents, not the cops."

Piper jogged down the hall and went into the den. When she spotted the envelope still sitting there, she let out a cheer and grabbed it. She pulled out several sheets of folded yellowed parchment, from which a two-inch long brass key fell out onto the desk with a musical *ping*.

Fancy handwriting in dark brown ink warned her father of a collection of magical creatures (many quite dangerous) under the mansion grounds.

Each creature, no matter how dangerous, is secured by magical wards and cannot leave its enclosure. The gnomes take care of feeding and cleaning up after them, so you would not need to really do much but be aware that it exists, and be on guard for thieves and saboteurs. They are really quite helpful and also maintain the house. If you are wondering why there are no servants, it is because I have befriended these gnomes who seem to regard me as their king. They will be able to tell that you are my descendant, and should be readily willing to aid you as they have aided me. It has taken me almost sixty years to establish the collection, and if you are reading this letter, something went wrong during an expedition and I am no longer alive.

I realize you are probably rather cross with me for disappearing, but your mother objected to my work. She was too soft-hearted, and couldn't differen-

tiate these creatures that merely appear to be people from actual people. Unfortunately, for sake of security, I could not allow her to remember any of this. I did, however, give her the life she wanted, free of guilt. It is my hope that you will come to understand some day and forgive me.

The enclosed key opens the main control panel in the office, as well as many other things. I am rather forgetful, so I have one enchanted key that opens all the locks. Don't pay any attention if the lock does not appear to go with this key. It will work.

More writing, in a modern blue ballpoint pen continued past that point.

One more thing. A Boggart has managed to escape its enclosure and is presently loose in the manor grounds. This creature is annoying, but not deadly. They love playing pranks (which may cause minor injuries), but should not present a mortal danger. I will deal with the escapee upon my return, but if you're reading this, then I committed an error in my hunt. Should you desire to re-capture the boggart, there are notes down in the menagerie control room about how to trap one. If you have no interest in such endeavors, you can protect the home by hanging an iron horseshoe over the door. Also, a pile of salt on the floor at the foot of your bed will forestall any midnight mischief.

"Wow. Dad read all this and didn't believe it." Piper repacked the letter in the envelope, then picked up the key, which she stuffed in her jean pocket. "Wait here. I'll be right back."

"Okay." Tristan wandered around the desk to the area by the fireplace, and flopped on a couch.

Piper ran upstairs to her room, shut the door, locked it, and got undressed. Opening the mermaid's cage required getting wet, and she didn't want to walk around in soaked clothing. She fished a bathing suit out from her dresser, a two-piece purple one her mother had picked up at a yard sale, and put it on. Wearing it made her miss her friends back in Syracuse, since she'd only ever put it on when swimming in Gwen's pool.

She pulled her jeans back on over the swimsuit, and stuck her feet in her shoes without socks before pulling her T-shirt back in place. After changing, she ran downstairs to collect Tristan from the Den.

They left via the back door, racing across the field to the secret tree.

Piper pulled it open. "Okay. Let's go get the mermaid out."

"Why are we only saving the mermaid?"

She backed into the tree and lowered herself onto the ladder. "I wanna save them all, but she's basically a person and she won't hurt us. Plus, her cage has a door. I don't know how to get the other creatures out. And the stuff we can't just talk to... I'll need to figure out how to help them without being eaten. We gotta bring my parents down here and show them it's real."

"Okay." Tristan stepped into the tree and let the door close. "I hope you can convince them to look. Your dad seemed really worried about you. He probably thinks you're freaking out."

"I am freaking out, but not about that." Piper stepped off the ladder and marched into the zoo once more. "I'm angry. Grandma was right. Jenkins Bailey was a... a... butthead."

"You wanted to say something worse, didn't you?" asked Tristan.

"Yeah, but I'm not allowed to swear."

He ran up to walk beside her. "But your parents aren't here."

"I know. I promised I wouldn't. It's not about getting caught, it's about meaning what I promised." She pulled her hair out of her face.

"But we're sneaking back in the house."

"One: I never promised not to. Two: Someone needs help."

Tristan gave her the side eye. "You're weird."

She shifted her gaze to him.

He grinned. "Good weird. I like it."

12

LEGENDS AND MYTHS

Piper found her way back to the mermaid's tank relatively fast. She darted in the door and up the stairs to the water-covered platform. The mermaid swam up behind the cage door again, gripping the bars, a miserable, forlorn expression on her face.

"Do me a favor?" asked Piper, to Tristan.

"Sure."

"The floor's all wet. Hold my stuff."

She pulled her T-shirt off. He blushed with a gasp, but as soon as he noticed her bathing suit top, calmed down. After handing him the shirt, she stepped out of her sneakers. Cold, but not unbearable water lapped at her toes. Last, she slipped out of her jeans and handed them over. Piper snugged her suit bottoms up a little, fished the key out of the jean pocket, and held it up to show the mermaid.

At the sight of it, the young woman did an underwater backflip and seemed to burst into tears, though she didn't make any sound.

"Don't let my clothes get wet," said Piper.

"'Kay." He held on to the bundle. "Don't get hurt."

"I trust her." Piper sat on the edge with her legs in the water. It took her a second or two to work up the courage to attempt diving thirty feet down, but she convinced herself and let gravity pull her into the water. "Wow it's cold."

"Hurry up. Don't stay in too long."

"Right."

She took a few preparatory deep breaths, then a really big one, held it, and dove under. The cage door sat at the bottom on the opposite side of the pool. Piper resurfaced and swam across along the top since it would be shorter to go straight down by the cage. When she reached the far wall, she braced a hand on it, inhaled a big breath, and ducked under again.

The mermaid reached between the bars, extending a hand up toward her.

Piper pulled herself downward, never having been in water this deep before. Gwen's pool only went about ten feet at the deepest end, less than half of this enclosure. Pressure squeezed her head and lungs, but she kept fighting to go down, hoping she could hold her breath long enough to get the door open.

When she could reach, the mermaid grabbed Piper's hand and pulled her toward the cell door. Up close, the blonde girl looked even younger, more like sixteen or seventeen. Tristan must've noticed her grab Piper's arm, as he shouted something she couldn't make out.

Piper stared into the mermaid's deep blue eyes, sensing nothing but innocence and sorrow. Close to the point of panicking and swimming for air, she grabbed a bar of the cell door and maneuvered closer to the lock. The keyhole looked like something out of an old Wild West jailhouse, made for a key so big you could beat someone with it. The letter said it would work, so she held the little two-inch key from the envelope up and inserted it.

Despite appearing not to touch the inner workings, it felt like the key made contact with a mechanism. When Piper turned it, a metallic *clank* resonated in the water. The mermaid pushed the door aside and glided a few feet out into the tank, grasping Piper by the shoulders.

Somewhere above, Tristan screamed.

Before Piper could even mentally react, the young woman kissed her on the forehead. The instant lips touched her skin, the near irresistible urge to swim up for air vanished.

"Thank you!" chirped a teenage voice in the back of Piper's mind. "Thank you so much! I was afraid you'd believe those lies."

Piper looked away from the young woman's bare chest, blushing.

She tried to talk, but that didn't work, despite feeling like she somehow breathed air.

"I can hear you if you think," said the mermaid. "And why are you embarrassed?"

You don't have a shirt on and you're old enough to have, umm…

"What's a shirt?" asked the mermaid.

Ugh. Never mind. How am I not drowning?

The mermaid grinned. "I gave you a gift, as a thank you for setting me free. I've been trapped down here for so long. I escaped once, but the old man captured me again and put me in the cage."

You've been locked up a long time? Piper wanted to cry at the thought. *Were you a little girl when he kidnapped you?*

"No. I'm almost ninety years old. I looked like I do now when he caught me in the sea. Once we grow up, my kind always appear young like this."

Oh wow. How long do you live?

She shrugged. "A few hundred years, I think. I've only been here for ten or so. It's hard to tell."

Piper looked down past her feet at the tank bottom. *I'm so, so sorry my grandfather did that to you. I didn't even know him.*

"Don't be upset. It isn't your fault. I can feel how guilty you are… and sad. I am overjoyed that a human cares about me."

She looked up. *Come on.*

The mermaid nodded and swam to the surface in mere seconds, towing Piper over to the platform. Tristan grabbed her hand, helping her climb out.

The instant she got to her feet, Tristan hugged her like she'd been gone for years.

Piper blinked. "Umm. Hi."

"I thought you were gonna get hurt."

The mermaid hauled herself up onto the concrete walkway like a beached dolphin.

"Can you change your tail into legs?" asked Piper.

"No," said the mermaid, speaking normally. "Why would you think I can do that?"

"More stories." Piper shrugged.

"So you can't walk?" Tristan looked at her, finally noticed she had no top on, and turned beet red in the face.

The mermaid rolled around to (somewhat) sit up, and shook her head. "No. That's how they caught me when I tried to run away before. I don't move fast on land at all."

"Can you pull yourself up a ladder?" asked Piper.

She responded with a blank look. "I don't know."

"How'd they get you down here?" Tristan offered Piper back her clothes.

"There's a whole room that moves up and down," said the mermaid. "Inside a big green place."

Piper glanced at Tristan. "An elevator… I have the key now. We can use the elevator to get her out!"

Tristan gestured at the girl's long fishy tail, easily eight or nine feet from waist to fluke. "It's mean to make her crawl on the floor."

"I'll crawl. I want to go home." The mermaid dragged herself toward the steps.

"Wait." Piper held up a finger. "Those carts!" She raised her hands at the mermaid in a stopping gesture. "Wait here a sec. I'll be right back. This will be *much* easier for you."

She ran down the steps into the corridor, bare feet clapping on red tiles.

"Uhh…" Tristan ran after her. "Aren't you gonna get dressed?"

"I'm soaked!" Piper kept jogging along. "As soon as I dry off a little."

"Oh."

Carrying her shirt, jeans, and sneakers, Piper ran down the hall from the mermaid tank, past the huge area full of little hillside homes, and around the bend to the corridor where all the pushcarts had been parked against the wall. She skidded to a halt, wet feet nearly sliding out from under her, by a long flatbed cart that looked big enough to hold the mermaid's entire tail.

Piper dropped her clothes on it and grabbed the handle. Tristan helped, and they wheeled the cart back around the hallways to the door by the mermaid's tank.

"Okay," called Piper. "Do you need help going down the stairs?"

"Maybe a little," said the mermaid. "It's scary being out of water."

Piper and Tristan walked up the steps, each taking one of the mermaid's arms. They supported some of her weight, easing her down the stairwell to the corridor. Once on flat ground, she dragged herself over to the cart and climbed onto it, curling her tail as much as it would bend to keep it from sliding on the floor.

"Where should we take you once we're outside?" asked Piper.

"There's a river not too far from here that I can use to swim back to the sea. If you can bring me there, I can go home."

"You got it." Piper smiled.

"How are we gonna do that?" asked Tristan.

She bit her lip. "My dad's pickup truck."

His jaw dropped open. "You drive?"

"Not legally… but my dad's shown me how… in parking lots."

"Little early, huh?" He chuckled. "Mine won't let me touch the car."

Piper grabbed the pushcart handle and pulled, but her feet slid over the wet tiles instead of moving anywhere. "Ugh. I think my dad was feeling guilty about always working and wanted to do something fun with me."

"Oh." Tristan grabbed the handle. "Which way are we going?"

"I think that hallway with the carts leads to like a cargo elevator. The tree we came out of was close to that weird building."

"Guess we can look. If that doesn't work, we go back to the food court and use that elevator." Tristan tugged on the cart and got it moving.

Piper's feet continued to slide more than anything, but she did her best to help pull. "That elevator is too small for this cart. If it's the same one we saw in the house."

"Oh."

Once on dry floor again, Piper stopped slipping around and they got the cart rolling up to a decent speed. The mermaid clung to the frame by the handles, a terrified but hopeful expression on her face.

It took about fifteen minutes to navigate the cart down the long expanse of tunnels. They kept going past the carts and around a left-ward curve to an open area, where dozens of wooden crates stood in piles. The far wall had an opening to a big freight elevator with padding on the walls. Tire tracks written in dirt crisscrossed the floor.

Piper steered the cart into the elevator and grinned victoriously. "Awesome."

"This is where they brought me in," said the mermaid. "I was in a much smaller tank. I couldn't even turn around."

"They?" asked Tristan.

"Your grandfather and the men who work for him. They tricked me into eating a poisoned fish that made me sleep."

Piper bowed her head, water running down the backs of her legs from her hair. "I'm really sorry, but he's dead now and can't do anything like that again."

The mermaid squeezed Piper's hand. "Do you know how to make this room go up?"

"Yep." Piper padded over to the control box and put the key in a tiny hole that appeared the correct size. When she turned it, both buttons lit up. She pushed the top one, which got the elevator trundling upward. "And… we're out."

Tristan looked around in wonderment. "Wow. I've never been in an elevator before without a door. That looks dangerous."

"Don't touch the wall or stick your hands out," said Piper.

"I'm not dumb." He grinned. "Just saying. I thought it was like the law or something that elevators have doors… or gates."

"Crazy, mean old rich grandpas don't obey laws when they build horrible zoos," said Piper.

About a minute later, they rose past the edge of the wall and the elevator came to a halt at a square room with more crates in stacks. It also contained a pair of golf carts, one with a flatbed trailer, and shelves of tools. Most curious, the tool shelf had tiny stairwells connecting each level.

"That must be for the gnomes," said Piper.

"What gnomes?" asked Tristan.

"The letter mentioned gnomes work here."

"Small men." The mermaid nodded. "They bring me fish to eat and cleaned the prison. But I think they were afraid of me."

"Grandpa butthead probably told them you'd eat them." Tristan shook his head.

Piper crossed the room to the wide garage door and put the key into a switchbox on the wall. When the buttons lit up, she hit the top one, filling the room with the painfully loud rattle of the door rolling up on its tracks.

"Hey," shouted Tristan.

She looked back.

"This isn't gonna work on grass. No way will we be strong enough to push it." He pointed at the golf cart. "Does that thing work?"

Piper ran over and hopped in the driver's seat. She flipped a rocker switch to the 'on' position, and a green light next to it glowed bright. "I think so."

The mermaid pulled herself across the garage, leaving a long, wet drag mark, and climbed up onto the trailer. Tristan grabbed the wad of clothes from the pushcart and hopped in. Piper pressed her foot down on the accelerator as gently as possible, having no idea how zippy the cart would be.

It moaned with the labored whine of electric motors. She pressed a little farther, and the cart rolled out onto the meadow at about walking pace. After steering toward the house, and getting a little more comfortable with the feel of it, she accelerated.

By the time they reached the fountain circle, the steady warm breeze had dried her somewhat. Her thick hair remained damp, her bathing suit as well, but not so much it would be uncomfortable to put her jeans back on. She parked the golf cart beside Dad's pickup truck, shut it off, and got out.

"The only thing that might be a problem now is if Dad took his keys."

"We could ask mine to drive us," said Tristan.

"Do we want to let him see her?" Piper pointed at the mermaid, who didn't seem to care about being seen.

"Hey." Tristan snapped his fingers. "Try the key on the truck. The old guy said it opens every lock, right?"

"Not *every* lock. Just the ones made to work with it." She poked the key at the truck door. It clicked uselessly against the lock. "Nah. It's not a magic super key." After pulling her clothes back on over the damp swimsuit, she stuffed the key in her jeans pocket. "I'm gonna go check the kitchen. There's usually an extra set of keys there in case Mom needs the truck."

"Okay. I'll help her climb in."

Piper ran around the fountain to the front door, a short distance away. Finding it locked, she about got angry enough to kick it, but remembered the key. The house belonged to Jenkins Bailey, so maybe the key would work on it? She pulled it out, stared at the old-fashioned skeleton key that should in no way fit the modern-looking keyhole on the door, and tried to push it into the knob. The brass key blurred on contact, sliding into place with the ratcheted sensation of key teeth bouncing over the guts of a lock.

"Wow. That's so cool."

Piper ran to the kitchen and squealed with delight when she found a set of keys in the bowl with a Chevy logo on the clicker. She ran back outside to find Tristan tucking a tarp over the truck bed to hide the mermaid.

Shaking from nervousness, she hurried around to the door and climbed in behind the wheel. A few things still reminded her she was a twelve-year-old of average-to-short stature. One of those things was sitting behind the wheel of a pickup truck. She scooted to the edge of the seat with an inch or two of butt-to-cushion contact. The tips of her sneakers reached the pedals, she could see over the wheel, and while frightened at the idea of driving for real (instead of a golf cart), she figured she could pull off a short trip without a problem. Especially way out here in the middle of nowhere.

Tristan pulled himself up into the passenger seat and put his belt on. "Be careful."

"I've done this before." She put the key in and started the engine. "Not driving a mermaid to the river, but… driving this truck."

"You know we're going to get in a buttload of trouble if we get caught." He gripped the seat. "You sure you don't want me to ask my dad if he'd drive us?"

"What if he doesn't believe us? We're supposed to be hanging out in the woods behind your house? We'd have to admit we went back here, and we'd get in trouble for that."

"Oh." He nodded, then sighed. "Right. Okay. Don't crash."

She pulled the gearshift down to drive, and eased the Chevy around the fountain circle.

"We could walk there faster than this."

Piper stared at the approaching gate. "I'm being extra careful. No scratches. No dents. No injuries."

"Okay. Just saying… if you keep driving this slow, your parents will be home before we even get to the river."

"Fine. Let me get comfortable with this first." She nosed up to the gate, stopped, flipped the gearshift into park, and hopped out to hit the button for the gate.

A pained squeal came from the truck bed.

"Are you okay?" asked Tristan.

"Yes," said the mermaid. "Scared."

With the gate motoring open at a frustratingly slow pace, Piper got back into position behind the wheel and waited. As soon as the gate stopped, she drove down the long, winding dirt path to Route 214.

"Turn left here," said the mermaid.

Piper glanced at the rearview mirror, wondering how the mermaid could know that without looking. Still, she felt confident in trusting such an innocent creature. In fact, she mentally chided herself for thinking of her as a 'creature.' *She's a person with different parts.* She flicked the turn signal, came to a full stop, and looked both ways. Once sure no other cars approached, she continued around a left turn and accelerated up to about forty.

"It's not far," said the mermaid. "We are moving so fast I can't believe it. What is this machine?"

"A truck." Tristan laughed. "We're going kinda slow really. Grandma Bailey could drive a little faster."

"Shut it!" Piper giggled. "I'm trying not to crash."

"Oh, crap," said Tristan, shrinking in his seat. "We're dead."

Piper looked over at him. "Huh? What?"

"Check the rearview." Tristan cowered down in his seat.

She looked up at the mirror, and her heart nearly stopped cold at the sight of flashing red and blue lights coming up behind them.

13

THE BEST EXCUSE EVER

Shaking, Piper eased the truck over to the side, hoping the cop was really in a hurry to be somewhere else. "Maybe he's going to a crime or something. We're not speeding."

The cop nosed up behind the truck, clearly after them.

"Damn." She flipped on the hazard lights and slowed to a stop on the shoulder.

Her stomach did backflip after backflip while they sat there in silence, waiting. Piper stared straight ahead, feeling like she floated away from reality. A *tap-tap* on the glass beside her made her jump. The huge police officer at her window tilted his head in confusion, and put the flashlight he'd knocked with back on his belt.

Piper hit the button to roll the window down. "Good afternoon, officer. I'm sorry. I didn't think I was speeding." She stared at the New York State Police logo on his shoulder, and shook even harder.

"I'd ask to see your license and registration, but something tells me you don't have one."

She stared pathetically up at him.

"How old are you, kid?" asked the cop.

"Twelve," said Piper in a small voice.

He put a hand on the door and peered in. His 'big tough cop' demeanor seemed to slip into 'concerned dad.' "Something going on at home? What are you doing driving off on your own? Go on and turn the engine off, step out of the truck."

She grabbed her chest, trying to slow her racing heart. "I'm sorry. I know I shouldn't be driving, but I didn't have any other choice. We found a kidnapped mermaid locked up in the basement and we're bringing her to the river so she can go home."

The cop stared at her, looking utterly stunned for a few seconds. "Wow, kid. That's gotta be the most original excuse I've ever heard, and I've heard some real winners."

"It's true," she whispered, while giving him her best 'please don't get me in trouble' eyes.

"You sure you're all right? Come on, now. Turn off the engine and get on out of there. You're safe. There's no need to get the law involved here if you don't give me any trouble. Your parents can deal with this however they feel proper. I just don't want a couple of kids who shouldn't be driving getting hurt, or hurting someone else."

Piper sighed at the steering wheel, inches from throwing up all over. What would her parents do? She'd *never* done anything this bad before. Shaking, she started to reach for the key to shut off the engine, but got an idea. "I'm not lying, officer. Look in the bed. She's right there under the tarp."

"All right. Turn the engine off, and I'll check out the mermaid in the back." He smiled as if humoring a kid playing games, clearly not feeling threatened by a pair of children.

"Yes, sir." Piper nodded, swallowed hard, and shut the engine down.

With a bit of a smirking grin, the cop took two steps to his right, and lifted the tarp. His expression turned to astonishment, then a glass-eyed stare.

The mermaid sat up until her nose almost touched the cop's. She swayed in a manner similar to how Mom acted around Dad sometimes right before they got all mushy. The officer blinked, leaning side to side to match her motions.

"Are they gonna kiss?" whispered Tristan.

Piper, still too terrified of getting in trouble to process anything, looked at him, mute.

A moment later, the cop walked back to his car and got in, gazing into space. The mermaid turned toward the kids.

He won't remember seeing us, said the mermaid's voice in her mind. *Hurry. We're almost there.* She lowered herself into the bed and pulled the tarp back over.

"She mind-zapped a cop." Piper didn't know if she should laugh or cry, but started the engine anyway. "That's so wrong."

"So is keeping a mermaid in a cage," said Tristan.

She covered her mouth and nose with both hands, breathing in and out until her heart no longer felt ready to explode. "Yeah. Okay."

One last look confirmed the cop hadn't moved an inch. Piper checked the mirror for approaching cars, saw none, and pulled back into the lane, accelerating up to fifty-five. Two minutes later, the mermaid's voice filled her head again.

Turn left when you can.

Piper slowed to thirty, and to a near-stop when she spotted a dirt road leading off to the left. They bounced and wobbled down that trail for a little while before she caught sight of a river on the right. She pulled over and stopped.

"It's kinda far," said Tristan. "This is a truck, drive to the edge."

"No way. If I get it stuck in the mud, we're dead." She killed the engine and got out, heading around back to open the tailgate. "We're at the river. We'll help you get across the grass."

Tristan walked over.

"Stand there." Piper pointed. "Put your back to the truck."

He did.

The mermaid realized what she meant to do and crawled to the edge, putting her arms around the kids' shoulders with her head between theirs. They half-carried, half-dragged her out of the truck and over the grassy field to the river's edge.

When the ground began to squish with mud, the mermaid squeezed her arms close, hugging Piper and Tristan together. "This is far enough. I can make it the rest of the way. Thank you so much for my freedom."

Piper sniffled. "I'm really sorry. I hate being related to someone who could be so cruel."

The mermaid brushed a hand over her hair and kissed her on the forehead. Nothing bizarre or magical happened this time. She gave Tristan a kiss on the cheek, which left him with a silly grin.

"Please be safe on your way home."

Piper nodded. Tristan kept gazing at her with a half-awake grin.

"Did you do something to him?" asked Piper.

"No, not on purpose. But he's a boy so maybe I charmed him a little without meaning to." She winked.

The mermaid dragged herself over the last few yards of muddy marshland and slipped into the water. A moment after, her head bobbed up quite a distance out toward the middle of the river. She waved goodbye and dove under. Her fluke broke the surface, a gleaming rainbow in the sunlight, and sank out of sight.

Piper started to walk back to the truck, but stopped when Tristan didn't move. "Hey. Come on."

"Huh?" He blinked and turned toward her.

"Your girlfriend's gone." She smirked. "In the river."

His face went crimson. "She's not my girlfriend."

"Then why are you staring with that stupid lovesick smile?"

"I dunno. Magic?"

He looked confused and guilty enough that she dropped it. "Like the cop."

"Yeah. I guess. But I remember her." He jogged to catch up. "Sorry for doubting her. You were right. The sign lied."

She smiled to herself, thinking about how worried he'd been when she got close to the mermaid at first. On a whim, she took his hand.

He didn't seem to mind.

14

LIVING MEDIEVAL

Piper drove back home, teetering at the edge of throwing up the whole ride. If another cop saw them driving, she'd have no magic mermaid to save her from being grounded until she turned twenty-one.

In a fit of unusual good luck for her, they saw no cops—not even any other cars—on the ride. She parked by the fountain, hopefully close enough to where it had been that her father wouldn't notice it had moved, and ran the keys back inside to the bowl.

"Be right back," said Piper.

Leaving Tristan in the kitchen, she raced upstairs to trade her swimsuit for normal underwear. When she returned, he'd helped himself to a glass of water. Thinking it a good idea, she had one as well.

"Now what?" asked Tristan. "We have the key. But I don't think it opens the other pens. Only that one with the mermaid had a door."

"Probably because it's a tank of water." She grumbled. "There's gotta be some hidden tunnels that connect to the back of each area, so the zoo workers can get in to take care of the prisoners."

"That could take forever to find."

"Yeah, but I'm going to try." She poured more water into her cup.

He nodded. "I'll help."

"But, you're right. It'll take a while to find it and we don't have time. We should go back to your place so we don't get busted."

"'Kay."

They finished their water, put the glasses away, and headed out the back door. A ten-ish minute walk through the woods ended at Tristan's house, where they entered via a sliding patio door to the kitchen.

A slim woman in her twenties with straight brown hair stood by the counter, mixing stuff together in a giant silver bowl. The pungent smell of onions and garlic made Piper's eyes water.

"Hi," said Piper.

The woman looked back at them. "Oh, there you are."

Piper leaned toward Tristan. "Is that your older sister?"

"Hah!" The woman laughed. "I'm his mother."

Tristan stared down.

"Oops." Piper winced. "Sorry. You look really young."

"Well, I had him when I was nineteen. Not the wisest thing I've ever done, but I don't regret it." She hugged Tristan with an awkward elbow embrace, since her hands had gunk all over them.

"Will you be staying for dinner?" asked Mrs. Wiley. "I'm making meatloaf."

Piper looked around. "Umm. I don't know. I guess it depends on when my parents come home."

"Well, if they're not back by the time we eat, you're welcome to join us." Mrs. Wiley resumed mushing things together in the bowl.

"Thank you." Piper forced a smile, still trying not to throw up thinking about the cop.

"C'mon." Tristan walked out, cut through an extremely brown living room (both the carpet and wood-paneled walls) and up a flight of stairs to the second floor. The door to his bedroom, made obvious by a *Full Metal Alchemist* poster, hung half-closed. "You like anime?"

"It's okay. Haven't seen much. Mostly, I read," said Piper.

"Oh. That's cool. The good ones all come from manga first."

"What?"

"Manga?" He picked up the fattest comic book she'd ever seen and handed it to her.

"Wow. I didn't think they made comic books this thick."

He gawked. "It's a graphic novel, not a comic book."

"Elitist much?" Piper laughed.

He grinned.

"I mean books, not… graphic novels. Like just words."

"Oh, yeah. That's cool." He pointed at a shelf over a desk where he had a few normal books as well.

"Wow, you have a computer."

"Uhh, yeah. Who doesn't?"

Piper raised her hand. "This girl."

"Really?"

She sat on the side of the bed. "Yeah. We didn't have enough money for it and I never really asked for one." Head down, she surrendered to nervous shivering. "Holy crap, I thought we were gonna get in so much trouble."

"Me too."

"Geez. I hope I can stop shaking by the time my parents are back."

"You don't break rules much, do you?"

She shook her head. "No, not really."

"Well, don't feel too guilty. You helped that mermaid. No one got hurt, and you won't do it again. Tell your parents the truth if they ask about it, but don't confess unless you're sure they know what happened. No good deed goes unpunished, right? It's not like we took the truck for fun."

"Yeah. I'll try." She crossed her arms and stared at the rug, trying to calm down. "Just helping the mermaid go free."

"Exactly. So… computer? You got the money now." He grinned, working his hands like a weasel about to find treasure. "If you want help speccing a system out, let me know."

"Doing what?"

"Speccing out. Choosing the specifications. You know, selecting components."

"I have no idea what you mean."

"What case, board, memory, video card… all the guts."

She nodded. "Okay. I thought a computer was just like a Dell or HP or something."

"Yeah, that's an option, but some people by the parts individually so they get a killer system." He flopped in the desk chair and frowned. "I don't have a lot of games since our internet connection is lame. Only thing out here is satellite, and it's so slow it's not worth playing anything online. I always get crushed."

"I'll pretend I know what you mean." She laughed.

Tristan whistled. "Wow. How did you do any schoolwork without a computer?"

"Library. Sometimes, Mom lets me use her laptop to type out papers."

"What's a library?" He tilted his head.

She rolled her eyes, laughing.

"What? I'm serious. What is it?"

"Really?" She gawked at him.

"Yeah. I don't know what a library is." He stood from the desk chair and sat on the floor near a flat-panel TV hooked up to an Xbox. "Wanna play something?"

"Okay." She slid off the bed and scooted over to sit beside him on the rug.

They started with a fighting game. She mashed buttons at random, and he beat her over and over again without even trying.

"Okay, bad choice. Something co-op."

Piper shrugged. "Okay."

"You're not at all upset about losing so much?" He tilted his head at her.

"Uhh, no. Why would I be? It's a game you've played a lot and I've never touched before."

He laughed. "Wow you're really cool. Like all earthy and stuff."

"Earthy?"

Tristan popped the disc out and put in a different one. "Yeah, like you're just at peace with everything. Most people get really angry when they lose at video games."

"I'm not at peace with my stomach right now." She rubbed it.

"Hungry?"

"No, terrified. Like my parents are going to come home and just know I used the truck."

"Relax. They won't have a clue."

"Crap!" shouted Piper. "The golf cart!"

Tristan put a hand on her shoulder. "I got it covered. My parents know we're inside now, so we can't leave again. Your parents are going to come here to pick you up. It takes about twelve minutes to drive from here to there. When they get here, tell them you gotta go to the bathroom. Delay them for at least five minutes. I'll run back there and put the cart in the green building."

She nodded. "Okay. That'll work."

The new game had little characters they viewed from above, wandering around mazes zapping monsters. She chose a wizard, while he picked a big guy with an axe. They spent about an hour running around blasting goblins and skeletons and other digital monsters before Tristan's dad poked his head in the door.

"Hey, little man. Time for dinner. Piper, your parents are here."

"Cool game." She put the controller down. "I'd like to play it again…" She waited for Mr. Wiley to walk away before muttering, "If I'm not grounded for the rest of time."

He patted her back. "Just relax and be normal. Think about how happy that mermaid is to be free. You're a really good person, Piper."

She bit her lip as a weird squishy feeling stirred inside her chest. "You're kinda cool too."

Tristan grinned and led the way downstairs. Piper's parents stood in the living room, chatting with Mr. Wiley about helicopters. Dad had no idea helicopters had frequented the mansion property, and explained he had no plans to bring any around.

"Hi." Piper ran over and hugged them both.

"Everything okay?" asked Dad.

"You look worried," said Mom.

"Umm." She stared down. "About that zoo stuff. I'm scared you think I'm nuts."

Dad and Mom exchanged a glance, then gave her a 'not here in front of other people' face.

"Ready?" asked Mom.

"Sec. I gotta go to the bathroom." Piper looked up at Mr. Wiley. "Can I use the bathroom?"

He pointed at a small corridor. "Go right ahead."

Tristan slipped into the kitchen.

Piper walked down the short hallway into a bathroom opposite a little alcove with a washing machine and dryer. She closed the door before sitting on the toilet lid with her chin in her hands. Eventually, she calmed down and decided to really use the toilet, despite not having to go too badly. A while later, two light knocks struck the door.

"You all right?" asked Mom.

"Yeah, I'm fine. Almost done. Strange toilet and all. Little hard to get started."

Mom chuckled. "Okay."

She flushed and took a nice long time washing her hands, before heading back out to the living room and thanking the Wileys for letting her stay. That done, she trudged outside behind her parents, feeling like a prisoner being led to the electric chair.

She hopped in the back seat of the Camry and put on the seatbelt. Her parents got in. No one spoke for a few minutes as the car wound among the forest roads. Piper held her breath as a state police car went by in the other direction, but she couldn't tell if the same cop drove it. Fortunately, it didn't whip around with lights flashing.

"How'd it go with the lawyer?" asked Piper.

"Fine. He was much less nervous at the office," said Dad.

"I'm too worn out to cope with my daughter having a mental breakdown right now." Mom looked at her via the rearview mirror for a second or two. "Can you hold it together until tomorrow?"

"Yes, Mom. I'm not nuts. Really. I'm okay. I know I was upset about moving, but so are cats. If you have cats and you move, they'll spend a week hiding behind the couch in the new place. Cats don't need a psychiatrist."

Dad laughed.

"I think I just needed a friend. Tristan's cool. I mean, I still miss Gwen and Jamie, but I guess if I gotta be out here, it's not that bad."

"We'll talk tomorrow, okay?" asked Mom.

"'Kay." Piper leaned her head back and closed her eyes.

When they reached the dirt-paved road that led to the house, she crossed her fingers and even tried to cross her toes. *Please be fast enough.* Piper held her breath as the gate came into view, not letting it out until she saw the fountain circle with no golf cart in it.

She slumped back, exhaling with relief.

Mom parked by the truck, in the exact spot where the golf cart had been.

Unable to believe she got away with doing something *so* bad, Piper kept her head down and followed them inside.

THEY HAD A QUICK DINNER OF PREMADE SOUP AND BREAD, WHICH TASTED pretty good for being canned. Mom hadn't recognized the brand, which meant it likely came from one of the more expensive stores they never bothered going to.

Piper didn't say a word about the zoo, or a boggart running around the house, or gnomes. Neither of her parents seemed in the least bit ready for any conversation like that, so she played it safe.

After dinner, she changed into her nightgown and spent a while lounging in the cushioned area by her bedroom's bay window, reading *Lord of the Rings* again. Only, this time, she considered it studying what might really exist, rather than fantasy. The day had worn her out too, so around 9:15 p.m., she decided to call it a night.

As soon as she looked at her bed, the memory of being trapped and unable to breathe came back strong. She recoiled as if the bed itself would bite her, toes gripping the carpet.

Wait. No. That bed didn't attack me… the boggart did. She furrowed her eyebrows, annoyed, until she remembered the letter. *A pile of salt at the foot of the bed!*

She hurried out into the hall and down the cold stairs. The carpet between the stairs and the kitchen offered a break to her bare feet, but she squeaked as soon as she stepped on the kitchen tile floor. Walking on ice would've been warmer. Piper took a small plate from a cabinet, poured a pile of salt on it, and hurried back to the warm carpet.

While sneaking down the hall to the stairs, she slowed at the sound of her parents' voices leaking from one of the living rooms. Curious, she padded up to the door, listening.

"I have no idea," said Dad. "It stinks like, I dunno, halfway between fish market and swimming pool."

"Do you think the kids did that?" asked Mom.

He made an odd murmuring noise. "I don't see how they could have. Or why. Pranks aren't in Piper's arsenal."

"She was on edge. I think she did something she's feeling really guilty about."

"Like what? You know, it's more likely she's worried about her little outburst. You saw how all the color drained out of her face the instant you said psychiatrist. But… I dunno."

"You look worried, Al," said Mom.

He sighed. "You know that letter from Pritchard?"

"The one you said was full of nonsense?"

"Yeah. What Piper said? That bit about the zoo full of weird creatures? The letter said the same thing."

Mom laughed. "Oh, there you go. She found the letter and read it. That's where she got it from. Piper's young and she has your wild imagination. The letter came from a lawyer, so to a child, it must obviously be true."

Piper narrowed her eyes. *It* is *true!*

"Yeah, maybe. The kids did look at those drawings too. You're right. Overactive imagination… but why does my truck stink?"

"Maybe there's some kinda animal out here that peed in the bed?"

"Hmm. Could be. Guess I'll just wash it tomorrow."

Piper slouched with relief. She crept away from the door and scurried back upstairs to her room. After placing the plate of salt on the floor at the foot of her bed, she ran to the bathroom to brush her teeth and use the toilet.

That done, she shut off the lights and darted across the too-large room to the bed. It wasn't *her* bed, but she couldn't deny its comfort. She snuggled in the cloudlike softness, again with the blankets up to her chin, and stared at the ceiling.

All those creatures remained stuck in the zoo, but at least she had the key now. They'd been locked up for years, another couple of days until she figured out how to help wouldn't be bad. Fingers crossed that the salt would protect her from the boggart, Piper closed her eyes.

Her mind filled with random creatures, flashes of falling down the dumbwaiter, and the dread fear of flickering red and blue lights in the rearview mirror.

It'll be a miracle if I actually sleep.

15

PETTY REVENGE

Mom's screaming woke Piper to a bright morning. She sat up in bed without a problem, surprised to find her comforter, blankets, and sheet uncursed. Mom continued shouting from the bedroom, sounding furious.

Heavy banging, like someone pounding on the wall, accompanied her yells.

Piper padded out into the hall, crossed to the catty-corner door, and eased it open.

Her mother stood on the far side of the bed by their wardrobe cabinets, fuming. All the drawers hung open and empty, every bit of clothing tossed haphazardly on the floor. The banging came from the door to their attached bathroom.

"Mom?" asked Piper. "What happened?"

Her mother whirled to glare at her, auburn hair like flames around her face. "Now I know why you were so guilty last night! What's this for? We trusted you on your own and you do this?"

"I didn't!" shouted Piper. "Why would I? I'm twelve, not six!"

Mom rubbed a hand back and forth over her mouth, so angry she shook.

"Besides," said Piper, trying to sound calm. "Was this stuff on the floor when you went to bed last night? If I snuck back into the house after you left to do this, you'd have found the mess last night."

"I..." Mom's fury receded under the weight of logic.

"Hey," yelled Dad. "Would one of you grab a screwdriver? The door is stuck."

"I got it," said Piper.

She darted back to her room on a whim, and took a pinch of salt from the pile. Mom gave her an odd look when she walked back into their room without a screwdriver. Piper went over to the door and put the salt into the keyhole.

"Try the door now," said Piper.

A soft *click* came from the mechanism, and the door opened. Dad stepped out, wearing only boxers, and examined the door. "What did you do?"

"Undid however she rigged it," muttered Mom.

"I didn't play a trick on you." Piper refused to shout again. She almost blurted 'oh, there's a boggart loose in the house playing pranks on us, salt wards it off,' but decided that would be a one-way ticket to a mental hospital—or at least a psychiatrist's office. "Umm, it just had a little thing stuck in there."

Mom rubbed her forehead.

Dad disregarded that she'd said anything at all, and kept fiddling with the lock. "Hmm. Must've been stuck." He patted Piper on the head and walked around the bed to Mom. "I'm going to check around the property today. Finally have a good look at everything, get a feel for what kind of condition it's in."

Mom nodded, gazing at Piper.

Before an argument could brew up, she backed out and returned to her bedroom. Once inside, she noticed her hair reeked of fishy swimming pool.

"Ugh."

Both because it made her feel disgusting to smell like that, and because if her dad sniffed that on her, he'd ask questions she really didn't want to answer, she ducked into the bathroom for a shower. A white furry bathmat provided an island of sanctuary from the cold, black tile floor. The bathtub appeared to be marble, but turned out to be fiberglass.

Piper hung her nightgown on a hook behind the door, and made faces at herself in the mirror until she felt reasonably confident she didn't 'look guilty' about anything. She stepped into the tub and pulled the sliding glass door closed.

"This is so weird." She opened and closed it again, never having seen a tub with a door instead of a plastic curtain before. "Okay, it is kinda cool."

Soon, she had a nice warm spray falling on her. Though she didn't remember bringing any of it, a shelf in the tub had three different soap bars, two shampoos and two conditioners. She sniff-tested each soap, opting for one with a lilac fragrance. Once she finished washing her body, she grabbed the purple shampoo and squirted a healthy glop into her hand.

It foamed like crazy, flooding the shower with the fragrance of lavender and making her head tingle. No way would Dad smell mermaid tank water over this stuff. The bizarre and disgusting thought that mermaids couldn't use toilets and just 'went in the pool' whenever they had to made her gag. That poor mermaid had been trapped in a small cave for who knows how long.

Eyes closed, she massaged the shampoo into her hair and refused to think about it.

The spray from the shower flashed ice cold in an instant, jabbing into her chest like a rain of needles.

Piper shrieked. Soap in her eyes, she flailed blindly for the door, scrambling in a panic to get away from the freeze. She tripped over the tub edge and fell out onto the bathmat, screaming from the sting of shampoo in her eyes, the full-body ice bath, and landing hard on her left arm.

"Hon?" called Dad from behind the bathroom door. The knob turned. "You okay?"

"Don't come in!" shouted Piper. "I'm naked! I'm okay."

The knob un-turned. "What are you screaming about?"

"The water went ice cold all of a sudden. I screamed because it was *really* cold."

"Oh." He chuckled. "I promise I didn't flush. Uhh, sounds like a plumbing problem."

Piper, barely able to see past the stinging shampoo, curled up in a ball, arms wrapped around her legs, shivering, teeth chattering.

"When you're done in there, I'll check on the pipes."

"Okay." Piper scowled as best she could without being able to open her eyes and muttered, "That boggart doesn't like us? Fine. I hate it too."

She wiped at her face, trying to scoop foam away from her eyes, but the burn continued. Had she not found the zoo, she might've decided the house absolutely not worth staying and demanded to go home. But now that she had a bunch of mythical creatures counting on her for their freedom, she couldn't let a stupid prank get the better of her.

A waft of warm steam drifted by.

"Oh, very funny." She fumbled around blind, eventually finding the tub edge and pulling herself up to stand so she could stick one hand in.

The water had gone back to its pleasant warmth. Not fully trusting it, she stepped back in for a quick rinse, only long enough to get rid of the shampoo and de-soap the rest of her body. She hopped out and grabbed a towel before the water could freeze her again.

"Ugh." She sighed at the ceiling. "I'm going to have to put salt *everywhere.*"

16

THE HILL GNOMES

Breakfast, the old standby of frozen waffles, passed in silence. Mom fussed over her at first, since her eyes had reddened from the shampoo. She didn't bother trying to blame the boggart, but told them the water came back to normal on its own. Dad found it hilarious that they sat in a multi-million-dollar house having frozen waffles, and laughed about that the whole time they ate.

Dad headed outside to roam the grounds afterward. Once Piper finished washing dishes, she went upstairs to help her mother pick up clothing, but found her standing there in shock, everything back where it belonged.

"Oh, I guess the gnomes put it away for you." She waved at the wall. "Thanks guys."

Mom pivoted around and stared at her. "Gnomes now? Piper, seriously, why are you doing this?"

"I didn't toss your stuff on the rug."

"Not that. I mean *this*. Acting out, making things up."

"I can show you it's real. If you will just trust me enough to come take a look at something."

"I..." Mom sighed, rubbing the bridge of her nose. "I can't process this, hon. Woke up to everything on the floor and now it's like it never happened? Did I imagine that?"

"No, I saw your stuff on the rug too."

Mom walked over and put an arm around her. "I'm sorry for yelling at you."

"Thanks. Come look. I promise it's real."

"Maybe later. I need to run to the store and I have a lot of work from the school year to finish up. It's already a week late. Principal Meade is going to wring my neck."

"It won't take long. Just a few minutes." Piper smiled.

Mom shook her head. "A few minutes later tonight then. I *have* to finish this stuff."

"Okay." Piper frowned.

A normal doorbell chime rang throughout the house.

"Wow. Dad fixed that stupid gong?" asked Piper.

"I guess." Mom shrugged.

"I'll get it." Piper hurried down the hall to the stairs, and made her way to the ground floor.

Tristan peered in the narrow window on the left side of the front door. He had a white T-shirt with a blond anime-style face on it, though she couldn't tell if it was supposed to be a boy or girl. When he spotted her, he grinned and waved.

Piper opened the door, beaming. "You did it!"

"Yeah. I think I got the cart around the corner of the house like five seconds before your mom drove through the gate."

She bit her lip. "Sorry. I couldn't delay them any more without being suspicious."

"Hey, no problem. I'm back. Ready to set more stuff free? Oh, awesome shirt."

Piper glanced down at fancy lettering reading 'I solemnly swear that I am up to no good.' "It felt appropriate. I tried to get Mom to come with us to prove I'm not making stuff up, but she's busy. I think she doesn't want to risk seeing something she can't explain. She probably thinks I'm 'using my imagination.'"

"I got an idea. That phoenix seemed to understand you. Maybe you can ask him to follow us into the house and let your mom see him? Then she'll have to believe."

"Maybe. We can try that. That unicorn-dragon one also looked really friendly."

"The Ki-Rin." He smiled. "Do we have to fall down the hole again?"

"Nope." She held up the key. "Elevator time."

Piper trotted off into the ground floor, walking past the stairs to the elevator at the approximate middle of the house. She marched in, pivoted like a soldier, and glared at the control panel. This keyhole also matched the key's design, so it did not appear strange or magical when she inserted it. A quarter turn to the right made the gem by the 'B' light up violet.

"Your house, you push it." Tristan winked.

No longer afraid of what she might find in some mysterious basement, she jabbed a finger into the button without hesitation. The doors slid closed, and the elevator sank with little fanfare. About a minute later, it stopped and she stepped out into the food court.

The same weird 'bugs crawling all over her feeling' returned. Piper shivered, idly scratching at her arm. Everything looked the same as she remembered. Calm and confident without the shock of a near-death experience in an elevator shaft, Piper noted that four tunnels headed out from the circular room, one at each of the primary compass points. Since the elevator faced the front of the manor house, and she knew the rectangular house went east-to-west, she figured the bhargest passage straight in front of them lined up with south. West, to her right, led up to the garden with attack plants plus the ki-rin, griffon, and such. The corridor a few feet to her left led to the north, but she figured it would go to the giant garden or the area around the mermaid, where they'd already been.

"What do we do now?" asked Tristan.

She pointed left at the eastern tunnel. "We haven't gone down that way yet."

"We didn't go left past the bitey plant place either." He rubbed his arm.

"Ehh… That can wait until I bring the sword down here." She chuckled. "If that thing tries to chomp us again, I want to trim it."

He nodded. "I like that plan."

She crossed the food court circle to the eastern passage. The mood changed, darkening after about thirty feet. Though it didn't feel colder, goosebumps rose on her arms and a sense of malice hung in the air.

"Whoa." Tristan held his arms up. "It's weird here."

"Yeah. Think it's magic?" Piper kept walking, but slowed.

"It feels like evil."

She glanced at him. "Do you think there's such a thing as actual evil?"

"No, it's made up like mermaids and phoenixes."

"Not funny."

"I wasn't trying to be." He managed a weak smile. "Yeah, there's actual evil. They call it math class."

Piper sighed. "My mother teaches math. I kinda like it."

He bit his lip. "Sorry. I'm, uhh, not great at math."

"You sound like my dad."

The long corridor proceeded in a relatively straight line, with only minor bends left and right. Padded benches against the walls every so often looked new and never used, as did a water fountain or two. When they approached a fork in the corridor a few minutes later, a trio of small figures appeared out of nowhere, and ran up to them.

They resembled potbellied older men with wispy white moustaches and beards. Fluffy eyebrows wagged back and forth over beady eyes, wide with urgency. The tallest stood perhaps an inch higher than Piper's knees, and all wore tunics and pants like medieval peasants. None of them had weapons, nor did they appear aggressive. Their faces, bulbous noses, and whimsical expressions were so much alike, she'd never be able to tell them apart.

"Hello?" asked Piper.

"Greetings!" chimed the three of them at the same time. "We are Hill Gnomes."

"Hi. I'm Piper and this is my friend Tristan."

He waved. "Hello."

"We thought Master Jenkins' son would be older," said Middle Gnome.

The middle gnome held up a finger. "And a boy."

"What?" asked Left Gnome.

Right Gnome pointed at Piper. "That's a girl."

"Yes, yes," said Middle Gnome. "Girl, boy, does not matter. You are Master Jenkins' descendant."

"Granddaughter, actually. But my father is here too. He's Jenkins' son."

"Oh. *Two* masters," cheered Left Gnome. "A grand day!"

Middle Gnome shook his head. "Tis a sad day. The mermaid has escaped. Master Jenkins adored her."

Piper folded her arms. "My grandfather kidnapped an innocent gi—woman, and held her prisoner."

The gnomes stared up at her, mouths agape.

"She didn't escape. I set her free. Holding animals in zoos is cruel, and holding *people* is even worse."

"Mermaids is not peoples," said Left Gnome, scratching his head.

"Mermaids is mermaids," said Right Gnome, grinning.

"Quiet." Middle Gnome held his hands out to the others. "Master Jenkins is gone. What he asked us does not matter."

Piper glanced at Tristan, who shrugged. She looked back at the gnomes. "I want to let these poor beings go home where they belong. Can you help me set them free?"

All three gnomes gasped.

"You mustn't let them *all* out!" whisper-shouted Middle Gnome.

The other two said, "Yes, yes, yes," at the same time, in the same tone.

"Why not?" asked Tristan.

"Some things here are evil. They belong locked up. Master Jenkins was foolish to collect them, but at least they are contained." Right Gnome wagged a finger at her. "Like the Night Gnomes."

The other two shivered. "Very bad. Very very very very bad," they said in unison.

"That's a lot of verys," muttered Tristan.

"Night Gnomes are dangerous," said Left Gnome. "They will try to hurt you."

"Creatures will thank you for their freedom by trying to eat you," said Middle Gnome.

The side gnomes both said "bugbear" at the same time.

"They eat children," whispered Middle Gnome. "You look like children, so it would want to eat you both."

Piper gulped.

"They don't *look* like children," said Right Gnome. "They *are* children."

"You should not let the bugbear out." Left Gnome shook its head so hard his little cap flew off.

Middle Gnome picked it up and handed it to him.

"Well, what about the innocent things?" Piper pointed. "Like the kirin or the phoenix?"

The gnomes shrugged and said, "They won't hurt you," in unison.

"Oh. There's a boggart loose in the house." Piper rubbed her left shoulder, which remained a bit sore from falling out of the bathtub.

"Yes, yes." The gnomes spun around and ran. "This way!"

They went left at the fork.

Piper chased them down that corridor, around a sharp left turn past an enclosure containing a foggy woodland. The corridor bent left again, and went by another enclosure with window on three sides around a dreary, swampy forest. Small figures among the weeds and brambles moved, but she didn't slow down to look at them. The gnomes kept scampering onward for another minute or two, sliding to a halt at the next enclosure along the hallway.

The glass here had been shattered, creating a hole big enough to drive Dad's truck through, though no fragments remained on the floor. Inside, a large square chamber held a gloomy pine forest and a single, small peasant hovel like something out of medieval Europe.

All three gnomes gathered around the sign, pointing at it.

Piper walked up and read.

Boggart

Found: England (Northumberland)

The boggart, normally invisible, is forced to show itself within the enclosure. It is said they appear only in mirrors, unless they wish to be seen. A most malevolent spirit, these creatures often attach themselves to a particular family, hounding them wherever they go, and tormenting them for generations. Their pranks are injurious and terrifying, but rarely fatal. One should take great care never to give a boggart a name, for then it will become destructive and beyond all ability to control. To rid one's house of a boggart, nail an iron horseshoe over the front door.

A sketch beside the writing depicted a haggard, hairy man-shape with long, scraggly hair, wild eyes, and claws. Piper sucked a sharp breath in her nose.

She grabbed Tristan and pointed at it. "That's the thing I saw in the glass."

"In the den?" he asked.

"Yes. That's definitely in the house!"

"The law man accidentally scratched the ward," said one of the gnomes. He pointed at the silver scrollwork on a remaining section of window.

"Law man?" asked Piper. "Oh, the lawyer?"

"Yes. The Pritchard," said a gnome.

"So he knows about this place." Piper folded her arms. "I guess that's why he wanted to get out of here so bad. He knew the boggart was loose."

"Few years," said a gnome. "The boggart is tricky. Master Jenkins could not catch him in the short time he tried."

"The Pritchard scratched the ward, broke the ward. The magic keeps things where they belong." A gnome nodded, making his beard floof up.

"Not where they belong. Where they were put." Piper frowned.

"Creatures cannot leave their enclosures while the wards are intact." Another gnome tapped the glass. "Do not break wards on the dangerous creatures, or they will hurt you."

A gnome reached up to hold her hand. "We will do our best to protect you, but please, do not die. We like young Master Piper."

"Umm." She managed a cheesy smile. "Dying is not on my list of stuff to do."

"Good, good," said all three gnomes at once. "We have much work to do. Feeding and cleaning."

"Cleaning and feeding," said one of them.

"Be wise. If you wish to undo Old Master Jenkins' work, consider what the creature will do to you if it is free," said the next gnome.

"Right…" She nodded. "Ugh, this just got complicated."

"Yeah." Tristan stuffed his hands in his pockets.

The gnomes raced off down the hallway.

Piper walked back the way they'd come, stopping at the enclosure with windows on three sides. Creatures only two-thirds the size of the gnomes, but still basically person-like, stopped what they were doing and all stared at the kids.

They wore tunics made of thin leather and hoods of green cloth that tapered to curled points at the top. Their eyes looked too wide for the size of their heads, tapered to narrow corners, and aglow with a nasty yellow shine. Somewhat oversized heads made them seem childlike, though they teetered at a point halfway between cute and creepy. Their sneering gestures and dark laughter didn't do much to endear them.

She walked along, unnerved by the pack of eight or nine little figures standing statue-still, moving only their heads so they could keep staring at her. When she reached the middle of the window, she glanced at the sign.

Brownies

Found: Western Europe (various countries)

Brownies are irritating trickster spirits common to the deep woodlands and bogs of England, Ireland, Wales, and Scotland. Some have migrated to other parts of the world by sneaking into ships and aircraft, though mixing brownies with aircraft often results in disaster. They have an irresistible urge to play pranks and cause trouble, though they are not as cute as they appear. Brownies take great delight in causing suffering and death, though they rarely cause direct harm, instead causing the unwary or careless to stumble across more dangerous circumstances.

"Geez. Evil little things," said Piper.

Three of the brownies inside the enclosure gestured at her. The silvery ward around the window flickered brighter for an instant. They did it again, causing the ward to flicker a second time. Growling, they flew into a rage, their 'cute' little faces twisted and turned red with anger. A pelting of rocks and glops of mud hit the glass.

"Wow. I don't think they like us." Tristan laughed.

"No. Not at all." She stared at the silvery pattern that formed a line along the bottom of the window. "Maybe I won't let them out. If they're going to hurt people, they belong in jail."

Tristan shrugged.

She walked off, stopping a few minutes later by the foggy woodland they'd first passed while chasing gnomes. The enclosure didn't appear to have anything alive in it other than trees and undergrowth, so she checked out the sign.

Forest Troll

Found: Ireland

One of the most dangerous creatures in my menagerie, the forest troll is a master of camouflage in the woods where it dwells. These beasts consider anything living that is not a troll to be food. They aren't particular about what they eat, and never seem to reach a state of fullness. They are incredibly resilient to physical harm, except for burning. On the expedition to collect this specimen, four lives were tragically lost. This exhibit is dedicated to my friends and colleagues, Jameson Fowler, Edward E. Brim, Alastair Dawson II, and Kit Thompson.

"Uhh, it's watching me," said Tristan, his voice soft and wavering with fear.

Piper looked up from the sign. One of the trees had eyes. She leaned closer to the glass, peering at the spot for a minute or two before she made out the shape of a huge, humanoid creature. Its skin had the color and texture of near-black tree bark, complete with patches of moss and white splotchy fungus. It had to be at least twelve feet tall and stood with its back against a tree, as still as a statue.

Evidently sensing it had been spotted, the troll advanced with a heavy stomp that shook the floor. Tattered bits of brown cloth wrapped its ankles and feet in a crude attempt at footwear, while a mass of green ivy hung from its belt like a loincloth. It raised a fist bigger than Dad's chest and pounded it into the glass, sending a resounding *boom* down the corridor.

Piper screamed, fully expecting a hail of razor-sharp fragments to slice her to pieces, but the window somehow held. The silvery writing glowed bright for a few seconds after the hit, electrical sparks dancing across the scrollwork.

"Let's go… standing here is a bad idea." Tristan pulled on her arm. "Like waving meat at a starving dog. That thing might be strong enough to break the window."

"Uhh, yeah." She scrambled after him.

Running without too much care for direction, Piper zipped straight across the food court and into the hallway leading to the bitey garden. This time, she decided to check out the right turn before it. A moment's walk down that passage led to an enclosure that had no glass, or even any sign of a wall. The opening, flush with the floor and ceiling, led to a verdant jungle scene with too many plants, trees, and hanging vines to see how deep it went.

"Look." Tristan pointed back at a silver writing on the floor. "We're inside the ward."

"Umm." She tensed her legs, ready to sprint the ten or so yards back to where it crossed the hallway, forming a square line around the walls and ceiling. "Maybe whatever's in here is nice if grandpa thinks people can get close to them?"

Rustling in the leaves made her jump and cling to Tristan.

"You're right. Probably friendly if it's open like this."

A group of white snakes flew out from the jungle on wings of multicolored feathers. Piper's brain jammed to a halt and she let out a shriek of terror. Snakes had always frightened her; even pictures of them made her squirm and look away. Snakes with *wings*—her mind couldn't even process that.

Tristan wrapped his arms around her and held her up as all the strength left her legs.

She somewhat noticed a cloud of blurry color orbiting around them. Every time her lungs emptied of air, she drew another breath and screamed again. Piper wanted to run, but no direction offered escape. With nothing else to do, she clamped onto Tristan with her arms and legs, hiding her face against his shoulder.

A horrifying few minutes later, his shouting broke through the chaos in her mind.

"They're friendly!"

Piper lifted her head from his shoulder.

A white snake face hovered almost nose to nose with her. Its dark blue tongue flicked at her chin.

"Aaah!" she whimpered, too frightened to move. "It's gonna bite me."

The snake shook its head.

Having a snake react to her words threw a plank into the gears of her brain. It hovered still in midair, upon slow-beating wings covered in bright feathers of orange, green, blue, and red.

"You're not going to bite me?" asked Piper, barely over a whisper.

The snake shook its head again.

"Awesome," said Tristan. "Can you guys talk?"

Several of the snakes shook their heads.

Piper relaxed a little and lowered her feet to the floor.

"Whew. Thanks." Tristan squirmed. "You're kinda heavy."

"I… what?" She glared at him.

"I mean. Not fat, just… well. You're older than me and I'm kinda small and standing here holding you for an hour…"

She smirked. "Right."

"I didn't mean to call you fat. You're not."

"Forget it."

The winged serpents gathered around them, flying merrily.

One swooped in and rubbed its head on Piper's cheek. She froze, inches from a panic meltdown.

"Did you get bitten by a snake before?" asked Tristan.

"No. I don't know why they scare me so much. They just do."

"They're really friendly." Tristan pet one as it glided past him. "I bet they want to go home."

The serpents all stopped, hanging still in the air, and stared at him.

"That looks like a yes," said Piper. "I'm sorry you're stuck here. My grandfather did this. He wasn't a nice man. I'm going to find a way to get you out of here. You shouldn't be locked up like this."

All nine of them nuzzled her at once. She shivered, paralyzed with fear, but a few minutes of flying snakes behaving like affectionate cats put a crack in her phobia. Not that she'd ever go out of her way to touch one of these creatures, but she regained her ability to breathe and move. Doing her best to remain calm while essentially wearing nine snakes, she tiptoed over to where the sigil crossed the hallway, and crouched.

Picking at it with her fingernails didn't do anything. She took out the key and tried to scratch the marks, but that also didn't have any effect.

"Grr. How did that lawyer 'accidentally' scratch these? They're like magic tough or something."

Tristan took a knee and gave it a try with his house key, scraping lines in the stone, but the ward didn't budge. "Good question."

"Hmm." She sat back on her heels and scratched her head. Two snakes peered around from behind and gazed into her eyes. "I bet he had a knife or something magical. The writing is magic, so we're going to need magic to break it."

The snakes nodded.

"Coatls," said Tristan from over by a sign. "Says they're from southern Mexico or Central America. Aztec stuff. Friendly and wise, and bring good luck if they like you."

Piper reached out and patted one on the head. "I'm sorry if I made you feel bad for being scared. You're really nice and friendly, and I promise I'll get you out. I need to find something to break the magic… guess you can't fly past this line?"

The coatls shook their heads. One stuck itself out, its nose glancing off open air as if a pane of glass blocked the way. Each time it poked, the silver writing flickered with light.

"I understand. We'll come back as soon as we find a way to break this spell."

They all gathered around Piper, brushed against her, and then repeated the gesture with Tristan before drifting back into their jungle canopy and draping themselves over branches to rest.

"Where do you want to go now?" asked Tristan.

Piper walked over the line, heading east again. "There's more stuff past where the boggart escaped. We should check everywhere."

"I don't like that hall. It's like your grandfather put all the evil stuff in one place."

"Maybe he did, like a theme or something. All the evil down one hall, the bhargest and the cerberus are both dogs… Griffon, phoenix, thunderbird… all bird related."

"And all nice. Well, mostly. Boy griffon *did* try to eat us."

"They are nice. His mate knows we want to help. She cried." Piper rubbed her throat, trying not to choke up at the thought of the female griffon allowing herself to be captured so they could stay together.

Glum, she trudged back down the 'dark' corridor. When they reached the troll's enclosure, it roared at them and beat both fists on the glass. In seconds, a dazzling array of sparks and lightning raced around along the silver warding. The lights weakened and faltered. Piper grabbed Tristan's hand and ran. As soon as they got out of sight, the troll gave up attacking the glass.

"Wow," muttered Tristan. "That thing is angry."

She nodded, one hand over her heart. "Yeah. And I really don't think it likes us."

The brownies made rude gestures as they walked by on their way toward the broken boggart enclosure.

"I don't like it here," said Tristan. "I mean this hallway."

"Me neither. But we have to look everywhere." She glanced back toward the troll. "It's okay. The monsters can't get out unless we set them free."

Tristan nodded. "Right."

17

MAINTENANCE MAN

Mr. Bailey mashed his thumb into the button repeatedly, but the huge green door wouldn't open. He took a step back from the metal box on the wall and frowned at the tire marks in the grass going straight up to the edge of the building. He pivoted to peer along the length of the path they took to the house, over two hundred yards of meadow.

"Do we have a groundskeeper with a Cushman?"

The tracks, mere depressions in the grass, would fade away in a day or two, so whoever went riding around on a golf cart couldn't have done so that long ago.

"Hmm. Well, if my father did have anyone working for him, maybe that's the 'ghost' Piper keeps hearing." He shook his head, chuckling. "Someone needs to tell this guy my old man's dead."

A glint in the grass caught his eye.

Mr. Bailey stooped to fetch what he thought might be a coin, but instead found a large purplish scale with rainbow highlights. It *might* have come from a fish, but he didn't think fish got that big. The scale had to be two inches long and an inch wide, which would make the fish about ten feet or more by his reasoning.

He thought back to his truck bed smelling like seawater.

Deciding things too strange to waste time on right at that moment, he tucked the scale in his shirt pocket and poked the door buttons again. Nothing happened.

"I'll need to call that Pritchard again." Mr. Bailey picked at a small keyhole by the buttons. "He clearly forgot to give me all the keys."

Amy yelled something, but distance reduced her words to meaningless sound.

Mr. Bailey twisted toward the house. His wife stood in the kitchen door waving at him as if to get his attention.

He didn't bother trying to shout over the entire field, and started walking. Amy stopped waving, and remained in the doorway watching him approach.

"The power's out," said Amy.

"Out?" asked Mr. Bailey. He leaned back to look up at the second floor windows, but in the middle of the day he couldn't tell one way or the other if the house had power.

"Yes, out. All the electricity shut down. I was right in the middle of next year's lesson plan."

"You're using a laptop… don't they have batteries?"

Amy folded her arms. "The battery has been dead for two years. It only works when plugged in."

"Time for a new laptop. You could've gotten a new battery. They're not *that* expensive."

She ran her hands up over her auburn hair and leaned into him with a sigh. "I always used it plugged in anyway. Didn't think it was worth the expense."

"If the whole house went dark, it's probably a breaker." He stepped into the kitchen and headed for the basement door. "Crap. Hang on. It's going to be dark down there."

"All right," said Amy. "Hey, have you seen Piper or that boy? They disappeared."

Mr. Bailey grinned. "It's a huge house. I'm sure they're somewhere."

Footsteps thumped by overhead.

"See? There they are." Mr. Bailey ran out to his truck, which still smelled like swimming pool and fish. He cringed. "Damn. What the hell is going on?" After grabbing a flashlight from the toolbox in the back seat, he jogged back to the kitchen and made his way to the basement.

Yellow, purple, and green light on the wall surprised him, since the power should've been dead.

"What on Earth?" He pointed the flashlight at a strange array of wooden cabinets loaded with crystals, jars of glowing something, and glass tubes. Two fat black cables spanned from it to a normal looking circuit-breaker box. "Wow. Guess they made power boxes way different fifty years ago. Never saw anything like this before."

Mr. Bailey approached the console, which looked like a combination of a NASA control panel and a child's playroom toy. None of the levers or gem buttons had any labels, but one particularly large T-shaped switch on the right looked important. It also happened to be tilted forward and down, which made him think of a blown circuit breaker.

"Hmm. Maybe the kids were playing around with this?"

He grabbed the crossbar at the top of the lever and pushed the large T upward. Of course, being a man, he couldn't help but spare a few seconds' daydream of pushing the throttle lever of a giant spaceship. Alas, the ordinary light bulbs hanging from the ceiling didn't come on when the switch went as far up as it could go.

"Just a toy… What am I doing?" Shaking his head, Mr. Bailey went over to the standard grey steel electrical boxes and opened the panels.

Sure enough, the master breaker switch at the top of the left side had thrown. Based on the size of the breaker box and number of other sub-breakers, he figured it a bad idea to just hit the main one first. One by one, he turned the other seventy switches off. The main, a plastic bar about four inches tall, fusing four separate breakers behind it into one switch, required two hands to throw to the left and reactivate.

"Wow, damn, that was stiff."

Working both rows at once, he flipped all the smaller breakers back on. About halfway down, Amy's cheer came from upstairs. Mr. Bailey grinned while flipping the rest of the breakers, closed the cabinet door, and headed for the stairs.

He paused, glancing at the strange console and the big old-timey lever he'd pushed upright. The console didn't look different, nor did it seem to do anything. It certainly had no effect on the house power.

"Bah. It doesn't do anything. Probably my old man trying to radio Mars." With a wave of dismissal, Mr. Bailey trotted upstairs.

18

CHAOS

Piper found herself slowing down to a sneak as they neared the brownie enclosure. Not that they frightened her anywhere near as much as the troll, but the twisted little critters unsettled her. The sign *had* lied about the mermaid, but she had at least appeared innocent and sad. The little brownies certainly looked malevolent.

The lights faltered and went off, leaving the corridor dark except for whatever illumination leaked in from the enclosure's fake sky.

"Whoa." Tristan grabbed her arm. A second later, he whispered, "Do you think the troll did that?"

"No. It hasn't been making noise." She turned to look back down the hall.

The silver warding lines around the brownie enclosure's glass flared brilliant white. The glow lingered a few seconds and popped like a camera flash with a significant *snap*. Something in the air changed. Piper ran her hands down over her chest. That constant tickle like bugs crawling around under her shirt had stopped.

"That weird feeling is gone," whispered Piper.

"Weird feeling?" asked Tristan.

"Like how it feels to walk face-first into a spider web, only everywhere… and all the time."

"Oh, that." He scratched at his shoulder. "Yeah. I stopped noticing it. You're right, it's not happening now."

She stared at the glass. Nothing appeared any different, but the air felt lighter. An energy that had been everywhere no longer existed. "Oh no," she whispered. "I think the wards failed."

Tristan's eyes widened. "Why?"

"Maybe the troll overloaded it. You saw those sparks. Grandpa used electricity somehow to make the magic work. Electricity isn't magic. The troll could've blown a fuse."

"No one makes fuses anymore. It's all breakers." Tristan pointed. "We should check the control room."

"Good idea."

A shrill nails-on-a-chalkboard screeching locked up the muscles in Piper's back. She cringed, twisting to seek out the source of the horrible noise. One of the brownies stood inside the window, scratching lines in the glass with its tiny claws. It flashed an evil smile at her, and disappeared. The others behind it winked out of existence one by one.

"Umm," whispered Piper. "We should run."

Seven brownies appeared in the hallway with a ripple of soft *pops*. They cackled and rubbed their hands together, leaning aggressively toward Piper and Tristan. Despite their being about a foot tall, her first instinct said 'run like hell.'

One brownie pointed at her.

Piper's feet slid together and the laces on her sneakers weaved into an impossible tangle of knots. Another did the same to Tristan. A third brownie snapped its fingers in Piper's direction. Her waist-length wavy brown hair flipped up and wrapped around her head, blinding her.

"Gah!" She grabbed at her face, but her hair wouldn't budge from her eyes.

A tiny voice cackled with glee.

Tristan screamed, "It itches!"

The deafening *smash* of a huge window shattering into thousands of pieces filled the corridor, along with the ghastly, deep roar of an angry troll.

"No!" shouted Piper, grunting and squirming to pull down the hair squeezing around her head. "That's the—" A serpent of hair slithered across her mouth. "Mmm! Mmm!"

Tristan fell over, bumping her leg. Piper hopped, flailing her arms for balance with her sneakers tied together. He flipped around, gasping and whining, saying "itch" over and over.

A chorus of tiny voices rose up chanting, "Here troll. Tasties waiting."

Heavy thumping footsteps got louder.

Piper tried to scream, but her hair tightened around her head, pulling into her mouth. "Mmm! Trmm! Ammm!"

Tristan scrambled upright and grabbed her hand. "The troll's coming!"

I know that! "Mmm kmmmn mmmt! Rmmmm!"

"Come on!" shouted Tristan.

Unable to pull her feet apart, Piper hopped forward. Blind, she trusted the hand pulling her past the brownies, who all giggled and cackled, and showered them with taunts, calling them tasty, clumsy, stupid and smelly.

Troll stomping sounded closer, gaining speed and volume.

The slap-squeak of sneakers on tile echoed off the walls as they hopped. Piper stopped fighting her hair and kept her left hand outstretched so she didn't plow headfirst into a concrete wall.

Tristan pulled her to the left while shouting, "Turn!"

She hopped after him, still trying to scream past a cord of hair in her mouth. The troll had to be getting close. Any second now, it would pound them into spaghetti sauce. How could a giant creature like that not catch a pair of kids with their shoelaces tied together?

A sharp pain jabbed her in the left thigh. Tristan yelped at about the same time. Another, about as bad as a bee sting, hit her in the chest. She swatted blind at the air, and another sharp sting hit her between the middle and ring finger of her left hand. Piper flinched, but it felt like something remained stuck in the tender skin. More stings bit her all over, and the air filled with teeny chattering voices speaking angry nonsense gibberish.

A whooshing passed by her head seconds before a metal *clank* echoed from the left.

"Wmm wmm amm?" asked Piper.

"Uhh, a little thing just threw a knife at us."

"Mmm!"

"I know! Hop faster. The troll's right behind us!"

Piper ignored the rain of bee stings as well as her fear of going headfirst into the wall, or tripping over one of the benches. Despite being unable to see, she hopped as fast as she could. Tristan gasped and wailed, complaining about itching. Soon, the sharp stings hit her only in the back, butt, and legs from behind, providing extra motivation to hurry.

The floor shook from the troll's heavy footsteps. Tears streamed out of Piper's eyes, soaking into her hair.

"Here, here, here!" shouted a small voice.

She stopped crying as a light of hope went on inside her. *The nice gnomes!* Two more pinpricks of pain hit her in the left leg, right below the butt. "Owmm!"

"There's a tiny fat man waving at us," said Tristan.

"I'm not fat!" shouted the gnome. "Get in here before you're troll food!"

Tristan put a hand on her back, guiding her to the left as they hopped for another few seconds. "Stop! Kneel down and crawl. It's a little tunnel."

Two small hands with the coarseness of an old farm-worker's callouses grabbed her left hand and pulled. Piper scooted forward on her knees, gasping at small jabs of pain in her back. The horrendously loud roar of an enraged troll filled the tunnel along with a heavy *slam* rocking the floor. Squealing from fear, Piper shuffled forward as fast as she could. A short bit of crawling later, the gnome stopped tugging.

"Safe here. Rest."

Out of breath from all the hopping and panic, Piper started to roll to sit, but stopped when the gnome yelled, "Wait!"

She froze.

Three sharp nips bit her in the rear end.

"Mmm!" she shouted.

"Okay. You can sit now," said the gnome.

Piper rubbed her backside and lowered herself onto it, sitting.

A small hand touched her cheek, and her hair stopped squeezing.

She spat a few times to clear her mouth and pulled it away from her eyes. As soon as she could see again, she gasped. A three-inch arrow stuck out of her left hand, the point embedded in the skin between her middle and ring finger. Grimacing, she grabbed it and tugged. It came loose with a drop of blood and a thread of pain that ran all the way down her arm to the elbow.

"Ow!" She hurled it aside.

She, the gnome, and Tristan, sat in a tiny tunnel only a few inches taller than the gnome. Sitting on the floor, her head almost touched the top. Dozens more tiny arrows studded her legs and arms, a few also sticking out of her chest. Tristan scratched and squirmed like he had the world's worst infestation of fleas. A porcupine coating of tiny arrows covered him as well.

"You have brownie curses," said the gnome. "They will stop soon."

Piper plucked an arrow out of her thigh and held it up. About the size of a toothpick, it had a teensy metal head and dark purple fletching. Cord thinner than sewing thread tied the pieces together. "What's this?"

"Bog pixies." The gnome shook his head. "Mean and angry, but annoying. They can't hurt you."

She held her arms up, since letting them hang down pressed more little arrows into her flesh. "This hurts."

"No. I mean real hurt." The gnome poked a finger into Tristan's chest.

The fervor with which he scratched lessened. A moment later, he stopped. "That sucked *so* much. I've never been so itchy in my life!' He'd scratched his arms raw, a few of the nastier fingernail marks oozed blood.

Piper cringed. "I hate those things!"

Tristan reached over and plucked arrows out of Piper's shoulder, arm, and side.

She winced with each one, but sat as still as she could while he cleared her back of tiny arrows. Piper looked over at him, noting that he hadn't removed a single arrow from his body yet. "You've got arrows stuck in you, too."

"Yeah. I know." He avoided looking her straight in the eye, a hint of red in his cheeks.

Piper plucked arrows from her legs, tossing them in a pile. Once she had no more projectiles lodged in her skin, she pulled Tristan around and plucked arrows out of him. While working, she glanced at the gnome. "What's going on?"

"Someone shut off the magic in the wards." The gnome shook his head. "Very very very very very bad."

Piper and Tristan said, "That's a lot of verys" at the same time.

Buzzing like the Godzilla of mosquitos approached from the right. An eight-inch tall creature with a rounded, misshapen head, potbelly, and spindly limbs glided into view. Its skin had a corpselike pallor with a purplish tint in places, and it wore a small skirt of dead leaves. Its face warped with anger, exposing three teeth as it shot another little arrow into the side of Tristan's head.

"Ow!" shouted Tristan.

The gnome made a flicking gesture at the miniscule archer—which exploded into a glop of purple ooze—while saying, "Bog pixie," in a contemptuous snarl.

Piper stared in horror at the 'blueberry yogurt' dripping down the walls of the shaft. The realization that this cute little gnome just killed something made her turn her head to stare at the little man with new fear and respect. *They've got magic! Could it explode us too, if we make it angry?*

Three more bog pixies appeared, but as soon as they spotted the gnome, screamed and darted back into the hallway.

"We gotta get out of here," said Tristan.

Piper pulled at her shoelaces, unable to make sense of the complicated knots. "We can't. Those stupid brownies tied our sneakers together. We can't hop all the way out… not with all that stuff coming after us."

"Oh." Tristan struggled with his shoelaces. "This is impossible. It's like there's more laces than there should be. I could cut it apart."

"It's not impossible." The gnome tapped a finger on Piper's sneakers, then Tristan's. Like living snakes, the laces squirmed and un-knotted, shrinking back to normal. "It's magic."

19

ALL FANGS BIG AND SMALL

Piper sat for a moment, rubbing her arms where the arrows had hit her, while listening to the angry, gleeful, and bizarre noises coming from the creatures loose in the hallway. Having the gnome here kept her from surrendering to panic. Despite his being only two-ish feet tall, his presence reassured her, like having Dad around.

"What is this tunnel?" asked Piper.

The gnome grinned, his white beard fluffing up. "Gnome roads. We take care of this place for Master Jenkins. Gnome roads will lead anywhere. Too small for trolls. Too small for people too." He tilted his head. "But you are small people."

"We still have to crawl," said Tristan.

"Crawling is better than being mashed up by a troll." Piper nudged him.

"What are we going to do?" He grabbed his head in both hands, staring down at the floor between his sneakers.

"Umm. Find the control room and turn the wards back on?" asked Piper.

"That would not put the bad things back inside their spaces," said the gnome. "Master Jenkins spent years learning how to capture them. You would need to learn how he tricked them all."

"Ugh." Piper glared at the low ceiling. "Forget that. I said I wanted to set everything free, right? So, maybe all we need to do is get out of here, and the creatures will find their way home?"

The gnome emitted an uneasy whine. "Maybe, but I don't want to go away."

"You don't have to!" Piper smiled at him. "Just the ones who are locked up and don't want to be here. If the gnomes want to stay, you can. But you're not prisoners."

"No." The gnome shook his head. "Never prisoners. We help Master Jenkins because we like to. Our home was eaten by metal beasts. All the trees, gone. The hills flattened." The gnome bowed his head and shed a tear. "Master Jenkins gave us a place to live like home. This is our home now."

"I'm sorry. I'm not going to make you leave if you want to stay." She rolled onto her hands and knees. "Can you lead us to the control room?"

"Yes. This way." The gnome's sorrow evaporated. He grinned, spun on his heel, and zoomed off.

Piper crawled after him, her shoulders brushing the smooth concrete roof. She couldn't really keep up with him, but the gnome stopped whenever he almost got out of sight, as if he could tell without looking. He never went so far ahead that they lost him.

They crawled long enough for her knees to ache, going past numerous offshoots filled with the smells of wet earth, rotten eggs, or spoiled meat.

"So, what do you do here?" asked Piper.

"We clean and make food for those who live here. Other gnomes tend to the house. We used to make food for Master Jenkins too, but with new humans there, we hide."

"Hiding? Why?" Piper almost yelled. "My parents think I'm crazy."

The gnome spun to face her. "Humans can be dangerous to gnomes. Like the ones who destroyed our home. We have to make sure they will not hurt us once they know we are here."

"I won't let them hurt you." Piper struggled to crawl faster. "I promise."

"Ow!" yelled Tristan.

She shifted to peer back at him. He grimaced in pain, reaching behind himself to pluck another arrow out of his backside.

"Stupid bog pixies!" Tristan snapped the arrow and dropped it.

A tiny voice giggled in the tunnel behind him.

"Hurry." The gnome beckoned with a wave and scampered off again.

Minutes later, Piper crawled up to an offshoot going left. Curious, she glanced at it as she had all the other turns the gnome did not take. What she had thought to be darkness, turned out to be hair studded with little ruby eyes. Tarantula-shaped spiders as big as housecats broke apart from a cluster and scuttled toward her.

Piper let out a shrill scream, scrambling into a rapid crawl without care for how much it hurt her knees. Lost to blind panic, she rushed to the next possible turn, no longer aware of where the gnome had gone. Tristan shouted somewhere behind her, which got her to hesitate long enough to look back out of worry for her friend.

He dragged himself after her, kicking at the colossal spiders nipping at his heels. Since he hadn't been bitten, her concern for him succumbed to panic, and she dashed forward, desperate to find any way out of the narrow passageway where she couldn't run full speed away from the huge, black, hairy spiders.

The tunnel took a sharp corner. Soon after, she darted down a branch off to the right. She regretted the choice in seconds, as the new tunnel plunged downward. She screamed as she went sliding on her chest over polished concrete without any way to stop. Air ran out of her lungs seconds before she shot out the end of the tunnel into a dark chamber, flying toward cloudy white walls.

Piper crashed into the (surprisingly soft) surface and stuck to it, arms and legs splayed out in an X. Her body had wound up oriented mostly sideways, her back to the wall. Her left leg pointed straight up, while her left arm extended out over her head. A light tug failed to dislodge her right arm, which hung straight down. Strands of hair snagged in the adhesive cushion, but not so much she couldn't move her head. She peered to her right, down at the floor.

The chamber she'd flown into spanned about three stories, with her glued to the wall close to the roof. Only the top third had a coating of the soft, sticky substance. Below that, dark bare stonework resembled a natural cave. The square chamber looked about fifty yards or so on all sides.

"Hello," said a pleasant male voice from below.

Piper whined out her nose. No spiders had come out after her, but neither had Tristan.

Motion caught the light at the bottom of the room. Piper dreaded that she'd see a spider the size of a truck, but looked anyway. What sat at the bottom of the room defied her worst nightmare.

A gargantuan snake, as big around as a telephone pole, slithered out from the darkness by the wall, coiling up beneath her. An oversized human head, veiny and bald, perched at the end of the snake body. Despite his grotesque appearance, his expression attempted to be comforting.

She would have screamed at seeing a snake that big, but its face pushed simple fear into pure terror that left her barely able to breathe and unable to make a sound.

"You should get down from there before the spiders come out of the tunnel and find you caught in their web," said the serpent.

This is spider webs!? Eww! Piper glanced up at her stuck arm and whined. "You just want me to come down there so you can eat me."

"You are assuming," said the serpent.

"What… are you?" asked Piper.

"Your kind has referred to mine as naga. We are keepers of wisdom."

She didn't like the way its gleaming emerald eyes fixated on her, and felt much like a white mouse dropped into a pet snake's tank. In fact, the naga peered up at her much the same way as the school snake had done to the mouse. Her second-grade class teased her for months about that. She'd cried so much over feeding the class' pet snake that the school decided to move it out of the classroom. *I wonder if that mouse was this scared when Mr. Hunt dangled it by the tail over the tank.*

"The spiders are coming, girl." The naga coiled itself to the right, slithering back and forth under her like an outfielder watching a ball.

Tristan's yell came from a small, square hole in the wall, catty-corner to where she hung. He shot off the end at an angle, tumbled over twice, and hit the webbing chest-first a few feet to her left.

"Oof!" said Tristan.

"Don't trust the naga," said Piper.

"What's a naga?" muttered Tristan.

"Look down."

He struggled for a few seconds before pushing himself off the webbing and staring downward. "Oh. *That's* a naga."

"The spiders are coming, children. You should climb down here so I can protect you," said the naga.

Tristan looked at her. "You're right. I don't trust it."

"You got out of the webs?" Piper blinked.

"They're not that sticky." His eyes went wide. "Crap! Spiders!"

Piper tilted her head up to look at the wall behind her. Cat-sized tarantulas swarmed out of the gnome tunnel. She let out a reflexive scream of fear.

"Come on." Tristan shoved his body off the webs, except for his hands and feet. "It's sticky enough to climb, but we're not trapped."

Motivated by fear, Piper grunted and pulled until her right arm came free. The webs had enough sticky to keep her body clinging while she rolled upward and grabbed a handful of mush. A few strands of hair pulled out, and her T-shirt almost ripped, but she got herself reoriented and hung from the wall by her hands and sneakers.

Tristan moved sideways, away from the spiders, which swarmed after them. Piper followed, feeling a bit like a suction-cup climber going up the side of a building, unsticking her hand, re-sticking her hand, then doing the same with her feet.

A spider rushed in at her, fangs poised to nail her in the leg. Piper shrieked and kicked the creature in the face. Yellow ooze leaked from a crack between two rows of eyes, and it fell. The naga snapped it out of the air before it hit the floor, and devoured it in seconds.

"Ugh!" Piper looked away before she threw up. "Spiders and snakes! Really!? Did grandpa build this room specifically to freak me out?"

"Over here," yelled Tristan. "There's another tunnel."

She shuffled along the webbing, eyeing the spiders, which now seemed hesitant to get too close to her. *They're smart. Oh, crap.* "I don't wanna go in another tunnel. The spiders will just follow us."

"There's a door down here," said the naga in a charming, soothing voice.

Piper looked down. One story below, an observation deck jutted out from the wall for zoo visitors. "There!"

She moved with purpose toward the observation deck, but slowed at a fleeting shadow above her. A spider had scurried around to a spot right over her head. She locked eyes with it a second before it let go, falling at her face, its fangs dripping.

With a shriek, Piper pushed away from the wall with her left hand and foot, swinging clear of the plummeting spider, which passed by close enough for its coarse hair to brush her cheek. She dangled by one handful of webbing, refusing to watch the naga eat a second giant spider.

Gauzy white stuff peeled off the wall, torn by her weight. She scrabbled for a grip and swung briefly on a vine of spidersilk back into the webbing. Tristan, several yards higher up, looked down at her and breathed a sigh of relief.

The naga stretched itself upward, slithering on the wall toward her, a broad smile on its too-human lips. Piper pulled herself up and away, not waiting to see if he'd reach her or not. She crawled past Tristan to the corner and onto the next section of wall. Spiders followed them around the webs, Tristan kicking another one to its doom at the bottom of the pit when it made a run at him.

Piper climbed to the right, moving to a position above the observation platform. From her vantage point, she had the frightening realization that it had no doors. Short of breaking the thick glass windows, it didn't offer an escape. "Dammit!"

"What?" shouted Tristan.

"It doesn't open."

The naga chuckled from directly below her.

Piper stared at her fingers, covered in gummy white spidersilk. "Okay. Gnome tunnel it is. We don't have a choice."

"'Kay," yelled Tristan.

She pulled herself sideways across the wall toward another square opening near the ceiling. "Do gnomes fly or do they just drop food in here?"

"Usually, they zap the spiders and make them fall," said the naga. "It has been quite a long time since I had anyone to talk to."

"We can talk from here. You're trying too hard to get us to go down there. You want to eat us." Piper didn't look at the serpent, keeping her gaze focused on the gnome tunnel much too far away for her liking.

"I'm merely lonely," said the naga.

"And I'm not a feeder mouse," muttered Piper before raising her voice. "If you eat me, I can't set you free."

The naga twisted around, peering up at her. "Now who is telling stories?"

"I mean it. Where are you from?"

"Your kind refer to the region as India. My home was in the mountains."

Piper grabbed handful after handful of gooey webbing, pulling herself closer to the gnome tunnel. "I promise I'll help you get back there, but only if you won't eat us."

The naga chuckled. "You're a small child. As much as I would love to entertain some possible truth to your intention, your ability to follow through is lacking."

"Haven't you ever heard of girl power?" said Tristan. "Give her a chance."

Despite being caught between spiders and a huge snake, utterly terrified, Piper laughed.

"Yah!" shouted Tristan. "Sneaky!"

A faint squealing came from a spider as it fell.

"They're getting closer." Tristan shuffled faster, gaining on her. "The spiders are angry."

Piper rushed the last few yards to the gnome tunnel and almost burst into tears at the sight of a closed hatch over it. The plain, black metal covering had a single keyhole in the center big enough to stick two fingers in. "No!"

"What's wrong?" Tristan pulled himself over and hung next to her.

"It's closed." She pointed at the hatch.

Tristan reached over her head and punched a spider off the wall before it could bite her. "You're too scared to think straight."

She cringed down and leaned against him. "Thanks. I didn't even see that one. What do you—oh, duh. The key!"

"Right. Don't drop it."

Piper glared at him. "Why did you say that?"

"Umm. I dunno." He pointed at a carpet of black hair creeping closer around the sides of the room. "No pressure or anything. There's like a million spiders coming."

"Oh!" She whined out her nose and jammed her hand in her pocket. The sticky coating of web made it difficult to pull back out, but also glued the key to her fingers. When she inserted the relatively tiny key into the huge hole, it blurred and shimmered. As soon as she felt the mechanism engage the key, she twisted, and the hatch pushed inward. "Yes!"

Piper shoved it forward and crawled in, turning to grab Tristan's arm and pull him in behind her. He grabbed the hatch and slammed it closed, bracing it with both legs. Scratches and clicks of spider legs danced across the metal.

"Holy crap!" wheezed Tristan.

"Yeah." Piper held her hand up. The key remained stuck to her fingers. "I don't think I *could* drop it."

"That was wild." Tristan laughed. "Scary as hell, but wild."

"Says you." She peeled the key away from her fingers before rubbing her hands together to wad up the spidersilk. "This is disgusting."

"The spiders are pretty squishy. They look scary but they're not tough."

Once she mostly got her hands free of stickiness, Piper lay flat on her back and breathed hard. "Can we rest a bit?"

"I think so. Are those spiders smart enough to find another way around?"

"I hate you." Piper muttered.

He didn't reply.

"I mean… I hate that you said that." She closed her eyes. "My legs are jelly from climbing."

"It's okay. Sorry. I wasn't trying to scare you, but… I don't wanna be here if the spiders find us."

With a groan, Piper rolled over onto her stomach and pushed up to crawl. "Yeah. Neither do I."

20

A PROMISE MADE

Random choices of tunnel eventually brought Piper to an opening. A grass-covered field, strong sunlight overhead with puffy white clouds, and clear blue sky almost fooled her into thinking she'd somehow managed to escape to the surface. The scent of meadow flowers and pollen rode by on a warm breeze.

Tristan poked her in the back. "Hey. Why'd you stop?"

She crawled out, stood, and dusted herself off, gazing around. Rolling hills stretched off ahead of them and to the right, and a dense forest stood to the left. Behind her, a square gnome tunnel opening occupied the face of a large boulder. "It's pretty here."

"Wow." Tristan got to his feet and hovered close beside her. "Are we outside, or is this another exhibit?"

"I think we're still in the zoo. We didn't climb up at all." She advanced a few steps from the tunnel, turning to look in all directions, but nothing broke the illusion of being out in the countryside. "This must be a huge habitat. I don't see any doors."

Tristan peeled bits of spider web off his arms and jeans. "I hope whatever lives here isn't hungry. At least we can run now."

"Come on." Piper started walking.

"Where are you going?"

"Straight ahead. We find a wall, then follow it until we get to a door. This can't be a real 'outside.'"

"Your grandpa was either amazing or totally crazy."

She frowned. "Both."

They walked for a few minutes toward the woods before a noise like a galloping horse echoed out from the trees. Piper crouched, trying to hide in the knee-high grass. Tristan did the same, leaning shoulder-to-shoulder with her. A pair of dragonflies skimmed by, circled once, and landed on a tall, purple stalk with the fuzziness of a dandelion.

A deer darted among the trees with the briefest flash of light brown fur. Piper felt foolish for hiding, but before she could stand up, it bounded back into view. She hadn't seen a deer. The creature that emerged from the trees had the body of a human boy, at least down to the waist. From there, the rest of him resembled a foal. At a guess, she figured the boy part for about seven years old. He had no shirt, his scrawny human half sinewy with muscle and a deep tan. Long brown hair hung within an inch of his horse body. He appeared to be pursuing a bright orange butterfly.

"Aww!" Piper stood. "It's a little boy!" Her lip quivered and she had to force herself not to cry at the thought her grandfather had put a child in a cage.

The young creature froze, wide eyes searching around for barely a second before he spotted her. Fear left him, and he forgot all about the butterfly, trotting over to them instead. He stopped within arms' reach. Piper blinked, surprised that such a young-looking child stood a little taller than her.

He reached out and touched her face, lifting a tear from the corner of her eye. He glanced at it for a moment before giving her a confused stare and tilting his head.

"Umm, hi," said Piper a bit over a whisper. "Can you understand us?"

The boy nodded. "Yes."

Guilt hit her hard. Piper looked down and couldn't stop herself from crying anymore. "I'm really sorry."

Tristan rubbed her back.

"Why are you sad?" asked the boy.

"Because you're trapped here. You're just a little kid." She wiped her face on her arm.

"Trapped?" The centaur boy furrowed his eyebrows. "What do you mean?"

"My grandfather took you away from where you live and put you here like a trophy." She scowled, anger edging out her sorrow. "I wish he wasn't dead so I could tell him how awful he was."

The boy shrugged. "This is the only home I have."

"Maybe he was born here?" asked Tristan.

"Do you have parents?" asked Piper.

"Yes." He smiled, turned his upper half toward the woods, and shouted a few words in a strange language.

Piper stroked her hand along his back, feeling the horsehair. He grinned and pet her hair like a cat in response.

A man's voice bellowed from the tree line.

She startled and looked over.

Two more centaurs emerged, a man and woman. The man's upper body swelled with muscles. Dark brown hair covered his chest and arms. His beard reached down to his navel, and long a shaggy mane rained over his chestnut back. To Piper's alarm, his expression shifted to anger at the sight of her. The woman's human half had a slender build, blonde hair, and a worried expression. Her horse half shimmered with a light golden sheen.

After the mermaid, it didn't shock her *that* much that the female centaur had no top on, but Piper still felt a little weird about it. The male charged out from the trees, thundering toward them while shouting in the non-English language the boy had used.

The young centaur raised his hands in protest, yelling back.

"Wait!" shouted Piper. "I want to let you out!"

His charge slowed to a rapid trot. He swooped in and picked Piper and Tristan up by a fistful of their T-shirts each, seeming not to strain at all to hold them off the ground with one arm. He glowered at her with gleaming golden eyes, then gave Tristan the same challenging stare. Piper's feet dangled way off the ground. This centaur had to be close to nine feet tall, with a body like a barbarian warrior.

Tristan hung limp, arms slack at his sides, with that same huge-eyed pleading stare he showed her before.

"Arzun," said the female centaur, walking up alongside him. Her eyes sparkled like pink amethyst. "They are mere children. Do not harm them."

The male raised Piper toward his mate and lightly shook her. "This filly bears the stink of the one who put us here."

Piper grabbed his wrist. "My grandfather. I hate what he did. It's wrong!"

"No. Don't hurt them," said the boy centaur.

"Quiet, Pazlin," muttered the man. "Go with your mother."

The female centaur moved closer, brushing her fingers at Piper's hair. "I sense the sadness in her. She does not wish to hurt our son."

"Nozara, you are fooled again." The male tugged Piper away from her. "The writing on her even claims to be up to no good."

"It's from a movie!" yelled Tristan. "It's only a quote."

Piper glanced at him. "It's from a book."

"Movie," said Tristan.

"Book," muttered Piper.

"Mooovieee," sang Tristan.

Piper would've laughed, but her present situation didn't lend itself to humor.

"Fine." Nozara folded her arms. "Look for yourself."

Piper pulled at the man's thumb, futilely trying to open his fist. "Please believe me. I want to help you!"

Arzun lifted her up even higher, nose to nose, gazing into her eyes. His sweat smelled of pine trees, his breath of fruit and berries. Piper thought about how horrified she'd been at her grandfather keeping what amounted to a little boy and his parents prisoner for amusement.

The centaur snorted. "Unexpected." He set her down on her feet and released Tristan as well.

Piper pulled her T-shirt down over her stomach and tried to smooth out the wrinkles his fist left in the fabric.

Tristan approached Nozara, the top of his head not quite as high as where her human half met horse. "Something happened and all the wards shut off. The troll is loose."

Both adult centaurs tensed.

"You are true in your intention," said Arzun. "I do not understand how you can hold opinions so different from your blood."

Piper shook her head. "I didn't even know him. Your son is so little.

He shouldn't be in a zoo!"

Nozara brushed a hand over Piper's cheek. "He has known no other place. It is kinder, I think."

"No. It is cruel." Arzun glowered at nothing in particular.

"Follow me," said Piper. "We'll take you to an elevator and outside."

Arzun shook his head. "The troll must be contained or destroyed first." He gestured at the meadow and forest. "Here, we have the vast meadow to keep our distance. In the hallways, the creature would kill us."

"But you're so strong." Piper glanced at his arms.

"My strength is nothing compared to a troll, and I will not allow harm to befall my son."

The young centaur, Pazlin, walked alongside his mother, rubbing against her.

Nozara appeared to sense Piper's upwelling of sadness at seeing a captive boy, and brushed a hand over her head. "We do not blame you, child."

"Despite that you are kin of the man who has done this to us," said Arzun, "I give you my trust. Return when the troll is no longer a threat, and we shall follow you."

Piper nodded. She hated leaving them here, but that did sound better than watching the troll catch and smash them in the hallways. Having hooves, the centaurs would likely slip and skid all over on the tiles and be easy prey.

"The troll isn't that fast. We ran away from it hopping." Tristan bounced in place.

"We had a big head start, and—"

"We got lucky," said Tristan. "The bog pixies shot the troll with arrows too. It slowed down to swat at them or it would've caught us."

Piper shivered. "Okay… umm. Oh, this is so stupid."

"What?" asked Tristan.

"Well… all we need to do is find whatever shut off the magic. Then, one of us gets the troll to chase them into an enclosure where the window isn't broken, and the other one turns the wards back on."

Tristan scratched his head. "This place doesn't have any cameras. We'd need radios for that."

"Umm. Maybe the gnomes can help? They have magic. Maybe they could turn it on at the right time."

"Maybe."

Piper looked up at the centaurs. "All right. As soon as we trap the troll, I'll come back."

Arzun bowed at her.

She looked off at the field. "Where's the closest way out?"

Both adult centaurs pointed in the same direction.

"Thank you."

"We shall wait here until you have made the way safe," said Arzun.

Nozara nodded. Pazlin waved, a broad grin on his face.

Piper hurried off over the meadow, wondering how the old man made this place with such realistic sunlight, wind, and terrain.

Tristan jogged up alongside her. "Wow, that was close. I thought he was going to hurt us."

"He was only being protective of his son. Plus, I evidently smell like my grandfather." She frowned.

"I don't think he means literal smell. More like a magic smell." He grinned. "Like he knows you're related."

"Yeah, I got that."

They walked in silence for a few steps before Tristan blurted, "I don't think you smell."

Piper laughed.

A large bug buzzed by on the left. Somewhere off to the right, birds tweeted. The forest drifted across the meadow up ahead, too thick to see past.

"That's it. The door's probably hidden behind the trees." She pointed and started to walk faster. "Come on."

Tristan grabbed her shoulder and held her back. "Don't run. That'll only make us tired. We're going to need to run from the troll."

She closed her eyes and shivered from fear. "Why do you keep saying scary stuff?"

"Sorry."

Piper shook her head, opening her eyes again. "No. You're right. It makes sense. Save running for when we need it."

"I hope we don't have to."

She held his hand. "Oh… we're going to need to run."

21

THE RIDDLE

The woods reminded Piper of the trees outside, between Tristan's house and the manor. Bird tweets came from everywhere, though none showed themselves. They walked for several minutes before a blurry haze in the distance resolved to a bright white archway over a pair of double doors, also pure white.

"Wow, that looks straight out of a game or something," said Tristan. "Like a portal between worlds."

"It basically is a portal between worlds. Fantasy forest here, cold zoo hallway on the other side."

"We hope."

Piper gazed up. "Do you have to keep saying spooky stuff?"

"Sorry. Can't help it. You know you'd have laughed if we weren't likely to be killed by a troll."

She jabbed a finger in his side, but giggled anyway.

He rubbed the spot, overacting pain.

A twig snapped to the left.

Piper gasped and stopped short, hesitating for an instant before dragging Tristan behind a thick tree.

"No sense hiding," said a man's voice, rich, deep, and melodic.

She peered around the trunk.

A man with long, curly brown hair, slender horns stretching

upward from his temples, and goat-like legs wandered into view. He appeared to be wearing furry pants, but she had a feeling the fur belonged to him. Dark eyebrows framed a handsome, chiseled face with a sharp chin. Except for the legs, he looked like the sort of man who appeared on the covers of the books Mom liked, but refused to admit she read.

"Hi," said Piper.

The beautiful man bowed, twirling his right hand. "Greetings. What brings you to this place?"

"Looking for a door," said Tristan. "We need to stop the troll from hurting the centaurs."

"Oh, that's quite noble. Trolls are such simple, stupid beings."

Piper stepped out from behind the tree and took a few steps closer. "Who are you?"

He raised an eyebrow.

"Umm. Did I say something wrong?"

"I am surprised you asked *who* I am and not what, considering who you are."

She peered up at him. "Who I am? And you're talking to me, so you're obviously a person of some kind. It's rude to refer to people as 'whats.'"

"Hmm. Indeed." He traced his fingers over her cheek. "My name is Orothien, and I am a satyr."

"Hello, Orothien. I'm Piper, and this is my friend Tristan."

"What are you doing down here in such a dangerous place?" He continued brushing his fingers at her cheek.

The touch sent tingles down her back, but not pleasant ones. This satyr seemed friendly, but a note of guarded hostility lurked below the surface. Despite wanting to back away from his touch, she couldn't bring herself to, like her legs refused to obey. "My grandfather was wrong to trap you down here. I'm trying to set everyone free."

Orothien smiled. "But, child, the wards are down. I already *am* free." His caressing hand ceased. Sharp taloned fingernails scraped at her throat and the back of her neck. "All that's left is for me to punish those responsible for my imprisonment."

"Get off her!" shouted Tristan.

"He's already dead," whispered Piper. "My grandfather's dead."

He teased the point of his thumb talon around her throat, the knife-sharp edge raking her skin. "Hmm, but you are his descendant." Claws stopped pressing into her neck. Again, he brushed his hand over her cheek in a gesture of affection that made all the hairs on the backs of her arms stand up. "However, since you truly wanted to set me free, I will give you a sporting chance. A pity your grandfather is already dead, so I cannot kill him for what he has done."

"I didn't even know him," said Piper.

Orothien turned away, walking around her in a slow, deliberate stride. "You are his descendant, so ending your life would satisfy my revenge. Or would you prefer I take your father's life instead?"

Piper didn't want to die, but she couldn't tell him to kill her father, so she remained quiet.

The satyr chuckled. "You are young, and perhaps innocent of this prison." He snapped his fingers. "I shall give you a fair chance, child. A proper fey challenge."

"Y-you're not going to kill me?"

Orothien grinned. "That all depends on you. Injustice demands *some* recompense. One does not cross a satyr without a debt being paid." He stopped walking circles around her, took two steps back, and adopted a regal stance. "Little Piper, I challenge you to a duel." Before she could protest, he held up a pan flute. "Of music."

"B-but... I don't know how to play them." She bit her lip.

"What?" Orothien's eyes shot open wide and he tilted his head in shock. A passing blue jay landed on one of his twelve-inch horns. "That is simply wrong."

Tristan grimaced. He twitched as if trying to lift his legs with his feet nailed to the ground.

"Why is that wrong?" asked Piper.

"You are named Piper, yet you cannot play the pipes?" Orothien threw his head back and laughed, startling the jay to wing. "I simply cannot allow that crime to exist."

She cringed. "Please don't hurt me."

"So sad. I must fix the tragedy of your name with all due haste." Orothien closed the distance to her with two quick hops. He bent forward as if to kiss her full on the lips and put a finger under her chin.

Piper wanted to break and run, but her body refused to move even to blink one eye.

An instant before his lips met hers, the finger at her chin pushed her head to the right. Orothien breathed into her left ear. The rush of air spun into a swirling melody of flute tones that washed over her mind. Once a momentary blur of confusion faded, she felt as though she'd been playing panpipes for years. Understanding of technique and tempo, of how to breathe and project the music came out of nowhere. Songs played and unwound in her thoughts, melodies she knew all the notes to, yet somehow had never heard before.

Orothien stood straight again. "There. Now you are worthy of your name."

"Wow…" She didn't quite know if she should thank him or still be terrified. "So, what shall we play for a duel?"

"Oh, no." He shook his head. "I have shared my knowledge with you, so it would be like dueling myself. A contest one can never win. If you fight yourself, no matter the outcome, you lose."

"Umm." She blinked. "Why can't I move?"

"Because, I do not wish you to move." Orothien smiled. "However, we shall still play, but this is no duel."

"Why?" She struggled, but her body refused to budge.

"The answer to that is always 'because.' There is never a reason not to play!" Orothien winked. He grasped her wrist, lifted her right arm, and placed the panpipes in her grip. With a gracious bow, backed up a few steps and produced another set from thin air, which he raised to his lips. "*Dance of the Wood Elf.*"

She knew the song, but shouldn't. She raised her flute to play, but didn't want to. Wood touched her lips, and she breathed the music into the pipes. Orothien leapt and spun into a dance, energetic, upbeat notes flying from his instrument. Piper reacted accordingly, knowing her smaller flute and smaller lungs couldn't overpower him. Training she'd never had took over and she played accompaniment, resulting in an intoxicating melody that could've pulled the most curmudgeonly old man out of his chair to dance.

Piper stood in place, playing her heart out while Orothien whirled around, prancing and jumping. Tristan threw himself into motion, spinning and jumping about, lost to the dance. He flailed like a marionette in the hands of an insane puppeteer. She and the satyr played and played, a song that seemed to have no end. Time blurred and spun, and before she knew it, the boy collapsed in a heap nearby.

Orothien twirled on one hoof with a high trilling note that ended the song with a grand finale. Piper played a little flourish under it, then lowered her arms. Her chest ached from so much pumping air, but otherwise, she felt only a little tired.

Tristan, his face covered in sweat, had passed clear out.

"What did you do to Tristan?" She threw all her strength against the paralysis that had kept her rooted to the ground, but discovered herself free when she hurled herself to the ground.

"Oh… that was graceful," said Orothien.

Ignoring him, she crawled over and shook Tristan, who didn't react. He still seemed to be breathing, which let her relax a little.

"What did you do to him!" shouted Piper.

"*We* made him dance. The boy is fine." Orothien waved dismissively. "He's merely tired."

"How did you do that?"

He walked over to stand beside her, shaking his head. "My my, child. You do not listen. *We* did that. The music."

Of course. She knew how to play *magic* songs that could charm people. Wonder flashed to anger. "You *made* me do that to him."

"Satyrs have many talents." He winked. "My favorite is charming ladies. Alas, you are far too young for me to elaborate on that subject." He stroked his goatee a few times. "But now that the pleasantries of music and the tragedy of your name have been corrected…"

Piper stood up, moving protectively over Tristan. "Duel?"

"No. We cannot duel now." He flicked his arm out and placed a razor sharp claw at her throat. "I could make it quick."

She held her chin high. "Umm. You don't really *have* to kill me, you know. I think my grandfather was horrible."

"Oh, but I must have *some* revenge, you see. I simply cannot let this go. I offer you a riddle, then. Solve it, and you shall keep your life."

"And if I don't accept, you cut my throat. Not much of a choice, really. Okay. I accept your riddle."

Orothien lowered his claw. "Excellent. I'm glad you accepted. You must believe that I take no pleasure in harming innocent children. But, a wrong must be answered for. I wish you the best of luck." He leaned close. "We often must do things we dislike because we must. I do not *want* to harm you, so please don't fail."

"I—"

He breathed over her face and the world went black.

An instant later, Piper's vision cleared. Where once had been forest, she lay sprawled in the dirt, staring at a cave wall. The panpipes hung around her neck on a leather cord and a small rolled-up paper dangled from her fingers.

She looked down at it. Shaking hands had a difficult time opening the scroll, but she managed to unfurl it and read.

And now, the riddle.

Piper girl who couldn't play,
Until I showed her the way.
Gone is her companion dear,
So far away, yet so near.
A boy, locked enclosure hangs,
O'er flaming breath, claws, and fangs.
The key she lost, I have found,
Dangles high up off the ground.
Above a beast not so mild,
Loves to feast upon the child.
Careful quiet in the cave,
Noise will dig her early grave.

Piper gasped and turned away from the wall, sitting up. The chamber held nothing but her and a dirt floor. Tracks that looked like her footprints led from where she stood to the only way out.

I walked here? I don't remember… Ooh! He charmed me! She gazed around at the plain grey stone, sure only that she remained somewhere within the zoo, clearly in a place she hadn't gone before… with something that would eat her.

Her heart thumped in her chest. The Satyr wouldn't kill her, but whatever lived here would.

22

DRAGON IN A BOTTLE

Fear and anger got into a fistfight in Piper's heart. She glared at the flimsy scroll in her hands.

"Gone is her companion dear," she whispered. *He's kidnapped Tristan!* "Locked enclosure... flaming breath." She stopped herself from shouting in anger. If she made too much noise, whatever monster she'd been trapped with would find her.

"They key she lost..." Her stomach sank. She threaded her hand into her pocket, and grabbed only cloth. "No... Why? Why would he steal the key?"

Her lip quivered. Before the tears started, she curled up and hid her face behind her knees. *Crying isn't going to help. He's going to kill Tristan too if I mess up. Grr!* She wiped her face and tried not to think about being scared. More than anything, she wanted to shout for her parents, but shouting would only get her hurt.

She stared at the footprints she must've left walking in here. *If I just walked right in, I can just walk right out.* Step by step, she traced her path back to the cave opening. A narrow passage connected the chamber to a larger cave. Both directions looked the same. She grasped some of her hair and held it out, noting that the strands drifted to the right.

Air's coming from the left. She went that way, keeping one hand on the stone beside her.

A heavy rumble from up ahead made the cave shudder. Piper bit her arm to stifle a yelp of fear, and leapt against the wall, tucking into a shadowy crag. Her body wouldn't stop shaking. The note made it pretty clear that the monster in whatever enclosure she'd landed in would tear her apart if it found her. Orothien wanted to kill her, or at least risk her life over some stupid riddle.

She fumed, angry at the pointlessness of it. Why should he punish her for something her grandfather—a man she'd never seen and didn't even like—did? It sounded as dumb as the samurai from a novel she'd read who killed themselves over small errors. They didn't have to do that either, over something stupid like 'honor' that people made up.

If she ever saw that satyr again, she'd give him a good yelling at… assuming he didn't just charm her and make her go jump in the lake.

The rumbling happened again, suggesting whatever monster she had to sneak past had quite a bit of size. She waited there in the shadows, listening and watching. Tristan was in trouble too, but the riddle didn't sound like she had to rush. Still, the less time she left him in mortal danger, the better.

Nothing happened for a few minutes, so she risked emerging from the shadows and creeping up the cave tunnel. Eventually, after a few turns and bends, she spotted daylight on the ground. With hard stone along the floor, she couldn't tell by footprints if she'd come this way, but there hadn't been any branching passages.

Sunlight, even fake sunlight, gave her hope, and she got up to a light run into a small bend—and skidded to a halt, nose-to-immense-nose with a dragon.

As big as a small house, it lay curled up like a housecat right outside the cave. Scales of dark crimson burnished black at the ends made it look lightly burned. Two pairs of horns jutted from the top of its head, one set huge, the other small and bent outward at a sharper angle. The long, pointed snoot drifted closer. Nostrils big enough to inhale watermelons whole blasted her with hot, wet air that stank of bad eggs. If it opened its mouth, she could've walked down its throat without ducking.

She stared silently for a few seconds before she lost control of herself and screamed. Panic took her, and she sprinted back into the cave, running so fast she missed the passage to the chamber she'd started in and skidded to a stop in an even bigger one, covered in a mass of dead vegetation that stank like moldy hay.

Rumbling approached, shaking the whole chamber.

Crap!

Rapid breathing made her dizzy. She spun, searching for a place to hide. Firelight reflected on the walls out in the cave, getting brighter… and brighter.

Piper spotted a pair of stalagmites jutting up from the floor near the wall. She ran over the spongy layer of vegetation and slid to a stop not a full second before the dragon entered the room. Two short jets of flame flared from its nostrils, seeming more a light source than an attack. It swung its car-sized head side to side, and zeroed in on her right away.

The dragon stared at her, motionless.

Piper flattened herself against the stone behind her, shaking. She'd never before in her life had an accident in her pants, but if that thing took one step closer, she probably would. Whimpering, she tried to hold as still and silent as possible. Maybe the satyr's riddle meant it would only hurt her if she made too much noise.

Damn! Why did I scream? That made it angry.

Sniffing, the dragon slinked into the cave, heading right toward her. The little rock spires she'd hidden behind wouldn't slow this thing down at all. She considered (for a split second) trying to crouch and hide, but instead, decided to try running.

Somehow managing not to scream (or wet herself) she sprinted to the left, hugging the wall. The dragon spun after her like a cat chasing a mouse. It thrust its right clawed hand out against the wall, blocking her. She yelped and backpedaled, going the other way—until its left arm blocked her again.

Trapped between two huge clawed hands, she rolled to put her back against the wall and stared up at it. Each of its eyes had to be as big as a house window, brilliant gold and full of thousands of folds and lines. She'd have thought it astoundingly beautiful if not for being seconds away from a gruesome death.

The way it stood, she could run under it, maybe duck to the side halfway down its belly. She looked back and forth between the floor beneath it and its face. The dragon tilted its head like a bewildered dog.

Huh? What? It's confused? Her heart beat so fast she felt dizzy.

"Hi," she said in a sugary voice. "Nice dragon. Pretty dragon. Who's a good boy?"

The dragon furrowed its eyebrows. "I am no dog. Simple human." He shook his head, grumbling about rude children.

Her jaw hung open.

"What are you doing here?" bellowed the dragon.

She dug her fingers into the wall. "Umm. Do you eat people?"

"Oh, heavens no." The dragon attempted to smile.

Piper slouched with relief.

"Humans these days are far too high in sugar, and I'm watching my weight."

She choked.

"Why did you scream before?"

"I'm sorry." She looked down. "You're a big… dragon and the satyr said you'd eat me."

"Oh, him." The dragon rolled his eyes. "Don't believe everything a satyr tells you. They always play games and spin half-truths, especially to pretty girls."

"You think I'm pretty?" She looked up, eyebrows together.

"I suppose, among humans. I am a dragon after all, what do I know of human looks?"

Piper folded her arms.

"That's better. Not so frightened now." He backed up a few steps and reclined on the floor. "So, why are you here?"

She told him about the satyr, the riddle, Tristan and the key missing, and being charmed into the cave somehow.

"Ahh. Satyrs and their pranks."

Still shaking somewhat, Piper approached and reached out to touch his chin. She yanked her hand back from scales much hotter than she expected before tapping them, and easing her hand down again onto a surface as warm as a new-drawn bath. Hot, but not to the point of burning. For a moment, she rubbed under his chin. Her fear shifted to awe that such beings as dragons were real.

"I am not a dog, but that feels quite pleasant."

"You're a dragon..."

He chuckled. "Rather observant of you to point out."

"You don't belong in this place. I'm going to set you free."

A somber sigh flooded the cave with a rumble of stinky air. "I cannot leave, child. I have grown too big to fit down the corridors. Your grandfather brought me here over fifty years ago, and even then, they had difficulty squeezing me through."

"There's got to be some way."

The last two feet of his mouth curled upward, suggesting a weak smile. "I fear not. But I have plenty of space here at least. Enough not to feel too crowded."

Piper leaned against the side of his face, rubbing a hand down the scales. "I'm sorry. He was so cruel. If there's anything I can do to set you free, I will."

"Oh, girl. You should wish for things within your grasp. Do not worry about me."

"My friend is in trouble. The satyr's going to hurt him, too."

"Is he now?"

"Yes. I have to solve this riddle or I'm going to die."

The dragon stretched out and reclined on his side. "Riddle? Let us hear it then."

She held up the paper and read it to him.

"As far as I know," said the dragon, "The chimera is the only other fire-breathing creature here. I can breathe flame, but your companion is not here, nor would I cook him."

"What's a chimera?" asked Piper.

"A curious creature indeed. It appears much like a lion, with the head of a goat sticking up out of its back, and a long snake for a tail."

She blinked. "*That* breathes fire?"

"Yes. The goat head does. The lion simply bites, as does the serpent."

"Is it smart? Would it hurt Tristan?"

"No more so than a lion or a goat would be, and it would likely attack him, yes. The two of you are small and would be prey to it." The dragon leaned close and inhaled through its nose so hard her hair whipped forward. "And you smell rather tasty."

She pulled her hair away from her face, tucking it back behind her shoulders before smirking. "Thanks… I think. So I need to find the chimera and I find Tristan."

"You should get your key first. The riddle mentions a cage. I'd wager it locked."

Piper slouched, staring down at her sneakers. "Why did he do this?" She whined. "Okay. The key." She held up the note and read, "The key she lost, I have found, dangles high up off the ground. Above a beast not so mild, loves to feast upon the child."

"Hmm," said the dragon.

"I didn't lose it. He *stole* it." She grumbled, rubbing her leg over the pocket.

"Indeed."

"He hid the key somewhere another monster will eat me. Wow. Spiders, that naga, the troll…"

"I believe"—the dragon raised one clawed finger—"he refers to things which *prefer* to eat children. The troll would eat a car tire if it found one."

Piper laughed. "It's weird to hear a dragon talk about cars."

"Why is that strange to you?"

"Umm. Because." She shrugged. "We only see dragons in stories about long ago when cars didn't exist. Bugbear!"

"That's one, yes. I believe there is a lamia around as well."

"Never heard of that." Piper re-read the riddle.

"Tragic story. One tale claims a woman named Lamia was cursed long ago by the gods' jealousy and transformed into a demon, forced to feast upon children. They say as a mortal woman, she became a mistress to a god. The god's jealous wife stole all of Lamia's children, and out of her grief, she became insane and began to devour the babies of others."

Piper gasped, covering her mouth.

"Others believe there was no single woman named Lamia, but lamiae are creatures named for this mythological event. Nocturnal spirits who sneak into unsecured houses and feast upon babes."

She shivered. "That's… horrible. It's also really weird to hear a dragon call something mythological."

He laughed, rattling the air in her chest.

"Okay, so bugbear or lamia is probably where the key is. How could something love to hurt kids?"

"The lamia does not love her nature. She laments it constantly."

Piper pointed up at him. "It's gotta be the bugbear then. The riddle says 'loves to feast upon the child.'"

The dragon's eyebrow ridges climbed. "Indeed. A good point."

She shook with nervousness. "What should I do if the bugbear sees me?"

"At that point you would have two choices. One: run away. Two: be dinner."

"You're not helping," deadpanned Piper.

He smiled. "Am I incorrect?"

"No, but it's not helpful." She rolled the riddle paper up and stuck it in her pocket. "I have work to do. I'll be back. If I can find any way to get you out of here, I will."

"I appreciate the notion." The dragon heaved a sigh out his nose that blasted her with warm air, knocking her back a step and fluttering her hair. "But do not burden yourself with such a futile task."

She turned toward the cave exit. "I can't give up before I even try."

He closed his eyes. "I wish you luck saving your friend. Be careful."

If I was careful, I wouldn't be down here at all. "I will."

Piper hurried up the cave to the exit, where it opened to a rolling grassy plain. Like the centaur's enclosure, this one had so much space she couldn't see the exits. Distant mountains behind her appeared miles and miles away, impossible and surely not real. She looked around for a moment more before hurrying forward. She'd eventually find a wall.

Ten minutes of walking later, the endless plains in front of her blurred to a silvery mist and then into a plain, grey wall.

"Eep!" She stopped, standing in a four-foot wide space with concrete in front of her and puffy white cloud behind her. Piper backed up into the mist. Two steps, and the wall disappeared, again looking like miles of plains. She advanced again, and turned to blink at the cloud wall. "Wow. It's some kind of illusion. This is actual magic."

In the plain space outside of the enchantment, the physical wall followed a long, sloping curve. One side bent out of sight behind the fog so far away it hurt to think about walking that far. The other bend, much closer, only looked to be as long as her new backyard. *This room is huge… well… okay, dragon. Needs a lot of space.* She decided to head toward the nearer bend, but stopped a minute later when she reached a gnome tunnel. It didn't have a hatch, but she figured it didn't need one since this cage's occupant, a dragon, could never possibly fit in there—unlike the spiders or the naga.

With brownies and bog pixies likely roaming everywhere, she thought it wise to stay out of sight as much as possible. Still, she had no idea where she was in the zoo or where the bugbear lived. Considering it sounded like an 'evil' creature, her grandfather had most likely put it down the same hallway with the troll, brownies, and such. They had never made it past the brownie enclosure, but that hallway had kept going.

"Gnomes?" yelled Piper. "I could really use help."

She listened to her voice echo a few times, but no little old men appeared. Then again, they didn't exactly rush to show themselves before. With chaos in the zoo, they probably had quite a bit to do and couldn't spare the time to talk to her.

Piper crawled into the gnome tunnel, her panpipes swinging from the leather cord around her neck. "I've got a lot to do, too."

23

THE SMALL MATTER OF A KEY

The gnome passage hit a fork about three minutes later. She started down the left branch, but when the gossamer whiteness of spider silk became obvious up ahead, decided to backtrack and go the other way. A voice, belonging to the naga, echoed in another offshoot on her left not far from there.

She ignored that one.

Three openings later, she decided to check out a left turn and crawled maybe fifty yards to a room full of steel cabinets. She climbed out and stood, grateful for the momentary freedom from the tight passageway. A long counter ran along the wall to her left, a huge industrial stove with a flat grill section on her right.

This is one of the places in the food court!

She trotted to a door and looked out at a space behind a counter. An empty cake stand stood by an old-fashioned cash register. Two cooler cabinets on the left held nothing but shelves. Beyond the counter, the food court hung in dark and eerie silence. Without a creature enclosure nearby, the only light came from a few feeble crystal lamps. Enough to see the corners of surfaces, but little else.

"Nyrx!" shouted a tiny voice.

Piper spun to her right and locked eyes with a pudgy, misshapen bog pixie. It nocked an arrow while filling its lungs, probably to shout for more pixies.

She raised an arm to protect her eyes and charged at it. A bee sting hit her in the forehead, but she managed to grab the pixie out of midair. Instead of making noise, it bit her finger. Snarling from pain, Piper refused to let go and rushed a few steps left to stuff the hideous little critter into the cake stand. After slamming the glass lid down over it, she backed away and plucked the arrow out of her forehead.

"Ow," she muttered, when the point unstuck from bone. "Little b… bugger."

The bog pixie pounded his tiny fists on the glass, shouting and screaming, but only a muted chattering made it past the heavy glass lid.

I better get out of here before its friends show up.

She ran back into the kitchen and slid into the gnome tunnel. Having a frame of reference allowed her to do precisely what she didn't want to: travel *toward* the hallway where all the evil things lived.

For what felt like hours, she crawled and crawled, avoiding any passage with too much noise or the chittering of small, sinister creatures. Once or twice, she randomly chose a turn, while trying to maintain a mental sense of direction.

Eventually, a whiff of seawater attracted her to a passageway that ended at a hatch. Fortunately, it wasn't locked, and opened with the simple turn of a handle. She crawled out into a tall chamber full of giant pipes, as well as three bulbous tanks. Metal grating stairs on both long sides of the rectangular room led up to grid walkways by heavy doors that looked like they belonged in submarines, thick and concave with wheels in the middle to open them. The ceiling hung a good five stories over her head, and the smallest pipe appeared wide enough for her to slide down inside it. Valves and control mechanisms stood along the narrow wall at the opposite end, near some metal cabinets.

She gazed around at huge pumps, components she assumed to clean the water in the mermaid tank, and some electrical boxes up near the ceiling. In a hurry, and tired of crawling, Piper ran up the nearer stairwell to the door, at about the second story level along the wall. Grunting and straining, she eventually managed to get the wheel to turn, and heaved her whole body into the door to push it outward.

As soon as she could slip past the gap, she did so, and crept to the end of a short hall, peering into the corridor beyond. Far to her left sat the empty mermaid tank. To the right, the 'public' zoo passageway led off to an eventual T with another right turn a short distance from the end. Nothing moved or made noise here, so she decided to risk running around in the open for the sake of speed.

The right turn connected to a passage with a long, unbroken window. Behind it, an arrangement of pool and rocks looked like a cross between a seal pit and a section of rocky coastline by the ocean. The sign read "Coming soon: Selkies."

Whew. He never caught any.

She continued straight to the T. Another window spanned the wall in front of her, with a landscape of tundra and boulders and distant ruins that reminded her of a movie she'd watched set in ancient Greece. Piper tiptoed over to the sign only long enough to see the word 'Lamia' at the top before the overwhelming need to get away from it made her run.

I've gotta be close. Grandpa groups stuff together. Both kid-eating monsters should be in the same place.

She jogged down the curve, slowing so her sneakers didn't make quite so much noise. Soon after the hallway straightened, an enclosure window began. This one peered into a dark pine forest with patches of fog here and there. The scenery fit what her imagination had conjured up while reading a Victorian vampire novel awhile back, where everyone still had horses instead of cars. It didn't call out any particular location, and could've been the Pacific Northwest as easily as some place in Germany.

Piper held her hands over her chest as if it might keep her heart from exploding. Inch by inch, she made her way along the window to the yellow sign.

Bugbear

Found: Wales

The frightening bugbear has been a creature of myth and legend for generations, often used to scare misbehaving children. They love to feast upon human flesh, especially that of young children, though they are brutish and slow to react. In open land, they can outrun even horses, and have been known to wipe out entire parties of twenty men sent to destroy them. Note to visitors: Please do not allow small children too close to the glass, as it may enrage the creature.

She gulped, but forced herself to lean up to the glass. Deep in the woods, stood a dark wooden cottage covered in claw gouges and moss. A glint of brass above the roof drew her attention to something tiny hanging from a branch.

The key!

A distant brownie screeched, followed by an explosion of even smaller voices cackling.

Piper spun to put her back to the window. She resumed breathing again a few seconds later when she didn't see any creatures approaching. Fanning herself, she studied the bugbear enclosure. The corridor turned a corner to the right a good distance away, and the window followed. All the noises of bog pixies, brownies, and other voices came from that direction, so she did *not* want to peek around. If anything saw her, she'd be in a heap of trouble. She felt like a spy who'd snuck deep into an enemy base. Her grandfather had put all the bad creatures in one place, and she'd made it to the innermost point.

Not the place she wanted to be.

Near the end of the curve where the bugbear window started, she crawled into a gnome tunnel she hoped would let her enter the most dangerous place yet. None of the enclosures, except for the mermaid's, had 'people doors,' so she didn't even bother hunting for one here.

A forty-yard crawl brought her to a right branch, which led out to the forest inside the bugbear's room. She wondered if it lacked the strength to break the heavy glass like the troll, or if it chose to remain here. Maybe it had already gotten out somehow via magic and she didn't even have to worry.

The damp air smelled like dirt and dead plants, and the ground left her hands wet from crawling on it. A few feet from the gnome tunnel, she stood and dusted her hands off before sneaking up to the nearest tree. After listening to silence for a minute, she hurried from there to another tree, and hid behind it, peering at the cabin.

Her key dangled on a string above the roof, from a branch attached to a tree behind the house. Getting to it would require climbing either the tree or the house, neither of which sounded fun. She moved ahead to the next nearest tree, and hid behind it.

The cottage door swung open, revealing a huge black bear. Its face had somewhat-human features, expressive eyes and a mouth somewhat like a bear's snoot. A snarl exposed fangs as long as table knives. Its right eye emitted a dull, golden glow, though a deep scar ran down its face over the left eye, which didn't emit any light. The bugbear reared up on its back legs, taking on a stature a little closer to human. However, its long arms, an extended chest that would make professional bodybuilders feel tiny, and shortish legs, made the creature far more bearlike than man. Malice radiated from the creature. It sniffed at the air for a second or two before loping forward, heading straight at her, drooling and snarling.

Piper pushed herself off the tree and ran as hard as she could to the gnome tunnel. She dove to the ground and slid in on her chest, a clawed hand scratching at the concrete inches behind her sneakers. Scrambling back on all fours, she shrieked and kicked, staring at the thrashing paw that almost couldn't fit in the tunnel.

It hadn't looked *that* big from far away, and she certainly hadn't expected it to cross sixty yards of forest in the time it took her to run thirty feet. Dizzy from fear, Piper curled up on her side and wept.

The bugbear gave up trying to reach into the gnome passage a few minutes later and withdrew its hand. Piper twitched with every *snap* of a twig or rustle of leaves as it walked off. Once her breathing slowed to normal, she rolled up onto all fours and started to crawl back to the hallway. Too much. Too scary. She needed her parents.

She stopped after three feet.

"I can't just leave Tristan." She looked back and sighed. Head bowed, she took a few deep breaths, searching for courage, then turned around and crawled once more toward the bugbear forest. "I can do this."

As soon as she emerged from the tunnel, the bugbear raced out of the cabin, sniffing the air. Piper managed not to scream and ducked out of sight, scooting away from the opening. She *did* scream soon after, when the enormous black clawed hand filled the passage.

Piper crab-walked away from the scratching claws, her head swimming with anger, fear, and grief. "This isn't fair! That… that thing can smell me! How am I supposed to get that key!? I can't even get five feet out of the tunnel!"

Eventually, the bugbear tired of grabbing at air and withdrew its hand. It lingered by the end of the gnome passage, sniffing and snorting for some time. Piper curled in a ball, crying with her face pressed to her knees. She wouldn't be able to find Tristan and save him before the chimera killed him. All he'd ever wanted was a friend, and being *her* friend cost him his life.

She tried to think of a way to reach the key, but nothing that wouldn't get her eaten came to mind. Somewhere, Tristan sat in a cage, with only a matter of time before her failure would kill him.

"Stupid satyr! How am I supposed to sneak past a monster that can smell me from a mile away!? I'm trying to *help* you. Why are you so mean?"

Lost to grief, Piper sobbed.

A soft bell-tone chimed nearby a little while later.

She sniffled, lifted her head, and pulled her hair away from her eyes, peering at a floating orb of blue light. It pulsed brighter while emitting another bell-tone.

"You're a wisp."

It chimed again.

"Can you help?"

Another chime, and it wobbled in place.

The sign said something about wisps leading people to what they want. "Should I follow you?"

The wisp drifted away down the tunnel, leaving the bugbear area.

"That's the wrong way," whispered Piper. "The key is inside."

It chimed.

"Okay, fine. I trust you." She rolled onto her hands and knees and crawled after it.

The wisp glided out of the tunnel into the hall. Piper scrambled to her feet and ran after it, the pan flute bouncing left and right in time with her stride. The glowing ball whipped around the corner by the lamia pen and took the left past the empty selkie enclosure. She ran to the end, following the intense blue light saturating the hallway.

It didn't seem to care about being seen, but maybe it had some way to keep the bad stuff from noticing her running around in the open. The wisp shot up the hallway toward the mermaid's tank, but hooked a left into the giant garden.

Huh? Why is it going there?

The wisp hovered by the archway until she caught up to it, out of breath from sprinting. When she got close, it glided into the garden at a walking pace. She followed it among trees for a few minutes until it came to a halt in a thick, shadowed grove, lush with the fragrance of flowers.

"Okay… I'm here." Piper looked around. "What are you leading me to?"

The wisp chimed twice.

Whispering came from the trees around and above her from dozens of tiny voices. Piper raised her arms to guard her face and fell into a squat, dreading a rain of tiny arrows. An instant before she burst with an angry shout at the wisp for leading her into a trap, the branches came alive with bright colors.

A small army of eight-inch figures, no taller than the bog pixies, but *much* prettier, crept into view. They reminded her somewhat of elves, with slender bodies and pointy ears, plus dual dragonfly-like wings. The males wore skirts made of leaves, while the women had tiny dresses woven from grass blades. Despite being somewhere between beautiful and cute, they all looked furious and pointed tiny longbows at her.

"Please don't shoot me," said Piper.

The wisp disappeared.

"Who are you?" shouted an angry female with pastel pink hair.

Two men, also with pink hair, glided down from their branch and seemed to be aiming at her eyes.

She hid her face against the bend of her left elbow, covering her eyes. "My name is Piper. I'm trapped down here. My friend's been kidnapped by a satyr and I have to get a key back from the bugbear."

"Why are you here?" asked a male voice, close to her ear.

"Uhh, the wisp led me here."

Whispering drifted around above her for a moment.

"He meant what are you doing in this place," said a female.

Piper peeked over her arm at another girl-pixie with dark violet hair and a silver bow held sideways at her hips. "I found this place only a day ago, and I think it's horrible that my grandfather put you down here. I want to set every one of you free so you can go home where you belong… except maybe the evil stuff trying to eat me."

The mood among the tiny elves lightened, and the rest of the bows lowered.

"You wish to help us flee this place?" asked the pink-haired woman.

"Yes." Piper nodded. "It's cruel. But, the satyr stole my key and my friend is in danger, and the wisp brought me here. Can you please help?"

The group drifted closer and hovered in front of her face, the steady droning of their wings creating a gentle breeze against her cheeks.

"There are magical wards that trap us here." A yellow-haired man pointed to the left.

"Aren't they off now?" asked Piper.

"The ones surrounding this garden are," said the male pixie. "There are others. Another set surrounds this prison, and a third enchantment covers the grounds outside that we cannot cross."

She narrowed her eyes. *The satyr isn't as free as he thinks he is.* "Wait… I took the mermaid out and brought her to the river. Nothing stopped her from leaving." *She did seem really scared by the gate.*

"We cannot cross the ward," said the pink-haired woman. "How did you get the mermaid past the enchantment?"

Piper shrugged. "Umm. Does the ward stop when the gate is open?"

"No," said the male with pink hair.

"We put her in a truck and drove out."

All of the pixies made a collective, "Oh" sound.

The lemon-haired woman grinned. "A human can bring magical beings across the ward, but we cannot cross it ourselves. If you held me and went past the wards, that would work, but it would cause me pain."

"That's why she whimpered." Piper felt bad for hurting her, but the mermaid wanted to go, and never complained or warned her it would cause pain.

The pixies nodded.

"I need to save my friend, and I need the key to do that. I also need the key back to help you escape. Can you do anything to help me get past the bugbear? I promise I will turn off all the wards so you can go home."

"I will help," said the pink-haired woman. "It is dangerous for us to leave this garden, but for a chance to return to our homes, I will take the risk." She landed on Piper's shoulder.

"Thank you! What do I do?"

"Go back there. I will use my magic when we are closer."

Piper waved to the cloud of floating tiny elves and ran back the way she'd come in. It felt ridiculous asking a tiny woman for help against a massive bear-shaped monster, but she had no better ideas.

Thinking that she might need to save her energy to run from the bugbear, she fast-walked down the corridor past the selkie room, and headed around the corner again to the gnome tunnel. Two bog pixies hovered near the corner, both whirling around at the squeak of her sneakers.

The pixie on her shoulder zipped into the air, firing two arrows in rapid succession. Both bog pixies spiraled to the floor, crashing with a sound like dropped steaks. Piper didn't stare long, and scurried out of sight into the tunnel. Once she'd crawled a few feet away from the opening, she blinked at the friendly pixie.

"You fight with the bad ones?"

"Yes. Meadow pixies and bog pixies are deadly enemies." She puffed out her chest. "Meadow pixies are much stronger, but there are lots more of them than us."

"I don't like them either. They shot me a bunch of times."

The meadow pixie giggled. "Pixie arrows don't hurt humans much. They are foolish, but they do like to cause pain."

Piper scooted close to the end of the tunnel. "If I go out there, the bugbear will smell me. I need to get that key up over the house."

"Wait here." The meadow pixie zipped off in a streak of pink light.

The little energy comet shot over to the key, but bounced away with a bright flash and a *crack* like a gunshot.

"Oh no!" Piper gasped.

A moment later, one rather ticked-off pixie flew back into the tunnel. Aside from some mild scorch marks, she didn't look hurt. "Stupid satyr."

"I know, right?" Piper grasped her like a Barbie doll and wiped smudge from her face.

"Only you can touch it. It's enchanted." The pixie glided up from her hand. "Time for magic." She booped Piper on the nose.

In seconds, the little woman grew to adult height. Piper found herself not quite as tall as her shoulders, kinda like Mom. "Wow. Are you going to fight the bugbear?"

"No." The pixie pointed at the walls. "I'm not big. You're small."

Piper looked around and noticed the gnome tunnel had become a giant passageway. "Whoa…"

The pixie walked up behind her, wrapped her in her arms, and took off, wings buzzing. They made it about twenty seconds before the pixie ran out of energy and crashed into grass up to Piper's neck.

"Sorry," gasped the pixie. "We're not good at carrying things."

"Well, the bugbear didn't come charging after me, so maybe I'm too small to smell. That'll work." She pulled the pixie back to her feet. "We can walk."

The bugbear's cottage had probably been about fifty yards away from the end of the gnome tunnel. Being seven inches tall made the distance feel more like fifty miles. Piper shoved grass blades almost as thick as her arm out of her way, climbed over roots, and almost fell into in a lake that normally would've been a puddle barely up to her ankle.

Dirt shifted, exposing a brown furry spider as big as a horse. It came running at Piper, but slid to a stop, dead, with two arrows sticking out of its face.

"Gah!" Piper yelled, shaking. "Holy crap… how can you stand being this small!"

The pixie shrugged. "It's what I am. But we usually don't walk. These hiding spiders can't reach us. They also don't live where I'm from. This is an evil, unnatural forest."

"It's fake," said Piper. "My grandfather tried to copy where the bugbear's from, but it isn't real."

"Illusions." The pixie nodded. "How does a human have so much magic?"

"I don't know." Over about twenty minutes of walking, Piper told the pixie all about the inheritance, moving, never having met the grandfather, and the boggart loose in the house.

"Sorry," said the pixie.

"What for?"

"The boggart is our fault." She grimaced. "My brother hid in the human's pocket to escape the garden. We were trying to escape. He broke the ward on the boggart's glass, hoping it would… umm."

"Kill him?" Piper stopped to look back at the pixie.

The pink-haired woman pouted at the ground.

"It didn't, but it's all right. If someone locked me up in a place like this, I'd want to kill him too."

"Thank you for forgiving us." The pixie smiled. "You should hang a horseshoe over the doors to get rid of it."

"That will really work? I read that, but I wasn't sure if it would… 'course, the salt did."

"Yes. Boggarts will play mean games on people in bed. Put a pile of salt by the foot."

A loud growling snort startled Piper into a low crouch. The bugbear's house, more of a huge skyscraper now, sat a short distance away across a clearing of dirt. Its creepy bear-man face poked out of the door, sniffing the air.

Holy crap. It can still smell me and I'm like mouse sized.

The pixie pointed left. Piper scurried out of the grass to hide among the roots of a tree. Sniffing still, the bugbear crept out of the house, drifting toward her.

"Bugbears smell children doing bad things," whispered the pixie. "Running away from home, stealing, staying out too late."

Piper looked at the… not so little woman. "I'm not being bad. I'm trapped in a dangerous place."

She shrugged. "It still smells kids who run off alone."

Grr. "Help me, please," whispered Piper.

The pixie zipped into the air, shot the bugbear in the nose, and dashed off into the trees. Enraged, the massive creature bounded after her, shaking the ground so hard it knocked Piper over. She stayed down, hiding behind the roots until the earth ceased shuddering. Hoping the bugbear had gone far enough away, she sprinted around the tree and bee-lined for the open door. Being this small, she had no chance of climbing the tree, so the house would have to do.

Inside, the place stank like wet dog and spoiled meat. The sickening thought hit her of what the gnomes fed this thing. Hopefully, they brought it beef or venison or something, and not delinquent children. The gnomes seemed far too nice to do something so awful.

Piper hurried across floorboards as wide as cars, careful not to step in the gaps between them, which could trap her foot, breaking her ankle. She ducked under a strut between the legs of a chair, hiding in the shadow of the table while searching for a way to go upward. A dormant fireplace with a chimney looked like a decent option, if the bricks could give her a place to grab onto. Then again, if she slipped, a seven-inch-tall girl falling down a chimney wouldn't end well.

She scurried over to a foul-smelling bed and climbed the blankets up to the mattress. Trying to run across a hay-packed cloth bag sent her falling face-first several times, but she made it to the pillow end and shimmied up onto the headboard. From there, she walked to a little night table that held a bowl of bones, which looked enough like beef that she didn't freak out.

After scurrying across the table, she jumped up and grabbed the edge of a shelf. Grunting, she climbed up until she got a knee on the wood, and rolled forward, out of breath. While she lay there gasping for air, the bugbear wandered back in. It stopped three paces in and started sniffing.

She scooted behind a candle bigger than a refrigerator, flattened herself against it, standing pin straight and still.

Snorts and stomps continued for a while before the bugbear lumbered outside again. Piper darted to the end of the shelf, searching for somewhere to go, but nothing looked like a route to keep climbing.

The pixie zoomed in.

"Here!" shouted Piper.

She flew to the shelf and landed. "Hurry. He's right outside."

"Can you fly me up the chimney?"

"I think so."

Piper approached the edge and held her arms up.

The pixie grabbed her from behind again and leaned forward, falling. Loud buzzing from her wings followed them across the room in a barely-controlled corkscrew flight. Piper screamed, closing her eyes and bracing for a crash into the stone mantle. Her breakfast almost erupted out her nostrils at a sudden shift in direction from forward to straight up.

When no painful stop happened, she opened one eye. The pixie strained to haul her straight up inside a huge brick tunnel covered in soot. Her new friend ran out of steam right as they reached the end, unable to summon the strength to fly over the top. Piper grabbed the brick's edge, and pulled, dragging them both to a safe perch atop the chimney.

The pixie rolled onto her back, panting. "Escaping is exhausting."

"Yeah." Piper stared up at the fake sky, her head spinning from the fear of almost falling to her death. "We made it. Thank you."

"I see your key."

She sat up. The key she'd found in grandfather's letter hung from a branch on a twine cord, dangling over the edge of the roof, right above the front door. Piper walked around the rim of the chimney, refusing to look down into the gaping shaft. The branch went by the side, about ten (relative) feet below her. If she missed, she'd land on a thatch roof that looked reasonably soft, and probably wouldn't hurt too much despite it being close to a three-story fall.

"I'm gonna jump," said Piper.

The pixie flew over to land next to her. "Okay. You are brave. Most humans are scared of heights."

"We're more scared of falling than heights." She let out a nervous laugh. "That, and I'm not really athletic. I'm more of a book nerd."

"What's a book nerd?" asked the pixie.

"I sit around and read instead of play sports."

"Oh. I can help you jump."

"Aren't you tired?"

"Yes. Very tired, but it's not far and jumping is easier than flying."

"I think I can make it. Catch me if I miss?"

"Okay," chirped the pixie.

Piper squatted, lined up on the branch, took a deep breath, and jumped.

Time seemed to slow for the second and a half she sailed into the air. The branch flew up and mashed into her gut, knocking the wind out of her. She clung, legs dangling, seeing stars and unable to do anything but cling for a while.

"Are you okay?" asked the Pixie, hovering nearby.

Piper wheezed.

"That sounds like a no." The pixie grabbed on and pulled her up to sit on the branch. "You didn't miss, but landing on your belly was probably not smart."

"Yeah," rasped Piper. "Ow. That hurt."

"Almost there. I'll help you balance."

It took a minute or two for the pain in her stomach to fade enough to let her stand. Holding the pixie's hand while she flew alongside, Piper balance-beam walked along the branch. Easy at first, the task became difficult once the wood narrowed nearer the key. Soon, she balanced on a twig only as wide as her sneaker.

Piper lowered herself to sit, wrapped her legs around the branch, and scooted forward inches at a time with the pixie hovering nearby to help if she fell. Finally, she reached the knot in the twine, dismayed to find the cord thicker than her wrist. She grabbed and pulled, but may as well have been trying to lift a boat anchor.

Damn. Of course, the key's huge now. It's like 200 pounds to me. "I can't lift it."

The bugbear growled from within the cottage and stormed outside, roaring. Frustrated, it let out a bellow of pure rage and slammed the door, shaking the whole world. Piper slipped to the side, falling off the bobbing branch. She got a hand on the twine and swung, wrapping her arms and legs around it before sliding to the bottom, hanging next to the key. Eyes closed, she held on with all her strength, refusing to look down, or anywhere else, until the swaying stopped. Once her fear of falling subsided, she lowered her legs to stand on the bit at the key's end, clinging to the key and twine, swinging with the motion of the branch. From that dangerous perch, she gazed down at a fall equivalent to jumping from a thirty-story building.

She tried to shout for help, but only managed a voiceless rasp, her throat closed up tight.

The bugbear sniffed again, roared, and tromped up and down. It clearly smelled her, but couldn't find where the scent of 'child' came from.

"Hold on!" yelled the pixie.

Piper looked up. The pixie had landed on the branch where the twine looped around. She studied the situation, then dropped into a dive. Piper clung to the key, watching the comet of pink light fly away, turn, and come sailing back straight at her.

Uh oh. This is going to hurt.

She cringed.

The pixie crashed into her like a football linewoman, dragging her, the key, and the twine back up the branch far enough that instead of a deadly fall, she dangled only about twelve feet above thatch.

With stars dancing and popping in her vision, Piper muttered something intended to be "Good idea."

Once she could see straight again, she climbed up the twine to the knot, which had migrated down to hang about halfway between the key and the branch. Piper clung to the rope with her legs and attacked the knot. Being able to grab the exact point of cucumber-thick twine she needed to move with both hands made untying it a simple matter. She gave it a final shove and held on tight. As the knot unfurled, the key fell straight down. So did Piper.

Unfortunately, the thatch roof didn't hold even the weight of a shrunken twelve-year-old, and she punched through it like a rock. Screaming, Piper fell head over heels into the house, but landed on the bed. Striking the hay-filled stinky mattress hurt enough to stun her, but nothing felt broken.

"Ow," she muttered.

The key lay a few feet away, the bundle of twine beside it. She crawled over and grabbed the key, as tall as her waist and as thick as a broom handle. With great effort, she dragged it across the mattress until it fell to the floor with a deafening jangle of metal. That done, she ran to the corner and slid down the blanket to the floor.

And the bugbear tromped in.

Stifling a scream, Piper darted under the bed.

The monster walked right past the key without noticing it, and hurled itself down to sit at the only chair by the table. It radiated fury, its stomach rumbling. Every so often, it sniffed, but didn't get up again.

Maybe it thinks it's going crazy. It doesn't believe what it smells. She grinned. *Good. It'll stop chasing me. Now… how am I going to carry that key out of here? I can barely move it. And I'll never outrun that thing this small.*

She tapped her fingers on the floor, thinking, waiting.

Come on. Go away. Where's that pixie? Do something to make him leave!

Out of nowhere, a queasy sensation rippled around in her gut. She bit her arm to stop from burping, lest it hear her. Tingles spread over her from head to toe. The bed lowered itself on top of her. She rolled onto her back, raising her hands to catch the crushing ceiling, but realized the bed hadn't moved.

She grew.

When the world stopped moving, Piper found herself lying under the bugbear's foul-smelling bed, back to normal size.

Oh… bad timing.

The creature sniffed again in earnest, standing and running around the cabin, pawing at shelves, chairs, and the walls. She held as still as possible. Despite under the bed being the most obvious hiding place in the world, it seemed likely to fool the bugbear. It roared at the walls, long ropey threads of white drool flying off its fangs.

She cringed.

It stood in the middle of the room, huffing and snorting, wide-eyed. Like a cat chasing night spirits, it whirled without warning and charged outside.

Time to go!

Piper scooted out from under the bed and grabbed the key. She snagged the twine off the mattress and re-tied the key into an amulet, which she hung around her neck before running to the door.

She pulled it open and screamed at the bugbear, who stood right in front of her.

It roared in her face, blowing her hair back and pelting her with a few glops of drool. Her knees turned to jelly and she stumbled backward in time to avoid a raking claw that ripped a hunk of wood out of the doorjamb.

The bugbear chased her across the room to the corner, towering over her. She tried to dart around it, but it swatted her into the wall, miraculously not drawing blood with its claws. It leaned down, reaching for her.

Piper screamed louder than she'd ever screamed before.

A fizzling *pop* came from the back of the bugbear's head. It spun to look behind it, revealing a bald spot about an inch across that emitted smoke. The pixie hovered in the doorway, holding her bow up.

The bugbear snorted, evidently considering the pixie a pointless nuisance.

As it turned back toward Piper, the pixie yelled, "Make it dance!"

What? Piper looked down at her chest, at the key sitting on top of the pan flute.

The bugbear leaned closer, drool rolling off its teeth.

She grabbed the panpipes and played a few disharmonic notes, too terrified for her fingers to work properly. The bugbear cringed from the harsh sound, flinching away. She managed a few more notes, closer to key. Snarling, the black-furred monster advanced on her again. Fear exploded to a point beyond being scared. As though the music came from instinct, she breathed the *Wood Elf's Dance* into the panpipes.

The bugbear twitched, twisted, and lurched to one side. Piper curled up in a ball, cowering in the corner of the hut, but she kept on playing. The monster's foot tapped, then its leg bobbed. About forty seconds into the music, it hurled itself fully into an acrobatic dance. The monster went spinning around and around the cottage, thrashing the shelves, smashing the table, and tearing down the walls.

Witnessing her song have such a real effect on the creature eased her fear aside. With confidence, her music gained power. She remained huddled in a ball, but played with command rather than feeble hope. Moaning in agony, the bugbear continued leaping and swinging about. Minutes later, the great beast collapsed in a heap, half-lidded eyes crossed. It emitted a long, labored moan, and appeared to fall asleep.

Piper kept playing for a little while more, but it didn't move. Awestruck, she lowered the panpipes back to hang on their cord and pushed herself up to stand. Only a hint of waist-high wall remained of the cottage, the massive creature's inelegant dance having trampled it to rubble.

"Wow." *Guess the satyr expected me to do that instead of finding faeries...* She crept to the gap where a door used to be, cast a final look back to make sure the bugbear remained sleeping, and ran like hell for the gnome tunnel.

24

NOT SO ITSY BITSY

Piper hurried down the dark hallway, clutching the key to her chest in both hands. She possessed the means to get Tristan back, but still had no idea where the satyr put him. The dragon thought the chimera the most likely option as only two creatures in the entire menagerie could breathe fire. Clearly, Tristan had not been in the dragon's enclosure, nor would the dragon have munched on him if he had been. She grumbled at the idea of locking up a creature like a dragon, and growled louder when she thought about how resigned he'd been to his fate.

Her present problem, however, had somewhat more urgency than feeling sad for a dragon who'd given up hope of ever being free. She had to find Tristan before something roasted him. Alas, she hadn't seen a chimera anywhere. However, the zoo did have multiple hallways and turns she hadn't been down yet. This of course presented the issue of not finding him fast enough or running into dangerous creatures while searching.

When she reached the opening to the giant garden, she gently cradled and hugged the meadow pixie as best she could a woman the size of a Barbie doll. "Thank you for helping me. As soon as I find my friend, I will go right to the control room and turn the rest of the wards off. I'll carry you all out myself if I have to."

"Please be careful," said the pixie. "We are all counting on you."

"I swear I'll help."

"No. We believe you." The pixie smiled. "But if you get hurt…"

"Do you know where the chimera is?"

"Keep going straight until you reach a fork. Turn right at the fork and take the second passage to the left."

Not having to roam aimlessly in search of the chimera filled her with hope. "Awesome! Okay. I'll be back!"

The pixie waved farewell and zoomed off into the garden.

Piper hurried along the zoo hallway, dodging smashed benches that lay scattered around, some thrown into the walls hard enough to crack the stone. The mess suggested the troll had come by. She weaved among the debris, careful to watch where she stepped so she didn't cut herself on anything in the dark. The lights still hadn't come back on, and she doubted they would fix themselves.

The hallway darkened like a train tunnel, with only a distant light at the far end. Unable to see, Piper raised both hands and moved at a determined, but careful pace. Every few steps, she stumbled over a piece of debris or slipped in puddles of unknown substances. Here and there, she caught a whiff of sweaty socks, then a strange sweetness part way between wet wood and strawberry, and finally, the unmistakable (and overpowering) stench of poo. The idea of stepping in a cerberus turd (which probably would've been as big as a golden retriever) caused a simultaneous giggle and noise of disgust.

Clank—sudden pain exploded in her left shin.

She jumped back, hopping on one leg and clutching the spot. "Ow… that's a chair."

It hurt so much she almost fell in place and rubbed her 'wound,' but taking too long could hurt Tristan. Gritting her teeth, she forced herself to limp onward. The closer she got to the end, the more a view she had of the junk all over the floor, and the faster she went.

When she finally emerged in the food court, which also had been trashed, she promptly checked her shoe soles. Fortunately, she hadn't stepped in the *truly* bad stuff, only some pale grey ooze that gave off the wood-berry smell.

The food court didn't technically count as a 'fork,' so she kept going straight, climbing over equipment that had been torn out of the various restaurants and shops to make her way out the eastern passage.

Her chest tightened in fear as soon as she started down that stretch. This hallway led to the bad place where the troll enclosure, the brownies, and the bog pixies lived. She remembered the fork, where she and Tristan had gone to the left. At any moment, the troll might appear. Piper kept her eye out for gnome tunnels in case she needed to hide on short notice.

A long and scary slow walk in the dark brought her to a Y split where the air stank like sweaty clothes. Deep, raspy breathing from the left passage set butterflies loose in her gut. The troll had to be close. She slowed to a creep, setting her feet down with the precision of a surgeon. One tiny squeak of a sneaker sole could kill her. Not until she passed the split and had plenty of wall between her and the troll did she take a full breath.

Crystals set into the walls near the ceiling gave off a feeble amount of light, enough to hold back total darkness. She wondered if they operated on magic since this place had apparently lost all electrical power, or if they took batteries. The hallway curved around to the right. In a few minutes, she reached an opening in the wall with a wide window at the end of a short platform. One look through the glass at a wall covered in white webbing told her she'd found the naga's room, the observation platform she couldn't open from inside.

Having zero desire to let the naga to see her, she swung all the way to the left against the wall away from it and hurried past. At the muttering of tiny voices up ahead around a leftward corner, she skidded to a stop, fearing bog pixies. She listened for a moment to the confusing chatter, unable to make out words. The tone, however, sounded frightened and pleading. Nervous, Piper crept up to the corner and peered around.

Light shone in from an enclosure window along the right side some thirty yards away. Not far beyond that, three webbed lumps stuck to the wall, writhing and squirming above a webbed-over gnome tunnel opening. Around them, dozens of hairy legs lay scattered among puddles of yellow and green goop. The overall size and shape of the wriggling lumps added to the sound of the muffled voices horrified her.

The gnomes!

She cringed at the remains of at least twenty cat-sized spiders, likely exploded by the same magic the gnome used on the bog pixie that shot Tristan. Worried, she rushed forward onto web-covered tiles. The sticky padding tugged at her sneakers and made it difficult to walk. When she reached the gnomes, she reached up toward the narrower end and grabbed at the webbing. Ignoring her disgust, Piper thrust her fingers into the sticky mess and closed her fist.

A sharp tug ripped away a patch of spider silk, exposing a gnome's face.

"Huzzah!" cheered the gnome. "We are saved."

"Hang on. I'll get you out of—"

"Look out!" shouted the gnome.

Piper spun around.

A massive, furry spider crawled out from the enclosure behind her. What she thought had been glass had been an opening. The arachnid's body would make a cow seem small. Curved fangs as long as swords on its chelicerae dripped with amber venom. All eight of its glowing red eyes stared at her as it emitted a bone-vibrating hiss.

"Crap," said Piper.

She bolted off down the corridor, stumbling and nearly tripping from the webs sticking to her shoes. After ten steps, both sneakers had pulled off her heels, throwing her into an ungainly leaping stride to keep them on. The enormous spider chased her for only ten or fifteen seconds before walking backward to guard the trapped gnomes.

Piper slowed to a stop, gasping for breath, and squatted to fix her heels back into her shoes. "Wow. That's a giant tarantula. I'm not equipped for that… Maybe I can get the centaurs to help or something. Spiders wrap things up like that to eat later. The gnomes shouldn't be in *immediate* danger. Not like Tristan."

Swearing to herself that she'd find some way to help the gnomes, she kept going straight.

A minute or two of walking later, a passage led off to the left beneath an ornate sign bearing the words, 'Dragon's Meadow.' *Okay. I know where that is. I must be in the southeast end.* She trotted past it, since the pixie told her to take the second left. The corridor curved gently to the right, and after another few minutes, she hooked a left into the next offshoot.

And ran straight into a cloud of bog pixies.

They erupted in a chittering storm of tiny shouting voices and rained stinging arrows down on her.

Yowling from bee stings, Piper shielded her eyes and forced her way through them. One landed on her shoulder and bit her ear. Another flew down and sank its little fangs into the back of her left knee. She stumbled as the leg gave out, and grabbed the one chewing on her ear. It wailed as she yanked it away and threw it at the wall with all her anger.

The pudgy, pod-shaped creature bounced like a rubber doll off the concrete and laughed at her.

"Ow! Stop!" She flinched from an arrow hitting her in the back, then shot upright on her knees with a yowl when one stuck in her backside. Another arrow pinned her left ear to the side of her head, making her scream in pain. "Stop! Stop it! You're horrible!"

They laughed at her.

She curled up in a defensive ball, and wound up staring at the panpipes. *Ooh. Yes.* A wicked grin spread over her lips despite the constant pelting of stinging miniature arrows. She sucked in a deep breath and played *Wood Elf's Dance* again. In seconds, the bog pixies wailed in agony. They dropped their tiny bows to clamp their hands over their ears, crying out in a chorus of mutant baby screams.

Since the arrows had stopped, she stood and played even louder, pouring notes into the world faster and faster, a beating, driving cadence that whipped the bog pixies into a midair frenzy. Miniscule voices wailed.

"Too happy!"

"Awful bright music!"

"Make it stop!"

"No dancing. Argh! It is play! Cheerful bad!"

She ignored their pleas, and played until the last bog pixie fell from the air, landing with a splat. Spiteful, she got a running start and punted one. It flew a ways off, hit the wall with a meaty *slap*, stuck for a second, then peeled away and hit the floor.

Arrow by arrow, she plucked the stingers out and broke them in half. The one through her ear into her head hurt the most, and after she removed it, she kicked another bog pixie down the hall. Hitting them didn't appear to inflict any real harm, but it made her feel better.

"I don't know how I feel about the satyr." She frowned at the pipes. He had evidently given her magical music, and a reasonably potent weapon, but also put her in a dangerous predicament and threatened Tristan's life. "Is he trying to help or hurt us? Ooh. I don't understand satyrs."

Still picking arrows out of her legs and arms, she stormed off down the hall, grumbling.

25

THE LITTLE NATURALIST

The hallway dead-ended about a hundred yards away from the corner. An opening into an enclosure spanned the last third of the corridor. Fragments of broken glass littered the floor, glinting in the weak light from crystal lamps overhead. Walking slow to minimize crunching, Piper crept to the end of the window and crouched behind the wall beneath the missing window. She gripped the top and rose up only enough to peer over at a landscape of sand and scrub brush, like somewhere high in the mountains of an arid country.

Two small mesas flanked a grove of thin cypress trees maybe ninety feet in from the hallway, over wide-open dirt with nothing to hide behind. The chimera reclined near the center, next to a small pond fed by a little waterfall cascading down the left mesa. Its lion face rested on its paws, eyes closed. The goat sticking up from its back kept looking around as if on guard. She couldn't see the tail, which curled up behind it.

From one of the taller trees hung a shiny, rectangular brass cage, far too close to the chimera for her to dare risk approaching it.

Tristan sat cross-legged inside it, since it wasn't tall enough to let him stand. Thick bars blocked her view of him for the most part, but he didn't move much nor appear to be panicking.

"Grr." She glared.

Even shrunk to the size of a pixie, she'd never be able to get to the cage without being seen. The chimera *might* not be dangerous, but her luck never treated her that well. She could try the panpipes, but the magic would hit Tristan too, and she didn't know how long it would leave him unconscious, or if it would even work on the chimera.

I'm never going to get to Tristan without that thing spotting me. She glanced back down the hallway toward the trapped gnomes and the Spider of Unusual Size. *Oh, that's so stupid and reckless… Dad would kill me.* A chuckle slipped out. *If the chimera doesn't. I gotta do something before it realizes Tristan is there.*

Piper stood in clear view. "Hello. Are you a nice chimera?"

The goat bleated at her. A long, green snake rose up behind the creature and hissed. The lion's eyes opened.

"Nice kitty-goat-snake." She smiled. "Sorry for waking you up, but can I go talk to my friend?"

The chimera sprang to its feet, and the lion's roar drowned out the goat's continued bleating.

"Guess you're not a nice kitty." Piper gulped and raced off down the hall.

Scrabbling claws scraped over tiles like a giant housecat trying to run on a kitchen floor but not getting anywhere for the first few seconds. Her plan *did* involve the beast chasing her, but thinking about it and having it happen carried two entirely different levels of fear.

Blasts of fire lit up the air behind her, but only a hot breeze reached her.

Whining out her nose, she poured on speed and shot past the sleeping bog pixies, rounding the corner and heading to the right, back toward the huge spider. Snarls and goat bleats pursued, getting dangerously close, but she dared not look back.

She whipped around the bend in the corridor and charged straight at the titanic spider. Fortunately, it had drifted far enough away from the gnomes to keep her idea in the realm of stupid and dangerous, instead of suicidal.

At the sight of her, the spider raised its fangs and hissed, the hairs all over its body standing up. Pumping her arms and legs, she sprinted for the gnome tunnel opening, blasts of fire at her back a little too warm for comfort.

Piper threw herself forward into a dive, plunging into the gummy webbing over the end of the gnome tunnel. As her shoulder hit the floor, a sharp pain pierced her right calf along with pressure like a man's hand squeezing her.

The webs stopped her slide; she looked back and screamed at a huge green snake head clamped onto her leg. Glowing ruby eyes with far more intelligence than a snake should have stared at her with menace, as if saying 'hah. Got you.' She gasped at it, but couldn't tolerate the pain of pulling away while three-inch fangs remained in her calf. With nothing else to do, she wrenched her arm away from the webs and punched at the snake.

It didn't seem impressed, and the hit made the fangs flare in agony.

Piper screamed and shrieked, clawing at the head in an effort to pull the jaw open.

Out in the hallway, the lion roared. Spider hisses followed. The snake's evil stare shifted to a note of concern as it glanced toward the outside. A roaring rush like a flamethrower accompanied a flare of light and heat. The great spider let off an enraged squeal. A second later, the snake detached itself from her calf and whipped out of the tunnel. Spidery hissing and goat bleats traded back and forth.

Piper struggled to drag herself out of the gummy webbing. By the time she got herself free, the spider/chimera brawl had migrated about twenty feet away into a tangle of fangs, claws, and fiery spouts. She didn't know what to be more frightened of: watching a chimera breathe fire, or seeing a spider so big the lion-goat-snake creature looked like a Pomeranian picking a fight with a Rottweiler.

Whimpering at the pain her leg, she reached up and ripped the gnomes down from the wall, dragging their cocooned bodies into the tunnel to safety before tearing them free.

"You have our thanks," said all three gnomes at once.

"Who do you think will win?" asked one gnome to the other two.

The remaining gnomes tapped their chins in thought, watching the brawl.

"Can you debate that later please? I need to get to the chimera's enclosure, fast."

"This way," chimed all three gnomes.

One snapped his fingers and all the webbing disappeared from the tunnel and Piper's clothes.

They hurried off, down the tunnel.

She crawled after them, alarmed that her right knee didn't hurt when it hit the floor over and over. Soon, the leg burned, and the pain migrated up into her hip. Her mouth dried out. The gnomes took a branching passage, leading her along. By the time they crawled out into the desert landscape of the chimera enclosure, her right leg wouldn't move, dragging along behind her like dead weight.

Piper forced herself to stand and hopped on one leg over to Tristan's cage. "Hey. Are you okay?"

He waved at her. "Yeah. This is so cool."

"Cool?" She blinked. "I almost got killed like five times to get you out of there, and you think it's cool?" Lightheaded, she grabbed the bottom of the cage so she didn't fall over.

"Crikey," said Tristan in a bad accent. "Today, we're observing the desert thingamagig. It's got the body of a lion, the 'ead of a goat stickin' out its back, and a snake for a tail."

"Stop that." Piper reached up with the key and opened the cage door, which swung open with an ear-piercing squeak.

He jumped down. "Thanks. It was like a shark diver being in a cage. I mean, I couldn't get out but the cage also protected me from it."

"Right." She swooned to the side.

"Umm. You don't look so good."

Piper grabbed her stomach. "I feel kinda sick."

"Ack!" yelled a gnome, pointing at her leg. "The chimera bit her."

"Snake venom," shouted another gnome.

"Quick!" The third gnome bounced up and down. "Go to the dryad!"

Tristan looked her up and down. His smile disappeared. "You're like way pale. Come on." He threw an arm around her back and ushered her to the window. "Gnomes. Help us!"

Piper stumbled after him, mostly hopping on her left leg. "It's not good that my leg stopped burning, is it?"

"I don't think so." Tristan lifted her up and over the windowsill.

"Everything's getting spinny," said Piper. She gripped his shirt tight. "Hurry up."

26

TOO DANGEROUS

The gnomes zipped off to the left upon leaving the chimera hallway. Piper growled past clenched teeth as her leg alternated from numbness to feeling like someone had lit her on fire. She hung most of her weight on Tristan when it flared up, letting him drag her up the corridor to a T intersection.

He followed the gnomes to the right.

"Duck," yelled one, while running past a long, broken window.

Piper glanced past Tristan at the enclosure, which contained jungle, and another leonine creature with huge dragon-like wings and a frighteningly human face. It offered a disinterested sneer and flicked its long tail at them, hurling a cluster of spines.

Tristan shoved her down and jumped on top of her. Clicking and clattering, like a handful of pencils thrown against the wall, came from the left. Tristan dragged her back to her feet and mostly carried her for a little while until he gasped, "It's not chasing us."

"Manticores are lazy," said all three gnomes at once.

"Right here," yelled another gnome.

Piper loped along with Tristan helping hold her up. Her right leg had gone stiff, so she used it a bit like a crutch. They rushed in among the garden full of bitey plants. Groups of bog pixies and meadow pixies weaved in and among the flora, trading arrows and even getting into tiny swordfights. Neither side paid any attention to them, though a few stray arrows landed in her arm.

The gnomes led them past the end of the garden, across the food court circle, and out the north passage next to the elevator. Piper recognized the hallway as the one she'd come down not long ago on her way to find Tristan. A few agonizing minutes later, he dragged her through the opening of the giant garden. Her chest tightened, like the male centaur squeezed all the air out of her.

"Can't." She forced herself to take in air. "Breathe."

"Dryad!" shouted Tristan. "Please help! Piper's been poisoned!"

Wood creaked in the distance. Tristan pulled her along over meadow grass, but stopped short with a startled yelp as the dryad rose straight up from the earth in front of them with a burst of green light.

He eased Piper to sit on the ground, and flopped next to her, gasping for air. She gazed up at the clouds, feeling as if she could float straight up and join them.

The dryad hovered over her, placing one hand on her leg. Almond-shaped eyes of glowing green light radiated concern. "What happened?"

"Chimera tail," whispered Piper.

Where the dryad's wooden hand touched, her leg became cold. The iciness spread up her leg into her belly and down to her foot. Mint flooded her mouth and lungs, so strong she gagged on it. Her slow, hazy thoughts sharpened back to normal. After a moment, the dryad pulled her up to lay on her side.

"You must let the poison out."

"Wha—" Piper lurched and threw up a spray of glowing-yellow ooze that reeked like an untended litterbox. Smelling that, plus thinking it had been inside her, made her throw up again out of disgust.

"Eww," said Tristan.

Piper sat up and wiped her face on the back of her arm. Her right leg remained sore, but no longer burned. The spot where the fangs had pierced itched like mad, but didn't show any evidence of injury—at least what she could see through two small holes in her jeans. She leaned up and hugged the dryad, the small woman's body still as hard as an actual tree. "Thank you."

"You are welcome, child. We cannot let your life end yet." The dryad winked. "You've promised to let us go."

"Yes. I will definitely set you all free." She offered a sheepish smile. "I'm still trying to figure out exactly how to do it though."

"I understand," said the dryad. "We believe you will succeed. Your motives are pure, and there is much greed that remains to be unwound. You should drink from the pond over there."

"Is it magic water?" asked Tristan.

"No." The dryad smiled. "But the venom makes you thirsty. If you do not drink, you could yet suffer harm from it."

She rubbed her neck. "Yeah, feels like my mouth is all cottony."

"Let's go." Tristan helped her upright.

The dryad smiled, and sank into the earth.

Piper stumbled for a few steps until her right leg stopped protesting. Still with a bit of a limp, she headed for the indicated pond. The gnomes trailed after them, looking around and muttering complaints about how much of a mess the troll had made of the place.

Tristan joined her at the pond's edge, also drinking. Rather than waste time with handfuls, Piper held her hair back and stuck her face in, slurping up water until her stomach could hold no more. She sat up with a gasp, shivering from the chill, but also feeling invigorated.

A yellow sign off to the right caught her eye.

She wobbled upright and walked over.

Unicorn

Found: New Zealand

The magnificent unicorn is a creature of legend. Only the innocent of heart may approach it, all others can search, though they will never see. Rumored to have great powers of healing, these beasts are one of the most powerful magical creatures known to exist, and also the most elusive.

Piper rolled her eyes. Another sign claiming a creature existed that no one could see sounded like a con game. She started to walk back to Tristan, but stopped when she caught a flash of white in the trees on the other side of the pond.

"Oh, no way," she whispered.

Worried and curious in equal measure, she speed-limped around the pond and headed into the trees. Barely ten seconds later, a pure white horse with a long, silken mane, silver hooves, and puffs of the same silky hair on its feet trotted into view. From the top of its head, a long, pearlescent horn stretched to a needle point.

Piper froze, deciding to let it approach her if it so chose rather than try to walk up to it. "Oh, no. You're real and you're stuck here." The unicorn's presence affected her emotion, pushing it out of control. She fell to her knees, sobbing into her hands and muttering apologies for what her grandfather did.

A wet, warm nose nuzzled her head.

Piper looked up at the face of the unicorn standing right in front of her. "I'm so sorry. How… How did such a horrible man trap you?"

The unicorn bent down and tapped its horn to the top of her head. Fleeting visions flickered in her thoughts:

A little girl with black hair, no older than six, walking out of the trees in a pretty white dress.

The child reaching up toward her.

Ruby, hanging from the girl's necklace, flashing bright.

Pain.

Paralysis.

A view from ground level at a man carrying the crying child away while she wailed and screamed, "Leave him alone!"

Piper stood and wrapped her arms around the unicorn's neck. Her grandfather had used a little child as bait. A necklace he gave her worked like a trap, stunning the unicorn long enough to be captured. She'd disliked what her grandfather had done before, but now, she hated him personally.

The unicorn shook its head.

"What? You don't want me to hate him?"

It snorted, gazing at her with sorrowful black eyes.

"I know. It's not innocent to hate someone. I'm twelve. I'm not going to be innocent for too much longer."

The unicorn nosed at her heart and shook its head again.

"What do you mean it's a choice?"

He rubbed his cheek against hers.

"All right. I'll try. Do you know what I need to do to open the zoo?"

The unicorn pointed its horn across the pond.

"Go that way. Okay." She reached up and ran her hand down its rabbit-soft mane. "Thank you. I'll come back as soon as I can. When you get home, please let that girl know you're free."

The unicorn nodded. It glanced at Tristan and patted its hoof into the ground.

He crept closer, leaning back, eyes wide as if afraid of the large creature. "Umm. Hi."

It snorted at him.

Tristan shot Piper a sheepish look. He bowed his head and pulled his right arm out from behind his back, revealing a horribly burned hand.

Piper clamped both hands over her mouth not to scream.

The unicorn tapped the tip of its horn to Tristan's injury. Golden light surrounded the burn, and faded, revealing whole fingers. He stared up in shock.

His 'no problem' attitude when she let him out of the cage, his dragging her to the dryad, not even saying anything about his hand hit her all at once. Piper grabbed him with a crushing hug.

"I didn't want you to feel bad." He hugged her back, somewhat limply.

"You didn't even say anything."

"The chimera tried to burn me. I stuck my hand through the bars like an idiot…" He shrugged. "It's okay."

"No, it isn't. You got hurt because of me."

The unicorn snorted.

"He's right." Tristan grinned. "I got hurt because of the satyr, not you. Or because I was stupid."

Piper stared at him for a long moment. When she glanced at the unicorn, it twisted its head back and forth and attempted to smile at her. "Come on. We have to get out of here, and find a way to send everyone home."

"Yeah."

Piper bowed to the unicorn and hurried off in the direction it had pointed. They ran across the giant garden and entered a swath of forest. Out of nowhere, two swarms of pixies rolled in, both meadow and bog, locked in battle. The bog pixies dove on Piper and Tristan, swiping tiny swords, biting, and shooting them with arrows.

She screamed and swatted, grabbing bog pixies and hurling them away. Tristan got in a few solid punches, but his attacks only knocked the hideous things around and made them laugh. Tiny stings and papercuts hounded her no matter how she squirmed, ducked, or waved her arms. Every so often, a bog pixie tormenting her would freeze in midair with a silver arrow sticking out of it, hang there for a second, and plummet to the grass. Every direction in the woods appeared to be the same in the chaos of beating wings and stinging arrows. Trying to protect her eyes, Piper curled up on the ground with her arms crossed over her face.

A few painful minutes later, the assault ended.

Only meadow pixies remained hovering around them.

"Are you all right?" asked one.

Piper stood. "Ow. Yes. Just annoying."

The meadow pixies swirled around them in a swarm of flashing white and purple light. Tiny hands plucked arrows from Piper and Tristan's bodies and mended wherever bog pixie swords left cuts.

"We have been talking," said a blue-haired female. "Perhaps you have agreed to too big a task. Some of the monsters here are too dangerous for a human to be near, much less a child."

Piper shook her head. "I have to try. I promised I would fix what my grandfather did, and I will do it."

The pixies gave her somber looks.

A lavender-haired male flew up to her. "You are a child. We will understand if you cannot finish this task."

"I understand, but I'm not giving up yet." She took Tristan's hand. "There's been too much pain already to just walk away."

He nodded.

"Thank you for chasing off those awful bog pixies."

They mumbled amongst themselves.

"Back soon!" yelled Piper.

They jogged for a little while in the direction the unicorn indicated, which led to another gnome tunnel. She crawled in and made her way along a wavy passage for a while until it let her out in the room with all the pipes and pumps. The stairs she'd climbed before were missing, most of the pipes had dents and gouges, smoke peeled up from holes in one of the pumps, and sprays of water rained everywhere.

"Uh oh. That doesn't look good," said Tristan.

"The troll," said Piper. "He's been here. The gnomes have to have a garden or a farm. This is way more water than necessary for just a mermaid tank. The troll broke it too much. I think this place is doomed. We're not going to be able to fix it."

"So?" Tristan shrugged. "We're gonna shut it down. Who cares if it breaks?"

"Yeah. I just don't want anything to die before I figure out what to do." She started up the only remaining stairway to the door that would lead back to the hallways, but a distinctly trollish grunt made her jump back. "Crap! Run!"

The heavy armored door at the top squeaked. Four thick, grey-green fingers curled around the edge, and the troll's ugly face peered in at her.

"Run!" shouted Piper again. She darted across the bottom of the water room and scrambled into a gnome tunnel.

Tristan, screaming, barreled in behind her so fast he rammed his head into her back end.

She fast-crawled away from the roaring rage of an angry troll. The passage had no branch offs, and came to an end minutes later at a dirt field. Piper crawled out, stood, and blinked in surprise at a strikingly pretty black-haired woman sitting behind a cluster of boulders a short distance away, gazing at her.

Gold bands encircled her upper arms, a matching gold choker at her throat. Pure white cloth wound about her neck into a halter-top, leaving her shoulders and stomach bare.

When Piper's memory clicked, she about fainted in terror.

"Oh, hi," said Tristan, waving.

"Wonderful! Visitors!" The woman smiled, holding up an ornate kettle. "Come closer and have some tea."

"Umm. No thanks." Piper pointed at the enclosure window off to the right. "I've gotta get home, like fast. I don't have time to stay. I don't like that you're trapped here, but I don't want to be your dinner either."

Tristan glanced at Piper. "Huh? She seems nice."

"That's a lamia," whispered Piper. "Lamias eat children."

The woman burst into tears, sobbing into her hands. "I'm so lonely."

Piper grabbed Tristan's hand and edged toward the window, whispering, "Don't trust her. She's trying to trick us." She raised her voice. "I know you can't help it and don't want to hurt us, but I'd rather not die. Thanks."

The lamia stopped crying and stared at her.

"Oh, crap," muttered Piper. "Run."

"Feasting fills me with such sorrow!" shouted the lamia. "I cannot control myself. Run, please get away before it's too late!"

Piper dashed to the window and jumped over the low sill, Tristan right behind her.

The lamia grabbed her head, wailing, rising up from behind the rocks on a great serpentine tail where legs should be. She hissed, snarled, and glared. Red-painted fingernails stretched out into nine-inch claws. All trace of sorrow or compassion fell away from her expression, the creature lost to pure, uncontrollable hunger.

An instant after her eyes lit with a red glow, the lamia flowed forward in a spiral, screeching.

Piper ran, dragging Tristan behind her by an iron grip on his hand. Her longer stride kept him stumbling to keep up, but she didn't care. She'd drag him if she had to before she let the lamia eat him.

27

A GAME OF CHICKEN

Glancing back over her shoulder proved to be a mistake. The lamia closed in fast, her human part hovering like a ghost while her serpent tail whipped side to side. Piper didn't waste energy screaming, focusing instead on running as fast as she could.

They tore past the bog pixie enclosure, a rain of tiny arrows pelting the wall behind them. The little horrors zipped out into the hall to chase, but a handful shot the lamia and laughed. Tiny giggles melted into wicked screams, but Piper refused to look again. A pixie arrow flew over her head, another stuck in her hair. She rounded a right turn, flinching as a pixie arrow hit the wall by her face, and darted down a short hallway with benches on both sides.

Tristan let go of her hand to pick up an empty magazine rack, which he threw at the two bog pixies coming after them. They glided above and beneath it, still laughing. The flimsy metal stand smashed onto the tiles with so much noise Piper thought her parents might've even heard it. She and cut left down a familiar hall that led to the giant garden.

The scrape of the huge serpentine tail sounded farther away, perhaps delayed by the pixies.

"Come on!" Shouted Piper, grabbing Tristan's hand again.

She dragged him into the garden. The bog pixies jerked to a midair halt, hurling curses, refusing to follow. Piper ran a short distance deeper into the forest and stopped, looking around.

"Why'd you come here?" asked Tristan, breathless.

"I... dunno. This place feels, umm... 'good' or something. I guess I thought the lamia wouldn't be able to get in here."

A baleful screech split the air behind them in an almost-parody of a woman's voice.

"Guess not," muttered Tristan.

Piper spun around and went wide-eyed at the sight of the lamia slithering into the garden without hesitation. Blotches of pale purple goop spattered her arms and chest, the same stuff that painted the wall when the gnome made a bog pixie explode.

"Whoa. She killed the nasties," said Tristan.

With a shimmering flash of blinding light, the unicorn appeared out of thin air in front of the kids. He pointed his horn at the lamia, emitting a low nickering rumble. The lamia leaned back and slithered side to side, growling at him. Piper took advantage of the standoff to catch her breath, stooped forward with her hands on her knees.

The lamia circled to one side, but the unicorn kept himself between her and the kids.

Piper patted his flank, overcome by gratitude. "Thank you... I think you're stronger than her, but you don't want to hurt her unless she forces you to."

Without taking his eyes off the lamia, the unicorn nodded.

"We should hide then." Piper patted his side, shot a 'go away' stare at the lamia, and hurried off, deeper into the woods.

Tristan muttered, "Thanks," to the unicorn, and followed.

Several minutes later, Piper spotted a small cave opening about the size of a gnome tunnel. When she got close, the mirage of continuing woodlands faded, as did the appearance of a cave. She stepped into the narrow space between the cloud curtain holding the illusion and a plain, concrete wall.

"Wow." Tristan looked around and waved his hand at the rolling cottony mist. "What is this?"

"Magic. I guess it's like a movie screen so it looks like the forest goes on forever. Come on." Piper ducked into the tunnel.

She tried to work out how to get back the other way to the control room, taking a couple of turns over about ten minutes of crawling before noticing gnome-like voices speaking gibberish. They didn't sound overly excited, angry, or worried, so she followed the sound down another tunnel.

"Gnomes?" called Piper. "Are you here?"

Two gnome-like beings waddled into view, but they resembled the hill gnomes only in size. These had jet-black skin, straight white hair, and glowing blue eyes; they didn't look like cute old men. Even their outfits, dark leather armor, radiated a sinister air. If not for being so small, they could've been warriors from an evil wizard's kingdom.

"Umm. Hi." Piper smiled and waved.

Tristan grabbed her arm from behind. "Those gotta be the night gnomes. Other gnomes said they're not nice."

Both night gnomes stood like statues, staring at her.

"Sorry to bother you. Don't mind us." Piper backed up.

One night gnome pulled a sword (really, a large knife) from a sheath hanging on its belt. The other drew a little throwing blade.

Piper muttered, "Crap," and dove away from the branching tunnel, scrambling to keep going straight.

The hurled knife hit the wall with a *clank*.

Tristan yelled, "Go! They're chasing us!"

"I am!" She tried to crawl faster. "I wasn't going to ask them over for tea."

A burst of magical light went off behind them. With a shriek, Piper threw herself flat to the ground. Tristan did the same, landing on top of her with his face mushed into the back of her knees.

With a sparking buzz, a baseball-sized sphere of energy shot over them and hit the wall of a curve up ahead, leaving a char mark. The near miss charged the air and made Piper's hair fluff out so much it blocked off the tunnel. One spark crept over her face like a prickly-legged spider.

Tristan pushed at her legs. "Go! Go!"

She scrambled up on all fours again and crawled around the curve, coughing on the smoky smell of scorched stone. Small tromping boots echoed in the tunnel drawing nearer behind them. Piper scooted down a rightward branch, eager to keep solid walls between her and evil little gnomes capable of throwing magic bombs… or whatever that glowing ball was.

I can't outrun them crawling. Gotta get out of here!

Another magical blast exploded on the corner behind Tristan, making him yell and shove forward into her legs.

A spot of light at the end of an offshoot on her left caught her eye. She stopped short, causing Tristan to crash into her and yell. Piper backed up two inches and hurried toward the exit. Tristan screamed.

She rolled sideways to look back.

Black gnome fingers had grabbed his ankle. Tristan reared back his free leg and stomped the gnome in the face as it raised a sword. His kick launched the little man out of sight behind the corner, shouting bad words. She grabbed Tristan's arm and dragged him closer, then flipped back onto all fours and shimmied the last fifteen yards or so to the exit.

And climbed out into an ordinary-looking forest.

The shuffle of gnomes approached at a run.

Piper started to reach for Tristan's hand, but stopped at a flash of bright green feathers among the trees. *The cockatrice! Oh, crap!* She leapt behind him, clamped her hands over his eyes, then closed her own and shuffled forward, pushing him.

"What are you doing?" Tristan grabbed her wrists and tried to pull her hands away, but she held on like his life depended on it. "Ow. Hey. Stop! I can't see!"

A loud chicken-like squawk came from ahead and to the left.

Two gnome voices shouted, "Get them!" much too close for comfort to the rear.

Piper shuffled forward, refusing to let go of Tristan's face and hoping not to crash into any trees.

The cockatrice let out a loud shrieking cry.

Tristan whined. "Uhh… what is that noise? Let go."

"No!" yelled Piper.

Gnome voices screamed in terror. For less than a second, the screams turned to cries of pain. Stony scraping, like big rocks brushing against each other drowned out the gnomes' wails until only silence remained. She imagined the gnomes gradually turning grey from the feet and hands inward, becoming statues, like a scene from an old movie she watched about Medusa.

"Keep your eyes closed," said Piper.

"Why?" He kept pulling on her hands.

"We're in the cockatrice pen. If you look at it, you'll turn to stone and die."

Tristan stopped pulling at her arms. "Crap... why didn't you just say that instead of grabbing me?"

She slowed down, swinging her foot out in front to search for trees before taking a step. "Because I didn't want the gnomes to hear me."

"Whoa... you basically killed them."

"Yeah, I guess. But they were trying to kill us... and technically, the cockatrice killed them." Her foot bumped a tree, so she maneuvered around it.

"Don't you wanna save all the creatures?" asked Tristan.

"I'll make an exception for stuff that tries to murder us." She nearly tripped on a root, but caught her balance and felt around it with her foot for a few seconds. "Watch out. Root."

"'Kay."

"Can you keep your eyes closed? Please! I don't want you to die."

"No problem. I don't wanna die either."

She didn't let go of him.

"Really. I can keep my eyes shut. You don't have to keep covering them."

Piper took a few more steps. "I know."

"So..."

Her cheeks warmed. "Well, maybe I'm holding onto you because I want to hold on to you, not to keep you from looking."

"Scared?"

An avian squawk cut the air behind them. Chipping, like a hammer on stone, followed.

"Yeah." Piper shifted her grip down, wrapping her arms around his chest. "It sounds like it's behind us."

"I'm scared too. Anyone would be. I bet our parents would be scared of stuff like this too." He paused for a second. "Does it hurt to be turned to stone?"

"I think so. The gnomes screamed."

He shivered.

She kicked another tree. "Ow. Tree."

The cockatrice made a cooing cry.

"He sounds happy now," said Tristan.

"Yeah, he's got lunch."

"Can we open our eyes if we don't turn around? He's behind us."

Piper stopped walking, thought it over for a second, and risked a peek. Thin forest covered the landscape for about forty yards ahead of them. Shards of broken enclosure glass sat off to the left. They'd been walking toward a back wall.

"Yes. Don't look behind us, okay?"

"Okay."

She unwrapped her arms from around him and held his hand instead, walking briskly toward the window. Tristan kept his head down, staring at the ground where he stepped and nowhere else. They headed for a gap in the glass barrier where an entire panel had disappeared, offering an easy escape to the corridor outside.

A reflection on the half-inch thick window captivated her for a moment. The ostrich-sized bird pecked at a pair of dark grey gnome statues, biting off chunks of stone before raising its head and shaking its whole neck so the nugget slid down its elongated throat.

"Crikey," muttered Tristan.

Piper grabbed his formerly-burned hand in both of hers and squeezed. "That's not funny. I'm really sorry you got hurt."

"It's okay." He wiggled his fingers. "The unicorn fixed it. It hurt so much I didn't even feel it."

"That doesn't make me feel less guilty."

He tickled her side. "Stop saying sorry. This is cool. I haven't had this much fun in forever. *Nothing* will ever beat this."

"You're really not scared?" She climbed up on the thick concrete windowsill, sat, and slid down into the corridor.

Tristan jumped down beside her. "Oh, yeah. In between moments of pants-peeing fear, I'm having a great time."

She couldn't tell if he'd been serious or sarcastic despite his huge grin. "We need to get to the control room."

He looked left and right. "Which way?"

In all the chaos, she couldn't remember what part of the zoo they'd wound up in. False outdoor sunlight lit up the end of the corridor on the right, while the left appeared darker. The control room didn't have any enclosures near it, so she figured it would be dark there.

"Umm, this way." She headed left.

"Do you know or are you guessing?"

Piper sighed. "Guessing."

"Well, it's all connected, right? We'll eventually find it."

"Yeah." She lowered her voice. "Just, watch out for trolls."

28

SEEDS OF DISCORD

Piper dodged broken benches, smashed water fountains, tossed furniture, and clumps of wires hanging from holes in the ceiling. The overall destruction made her think the place looked like a zoo after the end of the world.

After a while of walking, the corridor curved around to the right and the amount of debris lessened. She jogged up to a light run, eager to find something familiar. Another curve turned left, passing an enclosure full of bamboo trees. She glanced at the sign for the ki-rin, but the creature had evidently left the enclosure. That one had supposedly been quite powerful, so maybe he'd gone outside or managed to go home already.

"Yah!" shouted a small voice. "Now!"

Piper stopped short with an, "Eep!"

A mass of night gnomes leapt out from behind toppled benches and broken giant flowerpots, surrounding them.

She raised her hands. "You don't want to hurt us. Please. We're trying to find a way to let you out of here. I want to set you free."

"Lies!" shouted a gnome.

"She works for *him*," said another.

"I'm not lying!" yelled Piper, clinging to Tristan and looking around at the dozens of knee-high, angry creatures.

The coal-black gnomes almost vanished in the dark corridor. A legion of glowing eyes, like tiny blue gas-flames, closed in.

"All we want is to let you out of here. You don't like being trapped, right?" asked Tristan.

"Vengeance!" shouted one.

Flashes of whitish magic snapped like cameras among the crowd.

Piper tried to plead, but her mouth wouldn't open. Her body went limp, collapsing to the floor next to Tristan's. A scream happened, but only in her thoughts. Even her eyelids refused to move enough to blink.

Tiny hands grabbed her arms and legs, dragging her off. She could only watch passing tiles and debris slide by, her entire body numb. Red floor gave way to gnome tunnel. For what felt like an hour or more, the angry little army carried her along. Eventually, the featureless grey concrete became dark soil. Purple moss clung to the roots of blackened trees. A hundred miniature boots crunched the underbrush. The procession came to a halt and dumped her on the ground, face-first into damp mulch.

Tristan landed next to her.

The night gnomes gathered in a conference somewhere past her feet, leaving her lying on the forest floor for a few minutes. She still couldn't blink or feel anything. Fortunately, the magic that kept her from moving also kept her from messing her pants, as she had never before felt so terrified or helpless.

When the conversation of little voices stopped, the gnomes swarmed over her again. They rolled her over onto her back, dragged her a short way, and propped her up against a huge tree trunk. A gnome walked up to stand by her feet, rubbing his chin.

At a snap of his fingers, thin black roots sprang out of the ground, winding around her legs. Other roots encircled her wrists, tying her arms to the tree before coiling around and around her chest. Satisfied, the gnome nodded at her.

They positioned Tristan beside her, and the same gnome covered him with binding roots.

All twenty or so of the gnomes then wandered off to a rounded clearing within a village of creepy miniature houses. There, they began arguing with each other about what to do with their prisoners.

For some time, she could only stare off into the branches of the sinister trees as the bickering gnome voices blurred into a continuous mass of sound. Itching started between her eyes, shifting to a tingle, which spread down her face. She blinked rapidly, her eyes watering from being open so long. The prickling sensation swept down her shoulders, over her chest and onto her legs, taking away the numbness. Fortunately, the itch appeared to be an effect of the magic wearing off, and didn't continue.

"Ow," muttered Tristan, squirming.

Hard, pinchy roots had tightened around her wrists enough to make her hands redden. She made fists and pulled, rocking side to side. The vines holding her to the tree couldn't have been much thicker than spaghetti noodles, but didn't break.

"What are they gonna do to us?" whispered Tristan.

"Umm. They're fighting about that. 'Cut our heads off' sounds like it's winning, but 'tie them up and throw them in the lake' is right behind it."

"Ugh." He grunted, straining to break the roots. "I don't like either of those."

"Well, in that case, there's also 'cook and eat them.' One gnome keeps wanting to cut off all our fingers and toes, then pluck out our eyes and let us go. Another thinks we should be poisoned." She pointed with her tied-together feet. "That guy on the far right is demanding we be burned alive."

Tristan glanced over at her. "I think these gnomes can stay in the zoo. I don't wanna let them out."

She opened her mouth to reply, but clamped it shut when a huge, black, furry centipede as big as a carrot crawled down the tree and over her face. Legs like gentle needle sticks plucked at her skin. She whimpered out her nose, twisting her hands around and pulling at the roots tying her wrists to the tree.

"It's got big red pincers. I hope it's not poisonous," said Tristan.

You're not helping! She whined louder. Her eyes shot open wide when the millipede's rear end slid past, with pincers as long as her fingers less than an inch away from her. The terrifying insect crawled down over her chest, onto her thigh, and off to the forest floor. She leaned away from it as much as she could, squeezing against Tristan, and stared until it flowed out of sight among the mulch.

A loud gnome demanded they bury their prisoners to their necks and pour boiling water down their throats.

"I really don't like these things," said Tristan.

Shaking, Piper gawked at him. "How are you so calm right now? They're talking about killing us... and in really nasty ways."

"It's kinda funny. They're really little. Not that scary."

"Did you forget already that they can snap their fingers and paralyze us? We can't fight or run away if we can't move!"

"Oh." He looked over at her with the pale-faced expression of a five-year-old who just woke up from a nightmare. "Yeah, I did forget about that."

"Grr!" She closed her eyes, leaned forward, and pulled at her right arm until the roots bit into her wrist. A few snaps gave her hope. Desperate to live, she kept pulling. The inky strands broke in a rippling cascade. In seconds, her arm came loose from the elbow down, albeit with a new black root-bracelet. Other strands wrapped around her body kept her pinned to the tree.

"Awesome," muttered Tristan. He scrunched up his face and pulled at the bindings, trying to do the same.

"I got an idea." Piper grabbed the satyr's flute and raised it to her lips.

When she played *Wood Elf's Dance*, Tristan laughed and began rocking back and forth, but being tied to a tree, couldn't move much. The night gnomes stopped arguing and stared over at her.

Uh oh. It's not working...

She played harder, trying to will the magic strength.

One gnome, perhaps the one who made the roots, marched over to her. His wispy beard wobbled as he frowned. With the dour glare of a schoolteacher, he snatched the flute from her hand and snapped the cord away from her neck. After throwing the pipes off to the side, he slapped her across the face hard enough to have knocked her over sideways if she hadn't been tied to a tree.

Seeing stars, she barely noticed him repairing the roots that bound her right arm. Once the initial shock wore off, pain and humiliation conspired to bring tears. Piper reached for anger to stop herself from crying, and managed to weep in silence while keeping her head down in shame. Something about being slapped across the face felt like he made fun of her.

"Hey!" shouted Tristan, thrashing at the vines. "Don't you dare hit her! I'm gonna kick your butt for that!"

The gnomes laughed.

Once Slappy walked back to the group and the argument resumed, Tristan leaned his head close to hers. "Are you okay?"

"Yeah." She sniffled. "Well… the magic song won't work on them."

"Can you break the roots without making noise?"

"I can't. He tied me up again."

She fumed in silence for a few minutes while the gnomes kept bickering. The tone of the argument darkened. Some of the gnomes looked ready to hit each other.

"Wow. They're not going to be able to kill us," said Tristan. "They'll argue so long we'll starve first."

"Yeah, they're getting mad at each other now." She blinked. "I got an idea."

"What?"

"Trust me," she muttered, then yelled, "Cutting our heads off is a really stupid idea. Only a moron would do that. The best way to kill humans is poison."

The gnome who'd suggested poison grinned, while the group advocating beheading glared at her.

"Don't listen to her," yelled Tristan. "She's a witch and she doesn't want you to throw her in the lake. If you do anything else, she'll come back and kill you all. Dunking in water is the only way to kill a witch!"

Piper bit her lip to keep from laughing.

The 'throw them in the lake' group pointed at Tristan and shouted, "He's got a point. We should throw them in the lake!"

"No, poison!" yelled about five gnomes.

"Cut off their heads!" shouted the majority, about nine.

"Please!" yelled Piper. "You really shouldn't throw us in the lake. Poison is best, but it would be nice if you buried us up to our necks and made us drink boiling water."

"Oh, oh, please burn me alive!" yelled Tristan.

"Don't listen to him!" shouted Piper. "He's a warlock! Fire will only make him powerful and he'll destroy you all."

Several confused gnomes stared at them while the remainder kept bickering. The 'cook and eat them' group physically shoved the 'bury and boiling water' group off to the side.

"Ooh! Yes, you should eat us!" called Piper.

"She's lying again," said Tristan. "If you eat us, we'll take over your bodies and possess you."

"Most of them want to cut our heads off," whispered Piper. "Turn the rest against that idea."

Tristan nodded. "Actually, you should cut our heads off. Please?"

"Yeah," yelled Piper. "Head cutting works best."

"No!" roared one of the gnomes. "They're trying to trick us. They'll do something bad if we cut their heads off."

"Come on!" shouted Tristan, sticking his neck out. "Cut it off!"

"Don't listen to them!" hollered a big gnome.

The head-cutting group became belligerent, calling the other gnomes fools and morons.

"Now that's just rude," yelled Piper. "You gnomes who want to put us in the lake aren't morons for disagreeing with head cutting. How dare he call you stupid!"

"Yeah!" shouted a handful of gnomes.

All it took was one fist.

The gnomes erupted in a brawl, with the occasional magical blast zooming off into the trees.

"Now!" whispered Piper. She twisted her body up, straining against the roots. One or two snapped, but not enough to get free. "Ugh. He put extra roots on me."

"Can you reach my pocket?" asked Tristan. "I got a pen knife."

Piper focused on her left hand, which hadn't been retied double tight. The gnomes kept fighting, lost to the fury of an out-of-control melee. Making a fist, she braced her elbow against the tree trunk and pulled. Roots bit into her skin; she grunted past clenched teeth and kept straining until the thin black strands gave out. After two quick breaths to recover, she slipped her hand into his jean pocket. Vines pinning her upper arm to her body prevented her from reaching in too far, so she curled her fingers, pulling cloth up until she brushed something plastic.

"Is that the knife?"

"Yeah." Tristan struggled, but couldn't get loose. He seemed to have a heavier coating of roots, perhaps because the gnomes assumed he'd be stronger than her.

She got one finger in a keychain loop and tugged a red Swiss Army knife out of his pocket. Once she got a grip on it, she held it close to his hand so he could pick the blade open. A magic blast struck the tree a few feet above their heads, making her scream. She cringed from a rain of ash.

"Hurry up," muttered Tristan. "They're getting really into it."

She pivoted her wrist and sawed at the roots on his wrist. Once that broke, he ripped his arm forward, breaking several strands pinning his body to the tree. He grabbed and ripped the roots wound about her chest while she cut at the ones squeezing the life out of her right wrist.

One smooth slice down between her legs cut all the roots binding them together. She rolled up to kneel and cut Tristan the rest of the way loose.

"They're escaping!" shouted a gnome.

"Crap!" Piper folded the knife closed and pulled Tristan up to stand. "Run!"

Something tapped her on the back of the head.

She spun.

A coatl hovered behind their tree, her panpipes in its mouth.

The woods behind them erupted in a mass of rainbow feathers. Coatls raced into view from branches overhead, diving at the group of gnomes, spitting lightning blasts. The gnomes, disoriented from their brawl, burst into chaos. Some ran, some hurled magical bolts at the flying snakes, who darted aside with ease. One night gnome decided to charge at the kids, but stopped short when a lightning blast struck him from the side.

That gnome, a startled expression on his face and smoke peeling from its hair, fell forward like a toppled mannequin and didn't get up.

"Thank you!" Piper accepted the flute from the nearby coatl.

It nosed at the flute and flapped harder for a moment.

"You want me to play?"

The coatl shook its head and tapped her on the ear with the tip of its tail.

"Oh! You heard me play and came to help?"

It nodded, then jabbed its tail off to the left.

"We should run that way."

It nodded.

"Thank you so much." Piper brushed a hand over its head.

The coatl flapped hard and launched itself past them into the fray. Screaming, smoking gnomes ran in random directions, darting around trees in an effort to seek cover from the continuous pelting of lightning coming from the swarming, winged serpents.

Tristan looked at her.

"I'm changing my opinion of snakes." She grabbed his hand, and ran.

"Me too!" yelled Tristan.

She bolted across the evil forest to the enclosure window and leapt the concrete wall like a hurdle jumper. Sneakers clapped and squeaked on the floor outside. She swung around to the right and started to run, but skidded to a halt, eye-to-thigh with the mottled-grey troll.

"Umm. We shouldn't go this way," whimpered Piper.

"Why—Aaaah!" screamed Tristan. He jumped back, pulling on her arm. "Yeah. This way's a bad idea. Run!"

29

THE GIFT

Drool fell from the troll's lips as they curled back into a snarl, exposing dark yellow teeth. Its wild, black hair touched the ceiling, even though the creature stood somewhat hunched. A glop of saliva fell ten feet to splatter on the floor by Piper's sneakers.

The troll raised a length of eight-inch-thick pipe like a club.

Before it could swing, Piper did something she never imagined herself capable of: she ran *at* the troll, ducking between its legs. Hoping the confusion of having to turn around would buy her precious seconds, she sprinted for a rightward corner only a short distance away. Tristan, screaming, followed. He started to pass her, which made her feel slow. Piper poured on speed, holding even with him while the pounding *boom, boom, boom* of a stomping troll filled the hallway.

For all of its strength, the troll didn't have much speed. They'd even managed to get away from it with their shoelaces knotted together. Free to run, it almost felt easy to keep away from the thing… but she also doubted it would stop for anything.

She ran without much care for direction other than getting away from the troll, choosing or ignoring corridors without real thought. Piper eventually swerved down the corridor where the thick, armored door led to the pump room. Hoping it would stop a troll, she rushed inside. Tristan darted in behind her and helped pull the door closed. Slapping at the wheel in the middle of the door, she spun it, the gear-works pushing thick metal bars into the wall on all four sides. As soon as the wheel refused to turn any more, she stood up on tiptoe so the master key around her neck would reach the center of the wheel, and locked it.

"There." She shivered. "It's locked."

"What about the other door?" Tristan pointed across the room full of pipes at the other armored door, which had been bashed in and mangled.

The intact door in front of them swelled outward, like the end cap of a high-pressure pipe. The opposite one had been battered almost flat, but didn't look like it would ever open again.

"I don't think he'll get through that either."

Wham.

A dent appeared in the door, the ring of metal on metal deafening. Piper clamped her hands over her ears and started down the catwalk steps to get away from the door, but stopped when she noticed a few feet of water at the bottom of the room.

"No!" she yelled.

The troll kept pounding on the door, crimping the inch-thick steel inward.

Piper sat on the stairs, stuck between water and an angry troll. The gnome tunnel she'd been hoping to use for escape sat underwater, already flooded.

"I don't think it'll get in." Tristan sat beside her. "But… I think we're stuck."

"Stupid troll!" yelled Piper.

It kept beating on the door for a little while before the sound of its venting frustration migrated down the corridor. Soon, the banging outside echoed in the pipes overhead.

"What's it doing?" asked Tristan, looking up.

"I don't know." She frowned at the water. With a moment to spare, she tied a knot in the leather cord and re-hung the panpipes around her neck.

The troll bellowed louder. Every time it smashed something, she jumped.

"He'll get bored eventually and stop," said Piper.

"Yeah." Tristan nodded.

Plop.

"What was that?" Tristan peered over the side. "Something fell into the water."

"I dunno." Piper looked up.

A bolt the size of a stick of butter fell from a pipe fitting near the ceiling four stories overhead, and hit the water with a *ker-plunk*. Each time the slam of the troll's anger shook the wall, the huge pipe shuddered.

She pointed up and started to scream, but the voice coming out of her drowned under the roar of water a second later as the pipe join failed. The lower half wrenched away, twisting under the force of the geyser blasting from the two-foot-thick pipe.

"You should call a real plumber. I don't think your dad can fix that," said Tristan, his voice shaky with fear.

Piper leapt to her feet and backed up the stairs, away from the rising flood.

"Crap. We have to run!" Tristan ran to the door and grabbed the wheel, but couldn't turn it. "Unlock it!"

"The troll's out there!" yelled Piper.

"No he isn't. He's not *right outside* the door. We can outrun him."

She fumbled the key around, having to grab it with both shaking hands to get it in the keyhole. After unlocking the wheel, she grabbed on and turned, but it only moved an inch. "It's stuck!"

Tristan helped, but they only made metal *clank*. The troll had damaged the door so much the gears no longer lined up, and several had bent. He started to shiver and cry, but Piper took comfort in an odd source.

She faced him and put her hands on his shoulders. "This looks bad, but we're going to be okay."

"We're gonna drown." He grabbed onto her.

"No. We're not going to drown. We're going to wind up in a hole in the ground and starve."

He gawked at her. "The bhargest."

"Yeah."

Tristan kicked at the catwalk. "I think I'd rather drown."

"No chance. That's a horrible way to die."

"Like starving is better?"

She tried to look comforting, but trembled too much to be convincing. "Dying at all is pretty awful."

"Yeah. So... you think that vision is real? No matter what we do, we're going to die down here?"

Piper sighed. "I don't know. Maybe it was just trying to give us a nightmare. Or it just showed us what could happen if we make a mistake. We don't know it's a fact. It looked pretty evil. I think it just wanted to scare us."

"You know what I think?" yelled Tristan over the roar of water.

"What?"

He grimaced, leaning on the railing to peer over the edge at the flood. "I think you're just saying that to make me feel better, and you really think we're gonna wind up in a pit somewhere."

She stared at him.

Tristan looked up and smiled. "Thanks."

"Up!" Piper ran to the end of the catwalk opposite the stairs. She climbed to stand on the railing, holding onto a pipe for balance, and stepped onto the flat where another massive pipe elbowed.

He followed, standing behind her with his hands on her hips. "Umm. What's the point?"

"Air? What else."

"It's just gonna take longer."

"This room is huge. There might not be enough water to fill it the whole way up."

"Hope not."

She stared at the rising water, which climbed about an inch every minute. A strong fishy smell wafted by, suggesting this water came in from the mermaid tank. That enclosure had been pretty big, but only three stories deep. Piper looked around at the walls, and her heart sank.

The mermaid room was wider... this one's gonna fill all the way up.

Her hand tightened around Tristan's. No point saying that, since it would only freak him out. *How is the room even filling up? The water should be going out the gnome tunnels.*

"Hatch!"

"What?" asked Tristan.

"The gnome tunnels have hatches."

"Move!" yelled Tristan, pointing at the water touching the bottom of the pipe they stood on.

She grabbed small pipes as handholds, climbing them like a playground jungle gym up to the highest horizontal pipe in the room, a few feet away from the ceiling. With nowhere higher to go, she perched there, staring down in dread at the rising flood. Tristan crawled up and sat next to her. He had the eyes of a small, frightened boy, but his facial expression attempted to convey bravery. She swung her feet back and forth thinking for a while, trying not to pay attention to the roar of falling water.

"The hatches," said Piper. "The gnome tunnels should be flooding. There's at least two of them, and they're almost as big around as the pipe feeding water in. This room should be draining faster than it's filling."

"But it isn't," said Tristan, sounding sad.

"Right. Which means the hatches are closed. I'm going to try to open one."

"It's too far down," said Tristan, taking her hand. "We're gonna drown anyway. Can we drown together?"

Her throat tightened. "I promise I won't drown alone, okay? I have to try!"

Tristan bit his lip, but nodded.

With the water only two feet below them, she figured another twenty minutes would fill this room to the ceiling and be the end. She had no more time to delay. "Ugh. I hate swimming in my clothes."

"You left your bathing suit upstairs," said Tristan.

"Yeah." She took a deep breath. "Okay. Here goes."

Piper pushed off the pipe and fell feet-first into the icy water. She shrieked from the cold, and wound up dog-paddling for a few seconds until her body decided to obey her brain again. "Cold!"

"Yeah."

She peered up at him. Scared, his large eyes and round face made him look half his age. Seeing her friend look so defeated and hopeless lit a fire inside her. "Don't give up. The hatch is right there. I'm gonna go down and open it and the water will stop rising." *And I'm probably going to get sucked along with it.* "You'll be okay."

Tristan nodded. "Please come back."

"I will."

After filling her lungs, Piper dove under and stared at the alien maze of pipes. She kicked off and swam down and across, heading for a spot that looked like the gnome tunnel. About halfway to the bottom, with close to twenty feet of water over her head, she felt like she couldn't hold her breath anymore. Determined not to let Tristan drown, she forced herself to keep swimming down. A few strokes later, she became lightheaded and her body disobeyed her, blasting the contents of her lungs out in a stream of bubbles. In a panic, she tried to swim for the surface, but crashed into a tangle of metal tubing and lost track of direction.

Piper curled up, clutching her throat, lost to the terror of imminent drowning.

But took a breath.

Huh, what?

She opened her eyes. Still clearly underwater, she breathed as if she had air—just like she'd done in the tank after the mermaid kissed her forehead. *Is... I can breathe water! Is... that permanent?* Not wanting to waste time wondering about that right now, she looked around for the hatch. On the wall to her left near the bottom, another two-foot thick green pipe sported a giant wheel valve. She kicked her legs and swam across the room over the smashed catwalk to the far end, more or less directly below where Tristan clung for his life.

The pipe thrummed with the rush of water. Certain it fed the flood, she swung her legs up, bracing her sneakers on either side of the pipe, and grabbed the valve. She felt dumb for not doing this before until she realized that at only a few feet up from the floor, the valve had already been under the surface and out of sight.

A splash overhead made her look up.

Tristan had jumped or fallen in, and treaded water with only his head above the surface.

She couldn't budge the wheel trying to turn it from the outer ring. Shifting sideways, she grabbed one of the spokes in both hands and pulled it like a lever, pushing her legs against the pipe. The valve broke free, the wheel vibrating from the force of water rushing through the mechanism. A quarter turn at a time, she grabbed turned, grabbed, turned, fighting for every inch. Tristan's shout overhead sounded happy.

Grinning, Piper kept working the valve wheel until it jammed and wouldn't turn any more. The roar of water had stopped. She kicked off the valve and swam toward Tristan, surfacing beside him. Only a foot of air remained between the surface and the ceiling.

"It stopped!" yelled Tristan.

"Yeah." She explained the valve. "I turned it off."

He burst into tears and grabbed her. "I thought you drowned. You were down there so long."

"I can breathe water… the mermaid."

"What?" He leaned back, sniffling.

"The mermaid did this." She leaned in and kissed him on the forehead. "And I think she gave me a gift 'cause she was so happy I helped her escape. I can breathe underwater."

Tristan went bright red in the face. "Uhh. Cool." His stunned expression gradually became a bashful smile.

"Be right back. I'm gonna go open the hatch. Umm. I might get like sucked into the tunnels with all the water."

"You could die. Break your neck or something. Look for a drain first."

"Oh. Okay. Good idea. Wait here."

He nodded. "Duh. I can't breathe water."

"Butthead," she muttered, and ducked under, avoiding his attempt to grab her.

Piper swam again toward the bottom of the room, weaving among the maze of pipes in search of a drain. She did spot a small drain opening on the floor, but it would take hours for it to empty the room. A bank of controls for water pumps gave her the creeps, since they probably ran on electricity… but then she remembered all the power had been cut off. None of the rubber-covered buttons did anything when she pushed them, and all the displays had gone dark.

Kicking off a desk, she launched herself forward, pushing a drifting chair out of her way before gliding over to a bank of lockers behind a giant machine. The alcove had nothing of interest, so she backed out and swam across to the other corner, where the glow of crystals in another control panel lit the wall pink and orange. One peach-colored gem had the word 'emergency purge to lake' scratched into the metal under it.

That looks promising. She put her finger on the gem. *Please be magic and not need power to work!*

When she pressed the button, the peach light went out for a second and came back on. A sharp metallic *clank* rang through the water so loud her bones rattled. Sensing imminent danger, she grabbed the end of the console and launched herself like a torpedo into a bank of narrow pipes. Seconds before a strong current started, she wrapped her arms and legs around one and held on.

Small pieces of debris, papers, pens, coffee mugs, and notebooks shot toward the middle of the room and into a square hole that hadn't been there before. Piper held on as the current took on a cyclonic spin, trying to sweep her away and off down the drain. Head down, she clung to the pipe like a koala bear for a few minutes until the cold brush of air washed over her head.

Tristan's scream got loud, then faded, then got loud again.

She lifted her head to look toward his voice. He flowed around upon a giant whirlpool, orbiting the drain. Piper shimmied sideways, climbing from one vertical pipe to the next, making her way closer to the middle of the whirlpool. When she pulled herself onto the last one, she clamped tight with her legs and reached out to him as he rushed by.

"Tristan! Grab my hand!"

He went around the room again, scrambling to swim away from the center of the vortex. The current swept him past her, nowhere near close enough to reach. She *might* survive being pumped out to the lake since she could breathe—assuming the pump didn't have sharp blades or anything. Did magical pumps have turbines? Either way, *Tristan* would definitely drown if the current sucked him down the drain.

Before she could figure out if she had a chance of saving him or would only succeed in killing them both, he crashed into something underwater and jammed to a stop. From the look on his face, a pipe had probably hit him in the groin since he'd been going feet first. She cringed in sympathetic pain. To his credit, his grip on the pipe held. A moment later, a pitiful squeal came out of him.

Eventually, the raging whirlpool disappeared down the drain, leaving only about an inch of water on the floor. She leapt from her sanctuary among the pipes and splashed over to Tristan. He sat atop a U-shaped section of pipe, draped over it like a drunk cowboy on a rodeo bull.

"Are you okay?" She peered up at him.

He moaned, still red-faced. "I can't move."

Piper patted him on the shoulder. "Breathe. Just breathe, okay."

"We're alive."

She smiled. "Yeah."

He grunted, pushed himself up, and slid down, landing in a stumble that left him on his knees. "Ow, that hurt. Gimme a minute."

"Okay." She crept over to the drain, morbid curiosity demanding to be satisfied. Two panels of floor had opened downward like a trapdoor. A cube-shaped hollow four feet deep contained a metal mesh grid littered with office junk above an enormous pipe. "Whew. Guess we wouldn't have gotten shot out to the lake…" *Probably just crushed to death.*

Tristan limped over. "Okay. I'm good. Now what?"

She pointed at the armored door. "That is never opening again."

"So we're locked in?"

"No. Gnome tunnel." She trotted across the room, sneakers sloshing in puddles. "Here."

A square, black hatch blocked off the tunnel, flush to a rubber gasket. She wondered, if it had been open, would the whole zoo have a couple feet of water in it, or have flooded totally?

"My grandfather was an idiot. Who builds a zoo underground?"

Tristan shrugged. "Someone who doesn't want it to be found. Maybe he had to, or some of the creatures could've like used magic to go home."

She fished the key out of her shirt to unlock the hatch. "Yeah."

The metal plate peeled away from the wall with a squishing noise like a refrigerator door, exposing a dry gnome tunnel.

Tristan scooted in behind her and pulled the hatch closed. "In case it floods again."

"Okay."

"Where are you going?"

It took her a few seconds to process that they wouldn't drown. When the realization hit her, she trembled. Water dripped from her soaked clothes, gathering in a puddle around her hands and knees. "Hunting for that tree ladder. I'm done. I can't do this anymore without help. I want my parents. We almost died *again.*"

He squeezed her shoulder. "It's okay to be scared, but yeah… I think we need to bring your parents down here."

Piper nodded, wiped her eyes, and breathed deep and slow until she calmed down. Freaking out about another near-death experience wouldn't help. She could fall to pieces as soon as she had her father's arms around her. At the moment, she needed to keep her head on straight.

"I think I know where we are. This way." She pointed ahead, and crawled.

"Umm. There's only one way to go here."

"Smart alec," muttered Piper.

"I'm Tristan, not Alec."

She stuck her tongue out and raspberried.

30

CURSES

Piper climbed out from the tunnel into a well-lit hallway, though the light didn't come from the ceiling fluorescents. Easily a hundred yards wide, the hill-home enclosure straight in front of her flooded the hallway with false sunlight.

No hill gnomes were in sight, but at least the familiar scenery told her where to go. The hallway to the right led past the bathrooms to the control room with the tunnel out to the secret tree door. She bounced on her toes with glee and pointed that way.

"Yes! We're there!"

"I remember this place," said Tristan.

"Come on!" Piper ran full speed down the hallway toward the curve.

Her happiness evaporated halfway around the curve. A pack of brownies stood at the bathroom corridor intersection.

As fast as a reflex, she kicked her shoes off. Barefoot beat hopping.

"They're harmless, but annoying. Let's run past them," muttered Piper.

"Okay."

The brownies jeered and pointed at them.

Tristan's sneakers slapped together, their laces knotting. One pointed at Piper, but nothing appeared to happen.

"Hah! Nice try! I took them off!" shouted Piper. She started to run at the brownies, but her right foot caught her left leg and she fell flat on her chest. "Oof!"

The brownies cackled with delight.

She got up, took two steps, and tripped again, which sent the brownies into howls of laughter.

Tristan hopped over to her and helped her stand.

"Not laughing!" yelled a brownie with a nasty tone.

Two brownies pointed, one at her, one at Tristan.

Piper burst into uncontrollable giggles. Tristan grinned for a second and erupted with laughter.

"That's not funny!" shrieked Piper between giggles.

"I know!" Tristan laughed so hard tears flowed down his face. "This is horrible."

"Come on." Piper grabbed his hand, giggling, and made it three steps before her feet collided and she landed flat on her chest again.

Tristan's sudden laughter no doubt came from a curse, but it still felt too much like he laughed at her falling. Furious, she tried to yell at him to shut up, but wound up snickering too hard to talk.

"Troll. Troll. Troll. Troll!" chanted the brownies.

Two of the little blighters pointed at the floor, and a glittery golden doorway stretched upward. Piper lurched to her feet and tried to run past the brownies to the passage leading out, but she slipped and crashed down on her rear end.

"Ow!" She scrambled to get back up, but her feet kept shooting out from under her like they'd been painted with oil.

The gold portal stopped glowing, fading to reveal another section of zoo hallway… and the troll.

"Troll. Troll. Troll. Troll!" chanted the brownies.

"You evil little creatures!" yelled Piper, before bursting into laughter. "I'm trying to *help* you!"

Tristan held his belly, still laughing to the point of crying. "We're gonna die! It's gonna smash us."

"That isn't funny!" Piper giggled. "Run!" She wanted to cry at being cut off from the exit, but could only snicker.

"I can't. My sneakers are tied together."

She got to her feet, ran three steps, and landed on her chest again. "Oof! I can't walk!"

He cackled. "You look so goofy!"

"It's gonna kill us!" She pushed herself up again. When she tried to grab his hand, she missed and accidentally stuck a finger in his eye. "Sorry!"

He yowled in pain, but cackled.

"Come on!" she yelled, deciding against trying to take his hand. "Hop!"

"I'm a rabbit!" Tristan giggled, but hopped away from the troll, which finally seemed to notice them.

Piper attempted to walk with slow, careful steps, but the fourth time her right foot touched the floor, it zipped out in front of her like someone kicked her heel. She fell into a split that made all the brownies groan and grab themselves.

Tristan doubled over, cackling.

Red-faced with anger, Piper laughed. She scrambled up to a run... and sprawled out on her chest three steps later, sliding. The troll squeezed itself through the portal and growled. It snarled at the brownies. The little devils screamed in terror and disappeared in glimmering silver clouds an instant before the troll's fist mashed down on the floor where they'd been.

"They just teleported away!" Tristan slapped her on the back a few times, laughing. "They brought the troll here to smash us, and they just ran away!"

"Ow!" She giggled. "Stop that!"

Piper grabbed the floor and pulled herself forward, sliding on her knees. Tristan hopped along beside her. Moving that way felt too slow, so she leapt upright and hurled herself into a leaping deer-like stride. Every three or four steps, she wound up falling on her chest or side, but Tristan grabbed her hand and pulled her upright.

Neither of them could stop laughing. No way could they hide like this. It would hear them.

The troll stomped closer, hurrying along as fast as it could go.

She tried to run with big leaps again. Five strides later, she landed on her chin, sliding forward with her feet hanging over her head.

Tristan pulled his penknife out, giggling, and sliced his shoelaces apart.

"Get on my back!" he yelled, before howling with laughter.

Piper stood, but fell right away. He dragged her for a few seconds until she managed to find a moment of balance, then leapt onto him like a backpack. Tristan got his hands under her legs behind her knees, bounced her up a little, and stumbled into a run, carrying her.

Troll fingers closed at the ends of her hair, plucking a few strands. Her attempt to scream in terror came out as a wild peal of laughter. *This is* so *weird!*

Roaring in anger at the near miss, the troll punched the wall. The loud *wham* made Tristan flinch and wobble, nearly dropping her, but he kept his balance. He turned right at a T and kept going, hooking another right at the next T.

"Where you going?" yelled Piper, amid giggles.

"Hah! Away from the troll!" He snickered.

Fancy decorative banners lined the walls, hidden in the dark. Enough of the pattern showed to hint at Arabian décor, like they'd stumbled into a street from *Aladdin.* Tristan sprinted hard until he staggered to a slow, loping trudge.

"The troll's a ways back now." She giggled. "You can put me down. Even if I keep falling, we're faster than it."

He let her slip back to her feet. The first step she tried to take, her feet got tangled, and she went over, but he caught her.

"Wow you're like really clumsy." He giggled.

"It's not me. It's a curse!" She tried to scream in anger, but cackled like the wicked witch.

Every few steps, she slipped, but he kept her from smooching the floor again. The hallway bent to the right and swept in a graceful curve to another corner. Pounding troll steps continued to chase them, making Piper try to run too fast and fall more often.

"Almost there," said Tristan between snickers.

"Yeah."

When they reached the corner, Piper gawked at a dead end with a small display window. She wanted to burst into tears, but wound up erupting in a giggle fit. The small enclosure, only about twenty feet square, contained a single wooden table and an ornate bottle. Its bottom, about the size of a pumpkin, had eight faceted sides of rich, blue glass that slanted outward up from the base, then curved back in to a narrow stem a few feet tall that ended with a gem-studded stopper.

The walls remained plain grey concrete, but the bejeweled bottle more than made up for the drabness.

A loud trollish roar filled the hall, stabbing her in the eardrums. She clamped her hands over her ears and spun, pressing her back to the glass. The troll stepped out from the curved hallway, filling it wall to wall. Glowing yellow eyes fixed on them. Thick, forest-green lips curled back in a wicked grin. As if it knew they had nowhere to go, it strolled closer, in no obvious hurry.

Scared beyond reason, Piper giggle-screamed, "Help! Please! Someone help us!"

Tristan also shouted, "We need help! Gnomes? Anyone! Help!"

Their pleas amused the troll. A deep, rumbling laugh shook the air in her lungs. The troll advanced, step by step. No matter how hard Piper leaned against the wall, she couldn't make herself pass through it.

The troll drew back its left hand, glaring at Piper with a victorious sneer.

Tristan jumped in front of her. The troll flicked him aside with its right hand while hurling its left fist toward Piper's face. She attempted to leap out of the way, but her feet tangled her, and she fell straight down onto her butt.

A massive fist whooshed over her head, striking the enclosure glass and shattering it with a horrendous loud symphony of clattering shards. Tristan grabbed Piper's arm and dragged her away from the troll, shoving her at the wall to his left. The troll snatched him up by one leg, hauling him into the air upside down.

"No! Let him go!" shouted Piper. "Don't hurt him! Don't you realize we're trying to *help* you? Do you want to be stuck in this place forever? You want to go home, right?"

The troll sniffed at Tristan's hair.

He kept giggling. "He's gonna eat me. Help!" Tristan laughed.

Piper grabbed Tristan's hands and tried to pull him down, but lifted herself off the ground instead. She gave up on that and flung herself at the creature, punching it over and over in the gut—not that it noticed.

"Hit him in the balls," yelled Tristan, laughing as the troll held him higher and opened its mouth.

"Eww!" She stared at the dark 'skirt' of ivy around its middle. Cringing, she tried to punch where she thought he'd feel it.

The troll grunted and looked down. It bumped her with a knee, knocking her to the floor before hoisting Tristan up to bite his head off.

"Flute!" shouted Tristan.

With shaking hands, she clutched the panpipes, but between endless giggling, absolute terror, and magical clumsiness, couldn't manage a single on-key note. Tristan grabbed the troll's eyebrows, trying to hold his head away from its mouth. It grunted, annoyed, and pulled him away, stretching its eyebrows a few inches out until the boy's fingers slipped away and the hairy brush-like things snapped back into place.

"Help!" yelled Tristan, laughing.

"I'm trying." She giggled. "I can't play. I'm laughing too much and I keep fumbling the pipes."

The troll again lifted Tristan up to lower him headfirst down its throat.

An avian screech came from the end of the corridor. Orange flickering light brightened, rocketing closer.

"Help!" yelled Tristan.

Surrounded by a bloom of flames, the phoenix glided around the curve. Screeching, it hurled itself at the troll, raking at the immense creature's back with its talons. The troll roared, wide-eyed. It swatted at the phoenix with its left hand, but the agile bird darted around it easily. Tristan bent upward, reaching for the fingers clamped around his leg, each one thicker than his arm. He pulled and tugged, but couldn't budge them.

Piper kept trying to summon the *Wood Elf's Dance,* but barely got two notes out before laughter got in the way. The phoenix flapped its wings at the troll's face, trying to claw at its eyes, but every slash its talons made healed in seconds.

The troll cringed away from the phoenix and raised Tristan, snarling, opening its mouth wide enough to swallow him whole.

"No!" shouted Piper. She tried to leap upright, but both feet shot out from under her and she fell flat on her side. "Tristan!"

With a great screeching cry, the Phoenix darted around and dove straight into the troll's mouth. The monster's eyes swelled, bulging out of its skull. The fire coating the bird spread over the troll's face, igniting its hair. A second later, the phoenix exploded in a tornado of flames.

Piper cringed away, shielding her face. Tristan let out an *oof* nearby along with the dull *thump* of a body hitting the floor. The roaring wind ended with a soft *whump* and the stink of scorched meat.

She pushed herself up off the floor to sit, and gawked at a snowfall of ashes descending onto a large pile where the troll had been. A giant grey hand and most of a forearm remained attached to Tristan's right shin. Embers at the stump end crept upward, disintegrating the troll's arm inch by inch.

He pried open the fingers and kicked the limb away before the burn could reach him. In seconds, the arm crumbled to join the ashes.

Piper crawled over and sifted at the pile, hunting for any sign of the phoenix, but found only dust. Overcome by sorrow that such a magnificent creature had killed itself to protect them, she burst into sobs.

Tristan giggled, but chomped down on his arm to muffle himself.

"It's dead," wailed Piper. "I didn't want it to do that!"

He put an arm around her back. "So's the troll."

She twisted toward him, and bawled onto his shoulder while he patted her back. A few minutes later, a giggle slipped in between her sobs. "I hate brownies."

"Me too."

Piper turned back to the ash pile, tracing her fingers over the dust. "I really didn't want you to die. Thank you for saving us."

Tristan bowed his head.

31

WHERE WE DIE

Piper alternated between crying and giggling, letting her tears fall into the ashes. She couldn't quite find the desire to stand up. Not that she'd stay upright. She'd wait here until she stopped compulsively laughing—that would mean the brownie curse ended. Maybe then she'd care enough to move. The weight of the phoenix's death made everything else feel pointless.

If she hadn't decided to explore the attic, the beautiful bird would still be alive. Everything down here would still be sane and normal.

No. Cruel. She wiped her face on her hands, laughing and sniffling. *I still promised I'd set them free. I guess dead is free compared to being locked up.*

"Whoa," said Tristan. "Check out the sign."

Piper braced her hands on the floor, got her feet under her, and stood. She took three dainty steps toward the all-too-familiar yellow sign before her toes snagged on her heel and she spilled over. Tristan leapt to catch her, and pulled her upright.

"Wow. Clumsy curse really sucks," said Tristan.

She scowled, snickering. "Yeah."

Djinn

Found: Persia

The rarest find of all in The Menagerie of Jenkins Bailey, the djinn (or genie as westerners call them) has been the inspiration for many stories. While it is true that these powerful sorcerers can grant wishes, it is vital to understand that they should never be trusted. A djinn is a twisted being, tormented for thousands of years by its imprisonment in the decorative vessel you see before you now. The button here will agitate the vessel and make it appear, but it cannot harm you past the enchanted wards.

Do not, under any circumstances, use the word 'wish' in the creature's presence. No matter what you wish for, you will wind up regretting it. Djinns will look for the worst possible way to grant the request to exact vengeance against humanity for their imprisonment. They are a fabulous creature to behold, but they should never be trusted —or even spoken with.

Tristan glanced at a metal box on the wall with a single red button. He shrugged and pushed it, but nothing happened.

"Don't!" rasped Piper, then giggled.

"It's safe to *look* at him, but the thing doesn't work."

She folded her arms, snickering under her breath.

"Be careful," said Tristan. "You don't have shoes anymore and there's broken glass everywhere."

Piper curled into a ball. "Eep."

"I'll carry you." He grinned.

She looked up at him. "My hero."

He laughed, though it sounded genuine that time.

"Hey. I got an idea. Why don't you wish for the phoenix to be okay?"

She shook her head. "Didn't you read the sign? It'll do something horrible. Like, it'll turn back time and the phoenix won't save us from the troll, so we die instead."

"Let me think. I played a game with a wish spell in it, and the rules said it worked exactly like this, where it tries to be as bad as possible while still being what you asked for. The kid running the game wasn't too smart, so I came up with a way to ask for something that had no way to go wrong."

"What kinda game was that? I thought you said you didn't have any friends."

"I don't.... well"—he smiled at her—"I didn't. We played online through a chat on the computer. Just text though. Ever hear of D&D?"

"No."

"It's a lot like writing stories, but each character has their own author."

"Oh, neat. So... you think you can make a wish that'll not go wrong?"

"Yep. I just need a minute or two to think." He climbed up over the windowsill. "And the troll opened it for us."

Piper stood, sat on the sill, and swung her legs over, standing inside the small room. "Okay. But don't do anything stupid."

Holding hands, they approached the table.

Buzzing and beeping filled the room, along with flashing red lights.

The floor shifted, falling out from beneath them, opening in two halves around a small platform under the table. Piper dove at it, managing to grab the narrow neck of the bottle and drag it with her as the clumsy curse made her trip and fall off the other side of the island.

She flopped onto the inner half of floor, too smooth to grab hold of, and slid off it as it continued lowering. Screaming, she fell straight down and hit concrete a second or two later. Her right ankle and left elbow throbbed from the impact.

The djinn bottle smacked into the floor with a bell-like ping, so hard she expected it to shatter, but it bounced, rolling to a halt against the wall.

"Argh!" yelled Tristan. "I banged my knee."

"I think I sprained my ankle." She sat up and rubbed it, rolling her foot around. "Maybe not. It doesn't hurt that much."

Mechanical whirring started overhead.

The two halves of floor closed upward, sealing them in a square pit. The djinn bottle gave off a blue glow, like a giant nightlight.

Piper looked around at the walls, shaking. *This is the place we starve to death.* "Umm."

"Yeah." Tristan crawled over and sat next to her. "I know. Sorry. My fault."

"You didn't know it had a security system." Images of Tristan's too-skinny body danced across her mind. Knowing she'd never see her parents again, she bent forward and cried.

He let her weep for a while, rubbing her back until the hard sobs faded to soft sniffles.

"Don't give up yet." He managed a weak smile. "We still have a couple days to find a way out of here. But… hey. Even if we're going to die, I'm still glad I met you."

She stared into his big, wide eyes, choked up, and cried onto his shoulder for a while more. "I'm glad I met you too." She wiped her face on her arm and sniffled. "I'd prefer not dying though."

"Yeah. There's gotta be a button or something. Stand on my shoulders and look around."

"I'll fall and break my neck."

"We're not laughing anymore."

She stared at her legs for a moment. "Yeah. True." Piper stood and walked back and forth in the small space. "You're right. I'm not tripping over my own feet."

Tristan squatted by the wall. "Climb up and stand on my shoulders."

"Okay."

It took her a minute or three to work out the balance, but she managed it. As soon as she stood up straight, he grasped her ankles and rose to his full height. She reached up, but still missed the roof by several feet. Hydraulic struts on either side connected by hoses to sockets in the wall, but she didn't see anything that looked like a button or handle to open it.

"I don't think it can be opened from inside. This is a jail, basically… to catch thieves. I bet there's an alarm going off in the control room, but no one will find it."

He sighed.

"Down?" asked Piper.

She walked her hands along the wall to keep her balance as he sank into a crouch, jumping to the floor once he couldn't duck any lower.

They paced around for a while, searching the plain walls, then sat, staring at nothing.

"Are we gonna have to drink our pee?" asked Tristan.

"Eww," said Piper. "That's disgusting."

"Saw it on a survival show."

She cringed. "That's still disgusting. Why would we do that?"

"Maybe last long enough for someone to find us."

Piper leaned forward, holding her head in her hands. "They won't. I have the key to the elevator, and even if my parents had one too, the power is off. The only way down here is the tree door that can't be opened from the outside, or jumping down the dumbwaiter, which would kill them."

"Oh." His lip quivered, but he managed not to cry.

She stared at the blue bottle for a while before getting up the nerve to stand and walk over to it. "We're going to die anyway. Whatever this thing does won't be worse than that."

"Okay." Tristan got up and hurried over, looking hopeful.

Piper rubbed the bottle, but that didn't do anything.

"Guess it's not like the movies." Tristan chuckled.

She grabbed the stopper and uncorked the flask.

With a loud *pop*, a billowing cloud of glowing blue-violet smoke grew from the end of the long neck. Once it expanded to fill a space the size of a person, it flickered and flashed, solidifying into a man with dark brown skin, black hair, a turban bearing a tall blue feather, and a most impressive moustache and beard. His baggy pants gave off blue light, and he wore shoes of dark sapphire with long, curled pointy toes.

He glared at Piper, appearing quite unhappy to see her. "So… you seek to make a wish, do you? Hmm. I shall grant you *one*."

"Not three?" asked Tristan.

The djinn waved dismissively, three fat emerald rings on his fingers sparkling. "No. That is a myth. You get one, and you should consider yourselves fortunate for even that."

Piper narrowed her eyes in thought. This man/creature certainly looked mean and nasty enough to want to grant a wish in the worst way possible. She pondered what to ask, but kept circling around to the probable truth that using a wish to escape death would probably only delay her demise or change its form. No matter what she asked for, she would die.

I still made a promise.

She looked up at the djinn, meeting its angry stare without a hint of fear. "I know what I am going to ask for."

The djinn frowned. "That isn't making a wish. You are wasting time."

Piper clutched the bottle, both hands on the long neck. "Great djinn, I wish for all the creatures trapped in this horrible zoo to be transported back to where they belong—including you."

Tristan gasped.

For a few seconds, the djinn didn't move or react. His head tilted slightly to the side, the hard glower in his eyes softening. "Are you sure, child, that is what you wish for?"

Piper nodded with conviction. "Yes. I promised all the creatures who could understand me that I would set them free. It's wrong that they were put here, and I'm not going to be able to help them myself now… so, yes. I want to use my wish for that. I wish for all the creatures, including you, who are trapped in this zoo to be returned to where they belong."

The djinn smiled. "As you wish…" He swept his arms out in a wide arc, bringing his hands together in front of his face. "So shall I grant."

A brilliant flash of lightning blinded her. Woozy, Piper felt herself falling to the floor from the powerful magical discharge. Tristan let out a startled yelp that sounded like it came from miles away. She tried to call for him, but everything went dark.

32

BREAKDOWN

Piper felt as though she floated in darkness. Her head stopped spinning after a moment, and a soft fabric-like texture met her cheek. She let out a weak moan and opened her eyes to see carpet.

"Piper!" shouted Dad.

She dragged her arms up and pushed her chest off the rug. Her father swooped in and picked her up.

"What happened?" yelled Mom. "You were unconscious."

"Umm." She looked up at her father and around at the giant living room in which they'd watched *Zootopia* the other day. *I'm not gonna starve in a hole!* She leaned up and wrapped her arms around her father, yelled, "Daddy!" and burst into tears.

He carried her to the couch, sat, and rocked her for a while. Mom sat next to them, stroking her hair. She squeezed him tight, shivering as all the fear and worry of the past day melted out of her muscles. It hadn't even occurred to her when she made that wish, but technically, both she and Tristan were 'creatures trapped in the zoo' at that moment.

Overjoyed to be spared a starvation death, she succumbed to another few minutes of hard crying.

"What happened to you?" asked Mom. "Your clothes are all ripped up. Where are your shoes? There's… is that blood? What, did you to go jumping through thorn bushes?"

Piper giggled. "No. You wouldn't believe me if I told you, so what do you want me to say?"

"Try the truth?" asked Dad.

"Mom… Dad…" She sniffled and sat up. "Grandpa built a big zoo under the house. He put all kinds of magical creatures in it. Tristan and I fell down the dumbwaiter and discovered it. But the creatures don't belong in a zoo. I was trying to set them free, but something shut off the power and they got loose and some of them are really bad, like the troll who almost ate Tristan and the bog pixies who kept shooting us and the brownies who cursed us and…"

"Oh, my God," said Mom. She ran a hand over Piper's hair and pulled her into a tight hug. "Stop, hon. Please stop. That's it, Alan. We are going back to Syracuse. This house is not worth our daughter's sanity."

Dad looked down, grim-faced. "What really happened to your clothes?"

"We got attacked by bog pixies. These ugly little creatures with wings. They shot us with teensy arrows and cut us with little swords, and bit us. Brownies cursed us to tie our shoelaces together so I took my sneakers off so they couldn't do it again."

Mom shook her head at Dad. "Our kid's twelve and she's having a complete mental breakdown."

"I'm not," said Piper. "I swear. It's real."

"Oh, honey." Mom rubbed her back. "I'm sure it must all seem real to you." Her jaw quivered and a tear ran down her cheek. "Schizophrenia isn't the end of the world. It can be managed. We'll make it."

Dad glanced at Mom. "Let's not start jumping to conclusions. She's obviously had a fright. Maybe they did fall down the dumbwaiter, and she knocked herself out and she's had a really weird dream."

"Well…" Mom bit her lip.

"It wasn't a dream. The truck smells like a fish tank because of the mermaid."

Dad blinked. "What?"

"Oh, Piper, stop." Mom sighed.

She shook her head and told them about helping the mermaid

escape, getting pulled over, and the mermaid charming the police officer to forget them.

Mom gasped. "You drove! At your age? Dammit, Alan, you never should've let her try it that time."

"Hang on, Amy..." Dad raised a hand. "One, if she *did* take the truck and get pulled over, the police would've called us... unless you actually believe she had a mind-wiping mermaid in the back. So, either she dreamed it, or the mermaid was real."

Mom stared at him.

Dad fidgeted with his shirt pocket.

Piper glanced at him.

He picked at the shirt a second more, raised his eyebrows, and asked, "Was she pretty?"

"Alan!" said Mom. "Don't encourage her hallucinations. Sweetie, go take a bath and change. You look like you got mugged in the forest."

"Yes, Mom." Piper stood and trudged out.

Her parents began to discuss whether she needed a therapist, psychiatrist, or a hospital. Silent tears ran down her face, thinking she'd never see Tristan again, probably spending the next few years locked up in a padded cell. Maybe it *had* all been a dream.

A few steps up the stairs, a pin poked her in the back of the left shoulder.

"Ow!" She grabbed at the spot, felt something thin, and plucked a bog pixie arrow out of her shirt.

"Mom! Dad!" she shouted, running back to the living room, bouncing on her toes. "Mom! Dad!"

Still on the couch, they both turned to look at her.

"What?" asked Mom.

She marched up to stand before them, holding the arrow out. "Look at this! If I had a dream or if I'm making it all up, what is this?"

Dad took the little arrow and stared at it.

"Uhh." Mom stammered. "I-it could be a toy or something?"

"Ames..." Dad tapped the tip with his finger. "It's quite sharp. Who makes toys like this?" He handed her the arrow.

"I..." Mom stared at it.

"There's something else," said Dad.

Piper and her mother stared at him.

Her father reached into his shirt pocket and pulled out a large glimmering scale. "I found this outside by that strange garage with all the fake plants on it."

"So?" asked Mom. "A big fish scale."

"A mermaid scale," said Piper. "We had to take her out of the zoo on the freight elevator. There's like golf carts in there. One had a trailer, and we drove her around front to the truck."

Dad's eyebrows flared like he made a mental connection. "I saw the tire marks in the grass."

"Alan… Don't tell me you're believing this?"

"Let's just say I'm not inclined to think our daughter's having a mental breakdown. Why don't we give her a day to calm down? I'm sure if this zoo is real, she can show it to us."

Piper nodded. "Yes… but it should be empty now. I found a djinn and made a wish for all the creatures to go back where they belonged. That's how I wound up here… We fell into a pit and got trapped, so we counted as creatures stuck in the zoo."

"Wishes now." Mom rubbed the bridge of her nose. "I don't know what to say."

"Let her get cleaned up. Give it a day, and we'll see what she has to show us. Would you rather see something unexplainable, or have our daughter be schizophrenic?"

"I'd take unexplainable if it's an option." Mom sighed. "I'm just baffled."

"It's almost bedtime. You must be starving," said Dad.

"No. I'm not *starving*." She shook her head emphatically. "But I am really hungry."

"Go clean up and I'll fix you something to eat." Dad stood.

Grinning, Piper ran upstairs to her room. After closing her door, she undressed and headed into the bathroom. She got one foot into the tub before catching herself and padding back to the foot of the bed, picking up the plate with the salt pile, and setting it on the floor right inside the bathroom door.

"You are not zapping me with ice water again!"

33

IMAGINATION

Mom's screaming dragged Piper from a deep sleep. She whined out her nose and rolled over in the super-comfortable cloud bed.

"Piper!" shouted Mom. "Get down here!"

Uh oh.

She reluctantly left the warm embrace of bed and padded out into the hall in her nightgown. Mom grumbled and rambled from downstairs. *Eep. She's mad if I heard her all the way up here.* She hurried to the ground floor and followed the sounds of angry-Mom to the kitchen. Every knife, fork, spoon, kitchen gadget, plate, bowl, cup, and dish lay scattered around the kitchen floor. The cabinets and drawers all hung open.

Mom stood in the midst of the mess, also in a nightgown, looking ready to kill someone. "What is this?"

"A boggart prank," said Piper. "We've got a boggart loose in the house."

"Enough with the lies, Piper! Why are you doing this?" yelled Mom. "And clean this up right away."

"I'm not!" screamed Piper. "It's an evil spirit. I didn't do this!"

"Oh, evil spirt!" yelled Mom. "You expect me to believe you aren't simply acting out to make us go back to Syracuse?"

"I didn't do it!" shrieked piper.

"Ladies!" yelled Dad, hurrying in to stand between them. "Please!"

"So much for waiting." Mom folded her arms. "Young lady, you are going to see a psychologist as soon as I can make an appointment."

"Amy, we talked about this last night. I..."

"Don't care!" yelled Mom. "This is going to stop."

"Why do you think she did this?" asked Dad.

"Did you?" Mom glared at him.

"Of course not."

"Well then, I know *I* didn't do this, and there's only one other person in this house."

"Umm." Piper smiled sheepishly. "There might be gnomes. I don't know if they're still here. I guess if they think this is their home they'd still be here, or maybe the djinn sent them wherever they came from."

Mom shuddered, eyes closed.

"Ames, calm down. You know kids have imaginations."

"Piper has never made up stories like this. We messed up, Alan. She can't handle this. It's a bad idea to pluck children away from familiar environments, especially socially-inept children like Piper. It took her ten years before she made any friends at all, and we pulled her away from them."

"Mom!" said Piper, gawking. "Ouch..."

She sighed. "I'm sorry, hon. I just mean that you're not exactly the most extroverted kid in the world."

Kicking her toe at the floor, Piper bit her lip.

Dad hung his head, looking like a small boy who'd had his puppy taken away. "Maybe this house was a bad idea..."

I wished for things to go where they belonged. Piper smirked. *I guess I belong here. Or maybe I just belong with my parents.* Still, she didn't really hate this house so much anymore. Especially since moving back to Syracuse permanently would mean she'd never see Tristan again. Gwen and Jamie could still visit here, and she might still wind up spending school season in the old house.

"Dad..." Piper took his hand. "This house isn't that bad. I made a new friend, too."

He smiled.

"Mom, I didn't throw this stuff all over the place, but I'll pick it up."

"Boggart, huh?" asked Dad chuckling.

Piper squatted and started collecting forks. "Yeah. That's why you got trapped in the shower the other day. I had to put salt in the lock to make it open."

"I'm not hearing this." Mom paced around. "I'm… Alan, what is going on?"

Dad bent down and grabbed bowls. "I'll help."

"Fine." Mom pitched in as well, picking up knives.

PIPER DARTED TO THE SIDE, JUMPING TO CATCH THE FRISBEE. SHE ADJUSTED her grip and hurled it back at Tristan who had to run sideways and dive, but still missed. Since her sneakers remained somewhere in the zoo, she had a choice between dress shoes and flip-flops. The flops won. Though, a few minutes into Frisbee, she kicked them off. After he missed the catch, the red plastic disc cruised off over the meadow, settling in the grass a good distance away.

"Oops," said Piper. "Sorry."

He picked himself up and brushed dirt away, grinning.

She walked over to him. "I can't believe you didn't get grounded."

"I told them we fell asleep on the couch watching movies. Got a 'don't let it happen again.'" He winked. "They're so happy I'm not sitting around the house all day alone, they're letting me slide."

"Cool."

"What happened with the zoo?"

"I don't know. I'm gonna show it to them later."

He poked her in the side. "Can you still breathe water?"

Piper nodded. "Yeah. I had to test it to make sure I didn't dream everything. I took a bath and sat underwater for like ten minutes."

"That's so cool. You think it's permanent?"

"I think so. How many people save a mermaid's life?" She smiled. "I hope she's happy."

"Anything's gotta be better than a cage."

"Yeah."

She looked down. "I'm sad I didn't get to say goodbye to them, but it's better that they're free."

"Yeah." Tristan patted her shoulder. "Sorry about the—"

Bwaaawk!

"What was that?" asked Piper.

"It came from the woods." Tristan pointed. "Let's go look." He jogged off.

A high-pitched *bwaaa* echoed among the trees, even louder.

"Wait!" She jogged over to her flip-flops, stepped into them, then ran after him, following the squawk every ten or fifteen seconds. After a bit of searching around, she realized the noise came from the fake tree. "It's down in the zoo! Something's still stuck down there."

He poked at the false wood. "We can't get down there though. Did you try the elevators?"

"Not yet, no. Dad looked pale when I told them about the power going off. I think he might've done it on accident."

"Whoops." Tristan made a silly face.

Piper spotted a brass dot in the bark. "Whoa. Is that?" She leaned closer, poking her finger at a tiny brass keyhole. "There *is* a way to open this."

"Nice!" Tristan bounced on his toes.

She pulled the key out from under her T-shirt and inserted it. Though this keyhole appeared half the size of the key, it still worked. A left twist opened the side of the false tree, exposing the little room and the ladder down.

Bwaaak!

They both cringed from the loudness.

Piper backed into the booth-sized space and lowered herself onto the ladder. While fine for a sunny late-June day, her jean shorts and thin shirt left her chilly in the underground zoo passageway. She backed away from the ladder as Tristan dropped down to stand beside her.

The place felt *empty*.

Except for whatever squawked.

"It's all gone." She smiled. "There's no sound at all. No fighting pixies or cackling brownies."

"Good." He shivered. "Building this place was an awful idea. I hope ghosts are real so that unicorn can bite your granddad on the ear."

She laughed.

Bwaaak!

"Sounds like the cockatrice got stuck in a door," said Tristan.

"Why would it still be here?" asked Piper. "And that sounds too small to be a cockatrice."

"Maybe it thinks this is its home?" He shrugged.

She hurried along, her flimsy foam shoes snapped at her heels, echoing in the concrete tunnel.

The shrill cries led her past the space of hill gnome houses, which much to her surprise, had about twenty of the little old men relaxing in lawn chairs by the tiny doors. They waved at her as she walked by.

"Why are they all sitting around like that?" asked Tristan.

"The zoo is empty. There is no work," said all the gnomes in perfect unison.

She stopped and faced them, hands on her hips. "You guys can move outside if you want. Re-build these houses in the back field."

They perked up eagerly.

Bwaaak!

"Sounds like something's in trouble or scared." She gave Tristan a brief glance before jogging off, worried.

The noises led her to the right, down a hallway for quite a way, and another right—straight into the Arabian-decorated area. Being near the hole where she almost starved to death put her on edge, but that pit would only be a threat if she was stupid enough to climb over the windowsill again. And she would *not* do that.

Piper rounded the corner at the end into the little spur in front of the djinn room, and skidded to a halt on her flip-flops, her jaw hanging open.

There, sitting in the midst of the ash pile, sat a tiny bright-red bird with huge eyes and a little candle flame burning atop its head. Stubby wings flapped with excitement upon seeing her.

"It's *sooooo cute!*" Piper squealed and sank to her knees.

"Is that a… baby phoenix?" asked Tristan in a whisper.

She reached forward. "Come here, baby."

The small phoenix waddled toward her, chirping happily.

"It knows you."

Piper picked it up and cradled it. "He's… It's the same one! He came back to life." She squeezed the bird, making him squawk. "Thank you!"

The phoenix cooed and rubbed his head against her cheek. Despite the little flame, nothing burned her.

"Oh, awesome. Yeah. Phoenixes do that!" Tristan dropped to kneel next to her and pet the bird. "So, what do we do with him?"

Tears in her eyes, Piper smiled. "We take him outside and let him go home."

Tristan nodded.

She shifted her weight off her knees and stood. "Everything else is back where it belongs. It's time for you to be free."

Bwaaak! The phoenix flapped merrily, and rubbed his head against her cheek again.

Piper turned on her heel, eager to get away from the pit of starvation, and walked back toward the ladder out.

"Hey, why didn't the wish send him home?" asked Tristan.

She let out a sad sigh. "Because he was a pile of ashes then. When I made the wish, he was dead."

"Oh."

The phoenix nuzzled against the side of her neck as they walked down corridor after corridor, back to the passage leading to the tree ladder. Tristan went up first to hold the door. She cradled the bird in her left arm and climbed one-handed. As soon as she stepped out into real sunlight, the young phoenix spread its wings and cried joyfully at the clouds. His sapphire beak gleamed with the luster of a gem and the orangey-yellow feathers down his breast held the shimmer of a burning fire.

"Am I seeing things, or is he bigger?" asked Tristan.

"Umm." Piper held him out to arm's length and looked at him. When she'd found him among the ashes, he'd been smaller than a baseball. Now, he'd reached chicken size. "Yeah. He's getting bigger."

She sat cross-legged in the grass, thanking and petting the phoenix while he stood nearby. With each minute, the bird grew. Once the bird had grown to about three-quarters of the size it had been, the little flame atop his head spread down his back and along both wings.

The phoenix turned, his glowing eyes fixed on hers.

Understanding filled her. The phoenix brimmed with joy at having protected her and Tristan. Though he had hoped the troll's mortal fear of fire would've made it run away, he thought nothing of immolating himself to save their lives. He felt Piper bringing him outside to be a greater gift than what he had done for them. Respect and love radiated from the phoenix, but also a strong desire to go home.

She leaned down and touched her forehead to his. "Yes. You must go home. Thank you. I'll never forget you."

Tristan reached over and traced a finger under the bird's chin. "Fly safe, friend."

"Piper?" yelled Dad.

Her father emerged from the trees right as the phoenix spread his seven-foot fiery wings and leapt into the air. The toolbox in Dad's hand fell to the ground with a *clatter.* He stood still, gawking. With the roar of an inferno, the phoenix swooped around once, making a low pass over Piper and Tristan, let out a joyous cry, and streaked off into the clouds.

Piper put an arm around Tristan and couldn't help but cry happy tears.

Dad trudged over, still staring upward. "Was that a..."

"Phoenix," said Piper, sniffling.

"Crying?" asked Dad.

"I thought he was dead. He saved our lives." She wiped her eyes. "I'm really happy."

"A phoenix." Dad nodded.

"Mr. Bailey, look in there." Tristan pointed at the tree.

Dad walked over and pulled the tree-door open, peering down at the ladder. "Wow. Okay then." He sat next to Piper and pulled her into a hug, patting her back while she kept sniffling. "I believe you, hon. I guess all that stuff really did happen."

"Yeah." She wiped her eyes.

"I suppose I should ground you for driving." He ruffled her hair.

"I did it to save her, not for fun, but I should've waited for you to be here. So, if I'm in trouble, that's okay."

"I'll think about it." He kissed the top of her head.

Piper smiled and squinted up at the clear, blue sky. No sign of the phoenix remained.

"Anything else you want to surprise me with?" asked Dad.

"All the monsters are gone." Tristan stuffed his hands in his pockets. "But you have a small army of hill gnomes."

"Oh, and a boggart. We need to hang an iron horseshoe over the front door," said Piper.

"That'll work?" asked Dad.

"I guess so. The pile of salt by my bed worked." She explained her morning of being trapped under impossibly heavy blankets, then shrugged. "It's just a horseshoe, other than looking strange, what could go wrong if it doesn't work?"

"Okay. One iron horseshoe coming up. Your mother's not going to take that well."

Piper looked at him. "After we show her the zoo, a horseshoe on a nail will be nothing."

34

A FOREVER FRIEND

All things considered, Mom handled a brief walk around the zoo reasonably well. She decided not to speak of it, but also accepted that Piper had not developed a mental problem. Though, she did struggle with the gnomes showing themselves. That had been the first time Piper had ever seen her mother faint.

Evidently, the gnomes didn't really mind living in the underground fake hillside, but at her suggestion to move the houses, they lit up. For no reason other than it gave them something to do, the gnomes had spent the rest of that day reconstructing their homes in the backyard. As far as any potential visitors went, Piper and her family would tell them the miniature village was pure decoration. Since gnomes could make themselves invisible at will, only those whom the family desired to know the truth would find out.

Piper had fallen asleep that night debating if she should tell Jamie and Gwen about the gnomes when they got here. Phone calls had made the rounds, and parents had come to an agreement that her friends could spend a week, sometime toward the end of July, at the manor.

Dad put horseshoes up over both the front and back door, and at least for the day following that, the boggart hadn't caused any trouble.

Whether it remained here unable to play pranks, or had moved on, she didn't know.

She awoke, comfortable in bed the day after the phoenix flew home, feeling happy for the first time in months. Ever since she'd first learned she had to move way out to the countryside away from her friends, a note of glumness had tinted everything. While she would rather have her friends close by, she had Tristan to hang out with. And after everything in the zoo, this house did feel like home, albeit not quite as much as the tiny place in Syracuse did. Giant spacious awesomeness couldn't fully compete with where she'd learned to walk, or the place she'd spent the first twelve years of her life thinking of as a sanctuary from teasing. Still, this enormous manor house no longer felt like the enemy.

With a yawn, she rolled on her side to steal a few more minutes of sleep before her parents called her down for breakfast.

The window she faced had turned bright golden-green.

Piper scrunched up her nose in confusion. The green in the window moved. A narrow black stripe down the middle got wider.

An eye!

She bolted upright in bed, ready to scream, but held it back when she realized the massive eye belonged to the friendly dragon, perched outside. Piper ran across the room and pulled the window open.

"Hello," whispered the dragon, his voice deep enough to vibrate in her bones. "You managed to do it."

"It wasn't me. I just made a wish." She ground her toes into the rug. "But I'm glad it worked. You're free."

The dragon's eye closed a little. "Oh, it was you. *You* made the wish. Beings such as djinn are bound by ancient laws. Nothing they do happens out of their own wanting. You did, however, find the trick to making a wish work."

She flashed a cheesy smile. "Wishing for something good?"

"Almost. Your wish provided a direct benefit to the djinn granting it. Out of gratitude, he did not turn the wish sour."

"Oh. Well. I'm happy you're free."

"Yes. I have not touched real sky since I was but a hatchling. You have given me that which I never thought I would ever have. My feelings toward your family line have changed."

Piper frowned. "He wasn't in our family line. He's a dead branch. I never even met him."

"I understand. I have something for you." The dragon leaned his eye closer to the window. "Place your hands near the corner of my eye."

She cupped her hands together and leaned out the window until her fingertips touched his warm, red scale.

A small tear formed, rolled into her hands, and hardened into a transparent stone with a faint reddish hue, a lattice of deep red veins trapped within. At the top, a silver dragonclaw clasp appeared in a shimmer of light that raced around to form a necklace chain.

Piper held the amulet up, mesmerized at the way it flickered in the sun. "It's beautiful. Thank you… but it looks so expensive. I can't…"

"I insist as a token of my friendship, Piper Bailey. Wear it always. I thank you for my freedom, and I will never forget you." He grinned. "And dragons have long memories. If ever you would call upon me, you have but to speak to that pendant."

She pulled the chain over her head, letting the amulet settle around her neck.

"Farewell for now."

Piper brushed a hand down the side of his face. "Will you come to visit, or only if I ask for help?"

"I'd be delighted to visit… but I think your mother would have a difficult time coping with me."

She giggled. "Yeah. I'll have to ease her in to the idea of dragons."

He laughed, shaking the house. "All right, child. I must be off now. There is one more thing I would ask of you."

"Anything." She leaned closer.

"Do not let the world change you. You will grow up. You will grow old. But you will not die unless you let the hope and brightness you have inside you fade away."

Piper clutched the gem at her chest. "I'll be who I am, always."

"Good to hear."

The dragon backed up, winked, and sprang into the air.

She watched him fly nearly straight up into the clouds.

"Piper?" asked Mom. "What are you doing at the window?"

"Talking to a friend." She pulled the window closed and turned to face her mother. "Promise me if he comes to visit you won't freak out."

"Why would I freak out?" Mom tilted her head.

Piper scrunched her toes into the carpet and put on a cheesy smile. "Umm. Because he's a dragon."

Mom laughed. "Dragons. What's next? Come on, time for breakfast."

"Uhh, never ask 'what's next?'" She tucked the amulet under her nightgown and followed her mother out into the hall.

A warm tingle from the amulet made her think of the dragon chuckling. She gripped the gem, grateful to have made *two* new friends.

fin

ACKNOWLEDGMENTS

Thank you for reading *The Menagerie of Jenkins Bailey!*

I'd also like to thank J.R. Rain for his suggestion to write a story about a hidden zoo.

Additional thanks to:

Julie Rodriguez for your wonderful help editing.

Ricky Gunawan for the incredible cover and interior artwork.

ABOUT THE AUTHOR

Originally from South Amboy NJ, Matthew has been creating science fiction and fantasy worlds for most of his reasoning life. Since 1996, he has developed the "Divergent Fates" world, in which *Division Zero, Virtual Immortality, The Awakened Series, The Harmony Paradox, and the Daughter of Mars series* take place. Along with being an editor at Curiosity Quills press, he has worked in IT and technical support.

Matthew is an avid gamer, a recovered WoW addict, Gamemaster for two custom RPG systems, and a fan of anime, British humour, and intellectual science fiction that questions the nature of reality, life, and what happens after it.

He is also fond of cats.

Links

Please visit me on the web at:

http://www.matthewcoxbooks.com/wordpress/

Also, for news, updates, and exclusives, join my readers group on Facebook:

https://www.facebook.com/groups/137705036768984/

Find me on Twitter: @mscox_fiction

For contact or inquiries regarding this novel, please email at:
mcox2112@gmail.com

OTHER BOOKS BY MATTHEW S. COX

Middle Grade

- Tales of Widowswood series (fantasy)
- Emma and the Banderwigh
- Emma and the Silk Thieves
- Emma and the Silverbell Faeries
- Emma and the Elixir of Madness
- Emma and the Weeping Spirit

- Citadel: The Concordant Sequence (post-apocalyptic)
- The Cursed Codex (LitRPG – Fantasy / contemporary)
- The Menagerie of Jenkins Bailey (contemporary fantasy)
- Sophie's Light (Dark fantasy novella)

Young Adult

Caller 107 (contemporary paranormal – Note: strong language)

The Summer the World Ended (nuclear apocalyptic / family drama / contemporary)

Nine Candles of Deepest Black (witchcraft horror)

The Eldritch Heart (fantasy / LGBT)

The Forest Beyond the Earth (post apocalyptic)

Out of Sight (science fiction)

Adult Novels

(**Divergent Fates** universe – Science fiction / Cyberpunk / Paranormal)

- Division Zero series
- Division Zero
- Lex De Mortuis
- Thrall
- Guardian

- The Awakened series
- Prophet of the Badlands
- Archon's Queen
- Grey Ronin
- Daughter of Ash
- Zero Rogue
- Angel Descended

- Daughter of Mars series
- The Hand of Raziel
- Araphel
- Ghost Black

- Virtual Immortality series
- Virtual Immortality
- The Harmony Paradox

- Divergent Fates Anthology

(Non-DF novels)

- The Roadhouse Chronicles Series (post nuclear apoc/zombie)

- One More Run
- The Redeemed
- Dead Man's Number

- Faded Skies series (post-ww3 / sci fi)
- Heir Ascendant
- Ascendant Revolution

- Chiaroscuro: The Mouse and the Candle (vampire, drama)

- Temporal Armistice Series (urban fantasy)
- Nascent Shadow
- The Shadow Collector

- Wayfarer: AV494 (sci fi horror)

- Axillon99 (LitRPG)

- Vampire Innocent series (vampire, comedy-drama)
- A Nighttime of Forever
- A Beginner's Guide to Fangs

- Operation: Chimera (sci fi – with Tony Healey)

- The Dysfunctional Conspiracy (nonfiction memoir – with Christopher Veltmann)

- Winter Solstice series (urban fantasy – with J.R. Rain)
- Convergence
- Containment

- Alexis Silver series (urban fantasy – with J.R. Rain)
- Silver Light
- Deep Silver

- Samantha Moon Origins series (urban fantasy – with J.R. Rain)
- New Moon Rising
- Moon Mourning

- Maddy Wimsey series (detective / witchcraft – with J.R. Rain)
- The Devil's Eye
- The Drifting Gloom

- The Far Side of Promise (anthology)

Made in the USA
Lexington, KY
07 September 2018